Praise for *Chasing the North Star*

"What an exciting new legend Robert Morgan has created! And just when we need such a story. *Chasing the North Star* has the gravity of the old slave narratives, and the blood-chilling action of a contemporary action thriller. The language reflects Morgan's deep connection to the land and the tradition, and burns with conviction and insight and heart. Jonah Williams is a hero for the ages. Reading of his courage and humanity puts starch in your spine. A must read."

—Randall Kenan, author of *Walking on Water*

"Throughout these pages Morgan takes measured and artful steps to remind the reader that history, whether large or small, is made up entirely of stories. And so, too, is life . . . The writing is visual and powerful and even breathtaking at times."

—*Minneapolis Star Tribune*

"*Chasing the North Star* is an epic journey, and Morgan's vision of our dark past shines brilliantly detailed, deeply satisfying, and ultimately hopeful."

—Charles Frazier, author of *Nightwoods* and *Cold Mountain*

"One of those page-turners that's tough to put down. Not only does he expertly draw the physical landscape . . . but he gives the reader clear examples of the inner conflict that comes with any change, no matter how necessary."

—*Washington Independent Review of Books*

"Richly imaginative and thoroughly well researched, *Chasing the North Star* walks the reader through an extensive and thrilling escape filled with fiery insight and deep personal conviction . . . Morgan summons a narrative that clearly describes the people, culture, and emotions of the time . . . His personal connection to the land, including its history and features, enables the reader to experience the thrilling escape vividly . . . [It's] an epic journey, vividly detailed, acutely satisfying, and ultimately hopeful."
—*New York Journal of Books*

"A gorgeous book full of lush prose, compelling characters, and an epic journey across America ten years before the Civil War."
—*Chicago Review of Books*

"Adventurous, compelling . . . Generously laced with humor, it becomes a story of more than survival. It is a story filled with courage and hope."
—*The Greensboro News & Record*

"Morgan's latest is a grittily entertaining, smartly paced narrative about a fugitive slave . . . Morgan is a first-rate storyteller; he plots his novel extremely well, and readers will find this journey captivating."
—*Publishers Weekly*

"Not only is the subject matter riveting, Morgan's language enhances the tension and defines his characters . . . The novel shines its light on the simple humanity of two teenagers adrift in a time of such hate and fear that it soon erupted into a bloody civil war. Today, with racial and ethnic tensions again running high, this stark, terrifying story of perilous love and the search for peace is especially illuminating."
—*Knoxville News Sentinel*

"A powerful, gripping, and unrelenting tale of wilderness survival under the most dire of circumstances in the pursuit of freedom: another outstanding work of historical fiction from Morgan."

—*Kirkus Reviews*

"Morgan . . . presents the reader with a convincing and richly imagined experience." —*Booklist,* starred review

"As with Morgan's eight other works of fiction, this one is hard to put down once begun. But the story is far more complex than a simple tale of page-turning adventure . . . Morgan's rich grasp of historical detail makes Jonah's and Angel's experiences feel close, almost familiar, despite the distance of their historical period: these are people we can understand." —*Cornell Chronicle*

CHASING THE NORTH STAR

Also by Robert Morgan

Fiction

The Blue Valleys

The Mountains Won't Remember Us

The Hinterlands

The Truest Pleasure

Gap Creek

The Balm of Gilead Tree: New and Selected Stories

This Rock

Brave Enemies

The Road from Gap Creek

Nonfiction

Good Measure: Essays, Interviews, and Notes on Poetry

Boone: A Biography

Lions of the West: Heroes and Villains of the Westward Expansion

Poetry

Zirconia Poems

Red Owl: Poems

Land Diving: Poems

Trunk & Thicket

Groundwork

Bronze Age

At the Edge of the Orchard Country

Sigodlin: Poems

Green River: New and Selected Poems

Wild Peavines: New Poems

Topsoil Road

The Strange Attractor: New and Selected Poems

October Crossing

Terroir

Dark Energy: Poems

CHASING THE NORTH STAR

A NOVEL

ROBERT MORGAN

ALGONQUIN
BOOKS OF
CHAPEL HILL
2017

Published by
Algonquin Books of Chapel Hill
Post Office Box 2225
Chapel Hill, North Carolina 27515-2225

a division of
Workman Publishing
225 Varick Street
New York, New York 10014

First paperback edition, Algonquin Books of Chapel Hill,
April 2017. Originally published in hardcover by Algonquin
Books of Chapel Hill in 2016.
Printed in the United States of America.
Published simultaneously in Canada by Thomas Allen & Son Limited.
Design by Steve Godwin.

LIBRARY OF CONGRESS CATALOGING-IN-PUBLICATION DATA
Morgan, Robert, [date]
Chasing the North Star : a novel /
by Robert Morgan.—First edition.
pages ; cm
ISBN 978-1-56512-627-5 (HC)
I. Title.
PS3563.O87147C48 2016
813'.54—dc23 2015023738

ISBN 978-1-61620-645-1 (PB)

10 9 8 7 6 5 4 3 2 1
First Paperback Edition

For my grandson Keith

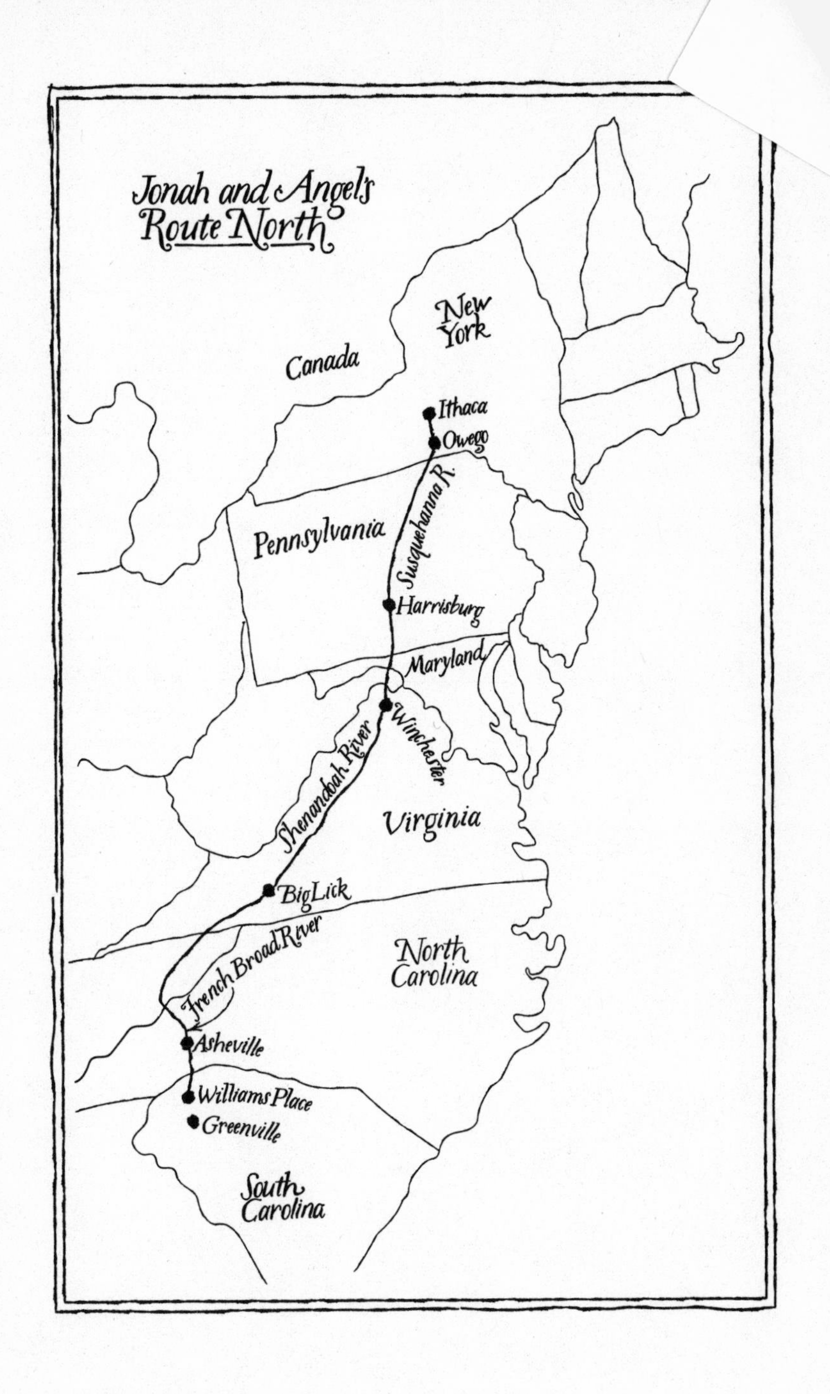
Jonah and Angel's Route North
New York
Canada
Ithaca
Owego
Susquehanna R.
Pennsylvania
Harrisburg
Maryland
Winchester
Shenandoah River
Virginia
Big Lick
French Broad River
North Carolina
Asheville
Williams Place
Greenville
South Carolina

ONE

JONAH

He was called Jonah because he was born during a terrible storm and his mama said soon as she let go of him and put him ashore in this world of folly and time the thunder quieted and the wind laid. Trees had broken off their stumps and skipped across fields like dust brooms, and the Saluda River spread wide over the bottomlands. Some of the slave cabins behind Mr. Williams's brick house got smashed to splinters by the high tempest.

But soon as Jonah was cut loose and washed off in a pan and wrapped up in a towel rag, his mama said the sky cleared and the moon came out and shined so bright you could see a needle in the light from the window. Everything the storm had ruined was vivid in the moonlight, including dead birds that had been torn from their roosts and snakes washed out of holes in the ground. Because Jonah arrived on the full of the moon in the middle of a storm under the sign of the Crab, his mama called him her moon baby. The granny woman that delivered him said he would always be darting away, running from one thing and then another. He'd be no more dependable than Jonah in the Holy Book.

THE DAY JONAH DECIDED to run away from Mr. Williams's plantation was the day he turned eighteen. It was in the middle of summer, a hot day in the cotton fields and cornfields. The Williams plantation lay in the foothills of South Carolina, north of Greenville, on land just below the cotton line. Higher in the hills the season was too short to grow cotton. Farther south the winter was too short for apple trees to thrive. Mostly Mr. Williams grew corn, which he sold to stock drovers in the winter to feed their herds of cattle, horses, hogs, or flocks of sheep or turkeys. Drovers came by every day on the Buncombe Pike, driving their animals through dust or mud to the markets in Columbia and Charleston.

Mr. Williams had built pens beside his big brick house, which he called Snowdon, to hold the herds and flocks, and the drovers paid two bits to sleep on the floor or four bits to sleep in a room upstairs in the big house. The house was called a stand or a tavern, and many of the women worked inside cooking and cleaning and taking care of the drovers. But in the summer they worked in the fields also. Mr. Williams called the plantation Snowdon, for a place in Wales overseas where his grandpa had come from.

Since the Williams Place was not a regular plantation, almost everybody did more than one job. Field hands chopped wood when firewood was needed, and they cut trees and sawed lumber when a new barn or stock shed was built. "I can't afford no field hands *and* house help," Mr. Williams liked to say. Everybody had to hoe corn in the spring and all the men had to clean manure out of the stables and pens and spread the wagonloads on the fields.

But Jonah the moon baby had been lucky, because Mrs. Williams picked him out as a boy to serve her and her children. Mrs. Williams was blonde and young and plump. She was young enough to be Mr. Williams's own child. She was from Columbia and she liked to wear lacy pink dresses and give parties for her friends from Greenville and Travelers Rest. She even gave parties for her children, Betsy and Johnny. And she liked young slaves to serve at parties for her offspring. She had special clothes made for Jonah to act as butler at frolics for Betsy and Johnny and the neighbor children of quality.

And because she paid special attention to Jonah, he paid special mind to Mrs. Williams. He volunteered to bring her the best strawberries from the patch just when they were perfectly ripe, and raspberries from the garden wall. He gathered chestnuts in the fall and roasted them on the hearth for his mistress. He carried her lap robe to the church in wintertime.

When Betsy and Johnny had their lessons, Jonah often got to sit with them. His job was to bring things the tutor and his pupils needed, a glass of water, a book from the library, an extra pen or pair of scissors. Jonah got to listen to the lessons and observe the writing on the slates, and in time he learned to read and count the same as Betsy and Johnny did. Jonah knew he was not supposed to be reading. Nobody but white folks were supposed to read. But every chance he got he listened to the lessons and he learned the letters and numbers. He tried to read newspapers left on the table, and the children's books left in the playroom.

It was Mrs. Williams who caught him taking a book from the master's library. It was a big book called *Robinson Crusoe* and he'd listened to the tutor read that volume to Betsy and Johnny. It was a thrilling book, with lots of words Jonah didn't understand. Day after day he listened to the tutor reading from that story, and when the book was taken back to the library Jonah promised himself he was going to slip it under his shirt and carry it back to the cabin to read himself by firelight.

Jonah knew where the book was. He'd replaced it on the shelf himself between smooth leather volumes with gold lettering on them. He had no trouble finding the book again and sliding it inside his shirt. He hoped to walk quickly down the hallway and take the side door out of the house. He would hide the book in a boxwood until nightfall. But just as he passed the dining room, Mrs. Williams called to him from the bottom of the stairs. She wanted him to carry a message to her friend Ophelia, who lived on the adjoining farm. She often called Jonah to deliver letters. But almost instantly she spotted the book under Jonah's shirt where the volume's weight pulled down the fabric.

"What is that?" Mrs. Williams said and pointed to the sagging cloth.

"Ain't nothing, ma'am."

"Don't lie to me," Mrs. Williams snapped. She made Jonah draw the book from his shirt and hand it to her.

"I won't have a thief in my house," his mistress said.

Jonah wanted to tell her he was borrowing the book for the tutor, but he knew the tutor would say he'd already read the book to Betsy and Johnny.

"You were going to take the book to the store and try to sell it," Mrs. Williams said.

Jonah shook his head and began to cry. He didn't mean to cry, but his knees shook and his jaw trembled. He had no choice but to say he was borrowing the book to read himself. As he said the words he felt something hot and wet running down his pants leg. He looked at the floor and saw a puddle of pee growing on the varnished planks. Mrs. Williams noticed the streak down his jeans and the puddle also.

"Shame on you, Jonah," she said. "Shame on you for deceiving us, and for stealing a volume from Mr. Williams's library."

Mrs. Williams was young and fat and soft, and she smelled like face powder and perfume. She took a handkerchief from the pocket of her dress and wiped his cheeks. She put her hands on Jonah's shoulders and looked him in the eyes.

"I won't tell anybody you can read," she said. "I won't tell anybody, if you'll promise me. Will you promise me?"

Jonah nodded that he would promise her whatever she asked. He was trembling and afraid he might be whipped and put in chains and branded the way Old Isaac was. If a slave fought and hurt another slave, he was whipped and put in chains. Even worse, Jonah was afraid he might be sold and sent away to live among strangers. Mrs. Williams said she'd tell nobody he could read if Jonah would return the book to the library and read to her from the Bible from time to time. She said he'd benefit most from reading the Good Book and she was going to give him his very own Bible so he could study it and learn more.

"Reading the Bible will teach you not to steal and deceive," Mrs. Williams said.

"Yes, ma'am."

"Reading the Bible will make you wise and useful."

The Bible Mrs. Williams gave Jonah was small enough to fit in his pocket. It had letters the size of gnats and hairs. But it was the prettiest book he'd ever seen, bound in rippling black leather. The edges of the pages were gold. The book had paper thin and crackly as cigarette paper or filmy bark on a river birch. Mrs. Williams made Jonah promise to read the book when he was alone. He could read it out in the woods or he could read it in the big house. He could read the book to her for his private lessons, and her private devotions.

"We will learn with each other," Mrs. Williams said. She made him clean up the pee on the floor and wash his pants at the well.

• • •

As Jonah read to Mrs. Williams from the Bible and learned more words, and learned the stories from the Bible, Mrs. Williams explained what words meant, words like *void* and *begat*, *serpent* and *multiply*. He stumbled through verses and Mrs. Williams explained when she could. Some of the words she didn't know herself. She said someday he could learn to look up words in the dictionary, but for now he should just keep on reading. She liked to close her eyes while he read, like she was dreaming of things described in the Bible. Sometimes she had headaches and put a damp cloth soaked with camphor on her forehead and kept her eyes shut as he stumbled through verses.

"This will be just our secret," Mrs. Williams said.

To help with his reading, Mrs. Williams let Jonah take newspapers back to the quarters. "Tell your mama they are to start fires with," Mrs. Williams said. "But before you burn the papers up, you can read every word."

From reading the newspapers Jonah learned about the Fugitive Slave Law, and he learned about the Great Compromise. Much of what he read he didn't understand. He read about elections and things in faraway Washington. He read about the Northern states, and at some point it came to him there was a place in the North, beyond North Carolina, where no one was a slave. He'd heard rumors about that. But an escaped slave could be arrested and returned to his owner. There were supposed to be no slaves up there, in the states to the north.

Jonah read many mysterious things in the newspapers before they got burned. He read about foreign countries and wars in places he'd never heard of. He read about places where the snow never melted, far to the north. And he read about governments with kings and ships that sailed to China. The newspapers were Mrs. Williams's greatest gift to him, besides keeping the secret of his reading. In the heat and dirt of the Williams Place, the newspapers were an inky threshold where he could enter a landscape that reached to the North Pole and to other times and people he'd never heard a whisper about before.

The day Jonah decided to run away from the Williams Place was the day his secret was found out.

Mr. Williams liked to be known among the people of the region, the other planters, the drovers, and the Negroes, as someone strict but fair. "Long as you obey the law and do your work I'll be fair with you," he liked to say. He almost never whipped a slave. He said whipping injured pride and injured property, instilled fear and resentment, and in the long run interfered with the work and harmony of the household. But Mr. Williams liked to remind his help that anyone who broke his rules and didn't do the work assigned would feel the lash. He kept a black snake whip hanging on a peg inside the barn door and from time to time it had been used on more than horses and oxen.

Jonah was caught the week Mrs. Williams was away visiting her sister in Flat Rock, twenty miles to the north, up in the mountains of North Carolina. A lot of families from Charleston and Columbia had homes in the highland community there. From late spring till early fall they stayed in the mountains to escape the heat and fever of the low country and central South Carolina. Everybody knew about the fine mansions there, and the wide, cool lawns and pine woods, the dances by the lake, the champagne lunches. It was a rainy summer day and no one worked in the fields. Summer was not a season when many drovers came along the Buncombe Pike, so things were quiet at the Williams Place. With Mrs. Williams and the children away, Jonah had no special duties. Mr. Williams was supervising work in the blacksmith shed, where iron bands were being fitted on wagon wheels. The ring of the hammers on steel was the only sound in the place except the tap of rain and the clucking of hens laying eggs in the chicken house.

For the past several months Jonah had kept his Bible in the loft of the barn. He'd found that the best hiding place because it was dry there and hardly anyone came up to the loft. He laid the Bible on top of a beam, and when he had a free hour in daylight he climbed the ladder to the loft and sat in the hay and read a few pages from the fine book. It was his favorite time of day, when he could pore over the words and say them to himself. It was his secret pleasure, savoring the words and stories.

He'd been so successful at hiding the book and finding time to read from it, Jonah had gotten careless. From the library he'd sneaked a volume of a new story called *David Copperfield* because he'd heard the tutor mention it. The book was in three volumes and he'd taken only one, hoping it wouldn't be missed. When he finished that one he'd exchange it for the next.

The books lay on top of the beam and he fetched them down and sat in the hay with his treasures in front of him. Rain on the tin roof was doing a tap dance that went on and on. In the gloom of the hay loft there was just enough light to read by. Jonah opened the Bible first. He would read a chapter there from the story about King David, and then he'd turn to the thrilling story about the other David and his friend Steerforth. Because of the hammering from the forge and the tap and hammer of the rain, he didn't hear the steps on the ladder to the loft.

Mr. Williams climbed up to the loft to get a piece of old harness hanging there. He planned to cut the harness into sections to use as pads on the brakes of his wagons. When he saw Jonah sitting in the hay he probably wasn't sure at first what the boy was doing. Jonah did know though that Mr. Williams resented that his wife was so fond of him.

"I can find some work for you, boy," Mr. Williams said.

Jonah jerked around, and as he turned Mr. Williams saw the books on his knees.

"What you got there, Jonah?" Mr. Williams said. He picked up the fine Bible and the volume of *David Copperfield*. He recognized the former as one that belonged to his wife.

"You have stole these," Mr. Williams said.

"I ain't," Jonah said, his teeth chattering.

Jonah saw that he was caught. He couldn't say that Mrs. Williams had given him the Bible, because he'd promised not to tell that she knew he could read, and that he read to her. And even if he could explain where he got the Holy Book, there was still the volume of the novel he'd taken from the library.

"What you doing with those books?" Mr. Williams growled.

"Borrowed them," Jonah said, his lips trembling. "Gonna take them back." But that was all he could say. There was nothing he could offer in his defense. And Mrs. Williams couldn't help him because she was away with her children in Flat Rock and would be gone another week.

"I'm a fair man," Mr. Williams said. His eyes pierced through Jonah like hot pokers.

"I know you are, sir," Jonah said and hung his head.

"But I won't have any stealing or lying on this place."

"No, sir," Jonah said.

Mr. Williams said it made him sad that Jonah was a thief. He wanted everyone on the Williams Place to live in Christian harmony and work in harmony. It hurt his feelings that Jonah would steal. "We are a family here," Mr. Williams said.

Mr. Williams had a chew of tobacco in his mouth and he spit it out on the loft floor and wiped a copper stain from his lip. He made Jonah precede him down the ladder and he followed, carrying the books under his right arm.

"You have stole books you can't even read," Mr. Williams said. Jonah wanted to shout that he could read, and that he'd read to Mrs. Williams, but he saw that wouldn't help him now. Since it was raining steadily Mr. Williams told Reuben the blacksmith to tie Jonah's hands to the railing of the horse stall. Jonah had to take off his shirt before he was tied up, and Mr. Williams made him drop his overalls also. Mr. Williams took the whip from the peg beside the barn door.

"This is for your own good," the master said. "I don't want you to become a thief."

Several slaves had gathered in the hallway of the barn to watch. Chickens pecked for corn in the dirt of the hallway floor. With his face against the planks, Jonah smelled manure and piss, and the dust of the old corn. His knees shook and his lips trembled. When Mr. Williams hit him the first lick, the sting flashed through him. The hurt was not as bad as he expected and at the same time it was worse. It was a hurt he'd known before, but the lash also touched a new raw place. He jumped and twisted and felt something hot on his leg. He was pissing on the planks of the wall and the piss splashed back on him.

"I won't have a thief on this place," Mr. Williams said again, and lashed him across the back, and lower down on the small of his back. The whip cut wires of fire in his flesh, as it fell on his legs and buttocks, and then on his back again. Jonah felt something else hot on his legs and thought it must be blood, but then smelled his own shit. The shit ran down his legs, the streaming, steaming shit of a coward.

Jonah must have fainted then for the next thing he knew he was being dragged out into the rain to the well. Buckets of cold water were thrown on him and rain pecked his face and shoulders.

"You clean yourself up and go back to your place and rest," Mr. Williams said and tossed a tow sack at Jonah to cover his nakedness. "I'm a fair man, but I won't have thieves on my place."

Jonah wrapped himself in the sack and limped back to the cabin. Other slaves watched him go by and didn't say anything.

"What you go and do a thing like that for?" Mama said as he came inside. "Why you steal from Massa Williams?"

Jonah didn't answer her. There was no use. He lay down on his cot in the corner of the room face down, and he stayed there all afternoon.

"I knowed you gone get in trouble with all that reading," Mama said.

"How you know I was reading?"

"'Cause I got eyes," Mama said. "You always pawing over and staring at them newspapers. I knowed you gone land yourself in trouble. I seen it coming."

When Mama hollered she had supper ready, fresh corn and green beans and new potatoes, he didn't move. He wasn't hungry a bit, not just because his back was hurting, and his legs, too, but because he was thinking. In the newspapers Jonah had read about slaves running away to the North. Most got caught by men with guns and horses and hound dogs, but some made it all the way. And if you made it to the North, people there would help you. He'd read about the Underground Railroad and abolitionists and he knew the song "Follow the Drinking Gourd," which meant follow the Big Dipper and the North Star.

As he lay on the cot with his back aching, Jonah thought and thought about what he'd heard and what he'd read. And along about dark, while Mama and the rest of the children were eating, he had an idea. In the lessons with the tutor, Betsy and Johnny had learned to read maps and Jonah had listened. He'd studied the maps himself and seen where South Carolina joined North Carolina. And he'd seen the chain of mountains leaning to the northeast and running all the way to the northern states.

The tutor said those mountains were wild and full of Indians and outlaws and people that made moonshine. The tutor said there were no plantations in the rocky hollows and deep valleys, only cabins and people who didn't even know how to read. The tutor said quality folks lived on the east side of the mountain chain, but only outlaws and squatters and trash lived in the mountains.

Jonah wondered how hard it would be to travel through such mountains. There were probably no roads and only a few trails. With rivers and deep hollows, cliffs and thickets, it would be almost impossible to travel that way. But at the same time it would be almost impossible for anyone to follow him. That was why escaping slaves headed for swamps and canebrakes, where they couldn't be easily followed. If he got into the mountains and became lost he could always follow the North Star. The problem would be to find something to eat, and to keep from being eaten by panthers, bears, wolves, and maybe Indians. It could take him months, even years to follow those mountains. But he'd rather take the risks that way than to stay here where he'd been whipped and shamed forever.

Now that Mr. Williams thought Jonah was a thief, he would always call him a thief. Now that he'd been whipped before all the others, Jonah would always be called a bad nigger. His fate had been decided suddenly that rainy afternoon in midsummer, when Mr. Williams climbed the ladder to the loft and Mrs. Williams was away.

Jonah lay on the cot and thought about what he could take with him. There were all kinds of things he'd need for such a journey. For one thing he'd need a knife and good shoes and strong clothes. He needed money and a map, and he needed a better hat. Mr. Williams only gave his slaves shoes in the winter time, cheap heavy brogans. Jonah needed shoes that didn't leave tracks, and he needed to travel fast and light. He could steal a knife from the kitchen behind the big house, and he might take a hat from the pegs inside the kitchen door. But he wasn't sure where he could find money. Mr. Williams kept his money locked in a box inside his bedroom.

Mama saved coins in a jar over the door of the cabin. But she would hear the rattle on the glass if he tried to take them out of the jar in the dark. He was ashamed to think of stealing money from Mama, but it was the only way he knew to get the funds for his long journey.

Jonah lay on the cot till all his brothers and sisters were asleep. He waited until he heard Mama snoring and then he quietly raised himself. Even if Mama woke she would just assume he was going out to pee. After lying on the cot all afternoon and evening it would make sense that he had to relieve himself. He slipped on his shirt and a pair of ragged overalls. When he reached the door he felt for the jar on the board above it, but the jar was not there. After a moment of panic, he walked his fingers along the wood and touched glass. The jar had been moved to the left from where he'd last seen it. He lowered the jar without rattling the coins and slipped out into the night.

July is the quietest month of the summer. The crickets have not appeared in the hills of South Carolina and the katydids would not start their singing until later, in August. Only an occasional cicada, or jarfly, buzzed in the trees. The rain had stopped, and a crust of moon shone through the clouds. Jonah hurried to the kitchen and took a hat from one of the pegs, then found the shelf where the knives were kept. He didn't want a large butcher knife, which would be hard to conceal, but he needed something bigger than a paring knife. There was a strong knife with a wooden handle that he'd seen the cook use for slicing meat. He felt in the dark for that knife, being careful not to cut his fingers on the blades, and when he found the right one he stepped quickly into the backyard and headed toward the road. He wished he had some shoes, and he wished he had a map, but he had to get far into the mountains before daylight, before anyone knew he was gone.

TWO

JONAH

By the time Jonah reached the woods, he was so scared he almost turned back. If he hurried he could return the knife and hat to the kitchen and replace the money jar over the door, slide back into his cot, and no one would ever know he'd tried to run away. For running away he could be whipped again, and put in chains in the smokehouse. Slaves that ran away could be branded with a red-hot iron also, and they sometimes had to wear leg irons, or a neck collar with spikes, and some had an ear cut off.

Jonah paused in the bushes at the edge of the field and decided he'd better go back while there was still time. Maybe Mrs. Williams would help him when she returned from Flat Rock. Maybe she would even say she'd given him the fine Bible, and that she herself had taught him to read it. Maybe if he was careful he could get by. And if his manners were good he could serve in the tavern and make cider and work in the distillery. Maybe if he was lucky he could even save money enough to buy his freedom one day.

It was the burning in his back and on his legs that stopped him from turning back. But it wasn't just the fear of another whipping that prevented him from retracing his steps across the field. Jonah knew that he could never be a good Negro again. He'd been whipped for stealing a book that was already his. He would always be called a thief at the Williams Place and he couldn't submit to that daily humiliation. If he didn't run away tonight, he'd run away next week, or next year. That was certain as the wet ground under his feet and the twinkling heavens overhead.

As soon as Jonah knew that he could not turn back, he remembered something important. He would need lucifers to start fires to cook whatever fish or game he could steal. And when it was rainy and cold in the mountains, he'd need them to build a fire to keep him warm. There was a box of friction matches in the kitchen near the knives. He'd been foolish to not grab the lucifers while he had a chance.

He was going to turn back to get the matches, but soon as he stepped out of the bushes a dog began to bark in the distance. No, he couldn't turn back. Jonah had to get as far as possible up the mountain before daylight. As soon as he found Jonah gone, Mr. Williams would get the sheriff and they'd form a party to go looking for him.

Rather than strike out through the woods and get lost in the dark, Jonah saw that he'd better take the Turnpike, at least tonight. He could travel faster and farther on the road, and now that he thought about it he saw it would be easier for men and dogs to follow his tracks in the woods than on the packed, much-traveled road. But soon as it got daylight he'd have to turn off the road and find a place to rest and sleep. It would be foolish to stay on the Pike in daytime. If he traveled by day he'd have to stick to the woods and thickets and skirt along the edges of remote fields.

The world of the night was a different world, as mysterious as Jonah's thoughts. He was as confused as he was determined. He was afraid as much as he was resolved. One of the things he was afraid of was snakes. He feared rattlers, but rattlesnakes rarely crawled at night and besides they warned you with the rattle of their tails before they bit you. He hated cottonmouths, but they stayed near water and were not seen often in the hills. What he feared most were pilots, copperheads, which did crawl at night and were said to be blind this time of year. Because they couldn't see, they would strike at anything that moved. Copperheads were silent and sneaky. They hid in the grass and weeds. They were called pilots because they slept through the winter in nests tangled with rattlesnakes deep in the ground, and when spring came they led the drowsy rattlers to water for their first drink. Jonah was afraid of wolves, too. He'd heard that in the mountains there were lots of wolves that killed calves and lambs. And there were panthers that lived in cliffs and preyed on anything that passed below them. And in the highest mountains there were bears. Bears could attack you at night while you lay sleeping. He'd been told she-bears were especially mean when they had little cubs.

When he reached the road, Jonah almost wished he hadn't decided to go that way. The heavy rain had left the ruts filled with muddy water. He stepped through puddles with bottoms slick as wet paint. Mud squeezed between his toes, and he stubbed his big toe on a rock. There was just enough light to see the way between the trees. The road itself was a shadow, a long tunnel of shadow.

Something else he'd forgotten while in the kitchen was to grab a few biscuits or a piece of cornpone, a little side meat. Anything left over from supper would come in handy when it got daylight and he had to rest and his belly was empty. Anything would do then, when he was hungry enough. Jonah had to stick to the edge of the road, out of the deep ruts. The edge of the road was firm ground, but overhanging bushes scratched him in the face and chest. He held out his arms and once got raked by a blackberry briar, or maybe a cat briar. Ticks hung on limbs and would drop on people as they passed; when it got daylight he'd have to search his hair and shirt and overalls and hat for ticks.

Where the Turnpike ran through bottomland along the north fork of the Saluda River, it was a plank road. They'd laid logs side by side in the dirt and nailed boards on top of the logs to make a smooth track. He could walk faster once he got on the plank road. But he'd have to watch out for splinters. Jonah didn't want to run, for if he hurried too much he'd wear himself out. Easy does it, he'd heard the tutor say to Betsy and Johnny. "Easy does it, Jonah," he whispered to himself. He'd walk until daylight and then rest and walk again. A horse can walk a hundred miles a day, the tutor said. But a man is lucky to walk twenty-five.

Despite the warning, as soon as Jonah reached the plank road he picked up his pace. The boards were wet and gritty, but they offered solid footing. He walked as fast as he could without trotting or skipping. While he walked on the planks it occurred to Jonah that this was a good season to be running away. Even though he'd not brought anything to eat, there would be fresh corn in fields wherever he went. Every place would have a garden, with new potatoes and beans, summer squash and tomatoes. If he was lucky he could slip into a garden and take what he wanted. It would be harder to find bread, whether biscuit or cornpone.

Cherries would be ripe in some orchards, as well as apples, and back in the mountains there would be blackberries along creeks and huckleberries on hills, around old burns. Jonah was not so confident when he thought about meat. He had no gun or other weapon except the kitchen knife. He might be able to make a snare or deadfall to catch rabbits.

Or if he was lucky he could kill a rabbit with a rock, or maybe even a groundhog. As he hurried along the level road across the wide bottomland, Jonah thought of something else he'd forgotten to bring. If he'd thought to take just one little fishhook he could have caught trout and other fish out of creeks. Jonah thought of the way Mama fried catfish in cornmeal so they were juicy and golden. He thought of the grits Mama would fix in the morning for his brothers and sisters, and his eyes got wet. He couldn't believe he'd run away, run away without making any plans, just vague hopes.

While Jonah walked, the stars grew brighter and he got his night eyes. He found he could see more if he looked sideways, out of the corners of his eyes, something he'd never noticed before. When he glanced that way, either to the left or to the right, the night was more vivid, the road ahead clearer. When he reached the other end of the long stretch of bottomland, the road turned steeply up the side of the mountain. He'd made such good time on the level plank road he was surprised at how quickly he got out of breath on the steeper grade. The road up the mountain was just dirt and rocks, and with every step he had to pull his weight up. Jonah had never been this far north on the Turnpike, and he'd heard that the steepest part, where it wound round and round and switched back and forth, was called the Winding Stairs. If he could reach the top of the mountain he'd be in North Carolina. Maybe because he was getting tired and out of breath, Jonah didn't hear anyone on the road ahead of him. Suddenly a lantern was turned in his face. He was stunned, and didn't know why he hadn't seen the lantern before.

"Where you going, nigger?" a man said.

"Going to my massa at Flat Rock," Jonah said in his flattest voice.

"Like hell you are," another man said.

"I be going to Flat Rock," Jonah said, his chin trembling.

"You're a runaway," the first man said.

Jonah saw the end of a shotgun poking out of the dark at him. He could hardly make out the face of the man holding it under his arm. "Ain't done nothing wrong," Jonah said.

The man with the gun laughed like he was at a frolic. "Everybody has done something wrong," he said. That was when Jonah saw the mule, loaded with heavy sacks strapped on either side. The sacks rattled and tinkled with jugs stopped with corncobs. The second man carried a shining jug in either hand. The man with the shotgun held the weapon under his right arm, which gripped the lantern, and he carried a jug with his left hand.

"Since you ain't done nothing wrong, and since you ain't a runaway, you can carry a jug for us," the man with the shotgun said. He handed Jonah the jug he carried. It was a heavy two-gallon jug. "You walk beside the mule," the man said.

The jug was so heavy it pulled Jonah down on his right side. He tried to hold it with both hands. He shifted the burden from his right side to his left side.

"Hey, that ain't fair," the man with the two jugs said. "You ain't carrying nothing."

"I'm carrying the gun and the lantern."

"Here, take one of these," the other man said.

"I've got to carry the gun to watch this runaway," the first man said. "Not to mention the lantern."

As they labored up the road, the two men argued. Jonah wondered if he could drop the jug and dive over the bank and dash into the woods. The risk was that the man with the gun would shoot at him, aiming at the sound of his running. These blockaders would not mind killing him. He had to study what to do. He didn't want to die before he even got out of South Carolina.

"You're a lazy bastard," the man with the two jugs said.

"Make the nigger carry one of them jugs," the man with the shotgun said.

"Here, take this," the other man said, and handed one of his jugs to Jonah. As he took the second jug Jonah saw that the lantern was only open on one side. That was why he hadn't noticed the light until they turned it directly on him.

With a jug in either hand, Jonah felt his arms stretched almost to the ground. Each jug must have weighed thirty pounds. He took shorter steps to keep from tripping.

"Carry them to the top of the mountain and we won't turn you in," the man with the shotgun said.

"Bet there's a re-ward for a young buck like you," the other man said.

Jonah didn't bother to answer them. They could do whatever they wanted with him. They had the gun and there were two of them. He was worn out from the whipping and the walking. And he was even more tired from the climbing.

"If we could collect a re-ward we wouldn't need to carry no liquor," the man with the shotgun said.

"We'd be rich," the second man said.

"You're already rich," the man with the shotgun said and laughed, "rich around the asshole."

As they climbed up the Winding Stairs the two men cussed and argued and threatened.

"This black boy would make a better partner than you," the man with the gun said.

Jonah's back and feet were sore. His arms ached from lugging the heavy jugs. He was too tired to run for it. He thought about how he was going to get away from the bootleggers. The road wound higher and higher. Jugs clinked in the sacks on the mule's back, and the men's boots ground on the wet clay and gravel of the road. They'd climbed so far it seemed they must be already up in the sky.

"How much is the re-ward for you, boy?" the man with the shotgun said.

"Ain't no re-ward for me," Jonah said. "I be going to see my massa in Flat Rock."

"What if we was to take you to your massa?" the other man said. "Reckon he'd give us a re-ward?"

Jonah didn't say any more; nothing he could say would help. As long as the men didn't know who he was and where he was from, they couldn't take him back to the Williams Place. But they could turn him over to a sheriff, who would put him in chains until Mr. Williams came looking for him.

"What's your name, boy?" the man with the shotgun said.

"People calls me Julius," Jonah said.

"Well, Julius, we're going to take you to Flat Rock to see how much your master will pay to get you back," the other man said.

JONAH FIGURED THESE BLOCKADERS would just as soon kill him as not, but as long as they thought there might be a reward they would at least keep him alive. Maybe he was safe until it was daylight. But as they followed the road higher up the mountain the men began to quarrel even more. The man with the shotgun said they couldn't take Jonah to Flat Rock: "Are you stupid enough to walk along the Buncombe Turnpike in broad daylight with a load of liquor?"

"Don't call me stupid, you dirty soap stick."

"After all this trouble you want to lose this liquor?"

"This boy may be worth ten times what the liquor is."

"And he may be worth nothing, you stinking polecat."

First light came just as they reached the top of the mountain. The road and the trees were still dark, but there was a faint glow faraway to the east. Jonah felt he was above the rest of the world, but he could also see there were mountains to the west higher than the ground he stood on. As it got lighter Jonah saw the second man had a pistol stuck in his belt.

"We've got to get off this road afore daylight," the man with the shotgun said. His partner said nobody would be stirring on the Turnpike at this hour, and besides, Jonah was worth more than ten loads of liquor. They cussed and argued and fussed back and forth, stopped in the middle of the road, and the one with the shotgun said they had to cut off on a trail there.

"What are we going to do with this boy?" the other man said.

"Ain't nothing to do with him except make him tote liquor."

Jonah wanted to drop the jugs and run, but he was so tired he knew they could shoot him before he reached the edge of the road. If one missed, the other was sure to hit him. Eventually the men decided they would tie Jonah to a tree. They had to get off the road, but they couldn't let him see where they were going because they were on the way to the place where they stashed their supply of liquor. The man with the pistol said they would kill Jonah if he told anybody he'd seen them.

"No, sir," Jonah said. "I ain't seen nobody."

"Damn right, you ain't seen nobody," the one with the shotgun said. He made Jonah take a drink from the small bottle he carried in his pocket. The whiskey flared in Jonah's throat and sent a blaze through his belly. Then they used a piece of twine to tie his hands to a persimmon tree.

"Anything else we can do for you?" the man with the pistol said.

"All I need is a box of matches," Jonah said.

"You want to burn down somebody's barn?"

"I just need to light my pipe."

"I'll give you some matches," the man with the pistol said. He gathered straw and leaves and heaped them at Jonah's feet. Then he poured some moonshine on the pile and dropped a match on top of it. Flames leapt up to Jonah's knees where he stood with his arms around the tree. He stepped to the side and stomped the flames as the two men laughed and headed off into the woods with their mule and clinking jugs. He heard their laughter echoing off the trees as he kicked dirt on the fire. By the time he'd stamped out the last burning leaves and straw, the woods were quiet and he couldn't hear the tinkle of jugs anymore.

The bootleggers hadn't bound his hands very tightly, and Jonah found that by leaning away from the tree he could rub the twine against the hard bark. By working his hands up and down, up and down, he wore the twine so thin he could break it. His wrists got scratched, but within a few minutes he was free.

It was almost daylight now, and he could see the trail the blockaders had taken along the side of the mountain, winding down through a kind of thicket. As the sun came into view, Jonah looked out from the ridge on a world he'd only dreamed of before. The first rays turned the mountain peaks copper, but the valley before him had fog along the streams and lifting out of coves.

Across the valley to the north a hill rose above a church steeple, and beyond that a higher ridge rippled to the west. Past that ridge other mountains rose into the early sun, like steps climbing one after the other. Mountain floated behind mountain to the edge of the world. It seemed impossible he could see so far.

Just looking at the distant mountains he didn't feel as tired or as hopeless. He was miles above the Williams Place, standing at the edge of a strange world. Surely in all the blue and copper mountains he could get lost and they'd never find him. He was so far up in the sky he must be close to the heaven they talked about in the Bible and in church. But no matter how thrilling the mountains and the view were, Jonah had to find a place to hide and rest, and he had to find a place to sleep, and something to eat. All he had was a knife and the coins in his pocket.

After following the trail through laurels for a way, Jonah climbed to the very top of the closest ridge. Under some oak trees he found a bed of moss, which, though lumpy, was softer than the ground. Jonah cut some limbs off a sweet shrub to cover and hide himself when he lay down.

He fell asleep and dreamed about dogs. A big dog like a cur lunged at him out of the dark, and when he backed away another dog gnawed at his leg. A dog barked in his ear. Another dog trotted toward him, one that appeared to be a mad dog. When Jonah woke he heard a dog barking, so it was not just a dream. The dog was far below him, somewhere down in the valley. By the sun he could tell it was late afternoon. A breeze stirred in the trees, but he could hear cicadas and a squirrel quarreling, and the dog barking. There was an ant on Jonah's chin and he flicked it away. Another ant prickled on his neck, and he saw ants on his pants. There must have been a nest of ants in the moss. He jumped to his feet and began to brush the ants away. He'd been stung on his legs and on his elbow.

The barking dog sounded closer than it had before. He listened, wondering if he could tell what kind of dog it was and if it was headed his way. Jonah knew they used bloodhounds to track runaway slaves. They used other hounds, too, and mean dogs like bulldogs and curs and Airedales. Jonah had once seen the sheriff come through the Williams Place looking for a runaway slave. All the Negroes had stood in silence as they watched the dogs go bellowing and yelping by, sniffing and panting, following a path along the edge of the field and past the last fodder barn. But when they reached the creek they lost the trail. The runaway must have walked right in the stream. Jonah had heard of all kinds of ways you could throw dogs off your tracks. The best was to run in a creek so far that the dogs lost hours trying to find where the trail continued on land again. But you could also run the length of a fallen log, then jump as far as you could, or swing on a grape vine across a gully. Any gap in a trail would slow the dogs down.

Best of all was to do what a fox would do: backtrack. An old slave named Elmer had once described that ploy to him. First you got a lead on the dogs, then you turned and walked back in your own tracks. When you came to a bank or stream you jumped as far as you could. If you were lucky the hounds would go right past. As soon as they'd gone by, you ran as hard as you could in the direction you'd come from, hoping the dogs would just be confused. Elmer had told him to never climb a tree, for if they spotted you there was no escape.

Best was to have hot pepper to sprinkle in your tracks, or gun powder, or meat with laudanum in it. But Jonah had none of those things in his pocket. If the dog was coming his way, he'd have to find a stream big enough to run in. His tracks could easily be seen in a spring branch or a swamp.

Jonah listened to the bark, but couldn't tell if the dog was really close. To reach a stream all he had to do was walk downhill, but he had to avoid roads and houses, and he knew there might be cabins on the slope or in the hollows of the mountains. It was better not to run, but to walk quickly and quietly. Before reaching the creek Jonah came to the edge of a little cornfield, tucked into a cove beside a branch. The corn smelled sweet as syrup. He stopped and listened, but didn't hear the dog anymore. He watched the rows carefully to see if anybody was around.

THREE

JONAH

The white field corn was not full in the kernel yet. In another week the grains would be bursting with milk. But the seeds were already sweet. Jonah pulled three ears and hurried back into the brush along the branch. If he left no shucks in the field no one would ever know he'd been there. If people reported things stolen along his route then someone might guess he'd come this way. They'd know the direction he was headed and Mr. Williams would send somebody to cut him off and bring him back to the Williams Place.

Jonah was so hungry he bit off the pulpy seeds and hardly chewed them. He swallowed like a dog gulping mush. But then he slowed himself down. If he ate the raw, green corn too fast, it would give him a bellyache and he'd end up sick. He slowed down and munched the sweet, fibrous seeds. The smartest thing is not to hurry, Jonah told himself.

When you have a long way to go, it does no good to get out of breath and confused. It won't help to wear yourself out when you don't have to. Mrs. Williams had more than once warned him not to be in such a rush. Hurrying was his weakness. He'd run away from the Williams Place in a hurry. A pain shot through his bones and through his bowels. He would never see Mrs. Williams again. And he'd never see Mama again. You fool, he said to himself. He put his arm across his eyes and cried hot tears. Whoa there, he said. Jonah was ashamed of himself for crying, and he was ashamed of himself for stealing money from Mama.

Later, as he ate the second and third ears, he listened for the bark of a dog. But all he heard was the slapping of the corn leaves in the breeze in the nearby field and the mutter of the branch. Chewed slowly, the corn got sweeter on his tongue. By the time he swallowed, the corn was sweet as molasses. As he chewed, the sweetness of the corn became part of him. He didn't know how it worked, but somehow the rich things he ate became part of his blood and then part of his flesh and bones. What he ate became his strength, and his future.

If it was a thousand miles to the North, and he could travel ten miles a day, it would take him months to reach his destination. He tried to recall the tutor's lessons in arithmetic. By any guess it would be late October before he got where he was going, and would be liable to be cold by then. He'd need a coat and shoes and heavy clothes. He'd need a place to stay warm. It would take money to buy the clothes. He could try to steal from clotheslines, but at some point he'd need more money than he'd taken from Mama.

Jonah pulled the jar from his pocket and looked at the coins. It was a little jar Mama had once put cherry preserves in. He counted the silver coins first. There was one silver dollar and no gold coins. It was all the money Mama had saved that summer from selling herbs out of the little garden behind her cabin. Sometimes Mr. Williams would give her a coin on her birthday, and every Christmas Mr. Williams gave each of them two bits.

Besides the silver dollar, there were two half dollars with pictures of eagles on them, and eight smaller coins, each worth two bits. Jonah counted fourteen little dimes and twenty-three nickels and eleven red pennies. As he tried to add the amount in his head he kept losing track of the numbers. But finally he separated the coins out on the ground and counted each pile and figured he had six dollars and sixty-six cents. It was a lot of money, and it was not a lot of money. It was more money than he'd ever held in his hands at once. But it would have to last him until he got all the way to the North. For that long trip he didn't even have a penny a mile.

Silver had its own smell. Jonah held the dollar and half dollar pieces to his nose. Silver tarnished like it had soot on it. What he could smell was the tarnish of silver touched by air. It was a smell of something faraway. Touching the coins left the smell on his hands. He dropped the coins into his hand and then back into the jar. And then he dumped the coins again one at a time into his left palm. Nickels had less smell on them, but pennies gave off an aroma when touched by his fingers. The pennies had big pictures on them and writing on their backs. They smelled of a special kind of spice and of secret places deep in the ground.

Coins were the most interesting objects Jonah knew. They were equal to whatever could be bought with them. A little piece of metal could be equal to a horse, or a wagonload of corn. A quarter could be equal to time, time worked for a white man, the time it took a blacksmith to shoe a horse, an hour spent with a whore, or so he'd heard from Johnny Williams.

"What do you mean, whore?" Jonah had said.

"You don't know what a whore is?" Johnny said. "A whore is a fancy woman you pay for, to hop. You pay by the hour."

"Where is such a woman?" Jonah said.

"Why, everywhere. In Greenville, in Charleston." That had set Jonah thinking in a whole new way. Time was equal to money, and a woman's body was equal to money an hour at a time. It seemed that everything was equal to money, including freedom.

But coins were like jewels, too. They shone and clinked with music in them. They had little faces carved on them, and birds and flags. A coin was a work of art, a thing of beauty. It had weight and texture to the touch. The feel of the coins of money delighted and thrilled Jonah. Money was different from anything else in the woods because it was a man-made sign. Jonah knew that he'd need more money for his journey to the North. But even with money he could be stopped and beaten and returned to Mr. Williams anytime. He himself had a price. He was worth so many dollars to Mr. Williams, and to other white folks. Maybe a hundred dollars, maybe five hundred, for he was, at eighteen, young and strong. A few coins were equal to him. If he ever got to the North he knew he'd have to make money, if he was to be free and happy. Money was equal to freedom, to a house, a horse, a field, a fine suit of clothes, a wife, a fancy woman. He would find money and make money. If he ever made it to the North, that's what he would do.

There was no reason to carry Mama's jar; it hardly fit in his pocket, and it made the coins rattle and clink. He was lucky the bootleggers hadn't heard the coins. What he needed was a leather poke, a little sack. He'd have to carry the coins in his pockets until he could find such a sack. The heavy coins would wear a hole in his pocket, and then he could lose them. As soon as he could, he'd have to find a safer way to carry his money.

As Jonah was putting the coins in his pocket, a thought came to him that sent a shiver through his bones and gut. The amount of the money was $6.66, which was the number that was the Mark of the Beast in the

Bible: 666 was the sign of the Anti-Christ. He'd heard the preacher talk about that evil number, and he'd read about it himself in the Book of Revelation. It was the sign of the end of the world and the Great Tribulation. Whoever was marked with the number wore the sign of Satan. Whoever had the Mark of the Beast would be damned.

Jonah thought of throwing all the money away. The number showed it was cursed because he had stolen it from Mama. It was the amount that had taken her so long to save, money to buy herself cloth for a new dress. The number of the Beast was his punishment for stealing and for running away. Jonah weighed the coins in his hand. They felt heavier than they had before. There was something crushing about the weight of the silver and copper. The value seemed bleached out of the metal and the magic of the pictures and faces faded. All the delight he had taken had melted away.

And then Jonah knew what to do. Taking a penny from the handful, he poured the rest back into his pocket. With a stick he scratched a hole in the ground, big enough for the penny to fit in. Quickly he covered the red cent with dirt and raked leaves on top of the dirt. He patted down the leaves so no one would ever know they'd been disturbed. He almost smiled as he placed sticks on the leaves. Now there was six dollars and sixty-five cents in his pocket. He had no number of the Mark of the Beast on him. He'd paid his tribute to the earth under his feet. He'd returned the metal to the soil it came from. Now the metal in his pocket was not as tainted. He carried on his person enough metal to last him for weeks and hundreds of miles.

It was late afternoon when Jonah crossed the creek on rocks. The stream was bigger than he'd thought at first, and when his foot slid on a mossy rock he crashed into water up to his pants pockets. The creek water was so cold it burned his butt, and he stood and splashed through the pool to the shallows, holding his breath. He didn't know why he held his breath, but he did until he reached the ground near the bank. As he approached the bank, a tree limb moved near him and he saw a long, dark snake like a corkscrew unwind itself from the limb and plop into the water near his feet. It was a water snake that went scribbling out into the current and downstream. But he couldn't tell whether it was a cottonmouth or not.

The far bank of the creek was covered with trees and bushes, briars and vines. It looked impossible to get through. He parted two bushes to find an opening. He hoped there was no poison oak or poison ash among the mess, and no copperhead hidden in the weeds. Turning sideways, stooping under vines, Jonah emerged from the thicket along the creek and saw a log house at the edge of a clearing. Someone was chopping wood and he listened to the knock of the axe, and the thud of the echo from the ridge across the creek. Between the creek and the cabin a cornfield fidgeted its leaves in the breeze.

It looked as if there was a vegetable garden close to the house, for he saw bean poles with vines on them reaching above the rows of okra. He was sure there'd be tomatoes and summer squash there, maybe onions and carrots. But the garden was near the woodpile and he dared not get close. An ash hopper for making lye for soap stood just a few feet from the woodpile.

Beyond the garden rose a little building with a chimney, which Jonah guessed was either a blacksmith shed or smokehouse. If it was the former there might be a box of matches by the furnace. If it was the latter there might possibly be matches by the fireplace, though that was unlikely since meat was cured in late fall, not in the middle of summer.

Bending low behind the corn rows, Jonah worked his way around the little patch, keeping an eye out for anybody who might be in the field or garden. Crack and thud, the axe went, crack and thud. As he got closer he saw a long barn by a rail fence and a pasture on the hill where several cows grazed. The manure pile beside the barn glistened with a halo of flies. With disappointment he saw the small building was indeed a smokehouse.

Staying close to the barn and then in the shadow of the smokehouse, he crept to the door and looked in. It was so dark he couldn't see anything inside except the shelves where the salted meat was laid and the hooks where the hams could be hung over the fire. There was an overwhelming scent of smoke and ashes, grease and salt. It was not a bad smell, but summer heat had made the air a little rancid. Jonah looked out of the corner of his eye into the gloom. A couple of hams that appeared to have been turned to stone lay on the shelf by the door. Another ham, carved down to the shank, rested on a small table. As his eyes adjusted to the shadows, he studied the shelves and benches and saw kindling wood and a bag of salt. An old butcher knife lay on the table beside the shank meat, and Jonah sliced off a slab of the meat and put it in his pocket.

Jonah backed out of the smokehouse and closed the door. The afternoon air appeared brighter after the shade of the building. There was no longer the sound of chopping. He stood perfectly still and waited to hear someone moving. A chicken walked by and a puppy ran up wagging its tail. The puppy twisted its behind to show how happy it was to see him. A door banged and Jonah hoped the wood chopper had gone inside. He waited a little longer, and then walked sideways with his back to the shed. Skirting the manure pile where flies the color of dew dilated and hummed a chorus of hallelujahs, he reached the barn and hugged the wall to reach the edge of the pasture.

With someone at the house he dared not get any closer. His back was sore and his feet were sore. He couldn't believe he'd been crazy enough to run away from the Williams Place where there was plenty to eat and a bed to sleep in. You must be dumb as a chicken, he said to himself. All he wanted to find here was a box of matches that would cost a penny at the Gap Creek store. He was risking his life just to find a few matches. It seemed he'd been a fool to run away from all the comforts he'd ever known and all the safety he'd known, too.

Jonah saw it was too risky to cross the fence into the pasture, because the pasture was open and on high ground where he could be seen from the creek valley. Keeping the barn between himself and the house, he followed the fence to the edge of the pines and ducked into the cover of the trees. He noticed a trail that swung below the barn and into the pines, and he followed it into a hollow. The trail ended at a spring below some laurel bushes where a gourd hung on a stick. There was a wash table on the bank beside the spring branch, with two wooden tubs and a washboard. A black pot sat on rocks over the ashes of a fire. A cake of soap the color of beeswax lay on the table. Jonah suddenly knew how thirsty he was. He'd not had a drink all day. As he reached for the gourd to dip a drink he saw something blue out of the corner of his eye. Running to the table he saw it was a paper matchbox.

Sliding the box out of its sleeve, Jonah saw the box was almost empty, with no more than ten or twelve matches inside. But he could not have been happier if he'd found a box of gold coins. With a dozen matches he could start fires for a week or more. He quietly slipped the box inside his shirt and then took a drink from the gourd. Then, with the matches close to his belly, Jonah climbed through the pines up the hill above the pasture. Before it got dark again he had to study about his plans. He had to be smart if he was going to make it through North Carolina to Virginia and then to the North. He had to be smart every minute of the day.

Since he had money in his pocket, Jonah had to figure out a way to go into stores and buy what he needed. The money was just a burden if it couldn't be spent. It would wear a hole in his pocket and be lost. Any unfamiliar black boy going into a store in a strange place would look suspicious. And it was possible Mr. Williams would send out posters with his name and description. He'd seen such posters on store walls in Travelers Rest, and he'd seen announcements in newspapers about runaways.

It occurred to Jonah that on rare occasions Mrs. Williams had written a note to a storekeeper in Travelers Rest and had Jonah or another servant carry it there and bring back the merchandise. If he had such a note he could take it into a store and buy what he wanted. What he needed was a pencil and paper. But to get the pencil and paper he'd have to go into a store. It seemed a problem that couldn't be solved.

Another problem that hadn't occurred to Jonah until now was that there were few plantations, therefore few slaves, in the mountains, meaning that everyone there would notice him. And the deeper he went into the highlands, the more suspicious he would appear. He hadn't thought of that before. He'd have to be even more careful than he'd planned. Deep in the mountains where they were not used to seeing black folks, everybody would notice him and remember him. But it was also possible that since there were so few slaves in the uplands, someone might be willing to help him. If they didn't have slaves themselves, they might not be sympathetic to Mr. Williams or afraid of the Fugitive Slave Law.

Jonah reached the top of the hill, where hickory trees replaced the yellow pines. There was less undergrowth, and he walked quickly along the comb of the ridge and down the other side. In another hour it would be dark and he had to find a place to sleep. The ants on the bed of moss had taught him how vulnerable he was when sleeping on the ground. Besides ants, the copperheads were crawling blind in the summer night. It was dangerous to hurry through the woods as it got dark, for he might step in a sinkhole, or walk over a copperhead, or run into a hornet's nest. Or worse yet, run into someone carrying a gun who would take him into custody. The woods were getting so dark he could hardly see the spiderwebs.

Suddenly Jonah saw something white looming in the trees ahead. At first he thought it was a tree in blossom, and then he thought it might be fog or white smoke. He slowed down and slipped from tree to tree, holding the money in his pocket to keep it from rattling. The thing had a shape, like a sheet draped over a frame. It had a tall pointed hat. Jonah edged from tree to tree, holding his breath in the dark shade of the thick woods. Whatever it was stood just on the other side of the trees. He pushed a chestnut limb aside and caught his breath. And then he laughed at himself and called himself an idiot. "Whoa there," he said.

For there stood a little white church with a gray steeple. It was a church made of logs whitewashed until they glowed in the twilight. The steeple was white, too, except for the pointed tip, which was gray with weathered, cedar shingles. It was a tiny building with a patch of graves beside it, small as a kitchen garden. The church reminded him of a toy, a playhouse, a dollhouse, but was just big enough so he knew it was not a toy, but a real place where people gathered for worship.

Finding the church made Jonah feel better. He waited and listened and heard nobody else. The windows were dark and the only sound came from a bird calling in the woods. The gravestones under the trees tilted this way and that way. Jonah darted out into the clearing around the church but didn't try the front door. Instead he circled to the back, where two wooden outhouses sat at the edge of the woods. There was a second door on the side of the church and he turned the knob. At first the door didn't give, but he shook the knob the way you sometimes shake a key to make it fall in place. The glass knob turned and the door swung in.

It was completely dark inside the little church, which smelled of old wood and dust and ashes. As his eyes grew accustomed to the dark, he saw the fireplace to the left of the pulpit. Benches were aligned on the bare floor. Jonah felt the matches inside his pocket, but decided not to light the lamp. A light might attract someone who happened to be passing. The air in the church was hot and stale. A lighted lamp would make it warmer still, and smoky.

As quietly as he could Jonah pushed two benches together to make a bed just in front of the altar. The benches were hard but clean, and they'd keep him off the floor. He was stiff and sore and his wounds were a little itchy. He found that if he lay down carefully he could rest on his back, but he'd have to lie still.

Lying so near the altar where sinners had prayed and backsliders had been reclaimed, Jonah knew he should pray also. It wouldn't hurt to ask the Lord to help him. A bug of some kind buzzed in the air above him, but Jonah was so tired he sank almost instantly into a long voyage of sleep in the isolated sanctuary.

WHEN HE WOKE JONAH thought at first how thirsty he was, and then how hungry. All he'd eaten yesterday were the three ears of partly green corn. Today he'd eat the meat, but first he needed a drink of cool water. Lying on the benches, he looked down at the puncheon floor of the little church. Years of wear around the altar had smoothed the wood until it was almost polished, but dust had collected in the cracks between logs. The dust looked bright as salt where early sun came through a window. Jonah thought of the sweat and tears from many revival meetings in late summer, as well as the storms of dust in the air even now whirling and wrestling in the sunlight, and settling hour after hour, year after year, on the bumpy floor.

As he sat up and rubbed his eyes, Jonah saw what looked like a black letter *Q* or an *X*, run around the pulpit and disappear. He knew it must be a bug or a fly, but it really looked like a black letter of the alphabet had fallen out of the Bible some Sunday and lay on the altar until he had disturbed it. He stood and peered around a corner of the pulpit.

A black widow spider sat under the shelter of the lectern. Its belly sparkled like a drop of wet ink, and its legs curved slender as buggy springs. Black widows could jump. Jonah knew he should kill the spider, for it might bite the preacher or song leader as they stood at the pulpit. But there was nothing in sight he could use. He needed a stick or a broom. Besides, he wasn't sure black widows spread a web and stayed in one place. Maybe they traveled and ate the insects they encountered. By Sunday morning the black widow might be far away. Jonah decided to leave the dot of venom where it was. The empty church was so quiet he didn't want to disturb anything.

Jonah did push the two benches back to their original places before he left. He wanted to be on his way, to hurry through the valleys and hollows, leaving no more trace than a breeze or a shadow.

There was a spring near most churches and Jonah soon found the spring behind this one. In fact it was a double spring, with two springheads coming from opposite directions out of the hill and merging into one branch. The southern head was sluggish and filled with moss and flies. But the northern spring rippled out clear into the basin, with sand dancing around the inlets and the overflow throbbing. He took a coconut shell from a stick nearby and drank the cold sparkling water, which tasted like it had run through rock and quartz and precious metals from deep in the earth. Jonah took a slice of the shank meat out of his pocket. If he started a fire he could slide the meat on a stick and cook it brown and crisp. It would taste like ham, salty ham. But the smell of the slab of pork was a little off, and when he looked at it closely he saw tiny worms like grubs in the fibers. The meat had been blown by flies. Even if he raked out the worms the piece would not be edible. He dropped the shank meat on the ground for the ants to find, and rinsed his hands in the branch.

With the coins rattling in his pocket, Jonah followed the spring branch down the valley. He wasn't sure anymore where the Turnpike was, but he wanted to avoid it in any case. If Mr. Williams came looking for him, that was the way he'd come. Even if he crossed the Turnpike or had to follow it a ways, he should stay on it only briefly.

Jonah wanted to go north, and north was to the left if you faced the early sun. The spring branch ran toward the sun, so he turned to the left and walked, and when he came to a field he saw a wall of mountains ahead, higher mountains. The steep ridge had cliffs like teeth along its top. The steepness and height made him weak with dread. He was tired from hunger. How could he climb such a steep barrier unbroken by gaps or low places? And yet, if he was going north, that was the way he had to go.

He crossed the field and came to a little creek that seemed to shiver right out of the mountainside ahead. Maybe if he followed the creek it would take him part way up the ridge, and lead him into a hollow where the climb would be easier. It was the sheer cliffs that scared him. The small stream wandered like a path through the woods. He jumped from rock to rock and bank to bank. Sometimes he had to duck under limbs, and twice he saw snakes slip off branches into the water. And then he came to a larger pool and saw several shadows hovering near the sandy bottom. Without a fishhook it seemed impossible to catch something so quick and slippery. If only he could drive one into the shallows of the little stream. Thinking of a narrow, shallow pool gave Jonah an idea. Stepping to the bank he began breaking sticks about a foot long. He gathered dead sticks and living sticks of sourwood and sweet shrub. He broke poplar limbs and maple limbs. With his knife he cut some river cane until he had more than a hundred sticks. He stripped off leaves and sharpened the ends of the bigger sticks.

Jonah studied the pool where the trout hovered near the bottom.

At the lower end the pool got sandy and shallow before spilling over a lip of rock. He began planting the sticks in sand about an inch apart. He made a line from the deeper water to a shallow depression. The sticks stood like pickets of a little fence. He made a second line starting about four feet from the end of the first and converging into a chute that led into the shallows. When finished, he had a funnel that narrowed into a passage no more than four inches wide. If he could scare a trout into the entrance of the funnel and drive it up the chute, he could catch it in the shallows with his hands.

First placing his matches in a dry spot on the bank, Jonah waded into the pool from the side opposite the trap. Trout flashed like bolts of lightning in the water. He tried to see where they went, but the shadows and mirrory sides turned too fast for him to follow. And then he saw something rippling the water between his rows of sticks. Wading quickly across the pool to drive them, he saw two trout indeed had gone into his trap. The fin of the bigger one sliced out of the water. It was a fat trout, maybe fourteen, fifteen inches long. Jonah stepped into the entrance of the funnel and the fish thrashed farther up into the neck.

The trout floundered right into the narrows of the chute and Jonah reached down to grab the bigger one. Because the fish was so quick and slippery he couldn't grab hold of it. Instead, he tried to scoop both trout up and heave them onto the bank. Jonah tossed one thrashing fish up on the bank. But the other trout had turned between the rows of sticks and shot between his feet and was gone. It was the bigger fish that escaped. But the other trout flipped and trembled among the ferns on the bank, and he seized it and held it with his fingers in the gills.

After he'd cut off the head, ripped open the belly, and raked out the guts, Jonah laid the trout on a log and scraped off the tiny scales, then washed the scales and slime away and impaled the fish on a sourwood stick. With the knife he shaved curls off a stick of dry pine and started a fire. Then he held the trout on the stick over the flames. Without butter or oil the fish had to roast in its own grease. As the trout browned in the flames, it filled the woods by the creek with the scent of roasting flesh. The fire made the place in the woods seem almost like home. The fire and the smell of the cooking fish inspired him with a new confidence.

When the trout was browned on the outside he took it off the flames. The flesh was too hot to eat, and he blew on the steaming sides. Jonah wet his lips and nibbled a morsel near the tail. To keep from burning his tongue he moved the bit of fish around in his mouth, and when he tasted the flesh he knew it was the sweetest thing he'd ever savored. Fresh from the stream, the trout had a vivid flavor he'd never known before. It was like other fish he'd had, but better, so much better.

As the fish cooled, he nibbled bits off the comb of bones. The fish tickled his mouth and sweetened his belly. He ate slowly, cleaning every bit of meat off the tines of bones. The warmth and strength of the fish flowed out from his belly into his veins and into his limbs. Jonah sat on the ground and leaned against an oak tree. He would wash his hands in the creek in a minute and move on. It was a thousand miles to the North and safety. It was so strange to think that he had to go all the way to Canada to be safe and free.

How strange that he was Jonah and not someone else, strange that he'd been born who he was and where he was. He could just as easily have been born in another time and place. He could have been born white and free. He could have been born a Cherokee Indian or a chief in Africa. He could have been born rich and in the North. Instead he'd been born Jonah Williams, a slave on the Williams Place, which Mr. Williams called Snowdon. And he'd been whipped for stealing a book that was already his. And he'd had no choice but to steal himself from Mr. Williams and run away into the night. The sores on his back itched and smarted. His feet were sore from all the walking he'd done. But he had a knife and he had matches and he had a gut full of trout. And he knew how to spend the money he had, if only he could find pencil and paper.

After he'd rested maybe half an hour, it was time to go. If he was going to climb the mountain wall, he might as well go ahead and do it early in the day. He washed the knife and washed his hands and placed the matches in his pocket. And he started following the creek deeper into the side of the mountain.

Around the next bend he came to a waterfall leaping off a rock shelf twenty feet above the pool. There was no choice but to climb up the steep side of the hollow, through ferns and spray from the falls, pulling himself up on roots and rocks, bushes and saplings. When he reached the shelf where the waterfall milked over the rim, he saw the cliffs far above. To reach the top he'd have to climb between the cliffs, crawling on hands and knees through laurels, looking out for snakes and stingworms on logs. As Jonah began to climb through briars and vines, he saw there was no secret to the labor of climbing but to go slow. Rising a foot at a time, one step at a time, he could mount to the summit, picking a way among rocks and brush. It would take him much of the day to get across.

FOUR

JONAH

Once Jonah reached the top of the ridge, he stepped out on a jutting cliff and looked to the north. A wide valley spread as far as he could see, to the chains of higher mountains to the west and north and east. The floor of the valley below was almost completely flat. The faraway mountains appeared to float in blue-white haze, and the air above the valley seemed to have smoke in it, the smoke of heat and full summer. Directly below the ridge where he stood stretched a wide pine woods, with clearings here and there and roofs of big houses and a church that looked as if it came from another country, a church of pink stone with a tower, sitting on a rise.

Jonah turned and walked out the ridge until he found a trail, which he followed down the steep north side. The path switched back and forth among boulders and trees, always going down, and Jonah felt the fish in his belly gave him strength. He jumped from foothold to foothold, swinging around saplings, banking off of boulders. It didn't take long to reach the valley floor.

There at the head of a creek valley he saw the first house. It was a long three-story dwelling with porches across the front, the biggest house he'd ever seen. The walls were painted blinding white. The big house had barns and outbuildings, slave quarters, and a woodshed behind it. A black woman was cooking over an open fire outside the summer kitchen. A large dog barked from a pen near the barn. Jonah stepped back into the woods and skirted the field and pasture that flanked the mansion. When he saw two more big white houses farther down the valley, he guessed he must have reached Flat Rock. Only Flat Rock would have such fine mansions deep in the mountains. He tried to recall the name of the family Mrs. Williams and Betsy and Johnny were visiting, but he couldn't. He knew Mrs. Williams had mentioned where they were going, to visit her sister, but he'd forgotten the name.

He picked his way carefully along the edge of the farthest outlying fields, his goal being to go around Flat Rock. Word of his escape might have already reached the community there. A man and woman on horses galloped near him, and he crouched in the ragweeds until they were past. As he walked on, Jonah heard voices and the clopping of more horses. When he reached the pine woods he could move faster, for there was little undergrowth or brush beneath the tall pines. He heard the creak of a wagon and the rumble of carriage wheels on gravel, and soon a road came into view. Two men on horses passed, and then a cart pulled by oxen. Jonah backed out of sight behind a large pine tree and watched.

Farther down the road another white house rose among pine trees. Its lawn was wide, and boxwoods lined the driveway up to the front porch. Flower gardens and trellises with vines decorated the yard. A white statue stood in an open space beyond the end of the porch. It was the fanciest yard Jonah had ever seen, and he knew that black men must have worked a thousand hours to make it that way.

In the other direction, going north, Jonah saw what looked like a store across the road from another larger mansion. No buggies were stopped in front of the store, but a horse was tied to the railing beside the entrance. As dangerous as it might be to go into the store, Jonah figured he'd have no better chance to get a few things he needed. He had to have a pencil and paper to write notes to use in other stores, and he needed bread or crackers. He also needed fishhooks, and, of course, shoes for the long walk ahead.

When a carriage drove by, Jonah stepped into the ditch and let it go past. He bowed to the white folks in the carriage as Mr. Williams had taught him to do. He wanted to show good manners and not call attention to himself. White people would hardly notice a Negro who was humble and good-mannered. After the carriage passed, he walked slowly with his head down. A slave was never supposed to hurry, or hold his head too high. He needed to pass through in such a way that white folks wouldn't remember he'd been there. As Jonah approached the store, a man came out the front door and mounted the horse tied there. When Jonah got closer the man said, "Can't you see the store is closed—it's Sunday."

Jonah's face grew hot. He'd lost track of the days of the week.

"Massa done told me to get him a tablet," Jonah said, like he was ashamed and afraid.

"Who told you?" the man on horseback said.

"Massa Charles," Jonah said. "He say git him a tablet so he can write he letters, sir."

"Why would he want paper on a Sunday?" the mounted man said.

"He say get him a tablet, all I know," Jonah said and shrugged his shoulders.

The man swung off the horse and tied the reins to the rail. He took a key from his pocket and opened the door. Jonah followed him into the shadowy store, trying to seem as though he was used to going there. The place smelled of leather and coffee. The man stepped behind the counter and pulled a writing tablet from the shelf. It was pretty, light-blue paper.

"Will that be all?" the storekeeper said.

"Massa Charles say he need a pencil, too," Jonah said.

"Why would he need a pencil if he writes with a pen?" the man said. The storekeeper took a green pencil from a box and laid it beside the tablet on the counter. "Now you get out of here," he said.

Jonah had thought he might ask for fishhooks and more matches, a loaf of bread, maybe even some shoes. And he was going to reach into his pocket for the coins, but he saw the storekeeper write something in his account book, charging the tablet and pencil to someone named Charles. If he asked for fishhooks or shoes on a Sunday, it would indeed look suspicious.

"Thank you, sir," Jonah said.

"You tell Charles we don't do business on Sundays," the man said.

"Yes, sir, yes, sir, I tells him," Jonah said and bowed.

Once he got outside, Jonah turned back south, the way he'd come. He knew it would look odd if he continued north. The storekeeper locked the building, mounted the horse, and rode north, and soon as he was out of sight Jonah turned in his tracks and followed him. He put the pencil in his pocket and the tablet inside his shirt. It wouldn't look right if he was seen walking along the road with a tablet of fresh blue paper. That was not the kind of thing a slave would carry on a Sunday morning.

Jonah followed the Turnpike over a low hill and saw another store on the right. It was smaller than the first, and had UNITED STATES POST OFFICE written over the door. A number of posters and handbills had been tacked to the wall beside the door. Jonah stepped out of the road to glance at the posters. One described a convict who'd escaped from prison in Asheville. Another offered a reward for a horse that had been stolen. And then Jonah saw his name on a handbill. RUNAWAY SLAVE JONAH WILLIAMS, the sheet said. There was a rough sketch of his face, and he was described as five feet eleven inches. A reward of one hundred dollars was offered for his return.

Jonah felt his heart race as he tore the poster from the wall and walked away from the little post office. He was worth a hundred dollars to anybody who caught him. Mr. Williams was willing to pay that much to get him back to whip and brand him. The poster in his hand took some of the strength out of Jonah's chest and legs. He grew tired as he crossed another hill and came down into a deep valley. He had to get off the Turnpike soon. If there was one poster there would be others at stores and post offices along the way. Maybe even some nailed to trees, for Mr. Williams would guess he'd gone north. As soon as he came to a side road Jonah would take that. He'd follow the mountain chain and he'd stay far from turnpikes and towns after this.

Jonah saw a pink church ahead to his left. Carriages and buggies and carts were parked in the yard, and saddle horses were tied to the trees outside. A crowd clustered outside the door. Jonah climbed the bank into some hemlock trees to get a better look. He'd been startled to see his name on the poster, and he was startled again to see Mrs. Williams among the crowd entering the church. Mrs. Williams wore a blue hat with a bright blue dress and a light blue shawl. Betsy and Johnny stood on either side of her. They almost certainly knew by now that he'd run away.

Jonah got as close as he dared as Mrs. Williams and the children disappeared into the church, which looked like something from a foreign country, maybe Italy or Spain, the pictures of which he'd seen in newspapers and magazines and books in Mr. Williams's library. A graveyard stretched across the hill behind the church, and when everyone had gone inside Jonah hurried across the cemetery and into the shrubbery nearby. A horse snorted and shook its bridle. As he got close to the wall of the church, Jonah heard organ music and singing inside, and he got closer to the window to hear better. It was the first music he'd heard in a long time; it made him think of sacred things.

Jonah sat in the shrubbery beside the church and listened, wishing he could be inside. Jesus had preached love and mercy; Jonah had read the words in the Book of John. But it felt to him that it must be only love and mercy for white people. If Jesus loved everybody the same way, why had he made some masters and some Negroes?

It was a question Jonah had puzzled about before, of course. But with his back sore and his feet sore and his legs tired and the poster folded in his hand, he listened to the wonderful music and wondered why the world was the way it was. He'd asked Mrs. Williams that very question once, and her answer was that the ways of the Lord are a mystery beyond human understanding. Sinful people and even good people were not meant to know why everything was the way it was. That's why they had to have faith. Only faith enabled them to accept the world as it was. Only faith allowed them to live their lives in harmony with God's plan.

Such talk did not make much sense to Jonah. The more he thought about it, the less he understood why God's plan would make some people slaves, and some crippled or afflicted in their minds. Only the beautiful organ music and the high trill of the chorus had any meaning. As the service drew to a close, Jonah knew he had to run. He could not be caught hiding in the shrubbery when Mrs. Williams and the children came outside, although he wished that he could talk with her again. He wiped his eyes and stood up.

Beyond the cemetery, the hill dropped steeply to a branch, and the branch threaded its way through a musty hollow. A wagon road ran out along the edge of the swampy area, and Jonah followed the tracks to the north. As he walked along the ruts of the wagon track, he thought about the kind of bag or sack he could use. Best would be a leather satchel with a strap he could hang over his shoulder. With such a bag he could carry extra things: a cup and maybe a kettle for boiling water, a change of clothes, a compass to tell him always which way was north. And he needed to carry things to eat, plus pepper to sprinkle on his tracks if dogs were chasing him.

As he thought of all the things he might need, Jonah began to laugh at himself. He was thinking as though he were a rich man, a free man, a white man. A leather case like he wanted would only call attention to himself. Everybody who saw it would assume he'd stolen it. A Negro with a fine leather case like a saddle bag would arouse everybody's suspicions.

What he actually needed was something so plain nobody would notice it, a flour sack or even a tow sack. With a tow sack flung over his shoulder, he would look like a Negro who had been to mill, or was carrying tools for his master. It was a tow sack he'd look for.

Something else Jonah knew he needed was a book to read, for he'd spend long hours, maybe days, waiting in woods and swamps, perhaps hiding in attics and barn lofts, waiting for a chance to move, and it could make a big difference if he had something to pass the time, to focus his thoughts, to take his mind off the fear he felt. And the best book would be the Bible, for it was big and had many different stories, and it would give him something to think about when he was afraid. A Bible would give him a place to go that was familiar, no matter where he might be reading it. The Bible was a home he could take with him, however difficult its message was to understand.

Walking at a steady stride and wondering where he might find a

Holy Book, or any book, Jonah was hardly aware of the hoofbeats coming along the wagon road behind him. And when he did notice the noise and turn to look back, the horse and rider were already in sight. It was too late to hide, for if he dashed into the woods that would only make him look more like a runaway. He kept walking, as if he was just going about his business.

The horse and rider bore down on him, passed Jonah, and then wheeled to confront him.

"Where are you going, boy?" the rider said. It was the man from the store who'd given him the tablet and pencil.

"Just taking the tablet to Massa Charles," Jonah answered. It was all he could think of to say.

"Charles Eliot don't live in this direction," the rider said.

"I be taking the long way, sir," Jonah said and bowed. "Massa Charles he told me not to be in no hurry."

"You're a thief and a liar," the storekeeper said. "I've seen your likeness on a poster." The man swung his riding crop and hit Jonah on the shoulder. The lash burned like a hornet sting.

The bank of the road was covered with big weeds, some twice as high as a man's head. Jonah leapt into the mammoth weeds and ran blindly, knocking stalks out of his way. The weeds crowded the bank of the little stream, and on the other side briars and grapevines tangled among the trees. Jonah splashed through the mud of the branch and up the bank, through briars and knots of vines.

"I'll catch you, you black bastard," the man on the horse called. If the rider had gotten off the horse, he could have chased Jonah through the weeds and mud and vines and possibly caught him. But Jonah was pretty sure the storekeeper would not get off the horse. The man would come riding after him and hit him again with the crop, but he wouldn't get down on the ground, on the level with a runaway slave.

Jonah saw he had the advantage of a rabbit or a fox in deep cover. The vines and briars and brush would keep out the horse and rider while he could hurry through. Without dogs the man could only follow him by sight. But Jonah's advantage would only last a few minutes, because the man would find a place to cross the branch and come riding after him into the woods. Beyond the vines and brush along the stream, Jonah saw only pine woods, with little undergrowth or scrub to hide him. He could run fast through the woods, but so could the horse and rider. He'd have to think quick. One thought was to wait until the horseman was in the woods, then plunge back across the branch, but that would gain him only a minute or two.

Looking around for the biggest pine tree, Jonah spotted a giant about a hundred feet away. The tree was so big and old, its bark looked more like masonry than something alive. The limbs near the ground had broken away, but about five feet up the stubs of limbs stuck out from the trunk, and a few feet above that living limbs reached out like spokes from a hub. Jonah jumped and grabbed the lowest limb. It broke and he fell into the pine straw. But he pushed himself up and grabbed for the next limb. Bracing with his feet on the bark, he reached the next stub and pulled himself onto the first living branch. Climbing a tree was just what Elmer had warned him not to do, but there was really no choice. The pine was smeared with drops and scabs of resin, and already his hands were sticky. Hoofbeats came closer and the horse and rider trotted into sight just as he slipped into the higher limbs.

The horseman passed by beneath him and Jonah climbed higher still. He was about halfway up the big tree when the man on the horse came back, searching behind every tree. Jonah stood very still on a big limb. If a twig broke, if a piece of bark or resin fell, he was lost. The man would simply wait until he had to come down. If he made a noise or moved, the man might spot him.

"I will catch you!" the man called out. Jonah couldn't see him so he wasn't sure in what direction the storekeeper was shouting. "We don't take kindly to thieves around here," the man added.

Jonah stood still while the tree sighed and stirred around him. The smell of the resin was fresh, but there was a kind of dust or mold on the white pine that made him want to sneeze. He put a sticky finger under his nose, and tears smarted his eyes.

"You might as well give up," the man hollered. "I can go back for dogs and track you down."

The bark of the tree close to his face looked more like the hide of some animal than a part of a tree. It was shiny and gray, with a tint of green. It looked like some kind of leather, but resin oozed through cracks, clear as honey.

"If I have to go get dogs to find you, I'll put you in chains," the man yelled. "Then I'll whip your black arse and turn you over to your owner."

Jonah hugged the tree like it was his mama. He was fifty feet in the air and safe for the moment. But he'd not be safe if the man brought dogs. They would smell him on the ground beneath the tree, and they'd follow him wherever he ran. But the next time the man called, he was farther away, and that suggested he didn't know which tree Jonah had climbed, though he seemed to have guessed that Jonah had climbed some tree. He was riding around the woods looking for Jonah up trees and behind trees and bushes.

Jonah waited until the man was out of hearing and slowly climbed higher in the pine. As he got near the top, the breeze picked up and limbs swayed back and forth. The air was fresher up there. When he got close to the very top, Jonah could see over the other trees. He could view the tower of the church and a tall white mansion to the left of the church hill. Turning to the north, he saw a wide, flat valley with a chain of mountains beyond, almost white in the haze. To the northeast there was a big mountain that was almost black. Reaching up above all the peaks around it, that summit seemed as ominous as an enormous, brooding bear.

From near the top of the giant pine, Jonah could see the wagon road he'd followed from the church hill. A horse with a rider trotted along the track. Jonah was pretty sure it was the man who had chased him. He hugged closer to the top of the tree, hoping he couldn't be seen at such a distance. In the breeze the top swayed back and forth, leaning far out and returning, rocking and returning. He thought that must be the way it felt to ride a big horse, swaying and returning, rising and falling.

If he had a horse he could travel three times as fast as he could on foot. With a horse Jonah could reach the North before summer was over. He'd have a chance to outrun posses and sheriffs and bounty hunters. But even as he daydreamed about stealing a horse, Jonah knew such a plan was impossible. If he stole a horse he'd be pursued as a horse thief and hanged. Added to that, the sight of a Negro on a horse traveling long distances would bring attention he didn't need.

But while he was daydreaming high in the pine, Jonah saw another picture in his mind. It was an impossible picture, but so pretty he couldn't help but study on it. If he had a good horse and a fine closed carriage, he could be the driver and act like he was carrying some important white person to Richmond or Washington. If he had the right clothes, everybody would assume he was the driver for a rich man. Who would look inside the closed carriage to see who the passenger was?

The idea was so attractive, Jonah kept running it through his mind. Of course he didn't have any such horse and carriage, and he didn't have any fine clothes, but if he did he might be able to pull it off, drive all the way to the North on the widest and best roads, and nobody would ever stop him. It was something to study on.

Another thought came to Jonah because of the tablet he carried inside his shirt. He wondered if it might be possible to write out a certificate saying he'd been freed by his owner. If he knew how such a document looked, he might be able to make one that would convince any sheriff or bounty hunter who stopped him. Of course he'd have to know what kind of paper to use, and what kind of pen and ink, and he'd have to know the words to write on such a document. If he had the right kind of papers, he could go anywhere without fear.

JONAH STARTLED HIMSELF FROM his daydream and began climbing down. He had to run before the man returned with dogs and more men on horses. He descended from limb to limb, and it seemed that with each step he lost more confidence. The limbs trembled with his weight, and his arms trembled as he grasped at the branches. Resin made his hands stick on the wood, pulling his skin like glue. As he dropped into the shadows of the deep woods, he wondered why he'd ever thought he could escape from Mr. Williams and from slavery. He was a thousand miles from Canada and at least five hundred from Pennsylvania. He didn't have a map, and he didn't have any transportation except his own bare feet. He only had money enough to last for a few weeks at most, and every time he stole something he might give away his whereabouts. The man at the store in Flat Rock had spotted him because of the poster, and because of the direction he'd taken. It was only a matter of time before somebody caught him and sent him back to Mr. Williams. Why had he thought he was smart enough to run away? Why had he thought he could be lucky enough to make his way all the way to the North? By the time Jonah reached the ground, he was overwhelmed by his own foolishness and doubts. It was because he'd learned to read and Mrs. Williams had encouraged him to read that he had such a high opinion of himself. If he was as ignorant as the rest of the folks at the Williams Place, he would never have thought of escaping.

All is vanity and vexation of spirit, and grasping for the wind, the Bible said, and now he could see clearly what the preacher in Ecclesiastes meant. Instead of humbling himself and accepting the facts, Jonah had let pride lead him into deeper trouble. It was his silly pride that tempted him to run away, and now he would be shot or beaten to death. There was pine resin on his shirt and pants, and more resin on his face and on his hands. He had to remember what would wash it away. Soap wouldn't melt the gum, and neither would hot water. He could scrub his fingers with sand, but that would only make the skin raw. Turpentine might melt the resin, but turpentine would burn his skin. Jonah recalled Mr. Williams rubbing his hands with something after they'd cut and trimmed a pine tree. It was an oil of some kind, mineral oil or olive oil. Or machine oil or whale oil for the lamps. Maybe even lard would dissolve the stiff, tight resin.

He had maybe an hour before dark, and Jonah couldn't wait any longer. Men with dogs might already be on their way to comb the woods. Perhaps they were already waiting for him to come out of the pine woods. Maybe they thought he would run over the next hill, and stood waiting for him there. He moved through the pine woods quickly, but when he reached a thicket with brush and briars he had to find a way around it, and he searched for a path or road. Vines and briars would slow him down too much. Once it got dark he should get on a road and walk as fast as he could. Jonah stumbled about a mile through brush before he came to a little road. He hid in the brush until it was almost dark, and then turned left and followed the road. He figured the sand and gravel in the tracks would soon wear away the resin on the bottom of his feet, but sand stuck to the resin and made his feet sore and his steps uneven.

He passed a house near the road, and a dog ran out from the woodshed and barked. Jonah held out his hand and whistled a little. Holding out your hand was a friendly gesture, and it usually made a dog stop barking or growling. He knew the worst thing you could do was cause a dog to think you were afraid or angry. Jonah held out his right hand and the dog quieted. In the twilight he could see the animal wag its tail. After a few moments Jonah continued on his way.

The breeze that comes at the end of a summer day cooled Jonah's face and blew under his shirt, making it easier to walk. He might be able to get to the far chain of mountains before morning. It was a wide valley, and he needed to get across it. Once he reached the mountain chain he'd be far from South Carolina and closer to the North.

Twilight was a peculiar time of day, a time when you could both see and not see. The world looked real and not real at the same time. In twilight everything appeared far away, but you felt it was close enough to touch. There was a comfort in twilight, as if you were safe and maybe hidden from danger.

Jonah tried to choose a stride that he could keep up for hours. He needed a pace that would take him mile after mile. It was no good to wear himself out too fast. It was long hours of steady walking that would carry him to the North. He felt he'd found his gait when he heard the dog barking again far behind him. The dog's bark could mean something was following him a long way back, for he'd gone at least a mile since passing the cabin. Jonah looked back and saw a light. He hurried forward and then looked back again. This time there appeared to be several lights, as if a group of men with torches was following him. Men carrying lanterns and torches could be foxhunters or coon hunters, but more likely they were hunting him. If they were on horses they could catch up with him quickly. If they had a pack of dogs they could follow him wherever he went.

If he stayed on the road they'd soon overtake him. If he ran into the woods the dogs might well find his tracks and lead the men right to him. What he needed was a stream. If he could discover a creek and wade in it for a few hundred yards, he might throw the dogs off for half an hour. Maybe he could double back and throw the posse off his tracks even longer.

Jonah looked back and saw the torches were getting closer, and he began to run. There may have been copperheads crawling in the tracks, but if there were, Jonah leapt over them. *One two three four*, he said to himself, keeping time with his running. *One two three four. Run out the kitchen door. Five six seven eight. Jump over the pasture gate.* As the road dipped into a little hollow, Jonah looked for a creek, but what he saw was a bridge, a plank bridge across a creek wider than any he'd yet seen in the mountains. His first thought was that if he got under the bridge maybe the posse would go right over him. And once they'd gone he'd double back the way he'd come.

But if they had dogs, the dogs would trace him to the bridge and sniff under the bridge and find him. Jonah would have to get in the creek and wade as far as he could, and then climb out and head through the woods. The creek appeared to wind between fields and rows of trees. The stream ran to the east, not to the north. Climbing down the bank through vines and brush, Jonah saw something at the edge of the water. In the gathering darkness it at first it appeared to be a little shelter, like a chicken coop or dog house. Then he thought it was a trough or box, the kind milk and butter are placed in to keep them cool. But when he touched the object, he found it was a little boat made of boards, with a paddle and one seat and a fishing line on the floor. Paddling the boat down the creek might be his best chance to get away. The posse would follow his tracks to the creek and not know in which direction he'd gone.

He tugged at the boat, but it was fixed to something. He lit a precious match to see what was holding the craft and found a rope from a ring on the prow tied to a sapling. He untied the rope and pushed the boat into the current and jumped in. Taking up the paddle, he pushed himself out into midstream. The water was so shallow, he could use the paddle to push against the bottom, pointing the little boat downstream.

In the dark he banged against a rock, and turned aside around it. He then hit a log or snag, and had to turn again. Without a light he couldn't avoid hitting objects. He pushed on and discovered he could see rippling water if he looked out of the corner of his eyes. Water rippled on a rock or snag or sandbar, so he tried to avoid ripples. Jonah found that if he paused and listened he could also hear the ripples. He paddled quietly, and then listened.

When he'd gone a ways down the stream he looked back and saw a cluster of lights milling around. The posse must have reached the bridge. They'd be looking for him along the banks of the creek. If he'd stayed under the bridge, he would have been tied up by now. He paddled as quietly as he could, going slow enough so that when he hit a rock it didn't make much of a thunk. The front of the little boat ground in the sand, and he pulled it back and turned aside and started again. The murmur of the water told him where a rock was, if he listened closely enough. Jonah had never used his ears in such a way before. He listened and paddled. Once he hit the side of the boat with the paddle and it sounded like he'd thumped a wooden drum. He stopped paddling and looked behind him, but the men with torches must have been making so much noise they didn't hear the knock.

A limb smacked Jonah in the face, and his eyes filled with tears. There was no way he could see every limb that reached out over the water. He bent forward, keeping as low as possible. He studied the water ahead to catch the gleam from the faint light given off by a bright, rising moon. All he had to do was follow the sparkle. Soon the men with torches were so far behind, they were lost to sight. He seemed to have reached a stretch of still, level water, with few trees on the banks. As he paddled he could watch the moon and the stars above. A dog howled in the distance. He saw lights on the hill to his left. There were so many lights it must have been a town.

The boat scooted along the still water, and from time to time something scampered down the bank ahead and plunked into the stream. After walking all day and climbing the pine tree, it felt good to rest on the seat of the little boat. His arms did all the work, guiding and pulling the paddle. He crossed his legs and almost knelt in the shallow boat, which nudged weeds here and a sandbar there. It was the easiest traveling he'd done yet, gliding over the water. He wished he could float and paddle all the way to the North. He wished he could get in a current that would sweep him hundreds of miles away from the posse with torches, from Mr. Williams with his black snake whip.

The creek made a slight turn and Jonah saw a light ahead, and it seemed to be out in the middle of the stream. He quit paddling and drifted, straining his eyes to see the light better. Had somebody from the posse ridden out ahead and now lay waiting for him around a bend in the creek?

It seemed that on either side of the creek there were open fields and no trees to hide in. He stopped the boat and listened. He heard no voices. He would sit in the boat and wait to see what happened. He could try to paddle back upstream, but that would be hard, and there were no woods to scramble into.

Jonah pushed the boat to the bank and pulled it up on the sand, working as quietly as he could. The bank was covered with briars and vines, and they tore at his clothes as he climbed to the edge of the field. From there the light ahead was hidden by brush, and he walked ahead as quietly as he could, watching for the light.

Keeping a clump of brush between himself and the light, he tiptoed up as close as he dared. He expected to see men with shotguns and torches, but instead he spied an old man wearing a straw hat and holding a fishing pole. The man was barefoot, and Jonah saw he was a black man. The man was so still Jonah thought he might be asleep. He held the long bamboo pole out over the still water of the creek. And then Jonah saw the pipe in the man's mouth and smoke curling past the hat brim.

"Howdy," Jonah said.

The old man turned to look at him, his eyes reflecting the lantern light. "Now ain't you a sight for sore eyes," the old man said.

"What creek is this?" Jonah said.

"This be Mud Creek, I reckon," the old man said.

"And where does Mud Creek go?"

"Go to the French Broad, and don't ax me where that go 'cause I don't know, 'cept maybe it go to the ocean."

"Does the French Broad run north?" Jonah said.

"Boy, you ax a lot of questions," the old man said. He looked at Jonah like he was trying to remember his face. "Ain't seen you 'round these parts before," he added.

Jonah figured he'd better not say any more. The old man would not believe his lies, and it would be foolish to tell him the truth.

"Reckon you could use some cornpone," the old man said. He unwrapped a cake of cornbread from brown paper and handed it to Jonah. Jonah took a bite of the pone. Nothing he'd ever put in his mouth had tasted better. The bread had cracklings in it and tasted like gravy.

"Fish ain't biting no-how," the old man said and stood up. He knocked the ashes from his pipe and raised the fishing pole until the hook baited with worms swung back within reach. Stripping the bait off the hook, he wrapped the line around the tip of the pole and stuck the hook into a joint of the bamboo.

"You be careful, boy," the old man said and picked up the lantern.

He seemed in a hurry to get away, and Jonah guessed it was because he didn't care to be seen with a runaway. A Negro could be beaten for helping a runaway. The old man carried the lantern and fishing pole across the field toward the town, and Jonah watched him until he disappeared among the row of houses.

After eating every crumb of the cornbread, Jonah walked back toward the boat. He climbed down the bank, but the boat was not where he expected it to be. He'd walked farther than he remembered to see what the lantern was. It took him several minutes to find the boat farther upstream.

With the energy the rich cornbread gave him, Jonah began to paddle again down Mud Creek. He couldn't see the mud, but he could smell it. In still stretches, the creek smelled of rotten things, rancid rags and fetid silt, dead fish and frogs, sick, festering things. He reckoned the runoff from toilets also seeped into the creek, and water from hogpens. He paddled quietly and quickly, hoping to get beyond the town and beyond the narrow, stagnant water. He reached a stand of trees again where the stream passed under low-hanging branches, and it seemed he was in a swamp, both from the smell and the glimmer of water that spread like wings on either side of the creek. Big trees leaned over his path. He ducked and turned aside, and rammed into a log.

It was hard to tell the path of the creek through the swamp, with water going out in every direction. Twice he ran into vines and brush and knew he'd strayed from the channel. He hated to think of the spiders and snakes all around him. It was better that the swamp was too dark for anything to be visible except for the trees that rose like shadows out of the glimmering water. Cobwebs brushed his face and caught in his hair and on his hat.

He crashed against a tree trunk and backed away. Something big dropped to the water and began swimming. It sounded big as a bear or panther. He kept still and listened to the splash get farther and farther away. Whatever it was moved quickly.

By straining his eyes, looking sideways to find openings, Jonah finally got to the other side of the swamp. The creek beyond moved faster, rippling on rocks, dashing between trees. To make up for the time he'd lost in the swamp, Jonah paddled faster. *One two three four*, he said to himself as he pushed the boat forward. *One two three four*.

Listening for clues of current churning around rocks, he aimed the little boat at the glimmer of water ahead, and moved faster than the current. *One two three four*, he said again, and pulled himself forward. *One two three four.* Jonah was so intent on finding his way among rocks and logs and sandbars he hardly noticed the darkness start to thin and the light in the sky making the trees seem farther away. He could see overhanging branches better, and once he passed under a footlog that was so low he had to duck. In the dark he would have smashed his head against the log, but now he could see it. Someone's toilet stood on stilts over the creek, and he swerved around it. Jonah rounded the bend and saw what looked like a long pool spreading wider than the creek. He paddled into the middle of the pool, and it was only when he reached the middle that he saw he was entering a much larger stream. He'd reached the French Broad, and though the spot where the creek joined the larger stream was still, the river got rougher just below.

The French Broad was maybe a hundred yards wide, and it frothed and jumped, galloping over rocks and trotting through troughs of shoal water. Water leapfrogged, overtaking itself. The river seemed to move at different speeds and in different directions all over the surface. The river appeared to be sorting and resorting its pieces.

It was a good thing the sky was lighter now, for he was going to have to be alert.

FIVE

JONAH

It seemed very strange to Jonah that a river could be called the French Broad. He'd heard of the Broad River, which ran out of North Carolina into South Carolina. It made sense that a wide river could be called the Broad River. But he could think of no reason why any stream would be called the French Broad. In the early dawn light he paddled fast around rocks and down dashing, slurping chutes. The river moved so fast through its many channels and currents, he had to look out for obstacles and paddle hard to stay ahead of the tide. His hands were getting sore where they gripped the shank and middle of the paddle. Resin still stuck in patches to his skin.

The little boat pitched and dipped and shot ahead. The river swung this way and that, around gravel bars and rocks, swapping sides, as though it was braiding and unbraiding strands of bouncing water. He passed a little dock built in a bend, and then the mouth of a sizable creek. As the sky got lighter still, Jonah knew he was going to have to pull to the bank and stop for the day. He was worn out and his hands and back were sore. His arms felt numb. And it would be dangerous to continue on the river in daylight, so he started looking for a place to land. Because he needed to pull the boat up on the bank out of sight, he knew it would be better if he turned into a branch or little creek. He needed a place to hide and a place to conceal the boat. He scanned the shore for a likely spot, and saw a hollow that opened back from the river ahead. Wherever there was a hollow coming down to the stream, there would be a branch. He began to turn the boat in the direction of the hollow on the right bank. Sure enough, a small creek fed into the river there, but its mouth was cluttered with overhanging brush and grapevines. Jonah had to bend low and pull the boat forward by grabbing limbs and vines.

Soon as he was out of sight of the river, he pulled the boat up onto the creek bank and tied the rope to a small birch. He was pleased to see that the fishing line had a hook and sinker on the end of it. He would indeed be able to catch fish in this river. A tow sack lay on the floor of the boat and he folded that for a pillow. Placing the cushion in the prow of the boat, Jonah found he had just enough room to lay his head there and rest his feet on the seat. That was more comfortable than lying on the ground where ants might bite him again. As he floated into sleep he kept feeling the dip of the boat, the thunk of the prow butting a rock.

When he was tired, Jonah often had long dreams, and that day, as he slept in the little boat, he dreamed of searching through pine woods on a hill. Seeing a red light ahead, he followed the glow. Suddenly it was night, and he came to a clearing where people circled around a bonfire. They'd thrown their clothes on the ground and danced naked, their bodies glistening like polished leather. Some danced with their hands on the shoulders of the person ahead, and others danced alone. Both men and women danced, and as they moved they sang in some language Jonah didn't understand. They shook their bodies and chanted.

A woman spotted Jonah and beckoned for him to join them, but he held back at the edge of the pine woods. "We're going underground," the woman said. She pointed to a rock in the hillside, which he hadn't noticed before. And beside the rock was an opening that looked like the entrance to a cave. The dancers took up sticks from a pile and lit them at the bonfire. They carried the torches around in a circle.

"We're going underground," another woman with large, shiny breasts said to him. She came to the edge of the clearing and took his hand. One by one the dancers entered the mouth of the cave. Rocks at the entrance resembled teeth. The mouth looked like it could close anytime it wanted to. Still chanting in the unknown tongue, the dancers slipped through the orifice one by one. The woman handed Jonah a torch and pulled him behind her toward the cave, drawing him as if he was under a spell. He stepped forward through the teeth, and could see ahead a long room that looked pink. The cave walls glowed like he imagined the flesh inside a throat or belly would. The torchlight flickered on the walls and ceiling. Pictures of animals and whirling dancers covered the walls.

"This be the way to go home," the woman said.

When Jonah woke he found his pants wet at the crotch. He had shot off in his dream and his pants were sticky. Whoa there, he said to himself. The dream that had been so intense and vivid was flying away from him. He could recall the color of the cave's insides and the brightness of the torches. The woman with the gleaming breasts had reached back and taken him by the member.

Whoa now, Jonah said again, and drifted back into sleep, dreamless and exhausted.

When Jonah woke again, it was late afternoon. Sunlight slashed into the upper stories of the trees above him. A crow called somewhere up the little creek hollow. And he could hear the mutter and lisp of the river nearby. The river passed beyond the brush at the creek mouth, and he heard the splash and crash of water over rocks. Jonah wished he had some cornpone left, and also some sidemeat. He thought of Mama cooking cornbread over the fireplace in their cabin. The pain of the thought surprised him. He bent over and hit the ground with his fist. You are never going to see Mama again, or Mrs. Williams, or anybody you know, he thought. You're a fool, and you're lost.

The sob that rose in his chest felt like it could tear him in two, and he flung himself down on the ground and cried harder than he had since he was five. Later, he was ashamed of himself. He remembered how, when she saw he felt low and worried, Mrs. Williams had sometimes given him things to perk him up, perhaps a piece of cake, or two bits to spend at the store, once a magazine from London with pictures. But Mrs. William was not here to see his tears and help him. And she never would again, either. Wake up, you silly chicken, he thought. You could cry for a week and it wouldn't put any food in your belly. Hunger forced Jonah to stand up and pick his way through brush and trees up the bank of the little creek. Before it got dark he would try to find a garden with new potatoes and dig a few. He'd have to get a pot and frying pan if he was to cook things. It was a long way to the North.

Jonah figured there must be a farm up the little creek hollow, and wherever there was a farm, there'd be a garden, and chickens also. It was too dangerous to steal chickens, but maybe he could grab a few eggs. Why had he not thought of that before? If he had a pot, he could boil eggs. He could steal a few eggs at almost any farm and they'd not be missed. If he got a pan he could fry eggs. He could even eat eggs raw if he had to.

Jonah walked through the dense woods beside the creek until he came to a field with corn and a melon patch. There was no garden. The house must be farther up the hollow, and the garden would be beside it. In the melon patch he saw both watermelons and musk melons. He turned over a few watermelons, but found them not ripe; a ripe watermelon showed white and yellow on its bottom. Most of the cantaloupes were green, also, but he found two with promising orange color in the rind. The smart way to check for ripeness in a musk melon was to look at the stem attached to the navel. The stems were just beginning to dry up, so the melons were almost ripe.

After carrying the melons to the creek and washing them, Jonah took them to a little opening in the woods. He sliced a melon and raked out the pulp and seeds. The inside of the cantaloupe glistened, and he carved off a piece, the orange meat dripping with sweet juice, and ate it quickly. He was hungrier than he'd thought. After eating the first slice, Jonah remembered that melon or almost any fruit on an empty stomach could give you the bellyache. The second piece he chewed slowly, mixing the melon with spit and savoring the sweet flesh. He would save the second melon for later. It would ripen even sweeter, riding in the boat down the river. Jonah decided to pick some of the field corn also and carry it with him. He could roast the corn by the river. He would take it with him and roast the corn when he stopped far down the French Broad the next morning. If he caught a fish with the hook and line he'd found on the bottom of the boat, he could eat corn and fish together.

By the time Jonah washed his hands and the knife in the branch and returned to the cornfield, it was already far into twilight. But it was easy to locate the fat, hard ears in the rows just by feeling them, and he quickly gathered half a dozen. That would do him for two meals. He'd leave the shucks on the ears to keep them fresh until time to roast them.

With the knife in his pocket and the corn under his right arm and the melon in his left hand, Jonah started back to the boat. The woods were dark, but all he needed to do was to follow the stream. As he stepped through the undergrowth he heard a low rumble, as if it came from the ground under him. It was more a boom than a rumble, and when it came again he thought it must be from the mountain to his right. The mountain swept up from the river into the eastern sky. He stopped and listened, and the sound came again, a deep bump, a bang like vast rocks inside the mountain had shifted and knocked against each other. The ground he stood on seemed to tremble when the sound came through. It was the lowest sound he'd ever heard, like a drum had been struck. The blow sounded again, a low thunder coming out of the earth, out of the ridge above the river. It was a stroke of doom from deep in the ground.

Once when Jonah was in Greenville with Mr. Williams, he'd heard a church bell ring out again and again, with a pause in between each note. Mr. Williams said it tolled in memory of the governor of the state who'd died. It was an eerie sound, like a warning—a reminder, that even while you went about your business, somebody was dying, someone was being mourned.

It was time for Jonah to push off in the boat and continue downriver before it got completely dark. He needed a little light to find his way among the rocks and chutes of the shoals. But the doom sounds from the mountain rang out so regular, he had to listen. They repeated on the count of twelve. Saying the numbers slowly, he got to twelve every time before the jolt came through the ground again. Jonah placed the corn and the melon in the boat and decided to climb partway up the ridge to see where the sound was coming from. Could there be a mill with a large hammer that crushed rocks? He'd heard of a hammer mill and the loud noise one made, but the jolt seemed to be coming from *inside* the mountain. Jonah climbed higher on the ridge. The river below appeared to wave white handkerchiefs from its shoals, but the woods were shadowy, except for a glow on the top of the ridge. When he looked at the shadows farther up the slope, Jonah saw a spark in the air just above the ground. At first he thought it was a lightning bug, but this spark stayed lit, and it had a yellower, warmer light than fireflies made. And then he saw another spark, and then another. All the ridge ahead was covered with the little lights. The sparks hovered a foot or so above the ground and seemed to light a trail to the top of the mountain. He climbed to get closer, but as he moved they moved, too, floating just off the ground. Whoa there, Jonah said to himself, for he knew he should go back to the boat and continue his journey. He should turn back, but first he had to know what the little sparks were. The ridge was so steep, he dropped on hands and knees and crawled. The trail of lights up the mountain was like something out of a dream, and he wondered if he was still asleep. But he'd wakened and found the cantaloupes and corn. He'd walked along the little creek, and he'd seen the sunset. Jonah could not turn back. He climbed over rocks and logs, and picked his way through laurel bushes. The lights retreated to the very top of the ridge, but still he couldn't turn back. He was far above the river. There was a faint red glow in the west, the river a ghostly band between the dark mountains. He seemed at the top of the world.

The points of light seemed to spill into the laurel bushes on the other side of the mountain. Slow down there, Jonah said. You can't lead me all the way to the top of the mountain and then disappear. But in fact the hovering sparks seemed to have burned out. Were they bugs or flies, or the glimmer of the swamp gas in the air? He'd heard of the will-o'-the-wisp that floated in the air above swamps, sometimes called fairy lights. But that was a bigger light. He'd heard of the light called a jack-o-lantern that appeared to people lost or hurt in the woods and led them to safety. But this light had just been sparkles.

Jonah searched the woods below him. The laurel thicket was black as a cellar. He'd been so busy following the trail of lights, he'd forgotten the boom inside the mountain. But it came again, a dull stroke that shook the dirt right under his feet. It sounded like the shudder of doom, from a cavern below the mountain, below the river, below the deepest well. As Jonah looked into the thicket, he saw another light. This was not floating sparks but a glowing mist, like a cloud of lighted vapor. It was a blue and orange light, the kind that comes from burning applewood. What are you doing here? Jonah said to himself. You're a runaway. You have been beaten, and if you're caught you'll be whipped again and branded with a red-hot iron. You can be attacked by dogs and sent back to the Williams Place. You have one chance in a hundred of reaching the North. And yet you follow a will-o'-the-wisp, or swamp gas, into a snaky thicket. The boom shoved through the ground again and the jack-o-lantern slipped farther into the thicket, as though lighting his way. Jonah followed a few steps, and then a few more. The light appeared to beckon to him. Its glow was strong enough to show him brush and roots and rocks to avoid. He took three steps and the boom sounded again.

The Israelites had followed a pillar of fire in the Bible. He'd heard more than once of lost or sick men following such a jack-o-lantern and reaching safety. If such a thing appeared to him, it must have a reason. He took three more steps and the strum deep in the earth sounded again. Jonah came to a kind of bench on the mountainside and paused beside a big rock. The jack-o-lantern faded and he was once again in complete darkness. He could see nothing and he was lost. The jack-o-lantern had led him away from the river and the boat. It must be a light of cruelty and not of safety. He'd been deceived by the glitter of the points of light and the will-o'-the-wisp. He would have to find his way back up the mountain and across the top and down to the boat.

The darkness around him appeared limitless, and the mountainside dropped away beyond the rock. He'd have to find a dry stick and light it for a torch. He would have to strike a match to find a stick, and he had only about ten matches left. Jonah took the box from his pocket and was about to strike a lucifer when he saw a red glow farther down the mountain. It was firelight and he wondered why he'd not noticed it before. The fire leapt and flickered, and he heard singing and chanting. It was odd he'd not heard them before. Maybe he'd been too busy watching the jack-o-lantern and listening to the bang inside the mountain. Maybe the wind had shifted.

Now that he'd come this far, he had to see what the chanting was about and what the fire was for. As soon as he found that out, he'd hurry back to the boat and continue his journey. He'd stay hidden and no one would ever know he'd been there. Keeping his eye on the fire below, Jonah skirted brush and trees, descending the steep ridge. He held on to limbs and dropped a step at a time on the steepest places.

When Jonah got close to the clearing where the bonfire blazed, he gasped. It was so much like the scene in his dream, he wondered if he was still dreaming. Black bodies glistening with sweat danced around the flames and chanted. Negro men and women pranced and shouted. A fat woman with enormous breasts saw him watching from the edge of the woods and beckoned to him. He stepped into the firelight.

"Ain't you got no jubilee?" the woman said. She grabbed his hand and pulled him into the circle of dancers.

"I've got to go," Jonah said.

"Don't your mama teach you no manners?" the big woman said. She pulled him along and he had no choice but to step with the dancers. He moved to the beat of the drum and the long, low beat inside the mountain.

"Don't you listen to your belly?" the big woman said. There were only black folks around the great blaze. Women shook their breasts and men thrust out their hips as they circled. The women shivered their hips and shook their breasts again.

"Boy, you got to learn some jubilee," the big woman said. Jonah saw she was not old, only fat. Her hips were big and her breasts even bigger. As the woman quivered her hips, Jonah felt the drum beat in his temples and in his veins. The boom shook in his belly, in his guts. He took off his shirt and threw it aside. The woman, as she danced before him, unbuttoned his overalls and he stepped out of them. The young fat woman raised her arms and shook from side to side. Slow down, Jonah said to himself, but he didn't mean it. He didn't want to hold back.

"Ain't you never been to jubilee before?" she said and grinned. "Boy, where you from?" When she shook her big hips, it made the earth move under him and he stepped faster.

"I've been around," he said.

"I show you round," she said and bumped him with her hip.

As he stepped to the drum beat, Jonah no longer felt tired or sore. He'd climbed all the way up the mountain and descended it. His hands were blistered from paddling the boat all the night before, and resin still stuck to his arms. His back was covered with scabs from the whipping Mr. Williams had given him. But tonight he felt both light and strong.

"Look like you run into a fence," the fat woman said when she saw his bare back.

"The fence run into me," Jonah said, "but I jumped over it."

"Maybe that fence come following you," the woman said.

There was a great wooden tub at the edge of the clearing, and the fat woman led him to it and dippered out a drink with a gourd. Jonah scooped up a drink for himself, thinking it was water. But the liquid in the dipper smelled of rotting fruit and something bitter and something sweet. It was a kind of beer. The cool liquid sparkled on his tongue, and he laughed as he dipped out another gourd full. As they began dancing again, Jonah noticed a cage near the woods that held chickens. But they were not like any chickens he'd ever seen. They were black chickens with wing and tail feathers that glistened blue and purple in the firelight.

A woman with her hair tied up in a yellow rag and a butcher knife in her hand took a chicken from the crate and laid its head on a log. With one whack she chopped the chicken's head off, but didn't turn the hen loose as the body jerked and the wings flapped and fluttered.

The woman with the yellow turban held the chicken high and let the blood from the neck drip into her mouth. Then she held the bleeding body so others could drink. When she came to Jonah, he opened his mouth, and several drops of black blood dripped between his lips. The blood was salty and rich. He'd never tasted anything so strong. It was the finest sauce and the finest gravy he'd ever tasted. It was better than communion wine at church.

Jonah licked his lips and laughed. The fat girl licked her lips and giggled also.

"Who let you have a party out here?" Jonah said.

"Ain't nobody let us have a jubilee," she said. "Nobody but ourselves."

"You're not afraid to be caught?"

The woman began dancing again. She held her elbows out on either side and snapped her fingers. She twisted and looked him in the eye, grinned, and said, "Boy, you don't know nothing."

"Reckon I don't," he said and grinned back.

"Time you learned a thing, or two," she said. Jonah would not have guessed anyone so fat could move so fast or so deftly. She must have danced a lot to be that quick and sure. Her skin gleamed in the firelight.

"Nobody ever make your little colonel happy?" she said and turned so he could see her left side. He wasn't sure what she meant until he saw her looking at his member.

"What?" he said.

"I thought not," she said and laughed. She pushed herself up against him and then backed away. The firelight made her skin look the color of honey, dark clover honey.

"Ain't no good less your little colonel be happy," she said and looked him in the eye.

Jonah felt something stir way down in his belly. It was a force pushing out and upward. The force started in the ground and came up through the soles of his feet and up through his legs and into his groin. The beat of the drum and blood of the chicken summoned a fountain out of the ground and into his loins.

"Let me show you something," the woman said. She took him by the hand and led him to the edge of the clearing, and just as they reached the trees she broke away and started running. He hesitated only a second and then ran after her. She dodged around a tree and stumbled. She squealed and jumped over a log and fell to the ground.

It was so dark in the woods he could hardly see her. "Come here, boy," she said, and when he stepped closer she took his hand and pulled him down on top of her. She was the softest cushion he'd ever touched. Her breasts and shoulders were like a cloud of warm vapors, and he floated on their comfort.

She took his spigot in her hand and guided it into a place that was warm and wet. He pushed hard into her and she said, "Whoa there, boy, easy does it. Don't make your little colonel sing out before he time." And she laughed and he laughed.

The fat woman rolled a little to the side and then back. She rolled a little farther and then back. "We make that little colonel sing for his supper," she said.

As she turned, it seemed her breasts were pillows.

Jonah had never felt anything as right or as comforting. It was as if he'd spent all his life crawling on his hands and knees to this place. He no longer felt the sores on his back or the blisters on his hands.

• • •

When Jonah woke there was just light enough to see the trees overhead. Birds were loud in the woods below. The leaves beside him were empty. He sat up and saw the fat woman was gone. He stood and walked down to the clearing and found ashes and burned logs where the fire had been. The tub of beer was gone. He was naked and leaves stuck to the dried sweat and pine resin on his body.

If his clothes were truly gone Jonah knew he was in deep trouble. For where could he go without clothes? How could he ever get anywhere to steal clothes or buy clothes if he was naked? A naked Negro would be arrested on sight. Jonah looked around the clearing and finally found his shirt wadded up in the dirt under the bushes. He dusted the fabric off and put it on. Then he searched under the trees and brush for his overalls. Panic began to wash away the sweet memory of the night before.

And then he saw his overalls half covered with needles under a pine tree. He brushed them off and felt in the pockets. The money was gone and the knife was gone. But the box of matches was still there in his right pocket. He'd lost all the money Mama had saved.

SIX

ANGEL

The first time I ever heard the word *jubilee* must be when I was young and Mama went off and left me in the middle of the night. I woke up in the dark and saw Mama standing in the moonlight coming through the window, wrapping a cloth around her head. "Where you going?" I said.

"Shhhh," Mama said. "Don't wake the little ones." Then Mama whispered she was going to jubilee, but she'd be back. She said if I didn't lie down and go to sleep again she'd whip me with a hickory stick come morning. I lay down and closed my eyes, and smelled the rose petals Mama gathered by the hedge in front of the big house. She'd crushed the petals between her hands and rubbed them over her neck and shoulders and breasts.

There was a murmuring outside when Mama went out the door,

and then I heard footsteps and laughing and people walking away from the quarters. I lay in the dark thinking about the name *jubilee* and what it meant. It must be special because Mama seemed excited, fixing herself up in the middle of the night like she was going to a revival meeting. When I opened my eyes, the moonlight was streaming down from the window. Moving slowly so as to not wake my brothers and sisters, I climbed off the cot and stood in the pool of light. The moonlight seemed to be calling to me, "Come out and see the world now. Night is the time to play and be happy."

When I opened the door and stepped outside, I saw that it was true. That moonlight made the ground clean, coating everything with blue velvet and blue frost.

I held out my hands to the moon and the moon said, "Look at what can be." I looked at the pine woods and the mountains beyond the woods, and they were blue and silky all the way to where stars reached down to the ridge beyond the river. I felt like I could walk on that carpet of blue light all the way to the edge of heaven.

"This is the way things will be," the moon whispered, as I sat down with my back against the cabin.

I must have gone to sleep sitting on the ground, for the next thing I knew Mama was shaking me and it was dark and the moon had gone down. "What you doing out here?" Mama hissed as she pushed me inside; I was so sleepy and surprised I didn't answer. I could tell Mama was hot and covered with sweat, like she had been running or dancing, the way I'd seen her do at the revival meeting. Her turban had come undone and she'd tied it around her shoulders. She smelled sweet like rotten fruit, the way the master smelled when he'd been drinking brandy.

"I'll whip you in the morning," Mama said. "I'll teach you to mind me." Mama got a dipper of water from the bucket in the corner and drank it and then lay down on her cot.

The worst thing about a whipping was having to wait for it. Mama knew that and I knew that. And I guess Master Thomas knew it, too, for he whipped one of the help from time to time when they didn't mind him. But that was a bigger thing, an awful thing, to see a man whipped with a blacksnake whip till his back was cut and he was bleeding down to his feet.

Mama might say as a warning, "I'm going to cut the blood out of you," but she never did it. She knew the worst part of punishment was the anticipation. The next morning after we ate mush with molasses and I washed up the bowls, Mama said, "You know what I need. Go get me that hickory."

It was a relief to finally go and get it over with.

"Better be a good switch or I whip you twice," Mama said.

Sad as it was to have to go after my own switch, there was a kind of dignity to it. All I had to do was get the hickory and bear the whipping and cry a little to make Mama feel I was sorry, and then it would be all right again. I couldn't stand for Mama to be mad at me. If Mama was mad at me, then the whole world seemed twisted to the side and empty.

After I brought her the switch, Mama made me go outside. I had to stand in the yard where everybody could see the whipping. She made me hold her left hand with my left hand and she whipped me on my legs and on my butt. The hickory stung my skin like a hot wire.

"How many times do I have to tell you to mind me?" Mama said as she swung the switch.

"I do mind," I said.

"Don't you sass me," Mama said and swung harder.

"I mind you, I mind you," I said and started to cry.

"You sass me, I cut the blood out of you," Mama said. She was so busy whipping me and my eyes were so full of tears, neither of us saw the master standing nearby, watching. His sleeves were rolled up like he was on the way to the field. When the crops needed tending, the master sometimes worked right alongside the help.

"Don't whip that girl—she didn't mean to do nothing wrong," Master Thomas said.

Mama stepped back and dropped the hickory to her side.

"Angel's too pretty to whip," Master Thomas said. "Her skin's too perfect and her face too pretty. What has she done?"

"She don't mind me," Mama said. "She sassed me."

The master put his hand on my shoulder and looked into my eyes. I shivered at his touch, yet I was pleased by it at the same time. I could feel the power in his hand, which is not the power of muscles and calluses.

"Angel don't mean to be bad," Master Thomas said. "Besides, she's almost a young woman." He looked me in the eyes and smiled and I tried to smile back through my tears.

"Would you like to work in the big house?" the master said. "I think you're grown up enough to work in the big house. Would you like that?"

I nodded, forgetting the sting on my legs.

That was how I came to live in the master's house, before I was grown up. Mama didn't say anything; she washed me up and had me put on my clean dress. Other women in the quarters gave me looks, and Jessie Mae who was a little older than me, said, "If Master want to fiddle with you, you better let him." But I didn't answer her.

I didn't look back at the folks watching me as I went into the big house, by the back door of course. Sally the cook said I would sleep in a little room in the attic. The room was hot in summer, but I could lie in the breeze from the window. She said I would have a new dress and a new petticoat, too.

Mrs. Thomas was an invalid, and stayed in her room on the second floor. She stayed in bed most days or sat in a chair by the fireplace and read her Bible or some other book. Her room always smelled like medicine. The mistress made me feel backward and shy, like I didn't belong there. She wore a cap tied around her head, and her face was as pale as paper. She patted me on the head, but looked hard into my eyes.

"Angel, you have come to help us out," she said.

"Yes'm," I said.

"This house needs all the help we can get," she said. Then she asked me if I prayed and I said, "Yes, ma'am, I pray at the meeting Brother Evan has down in the quarters."

"Do you pray to be a good girl?" the mistress said.

Then she sent me up to my room in the attic, a place no bigger than a closet with a cot and a scratched-up chest of drawers and a tiny mirror on the wall. But there was a blue dress lying on the cot and I knew it was there for me. It was a fine old dress the mistress might have worn. Now it had been cut down for me. And I looked out the tiny window; I had a view to the front yard and its row of boxwoods and the cornfields beyond the white gate, and the blue mountains across the French Broad River rising up into the clouds. And when I lifted the window, the breeze came across the fields and yard and whispered on my face and neck like it was talking to me in a low voice. I couldn't even see the quarters and hogpens from my window, only the sweet-smelling fields and mountains climbing on top of each other beyond the river.

What we had to eat in the quarters was grits and mush and sometimes maybe pinto beans and fatback, except when the garden Mama made each year came in. And then we had roastnears and green beans and fat tomatoes and new spuds and, later, sweet potatoes and collard greens. And after the hogs were killed, we got a little tenderloin and ribs, and for Christmas, some sausage.

But when I came down to the kitchen in the big house, Sally told me to carry a tray up to Mrs. Thomas. On it was coffee and white bread and honey, a piece of beef and a bowl of soup that smelled spicy and a slice of fluffy cake with white icing. It was the prettiest food I'd ever seen. I knew I wouldn't get to eat any of that stuff. When I got back to the kitchen they'd make me eat mush and soup beans, and maybe greens with a little fatback, like I always had.

But then Sally cleaned off a little table at the side of the pantry and told me to sit down there, and she brought me some of the same vittles I had taken to the mistress. I'd never seen such a feast, and I couldn't believe she meant that was for me. I thought any second she would tell me to take it up to the master. But she didn't.

"Master he say feed you real good," Sally say.

And that was the beginning of my being fleshy. Every morning, noon, and night Sally gave me the best food. I ate as well as the master and mistress.

So they fed me real good and treated me real good at the big house. Except I had to work at fetching things and cleaning some, and Mrs. Thomas told me to learn to sew, to let Arrie the housemaid teach me to sew. But I was no good at sewing, and got the stitches wrong and the seams all wrong, and the mistress got mad at me. She kept a walking stick beside her bed and she would hit me with that stick when I did something wrong. "Angel, you're lazy as a sow," she said and whacked me with that stick unless I stood back out of her reach.

"Sorry, ma'am," I said.

"Don't know how we can afford to feed you," she said.

Mostly I tried to stay out of the reach of that stick. I sometimes stood behind a chair, until her temper went away. And sometimes after she hit me she insisted on praying with me. I had to kneel beside her and hold her hand while she prayed. I reckon she was ashamed of getting mad, but that didn't mean she wouldn't do it again.

• • •

Now I knew there would be more to my coming to the big house than just eating plenty and carrying trays and emptying chamber pots. And though Mama hadn't said anything about it, she knew why I was sent for. I'd been living in the big house all summer and all fall, and the master was on a trip to Charleston for most of that time.

But in the late fall, when it began to cool off and the nights took on a chill, Master Thomas came back. He saw me in the hall and said, "Angel, you look like an angel," and he laughed. "You have rounded out."

He touched my shoulder, and I said, "Yes, sir."

"Come down to my room tonight," he said.

"Yes, sir," I said.

After I ate my supper in the kitchen and helped Sally gather up the dishes and pots and pans, and then dried them after she washed them, I took a pan of warm water up to my room and washed myself all over. Nobody told me to do that, but I knew it was what I should do. Then, after the house got quiet, I took a candle and walked down the stairs to the master's room.

He was sitting at a table reading a book, and when I came into the room, he turned toward me with a smile. "You are a pretty girl, Angel," he said.

"Yes, sir," I said.

"We must be friends," he said.

"Yes, sir," I said.

The master told me to pull my shift over my head, and I did it. He told me to come sit in his lap, and I did. He ran his fingers all over me, over my shoulders and the back of my head. He ran his fingers over my chest and over my nipples like I was some precious thing he just wanted to touch, like I was a mystery he wanted to figure out. Now Jessie Mae had told me the master would want to play with me, but I didn't expect him to be so slow and easy.

He rubbed my skin like he was spreading oil or butter on fine leather. His fingers whispered on my legs, rubbing me like he was polishing up a fine saddle. Nobody had ever touched me like that before.

"I want you to be happy," he said. "That's why I brought you up to the big house."

"Yes, sir," I said.

"I want you to have fine things," he said. He laid me on the bed, but he didn't ask me to do anything but lie there. What he did didn't feel too bad and it didn't feel too good, but just like something that happens to a young girl. And while I lay there with him on top of me, I thought about how he ran his fingers over my skin, and the look in his eyes. And I realized I had a value I didn't know about before, nothing huge, but a little bit of power was better than no power. And I began to think about what I could do, because my power and my value were in the softness of my skin and the shape of my shoulders and new breasts and the roundness of my butt.

When the master finished he rolled off me and lay there for a time holding on to me and breathing hard. By and by the master told me to go back to my own room. I got out of bed and found my shift and the candlestick and let myself out of the room and climbed the stairs in the dark. I cleaned myself and then sat by the attic window, looking at the moon over the mountains. I sat with my elbows on the window sill and realized I was not worried so bad anymore. For the first time in my life I saw I was not helpless, for I had something that people wanted.

After that when the master told me to come to him, I washed myself and slipped into his room after the house got dark. Sometimes he just wanted me to lie beside him and hold him, and sometimes he wanted to kiss me all over. Other times he wanted me to lie at his feet. The hardest thing, though, was when he told me he wanted me to whip him.

After that time, when I went back to my room, I wondered how the master was going to act the next day, after what he had made me do, after what he had done. I didn't see how he could act like a master after he begged me to whip him on his butt. But next morning, when he came down the stairs, he seemed just like he always did, giving orders to Sally and me and the other help, going out with his riding crop. As always, Sally told me to take the tray up to Mrs. Thomas, and I did.

THE FIRST TIME I went to a revival in the woods was three or four years after I moved into the big house. The meeting was at night and Mama said I should go, it was time for me to find my shouting glory. I told the master I had the bleeding sickness and couldn't be with him that night, and he believed me. He said he was going away tomorrow to buy calves, but he would be back in two days.

I walked into the woods after dark with Sally and Mama and a bunch of other help. The meeting was held in a little opening in the woods lit by lanterns, and there was a table and some logs to sit on. There were lots of black folks there from all the stations and plantations along the Pike. A band was playing as we walked into the clearing, a tambourine and drum, a washboard and a banjo. It was lively music and folks were clapping and hollering. The music stopped when the preacher, Brother Blakely, stood up by the table. He had on a long black coat and a tall stovepipe hat, and in his left hand he held something that looked like a big baby rattle. Every time he said a few words, he shook the rattle, and people would clap.

"Brothers and sisters, the Lord sees us tonight," he shouted. "Don't matter how much grief you've seen, don't matter how heavy your hearts have been, the Lord sees us here tonight."

"Amen, brother," someone yelled.

"Don't matter we been down to Egypt land in bondage," the preacher said. "Don't matter we got to wander forty years in the wilderness, for we got the promise of a new day and a better land. In my heart I know we're gonna see a better time."

The women started to shout and clap, and I joined them. And when the band began playing again, I found my feet moving. The banjo and drum and tambourine and groan of the washboard seemed to call something out of the dirt under my feet. I heard a beat way down in the earth, and my feet had to move to the beat. "The Holy Ghost come here tonight," Brother Blakely shouted, shaking the big rattle. "The devil's on the run and we gone have some fun. The devil don't dare show his pale face here tonight in our place of delight." I saw then that the rattle was to scare away the devil and all the evil spirits. Next to me I noticed Sally had taken down her dress, and her big breasts glistened as she danced. "Can't nothing stop us cause we're on the way to the promised land," Brother Blakely yelled. Other women took down their dresses, too, and everybody sparkled with sweat like they were covered with diamonds.

"Show the devil he can't claim our souls, because we're the children of the King," Brother Blakely shouted.

Suddenly I felt confined in the fine dress the mistress had given me, my spirit bound up and choked by the expensive fabric and embroidery. I undid the buttons, and when my breasts were bare I began shaking, then gliding forward and back. It was like the world was rocking under my feet.

"This sister has got the Holy Ghost," the preacher yelled and shook his rattle.

I danced toward the preacher and then away, saying things I didn't even understand, talking like I was in a dream. It was like my soul had been lifted up, and I knew I didn't need to ever be afraid again.

• • •

Now jubilee is something else entirely, and I didn't get to go to a jubilee till I was older. I'd heard about jubilee and knew folks went off into the woods to sing and dance and have fun, without a preacher, but it was a well-kept secret. I heard rumors of their doings on the mountain. And once Jessie Mae laughed and said to me, "Up there on the mountain they just trade each other around like different kinds of clothes." I asked her what mountain and she covered her mouth and said she wasn't supposed to tell.

"You talking about jubilee, girl?" I asked, and she gave me a look and wouldn't say any more.

When there was a secret, I had to find out what it was, so the next time I saw Eli, who worked in the stables, I asked, "When you gonna invite me to jubilee?"

He looked at me and said, "When you're big enough to keep your mouth shut."

"I'm big enough now," I said and shook my hips and breasts at him.

"White folks can't know," he said.

"No reason for white folks to know," I said.

"Next full moon," he said.

So one fall evening I slipped out of the house way after dark. The master had gone off to Raleigh to be in the legislature and I had the night free. Mrs. Thomas had taken laudanum to sleep, so I knew she wouldn't need me. Five of us from the Thomas Place gathered at the edge of the woods. We got a chicken out of the coop and a bucket of beer from the master's barrel and Eli took his drum. Then we walked all the way to a place called Sound Mountain. I'd heard about Sound Mountain all my life because it was a place that had lights in the woods that glowed sometimes and sparkled at others. Some people said the lights were ghosts of Indians, and others said it was swamp gas or the devil's light. And rumblings came out of the belly of the mountain like distant thunder or thumping on a log.

I got excited as colored folks from other farms and plantations and houses in the valley joined us along the way. Some carried chickens in sacks and others things in baskets. Two boys toted a washtub of beer. The moon rose over the ridge as we climbed the mountain, and I saw a pink glow in the trees ahead.

And then I heard the sound way down in the ground, a sound like two big rocks rubbing together. And then it came again, slow, like the heartbeat of a giant. And the next thing I knew I was walking in time to the beat, ten steps to the beat. It was like a pulse running through my body.

It was both scary and thrilling to be out from under the eye of white folks, the masters and owners. Most of the things we did were at the direction of white folks. But we were out there that night by our own choice and for our own pleasure.

When we came to the clearing halfway up the mountain, I drank a gourd of the cold beer, and then looked into the eyes of this big old boy from over at Swannanoa. I took another drink of beer and shook my butt and let my dress down to the waist. I looked in that big boy's eyes again, and he said, "You're sweet as a barrel of honey."

"Don't talk no trash to me," I said and giggled.

"You're sweet as an angel," he said.

"That's my name, Angel."

"Is that a fact?" he said and we started dancing.

"But I ain't no angel," I said.

"Thank goodness for that," he said.

Then he put his big hands on my hips as we started to dance.

I realized Eli must have put something in the beer, because I felt easy and mellow, and after two drinks I saw lights flash like blue and purple heat lightning, and the firelight got brighter, and people's shapes stretched and distorted. And when the woman named Carrie cut a chicken's throat and dripped blood into my mouth, I felt like I was drinking the blackness of creation. I looked about me and saw we were all brothers and sisters.

THE FIRST TIME I saw Jonah he was standing at the edge of the clearing, staring at our jubilee like he'd seen the devil coming out of hell with his pitchfork. He was so scared he looked gray. I felt sorry for him, yet I couldn't help laughing at him. Soon as I walked up and took his hand, I could tell he'd never been with a woman, because he didn't squeeze back but let me lead him like a child to the center of the yard where people were dancing. He rolled his eyes around like he had never seen women with bare bosoms before.

"Where you from, boy?" I asked. "How come you here?"

As I thought, he'd never heard of jubilee. He asked me who let us come out there in the night and dance, and I told him we didn't ask permission, we were just doing it for our own selves.

Finally Jonah took a drink of beer, and I helped him take his shirt off. That's when I saw all the welts down his back; that boy had been whipped and the blood had dried and the marks were still fresh. That's when I knew he was a runaway. He'd been whipped and he'd run away.

Lord, I said to myself, here you are dancing with a runaway and giving him beer and showing him jubilee. If he got caught you could be whipped yourself, and branded on the cheek, or have your ear cut off. But I kept on dancing.

He told me he'd run into a fence, and that was how he got those scratches and places on his back, and when he let down his overalls I could see he'd been whipped on the legs, too. And I knew he was just like all the other men I knew, always bragging and pretending he was something he wasn't.

But there was something about this boy I liked. Maybe it was because he had the gumption and craziness to run away. I'd never seen a runaway before. He was foolish enough to escape from wherever he came from, which meant he had more nerve than anybody else I knew. And I liked his looks, too. So I led him off into the bushes and showed him a real good time, and since it was his first time I wanted to make it special. I knew how to make a man happy, at least if he's got it in him to be happy.

SEVEN

JONAH

With his knife gone and his money gone, Jonah felt he was starting all over again. He had matches and he had the tablet and pencil, which he'd left in the boat. He had the corn and the musk melon he'd picked the evening before. He had the fishing line on the bottom of the boat. With daylight come again, he would have to stay off the river, waiting for the end of day and dark.

But Jonah didn't feel as bad as he expected to. There was a kind of lightness inside him, as if a burden had been lifted. He felt a calmness he'd not felt since before Mr. Williams had whipped him. He had strength because he'd been with a woman, a big woman, for the first time. And what a woman she was! He recalled the woman's body as the color of sorghum at its sweetest. And he recalled the way the woman had grunted and hollered out and presented herself to him. He'd learned something he didn't know before about women. It was a whole new way of seeing the relations between men and women.

While he was thinking about the woman and his experience the night before, a strange idea came to Jonah. What if he could find some white branch clay and rub it on his face and neck and arms? Then nobody at a distance could tell he was black. He could paddle out in the middle of the river and those who saw him would not suspect he was a runaway slave. They might think he looked pale or sick, but nobody would want to bother a sick boy going down the French Broad River in a tiny boat. Now slow down and don't be stupid, he said to himself. But the idea caught in his mind and he couldn't see anything wrong with it. "Whoa there," he said and laughed. He'd have to keep his hat on to cover his crisp hair, but otherwise no one could tell he was a Negro unless they got close.

The problem was to find a pocket of fine white clay. Most black folks knew where to find clay because they liked to eat a little once or twice a year, especially in the spring, to thin their blood and tune their systems. Only pipe clay would do, because white pipe clay had no grit in it. Such clay was found in creek banks and was dug out fresh each time it was eaten. The little creek where the boat lay might well have a clay bank.

Jonah climbed to the top of the mountain and then descended the other side to the creek. He rolled up his pants and waded out into the little stream, searching under grapevines and honeysuckle. Most of the bank was covered with brush. What he was looking for was a place where the bank had caved in. That was where a clay pocket was most likely to be exposed.

At a bend in the creek, Jonah found what he was searching for. The clay had leaves and dirt sprinkled on it, but he scraped that away with his fingers. And once the surface of the clay was clean, and he'd washed his hands in the creek, he dug out gobs of the white clay and stacked them on a rock beside the stream. To melt the clay he needed a pan where he could crumble the lumps and mix them into a kind of gray paint. But with no mixing bowl, he had to crush the clay in his hands and wet it to rub into a paste. He covered his forehead and nose and cheeks, his mouth and chin. He coated his neck and ears. And last he smeared the mixture on his arms and wrists and hands.

As the clay dried it would start to flake off. But he hoped enough powder would stay on his skin to fool someone who saw him from a distance. Jonah made his way down the creek, carrying an extra chunk of clay to use later. He loaded the corn and melon in the boat and was ready to push it out into the river when somebody stepped out of the woods. It was the fat woman from the night before, covered now in a kind of gown made from old feed sacks.

"What are you doing here?" Jonah said.

"I'm going with you."

"How do you know where I'm going?"

"You running away—I'm gone run away, too."

Jonah could feel the clay smeared on him beginning to dry. It made his skin stiff. "Who asked you to come?" he said.

"Boy, you need my help," the fat woman said. "You don't know nothing."

"Why you want to run away?" Jonah said. In daylight Jonah could see she might be only a little older than him. She might be nineteen or twenty.

"Tired of being a feet warmer for that old man."

"Have you got a name?" Jonah said.

"People call me Angel," she said, "but I ain't no angel." She broke out laughing, like she had the night before.

"Got no room for anybody but me," Jonah said. But even as he said it he remembered the night before and knew he wanted to be with this woman again.

"You don't let me come, I'll go tell the sheriff I seen you," Angel said. She got into the front of the boat and sat down. She was bigger than he was and he had no way to get her out of the boat. He'd planned to travel alone. That was the only way he could get to the North.

"You get out of there," he said.

"Thought you liked my company," Angel said and shook her breasts.

"How can you run from a sheriff with dogs?" Jonah said.

"I can run fast as you."

He had to get going, and he had to get away from her. He hadn't planned on this. He'd have to slip away from her the first chance he got. He pushed the boat out into the river and sat in the back.

It was so much easier to paddle in daylight on the French Broad. Angel weighted the boat down, so it was steadier in the water. He guided the little craft between rocks and skirted the edge of a trough of shoal water, then worked his way into the middle of the river, where he would be hardest to recognize. The river moved as fast as someone could walk. The blisters on Jonah's hands were still sore, but they'd toughened overnight. He gripped the paddle and his hands itched a little with healing. They passed someone fishing on the bank of the river and waved to him and the man waved back. Better to act friendly and not afraid. Who would think a runaway slave would wave at him? But he hoped he looked like a white man with a Negro servant. Soon as he stopped for the night, Jonah would take the hook and line from the bottom of the boat and tie them to a pole and do some fishing himself. His belly was empty and he'd love a roasted fish to go with the roasted corn.

"I'll paddle when you get tired," Angel said.

"You stay right there," Jonah said.

"You look like a ghost," Angel said and giggled.

"We'll both be ghosts if we get caught."

As he paddled between rocks and fast water, the river seemed to gather speed. He'd have to look and act quickly, and listen for the roar of rougher water or a falls ahead. Jonah wondered where the river would take him, now that he'd given up his plan to stay in the mountains and follow the chain to the north. A river ran away from the highest mountains. A river always moved toward lower ground, for water never flowed uphill. This river ran to the north, though, or the northwest, roughly in the direction he wanted to go. That was the way of hope. He'd follow the river as long as it tended to the north, and then he'd start walking again, if he could get away from this fat woman.

"I got to pee," Angel said.

"You wait till we stop on the bank."

She ignored him and stood up, pulling her gown up to her waist.

"Middle of the boat!" Jonah shouted and pointed to the gunwale just in front of him. If she sat on the edge near the front it would tip the little boat over. As Angel rested herself over the side and peed, Jonah leaned as far as he could in the other direction to balance the craft. He was relieved when she finished and crawled back to the prow.

Where waves splashed on his arms, the clay began to melt. Black dots appeared on his skin. And as the day got hotter and he began to sweat, the clay ran down his face. At first there were only streaks in the gray paint, and then spots and streaks between the streaks.

"Boy, you look like a corpse yourself," Angel said. Jonah ignored her.

When he came to a long stretch of river where there were no houses, Jonah pulled into the shallows and pushed the prow of the boat onto the shore. Rubbing bits of clay between wet hands, he smeared himself again, this time putting on a thicker coat. Maybe if there was enough clay on his face even sweat couldn't melt it.

"You ain't going to fool nobody with that," Angel said.

"What makes you so smart?" Jonah said.

"I was born smart," Angel said and laughed.

As soon as he pushed off into the current again, Jonah was glad he'd reapplied the clay makeup. A bridge appeared ahead, a long bridge made of poles and logs, with people and horses crossing it. He'd have to go under the bridge, within fifteen or twenty feet of the people crossing. He aimed for a section of the bridge near the middle of the river. He'd paddle with his head down and with luck nobody crossing the bridge would even notice him. And maybe they would just assume Angel was his servant.

And then Jonah saw the boys. They were barefoot and wore overalls held up by only one gallus. They wore straw hats and were skipping rocks into the river, making flat rocks hop across the surface of the splashing stream. Jonah stayed near the middle of the river, far from the boys who stood by the east end of the bridge hurling rock after rock. The rocks lit sparks of splash across the water, as if something invisible was dashing across on tiptoe.

It was too late to swing over to the west side of the river. Jonah paddled faster, trying to ignore the boys. The rocks they threw skipped in front of the boat and one hit the side of the craft. He didn't dare yell at the boys or go to the shore to confront them. Nothing could be stupider than to get into a fight with white boys. They'd see the clay and see that he was African. But if he ignored them they might think that was strange also.

Jonah kept his head low and paddled hard. Rocks came dancing across the water in front of him and beside him. Another rock thunked again on the side of the boat. He held the paddle in his right hand and raised his fist at the boys. They laughed and yelled and pumped their right arms at him. He was within ten yards of the bridge when a rock bounded across the water as if the river was made of rubber and smacked him on the cheek. Jonah's face stung and he tasted blood in his mouth. He spat and heard the boys laughing. Tears welled in his eyes, and he was glad he was so far from the bank no one could see the tears. The tears would melt the clay around his eyes.

Another rock danced over the river and hit Angel square on the shoulder. "Ouch!" she said and rubbed the place that had been hit. She shook her fist at the boys on the bank and turned to look back at Jonah. "See how much good your white clay does."

The bridge ahead was blurred by his tears, but he aimed between two sets of pillars in the middle of the stream. As he shot under the planks, hooves and wagon wheels thundered above him. And when he came out into the sunlight again he saw the boys following him along the east bank. Thrilled by their success at hitting him and Angel and the boat, they ran along the bank scooping up more rocks. "Hey!" he called to them and shook his fist, and the boys yelled back and slapped their knees. They threw rock after rock, and one landed in the boat and one hit him on the knee, but it had run out of speed and didn't hurt much. The current was sweeping them away and the boys couldn't catch up. Besides, they'd had their fun, and were ready to turn to some fresh amusement. Jonah spat out bloody spit. His jaw hurt and he hoped the rock hadn't broken a tooth or a bone. More likely it had bruised the gum and made it bleed. He dared not wash his cheek or mouth with river water. The river was moving faster and he couldn't take his eyes away from the rocks and snags. He paddled ahead of the current. As he came around a bend he saw the town ahead. There were houses on both banks, but more on the east bank. It must be Asheville, he thought.

In the bright daylight Jonah guided the boat just where he wanted to go. He could twist the paddle to the left or right to guide it. After two days he was sure of his strokes and shot the boat around rocks and dropped through charging chutes. His skill with the paddle gave him new confidence. At this rate he could go many miles in a day. He was moving fast in the right direction. All he needed was to get rid of his passenger.

"Is that Asheville?" he said.

"Don't you know nothing?" Angel said. "Sure it's Asheville."

A long, low building ran along the bank on his right, a warehouse of some sort. And beyond that, houses and brick buildings clustered on top of a hill. The banks were high as bluffs, and Jonah saw only three or four docks down by the water. He kept to the middle of the river, which tore itself apart on snags and gulped around rocks, gathering speed. He wiped more blood from his lip.

If God sees everything and foresees everything, then he must have foreseen I'd be hit by that rock, Jonah thought. If God is all-powerful, as preachers say, that must mean he intended for me to be hit by the rock. It was a thought so scary, he couldn't get his mind around it. If he followed that logic, it meant that God wanted him to be hurt. If God controlled everything, then he must have wanted Mr. Williams to accuse him of stealing and whip him. And God must want some people to be slaves and some to be masters. If God was in charge of everything, then he must know how much cruelty there was, and how hard most people's lives were. And he must have meant for fat Angel to get in his boat and slow him down.

Jonah rubbed his cheek and was already tired from thinking such thoughts. There must be something wrong with his logic, for the plan of things could not be as crazy as these thoughts made it seem. Why would everybody be brought into the world to suffer? It seemed that if there was a secret to things, that secret was cruelty. He paddled hard around rocks as the river seemed to move faster. The stream appeared to be running away from itself faster than a man could walk. He dodged a snag sticking up out of the riverbed. The river was running away as he was running away. The river was his partner. He guided the boat with an assurance that surprised him.

"Ain't you gone let me paddle?" Angel called back.

"No time to let you paddle."

"There'll be time if you hit a rock," Angel said. "Plenty of time then."

As the river gathered speed beyond Asheville, it seemed to have a different smell. Above the town the water had the scent of dirt and rotting leaves and sticks. It was the smell of mud. But below the town the smell was darker, in raw and seething white water, but with a hint of filth, as if something foul had spilled out of the ditches from the town into the river. He didn't see any filth, but the water appeared to be darker, as if it had soot in it.

Woe to us, Jonah whispered as he plunged into the gorge that wound between steep mountains. The river was going faster, and he paddled faster to stay ahead of the tide. If the current could catch the boat crossways, it would turn it over. The river moved at different speeds in different sections. He tried to find the zone where the boat could be controlled best. He shifted from one section to another, keeping the boat pointed downstream.

By the time it began to get dark, they were far down the river. When he came to a long stretch with no houses or cleared land in sight, he paddled to the shore and pulled the boat up on the bank.

"What you gone do now?" Angel said.

"I'm going to catch some fish," Jonah said.

"Then I'll build us a fire," Angel said.

He turned over rocks until he found some earthworms, and then he tied the fishing line to a stick and baited the hook. It took him half an hour to catch two fish, a trout about ten inches long, and one about twelve.

Without a knife it was hard to clean the fish. But he managed to rip open the belly with a stick and rake the guts out. He couldn't scrape away the scales without a blade, so he pulled the skin off a piece at a time. With the grease on his hands he rubbed off some of the scabs of pine pitch. And then he washed his hands and saw Angel had made a fire to roast both fish and corn.

"You took my money and my knife last night," Jonah said.

"Wasn't me," Angel said.

"Now I got no knife," Jonah said.

"But you got me to help," Angel said and laughed.

The corn was not fresh but the fish was, and both tasted mighty sweet. He took the bigger fish and gave Angel the smaller one. They ate the corn between them. Then he washed his hands again and broke open the cantaloupe on the edge of the boat. The melon flesh was warm but very sweet. Jonah gave half to Angel and ate until he was full and began to be sleepy. But before he slept he knew he had to plan his strategy for tomorrow. He'd eaten all his rations and he had no money and no knife. However, he did have the tablet and pencil. He was going to have to be smart and think of some way to use them.

"Put out the fire," he said.

"I want to sit by the fire," Angel said.

"You want everybody passing by to see us here?"

Jonah put out the fire and they sat in the dark listening to the river. The river sounded like hundreds of people talking in low voices, maybe praying, maybe telling stories or gossiping. Whatever it was saying, the stream wasn't speaking to him. The river talked its own talk and ignored him. Maybe it was the ghosts of Indians that once lived on the banks talking. Jonah wished he was a hundred times smarter and a thousand times luckier than he was.

A plan began to form in his mind, a scary plan, that went something like this: he'd have to find the name of a landowner out in the country and go into town pretending to be a servant to the landowner. It would have to be an owner far out in the country, for all the slaves closer to town would be known. He'd have to write a note that was convincing, otherwise he'd be arrested for attempting to steal. The note would have to read: "Please give this boy ten dollars from my account," and it would be signed with the name of the plantation owner in such a quick scrawl it would be hard to read.

His scheme was dangerous because it required him to go into a town in daylight and walk into a bank. He could easily be cornered there and seized. And there was always a chance that the signature he scrawled would not resemble the landowner's. It was such a risky plan that outright stealing from gardens and chicken houses might be safer. But he needed money for a knife and more matches, for shoes and bread. The alternative would be to go into a house looking for money, or to rob the till of a little store.

And he had to think what to do about Angel. As long as she was with him, everything was more complicated. But maybe he could think of some way she could be helpful to his plan. Angel had laid down on the other side of the dead fire and she'd been so quiet he thought she might be asleep. Remembering the night before, he reached over to touch her. He wanted to raise her gown over her hips. As long as they were traveling together, he might as well make the most of it.

"What you doing, boy?" Angel said and pushed his hand away.

"Last night you were more friendly," Jonah said.

"Last night be jubilee," Angel said. "Just because I come with you don't mean I be your concubine." *Concubine* was a word he knew from the Scriptures. It surprised him to hear Angel say it.

"I bet you can't even read," Jonah said.

"I can read your mind well enough," Angel said.

Jonah lay for a long time in the dark thinking how strange it was to have gone to jubilee and to have Angel beside him now. Nothing turned out the way you expected it to. He tried to reconsider his plans, and dropped off to sleep still studying his schemes.

THE NEXT MORNING AS soon as there was light Jonah woke and saw Angel was already up and in the boat. She sat in the front like she was determined not to be left behind. "How long have you been up?" he said.

"Long enough to see how lazy you is," she said.

She'd made a little fire, but there was nothing to cook over the flames unless he caught more fish. He knew he should get on down the river. Jonah put the fire out and pushed the boat off into the river and began paddling. His hands were still sore, but he worked steadily, avoiding the worst shoals, staying near the middle of the river, watching the stream ahead and the fields and ridges on either side as they came into view. As it got lighter he saw there was a heavy dew, and the first sun made the fields sparkle. He saw women milking cows at pasture gaps, and men chopping kindling wood. He passed a Negro woman starting a fire under a washpot. Farther on some men were cutting hay with scythes. They stepped and swung the blades in unison like people dancing together. And then a town hove into view. First there were a few houses close together along the road and riverbank. Then he saw a steeple, and another taller steeple. There was a brick building that must be a courthouse. Houses stood so close together, there must not be gardens between them. A landing pier stuck out into the river. From the boat he could see a tan yard, where leather soaked in troughs of acid, and a blacksmith shop. There was another, smaller church, and a store with flowers planted in front of it.

"Ain't you gone stop here and get something to eat?" Angel said.

"Won't do no good to stop here in broad daylight," Jonah said.

"Do you mean us to starve to death?"

"I got a plan," Jonah said.

"Yeah? I want to see your plan."

As Jonah paddled beyond the town, looking for a place to land where no one would see him, he began to think how hard it would be to follow through with his scheme. How would he find out the name of a plantation owner out in the country without asking people in town or at other farms? If he had to ask around he'd raise suspicions. If he didn't have the right name the people in the bank would not be fooled.

But would they give money to a black boy in any case? Jonah began to see how far-fetched his plan really was. In his dirty, smelly clothes they'd run him out of the bank anyway. No matter what kind of note he wrote, they'd chase him away in his ragged, dirty overalls. They might call the constable and put him in chains, for all would see he was a stranger. By the time Jonah found a place where he could go ashore, he'd decided his only hope was to break into a store and find some clothes and a knife and perhaps a little money. If he stole only a little money maybe it wouldn't be missed. And if he stole only a few clothes and a pocketknife they might not be missed either. A country store would be the best bet, for he could hide in the woods until dark and there would be few houses around it. And even if he was seen in a country store, he might be able to escape into the woods.

Jonah paddled on down the river, and after about an hour he saw a road running along the edge of the fields on the east bank. Far ahead a large white building stood by the road, and as he got closer he saw a sign over the doorway: CHITWOOD'S GENERAL MERCHANDISE. A horse and wagon were stopped in front of the store. A kind of shed stood beside the white building, maybe a cow stall or workshop. Jonah continued down the river for at least a mile, then paddled to the right bank, where a branch entered the river between birch trees and hazelnut bushes. He got out and pulled the boat up on the bank.

"You stay here while I go to that store to get some things," he said.

"How long you be gone? I come with you."

"If you come we'll both be caught," Jonah said. "You're a jinx on my journey."

"You ain't done too well on your own."

"I've made it this far," Jonah said. "You keep your fat butt here while I get some supplies."

"You the man," Angel said and laughed. "Reckon you the big boss man."

Jonah took off his clothes and washed himself in the branch water as thoroughly as he could. The clay melted away with washing, but some was left in the pores of his skin. His arms were dotted with gray spots the size of pinheads. When he was as clean as he could make himself, Jonah found his way through the woods to the edge of the field behind the store. There was no place to hide in front of the store, so he had to watch it from the back. From behind some sumac bushes he saw people on foot and horseback, in buggies and wagons, stop at the store. The building beside the store was indeed a little barn where the store owner kept his cow and horse. A set of stairs in back of the store led up to the second story, and Jonah figured the owner and his family must live there. He'd have to break into the store while the owner was upstairs.

Late in the afternoon Jonah dashed to a haystack closer to the store. He watched the owner's wife come out and milk the cow and draw water from the well. She gathered eggs from the little henhouse and scattered corn on the ground for the chickens. After she went back inside Jonah could smell bread baking and meat cooking. He was so hungry he felt sick. A little later a man, who Jonah thought must be the storekeeper, came out the back door and locked it. He placed the key under a bucket that sat beside the stairs to the second story. Jonah could hardly believe his luck: he'd seen the key, and knew where it was hidden.

While he was concealed in the dusty hay, time stalled and drifted.

He watched lights appear in the second story and he listened to whip-poor-wills in the trees by the river. A man on horseback thumped along the road, and chickens clucked and quieted in the henhouse. A dog sniffed around the stairs and then trotted out of sight. Jonah dared not approach the store until all lights were out. His only hope was to wait until the storekeeper and his wife were asleep. Even then he'd have to move an inch at a time through the dark, hoping the dog didn't return. The minutes passed so slowly, he wondered if time could pause in its tracks and go backward. Was time just something you only thought of, and not an actual substance itself?

Finally the light went out in an upper room of the store building. Jonah waited for a few minutes more and then stepped out from behind the haystack, his legs stiff from crouching and kneeling so long. Slow now, he whispered to himself. He tried to recall the way the yard looked in daylight, the place of the woodpile and washpot, the clothesline. He'd have to move so slowly that even if he ran into something it wouldn't make any noise.

A dog barked down the road and the whip-poor-will called again from the trees along the river. A horse moved about in the stall. Something snapped in the field behind him, as if someone had stepped on a stick or dry weed stalk. He paused and listened, but the noise didn't come again. Jonah had almost reached the stairs when a window opened on the left side of the second story. There was a whisper and splash and Jonah guessed the storekeeper was pissing from his bedroom window. When the swishing stopped he waited for several more minutes, until he thought he heard snoring through the open window.

His foot touched the bucket by the stairs and the metal rang a little. Jonah stood perfectly still and counted to a hundred, then he reached under the bucket and found the key. Feeling his way along the wall, he touched the door and located the keyhole. Once the key was in place, he turned it cautiously. The lock must have been old and rusty, for the wards groaned and rattled. The key froze as if blocked, and he had to jiggle it to make it turn farther.

As soon as the door was unlocked he replaced the key under the bucket. He planned to leave the store by the front door if he could, and when he closed the door he locked it from inside. The storekeeper must never suspect anyone had entered. The store smelled of harness and coffee and cloth, as most such stores did. There was also the scent of rope and molasses. Jonah knew he couldn't feel his way around the store without knocking something over. There would be too many things to trip on or send crashing to the floor. He struck a match and saw the racks of clothes, the shelves of cloth, the hoes and rakes. First he'd find the money, and then he'd take some clothes. He'd not be greedy, but select only things he needed most. With luck the storekeeper might never miss them.

Jonah slipped behind the counter and lifted the lid of the till. He shuddered when he saw the compartments were empty, all except the box where the pennies were kept. The storekeeper must have taken the more valuable coins and paper money upstairs. Slow now, Jonah said to calm himself. Slow down, old hoss. He knelt to search the shelf beneath the counter. A pistol and a shotgun lay behind some boxes. Also a long knife, a Bowie knife. He'd love to have the knife, and he could use the pistol, too. But if he took them the storekeeper would know, first thing, that he'd been robbed. And Jonah knew it was not a good idea for a Negro, especially one not known locally, to be caught with a pistol. He looked in the boxes under the shelves and found no money. Farther on there were needles and thread, thimbles and pins.

Harness hung on pegs behind the counter and a saddle sat on a kind of sawhorse. A set of saddlebags hung behind the saddle. Something about the way a saddlebag leaned caught Jonah's eye. The leather looked weighted on one side. The match burned down and he had to strike another. When he reached into the left pocket of the saddlebag, he felt cold, slick coins. That was where the storekeeper hid his cash.

Jonah was tempted to steal the saddlebag and all its cash. But if he did that, a sheriff and posse would be after him tomorrow. Most of the coins were small. He took three silver dollars and two half dollars, and he took a five-dollar gold piece, then dropped it back into the bag. The storekeeper might assume he'd miscounted the evening before if silver was missing. But gold would be another matter.

When Jonah looked at the clothes he thought of grabbing the best shirt and pants. But what he needed was work clothes that wouldn't call attention to themselves. He took a pair of jean-cloth overalls and a thick cotton shirt. He was about to look for a pocketknife in the box behind the counter when he heard a horse galloping, getting closer. Jonah backed to the wall where a cloth-covered coffin lay on the floor. He blew out the match and listened to the hoofbeats approach the store. The horse stopped and someone clomped up the steps at the back of the store and pounded on the door above.

"Who's there?" a voice shouted.

"It's Silas," a man shouted. "Mattie has the headache. She needs her laudanum."

Footsteps creaked on the ceiling of the store as the storekeeper hurried to get dressed. "Mattie has her headache," the storekeeper muttered.

His steps moved toward the back door.

As the two men came down the back steps Jonah knew he'd waited until it was too late. He should have escaped through the front door while he had a chance. He didn't have time now to find his way through all the shelves and tables and unlock the front door without striking a new match. He must hide. As the storekeeper fitted the key in the back door, Jonah lifted the cloth and lid of the coffin and lay down in it, with the overalls and shirt clutched to his chest. He closed the lid as the men stepped into the store.

A match was struck, and through the crack under the lid Jonah saw a lantern was lit.

"Hate to roust you, but Mattie has the headache terrible."

"Sure does smell like matches in here," the storekeeper said.

"You just struck one," the man named Silas said.

The weight of the men made the floor creak as they walked around.

"What size bottle?" the storekeeper said.

"Better make it two ounces this time."

Footsteps came right toward the coffin and then walked past it. Jonah cringed inside the casket and heard a cabinet open and bottles clink, and then the door was closed.

"When can you settle up?" the storekeeper said.

"I hate to run up a tab," the other man said, "but I ain't got no choice."

"Don't know how much longer I can carry you," the storekeeper said.

"Soon as the tobacco's in, I'll settle. You know I will."

"It's been a long dry summer," the storekeeper said.

The two men walked to the counter and Jonah heard the scratching of a pen on paper. "That makes seven dollars and eighty cents in all that you owe," the storekeeper said.

"When Mattie gets the headache she can't do a thing but sit in the dark with her eyes closed. If she don't get her medicine she gets the all-overs."

"Good night, Silas," the storekeeper said.

"Night," the man said.

Jonah listened to the door close and the key turn in the lock. He was awfully glad he'd thought to replace the key under the bucket and lock the door from inside. It was only luck that he'd thought of that. He listened to the horse gallop away and heard the storekeeper's steps above. The storekeeper and his wife talked for a while, and then the house was still. Jonah waited for several minutes, and then he waited some more.

When he raised the lid of the coffin, he smelled burnt coal oil from the lantern. As he got out he took care to prevent the lid from slamming down on the box. The coffin was covered with black cloth, but even so the falling lid would make a racket. He propped the lid with his elbow until he could lower it gently. Standing in the dark, Jonah tried to remember where the box of knives was, and the supply of matches. He'd seen the knives at the other end of the counter, but he'd not noticed where the matches were. If he could get a good knife and matches, that's all he would take. His only hope was not to be greedy. The storekeeper must never guess anyone had been there, at least not until Jonah was a hundred miles away.

Stepping a few inches at a time, Jonah felt his way around the clothes rack to the counter, and then along the counter to the box of knives. He struck a match and looked at the shiny specimens, penknives with ivory handles, larger knives too big to carry in his pocket. He looked at the treasure of middle-sized knives, with wooden handles, bone handles, mother of pearl. He'd never seen such a hoard of cutlery. He picked a folding knife that fit his palm. It had a red bone handle and one large blade. A kind of plaque was inlaid on the left side of the handle with BARLOW engraved on it. Jonah slid the knife into his pocket with a shiver of elation. He'd never before had such a fine knife.

It cost Jonah another match to find the matches. They were in a box on the shelf behind the counter to the left of the harness. There were two kinds of matches, some in blue boxes and some in red boxes. He took one of each. As Jonah eased his way to the front of the store he saw the big cookie jar at the end of the counter. Laying the other stuff down, he lifted the lid and took out a cookie. It was almost the size of a cake, wider than his hand, and filled with raisins. He slipped the cookie into a pocket of the overalls. There were stacks of sardine cans and sausage cans on the shelf, and he slipped a can of sardines into the overalls also.

When he reached the front door and turned the key the door would still not open. He wondered if it had a double lock, maybe one on the outside. Jonah felt along the edge of the door and found a bolt. The bolt was shot into its sleeve on the door jamb. He carefully slid the bolt back and eased the door open, then stepped out into the damp darkness. The storekeeper would find the door unlocked in the morning and maybe assume he'd overlooked it the evening before.

As Jonah started down the dark road, walking slowly to make little noise and not trip over rocks and ruts, he thought at first of going back to the boat with his supplies and money. As far as he knew, Angel was still waiting for him there. But with her accompanying him, he had little chance of ever making it to the North. Even on his own he had at best long odds. Together it was only a matter of time until they were caught. If he meant to make it to freedom, he'd have to go on his own. There was no other way to look at it.

The road ran along the river, near where the boat was pulled up on the bank. Jonah turned aside into the woods, and started climbing the ridge away from the river, in the direction he assumed was north or northeast.

EIGHT

ANGEL

As I sat in the boat waiting for Jonah, I thought about all the strange things that had happened to me so suddenly after the jubilee. It didn't seem possible I'd run away from the Thomas Place and everything I knew just to follow this crazy boy that wanted to go to the North. But there I was, waiting in the dark for him to come back. And I thought about how we had gotten together and all the silly things that had happened in the last two days.

After the jubilee Jonah must have been tired and worn out from the good time I gave him, for he slept on the ground like an old bear in winter time while we gathered up our stuff and had to leave. I didn't mind leaving and taking the money out of his overalls flung on the dirt, for I had given him lots of jubilee. But before we got back to the Thomas Place I started thinking and feeling bad, for he was a runaway and needed all he could get. He had the nerve to run away and I'd taken his money. And then I thought: if he can run away, maybe I can, too. It hit me like blue thunder out of nowhere. I knew I was at least as brave and smart as him. I had to give him back his money. And if he really knew the way up north, maybe I could follow. After last night I should be welcome company. And I liked him. I can't say why a woman likes one man better than another, but I knew I had a feeling for him.

I dropped back on the trail like I had to pee, and soon as the others disappeared around a bend I started back up the mountain. If I hurried I might catch that boy before he woke up. I hoped to find Jonah still asleep and slide the money back into his overalls. And then I'd wake him up and say I was going with him. And I'd show him the way to the river. I was going to find out where he had run from and where he was running to. I would offer to go along with him, and help him, and if that didn't work I'd go along anyway. For after all, how was he going to stop me? I was tired of being Master Thomas's bed warmer, and soon as I got older or had a child he'd kick me out of the big house to work in the fields like Mama and the rest of the help. I reckoned I'd done enough hoeing corn and stripping cane already.

But there was no boy at the clearing on the mountain when I got back there. By then it was daylight and he had already waked up and found his overalls and gone. He'd come down the mountain into the firelight and I thought maybe he'd climbed back up on the mountain. It was a steep slope with no trail and I had to pick my way through briars and blown-down trees and laurel thickets to the top. There was nothing on top but more trees, and I looked down and saw the river foaming over rocks way down below. And I thought: since Jonah hasn't come on a trail, he must be traveling by river.

I let myself down that steep mountain by holding to trees, and I fell and rolled over one time. And when I got to the bottom I saw a ghost wearing overalls and putting stuff in an old boat. And when I stepped closer I saw it was the boy himself all covered with gray paint or white clay over his face and arms. He looked like a corpse dug out of the ground.

"What did you do that for?" I asked him, and he said he was going to look like a white man. I laughed and he didn't like my laugh. I could see he was a serious boy.

"What are you doing here?" he said, and I told him I'd come to follow him. I was ashamed to tell him I'd taken his money.

"No you're not," he said, and asked how I knew where he's going.

"You're running away and I'm going, too," I said. He looked at me hard and shook his head. He was so mad he trembled a little.

"I will be good company," I said and patted his knee. He looked at me and then he looked away. A boy that's mad at you, a good boy, will not want to look you in the face. Mean men will look right into your eyes.

"Do you know how far it is to the North?" he said. "First you have to get over the mountains to Tennessee, and then over the mountains to Virginia. If you're lucky enough to cross four hundred miles of Virginia you have to cross Maryland after the Potomac River. And after that you cross the mountains of Pennsylvania. Then after a lot of miles you may get to New York. And from New York you still have to cross to Canada. I'll probably never make it by myself, and with you I don't have a shadow of a chance."

Right then I saw that boy was different from anybody I knew. He had all those names and all those miles in his head. That made me want to go even more.

"Where did you learn all those names?" I asked.

"I can read a map," he said.

"Can you read a book?"

"Sure, I can read anything, books, newspapers, maps. I read lots of books," he said, strutting in his voice.

So I said to myself: this boy is special, this boy knows where he's going. He's silly and proud like all men, but he's different, too. It wouldn't do any good to argue with him. I'd just walk over and put my fat behind on the plank in the middle of the boat. He wasn't big enough to get me off. He would have no choice but to push off with me sitting there, because if he hit me I'd beat him up. I was bigger than him. And besides, he was worried to get going, all covered with crumbs of clay like he'd been buried and rose up from the dead.

"I'll never make it to the North with you," he said, and shoved the boat into the water. "Never even make it to Tennessee with you."

"You'll never make it there without me," I said and giggled.

"We could be caught and whipped," he said.

"You've done been whipped," I said.

He didn't say anything else. He wanted to look like a white man covered with clay and paddling the boat, but I didn't think he could fool anybody. A colored boy covered with clay didn't look like anything but a colored boy covered with clay.

I TOLD MYSELF I'D have to stick to this boy like bark on an oak tree. I had run away from the Thomas Place and I didn't mean to go back there, and I didn't want to be whipped and branded either. Or have my ear cut off. He was my best hope for getting away to the North and freedom because he had that map of places in his head. Just like I knew the rooms in the Master's big house and all the shacks in the quarters, he knew the map and the way to those places and freedom far away.

That night after he caught two trout out of the river and we ate them, and then he put out the fire, I asked him how he learned to read so good, because no slave on the Thomas Place knew how to read, not even Eli. So he told me about waiting on his master's children and listening while they did their lessons and learned their letters.

"Does it come all at once, seeing what letters mean?" I said.

"Don't be stupid," Jonah said. "You learn a little at a time." He looked at me in the dim light like I had no more sense than a fence post.

"Ain't you the high and mighty one," I said.

He sulked like a man does when he gets his feelings hurt. Because he was not going to argue with a woman, a woman that couldn't even read. He was too important to snap back at me. We sat there as it got dark, listening to the mutter and whisper of the river. That river talked like it was telling a long story. "Where is this river going?" I said, but he didn't answer.

When I lay down on the ground to sleep, I thought, this boy is going to leave me the first chance he gets. He didn't know yet how much he needed me. He liked the loving I gave him the night before, but that didn't make any difference because he wanted to run off by himself. Only if I held back could I make him want me enough to take me along.

When he reached for me I pulled back, and then he turned away. And during the night while he was sleeping I got up to pee and put myself in the boat. Then at daylight I made a fire while he was still asleep. And when he woke up I was already sitting in the boat and he couldn't leave me.

Riding in the front of that boat while Jonah paddled down the French Broad River, I felt like the queen of the river. I wished I had a turban like Mama. I was right out in the middle of that water in broad daylight and anybody could see me. But we were moving fast. Jonah knew the way to the North, but he didn't have any money, and I was ashamed to tell him I'd taken his money. I was getting terribly hungry and we didn't have anything to eat. Finally we passed a store on the road that ran away from the river, and a mile farther on Jonah pushed the boat to the bank and stepped out.

"I will wait until dark and take what I need from that store," he said.

"I'm going with you," I said.

"No, you stay with the boat," he said. "I'll come back after midnight."

Now I knew you couldn't put any trust in what a man said. A man will as soon lie to you as spit out a watermelon seed. But I figured he had to come back to the boat. He was traveling by boat down the river. He couldn't leave his boat. But just to make sure I followed Jonah through the woods up the river and saw him hide behind a haystack watching the store building. All evening he hid there and I stayed in the woods and watched him.

He will get some good things to eat, I told myself. And he won't get away from me.

But I saw my mistake after it got dark. I waited a long time in the woods and then I moved closer to the house, but couldn't see anything. There was a flicker of light inside the store, but I couldn't tell if it was Jonah or the storekeeper, or somebody else.

Then I heard a horse clip-clop up to the store and I pulled back to the woods. There was lantern light and voices, and I thought maybe Jonah had been caught because a bright light came on inside the store. But I couldn't really tell anything, except that a horse galloped away from the store in the dark and then everything was quiet.

That's when I thought I'd better hurry back to the boat, for maybe Jonah had already gone back there. Maybe he'd fooled me and soon as it got dark he slipped back to the boat and went on down the river without me. Maybe it was all a trick to get rid of me.

Girl, you're not as smart as you think you are, I said to myself and started back toward the river. In the dark, limbs hit me in the face and briars raked my ankles. I held my arms out in front of me but still ran into a tree. I thought I heard somebody walking, and stopped still as a stump until the footsteps were gone.

It seemed to take me all night, but when I reached the river I followed the bank, knowing that boy had come back to the boat and left me. But then I stumbled on something in the dark and it was the boat right where I'd left it. The paddle was there and the fishing line was there. But Jonah had not come back. I thought he must still be waiting outside the store.

So I sat down in the boat and waited. And then I lay down, using my hands for a pillow. I must have gone to sleep, for next time I opened my eyes it was beginning to get light and the birds were singing in the trees along the river. I lay in the boat, but there was no sign of Jonah. First thing I thought is, that boy has been caught. For all his bragging about knowing how to read and knowing the map of the way to the North, he had been caught breaking into that store. He had been killed, or taken in chains to a jail.

A sick pain shot deep through my belly, for if Jonah was caught he might tell on me. People had seen me in the boat the day before. They might already be looking for me with dogs and guns. If they caught a colored girl in the woods, they could do whatever they wanted with her. I listened, but didn't hear anything but birds in the trees.

If I got in the boat and paddled on down the river, I might leave Jonah stranded, if he had not been caught but ran back to the river to get away. If I stayed any longer, I was liable to get caught myself, if they were out looking. It was an awful puzzle about what was the best thing to do. I wished I'd stayed at the Thomas Place where there was plenty to eat and all I had to do was carry trays and help Sally and let the Master have his ease with me. But I saw it was too far to go back up the river now. If I started walking up the river I'd be caught for sure, and they'd whip me and brand me on the cheek, or cut off my ear.

I sat in the boat and listened, and the longer I waited, the more I was sure Jonah had been caught and put in jail. And if he told about me, I'd be caught, too. And then I thought, no, he's still hiding and will come back to the boat anytime. He would come when it was safe, for he'd not leave the boat, which was the only way he had to travel down the river.

It never crossed my mind that he wanted to get away from me so bad he'd just leave the boat and start walking along the roads and trails. A young girl never thinks a man will leave her. I figured I was so special and I made him happy, and he needed me for his long trip to the North. A girl will fool herself, thinking a man needs her. I told myself I'd be good to that boy when he came back.

But after a long time I saw he was not coming back. He'd been caught or killed or had run off on his own and I had no way of knowing what had happened. I was miles down the river from the Thomas Place, and I didn't know where the North was, because I didn't have any map in my head.

Since I couldn't think of anything else to do, I pushed the boat into the river and climbed in. But guiding that thing and paddling was harder than I expected. Every time I paddled one way, it seemed to go another. The current pushed the boat sideways and I hit on a rock and was nearly thrown in the water. Everything seemed to go backward. The boat rammed into a log and tilted.

The open water in the middle of the river ran fast and dangerous and deep. I'd never learned to swim and knew I'd be drowned for sure if I got out over deeper water. I tried to steer the boat and hit a sandbar. After I pushed off of the sand and mud, I tried to aim for the still water in a bend. I tried every which way to make the boat go for me without getting far out on the river. But I kept running into brush and overhanging limbs. A big snake plopped into the boat and I flung it out with the paddle. A mud turtle the size of a dishpan sat on a log watching me go by. I brushed past a hornet's nest in a birch tree and one stung me on the shoulder.

Finally I saw it was no good. Jonah could made the boat work, but I couldn't seem to find the right way. If I tipped over on a rock in deep water I would drown and nobody would ever know what became of Angel. I didn't know where the river went anyway, though I knew that all rivers run to bigger rivers that go to the sea. Girl, you better get out and walk, I said to myself. You're not going anywhere in this rotten old boat.

When I saw a bare spot on the bank a little way ahead, I pushed the boat in that direction. When the point of the boat hit the mud, I jumped out and pulled it out of water. Soon as the boat was safe, I heard this noise halfway like a laugh and halfway like a belch, not quite like anything I'd ever heard before. I looked up the steep bank and saw this animal with big ears and silver whiskers under its chin and big old eyes like bubbles looking down at me. I thought it must be the devil himself making that funny noise. And then I saw it was the devil's own pet, a goat with a collar and bell on it.

I wasn't going to climb the bank with this goat looking down at me. He might butt me right back into the river. So I was stuck between the mud and the steep bank when I heard somebody singing up there in the trees. But it wasn't any kind of song I'd ever heard before.

"Who are you?" I hollered. The singing went on, and I climbed a little higher and saw this old man at the top of the high bank. He wore a straw hat and had the biggest mustache I ever saw. He said something I didn't understand and beckoned me to come up. He took the goat by the collar with one hand and waved me up with the other.

It took me some huffing and puffing to climb that hill, and when I got to the top the old man lifted his hat with one hand and smiled under that mustache big as the goat's horns. No white man had ever lifted his hat to me before, though I wasn't too sure this man was a white man. His skin was nearly as dark as mine, but his features looked white.

And then I saw this wagon in the clearing about half the size of a regular horse or ox wagon. The wagon was painted all kinds of colors, with figures like hex marks and pictures. And the canvas cover was also painted with pictures of trees and goats and hills and pretty houses with white columns. Buckets and pitchers, kegs and pans, hung from nails on the sides of the wagon. And hitched to the wagon were two goats in red harness, and three other goats with collars were grazing beside the wagon.

The old man smiled at me and pointed to his wagon and said something else I couldn't understand. And I thought he must be a gypsy or foreigner, maybe a Melungeon, or some kind of Indian. And then it came to me all of a sudden: this was the Goat Man that people talked about. I had heard tales all my life about a man who traveled with goats up and down the country from north to south and sharpened knives and soldered buckets and dishpans. Every few years he passed going one way or another, and then would come back again. I'd never seen him before but knew the stories.

"You're the Goat Man," I said and he smiled and nodded and said something that didn't make sense. But I reckoned he knew his name. He understood what people called him.

"Where are you going, Goat Man?" I said. He shook his head like he didn't understand me. But then he pointed to the direction that I thought was maybe north. His shirt had big, droopy sleeves and flowers embroidered on the chest. But the cloth was dirty. I don't reckon that shirt had been washed in a year.

"Have you got anything to eat?" I said. I was so hungry I was ready to beg, or drop to the ground. But he didn't understand me. The Goat Man was so short, he didn't come to my shoulder. He pointed to the boat like he was asking where I came from and where I was going. I didn't want him to think I was a runaway, but he didn't seem to understand anything I said.

"Goat Man," I said and rubbed my belly, and pointed to my mouth. He raised a finger like he meant to say wait a minute. Then he ran to the wagon and came back with a long, thin loaf of bread. I'd never seen bread like that before, shaped like a sausage. He broke the loaf in half and gave me a piece.

The bread was hard on the outside and soft on the inside. I could hardly bite it, but when I crunched into it I found it was the sweetest bread I'd ever tasted. I was so hungry I crushed the bread with my teeth and ate the whole thing quickly.

Soon as I finished the bread the Goat Man took two buckets off the side of the wagon and handed them to me and pointed toward the river. I hated to go back down to the water, but he had given me the bread so I took the buckets.

By the time I climbed back up the bank, sloshing the buckets of water, the Goat Man had a fire started, and he unharnessed the two goats from the wagon and all the animals were grazing on the weeds and vines. He put water in a pot to boil and make coffee, and he boiled more water to make mush.

I went to gather some sticks for the fire, for I was still hungry and I wanted him to let me stay. And since he talked in a strange tongue, maybe he wouldn't turn me in to the sheriff. I brought an armful of sticks and then I gathered another load. The Goat Man had a pan of tomatoes somebody had given him or he had bought or taken from a garden. And he had some sweet corn, too. He roasted the corn in the ashes for a few minutes and then stripped off the dirty shucks. And then he got plates and let me eat with him. The corn and tomatoes and mush tasted so good, tears came to my eyes. The old man took a drink from a flask but didn't offer me any. And I didn't care. I'd never eaten better vittles in my life.

NINE

JONAH

With the money he took from Chitwood's Store and the new pair of overalls and new shirt, the matches and fishhooks and sharp pocketknife, Jonah struck out overland until he reached the river he learned later was the Holston. He thought of looking for a boat to paddle up that river, which ran from the northeast, but saw the current was too strong. He could walk faster than he could paddle upstream.

Jonah followed the river to a village called Kingsport, and then took the road to the northeast. He found that with the new clothes he didn't look so much like a runaway. And he wrote a note on a page in the tablet that said: "This nigger boy is going to help my sick mother in Winchester. Please help him get there, Cyrus Page, his owner, in Knoxville, Tennessee."

Jonah had decided to say he was from Knoxville in Tennessee

instead of South Carolina, in case someone made inquiries and found that a boy like him had run away from the Williams Place. Twice he'd been stopped by a sheriff on the road, and each time, after reading the note, the sheriff had let him go. Jonah thought it was the words "help my sick mother" that worked the best. He was proud he'd thought of that detail.

And he'd learned how not to act like a runaway, also. Scared as he was, he tried not to show it. From time to time he remembered the saying, "The Lord helps those who help themselves." He walked right along the road like anybody else, as if he had nothing to hide. And when white folks passed, he stepped aside and took off his hat and bowed. He found that if he showed good manners, nobody was suspicious. A runaway slave was supposed to be angry and dangerous. Jonah was always smiling and cheerful, and took care to appear humble. If runaways were expected to be nervous and resentful, he would try to act the opposite. The wounds on his back had healed, and he tried to act as if they'd never been there. Jonah was pleased by his cleverness.

Every day he asked himself how a Negro would behave when traveling to Winchester, Virginia, at his master's behest. He wouldn't be expected to have much money. He would have good clothes but not fancy clothes. He decided that a boy like himself, if he was traveling legally, might stop at houses along the way and ask if he could work for his dinner. He could chop wood or slop the hogs. He could cut weeds and carry fodder from the corn fields. He had nothing to hide.

Through trial and error, he found the method that worked best. Along about dinnertime each day, he'd stop at the biggest house in sight and knock on the back door. When the cook or other black servant came to the door he would say, "Has you gots a little work I could do for some cornbread?" It was best not to sound educated. One cook who'd met him at the door when he talked proper had said, "What kind of high-talking nigga is you?" And slammed the door. After that, he'd always spoken as if he didn't know how to read.

Some cooks would say, "What you doing here in my yard, boy?" or "How come a lazy boy like you ain't out working in the field?"

But they'd usually end up handing him a piece of cornbread or a baked potato or two. Sometimes, but rarely, he'd get a biscuit with a piece of meat. They almost never asked him to do any work. In fact, they seemed happy to send him on his way as soon as possible. Maybe they suspected he was a runaway.

"Now go on, get out of my yard, before somebody see you," the cook might say, like she was the Queen of Sheba. But that was all right, for as far as he was concerned, she could be the Queen of Sheba.

It nearly always worked. It was the new overalls and manner of not being afraid that were effective. He acted humble, but not afraid. At suppertime they might give him a piece of cornbread and a cup of milk. And more than once he'd eaten watermelon with the field hands when they came back in the evening. They ate watermelon and sang hymns in the backyard until it was dark and the crickets and katydids had come out.

The rule seemed to be: don't ever act like what you really are. All is appearance and deception.

When Jonah reached the village of Big Lick, it was late August. The leaves on the trees were beginning to look old and dry, and the nights were not as hot anymore. The little town had a courthouse and several churches, a row of brick houses, and a tavern and hotel. Jonah had found it was better to knock at a more isolated house, for cooks were happier to feed him if they were not being observed by neighbors. He walked through the town and looked down the side streets, hoping to find just the right place, not too far out and not too close to the center of town, either.

There were many little houses on the streets and along some of the back alleys. High mountains swooped up on either side of the town. He saw more taverns with stables and stock pens behind them. He reckoned maybe lots of drovers and wagon traffic came through Big Lick. It was at the north end of town that he saw the big white house. It was not a mansion, but it had two stories, and dormer windows and a white picket fence in front. The house could be considered part of the town, but stood at the edge, in the country also. The main road ran to the left of it.

When he went behind the house to knock on the kitchen door, Jonah saw a long back porch on the second story. Three women sat in the sun there, their dresses pulled down off their shoulders so most of their bosoms were bare. Jonah looked away from them and rapped on the door. The cook who answered looked hard at him.

"Does you have a little work I could do for a pone?" he asked in his best humble voice.

"What you doing here, boy?" the cook said.

"Jus' a piece of cornbread and I be on my way," Jonah said.

"Humph," the cook said. She turned away and he saw he'd failed. It was time to move on. But then she turned back to him.

"You know how to peel taters, boy?" she said.

"Reckon I do."

"Wash your filthy hands at the well," the cook said.

When his hands were clean, the cook, who called herself Lonella, made him sit in the kitchen with a basket of washed potatoes and a pan for the peelings and another for the peeled potatoes. No one had ever put him to work in the kitchen before.

As he peeled and Lonella stirred steaming pots on the stove, she complained, seemingly to herself. "Can't get no help around here. Them trash won't help with nothing."

"I can help," Jonah said.

"What you say, boy?" Lonella said, as if he'd spoken out of turn.

"You put them taters in the pan and don't cut away all the flavor." He continued peeling and kept his mouth shut.

Slow down there, Jonah, he said to himself. Just hold your tongue.

"Now don't slice away all the meat in them spuds," Lonella said. "You know the good taste is right under the skin."

It had been a long time since Jonah had peeled potatoes. He scraped some of the thinnest skin off the small potatoes and sliced away the skin on bigger ones. The knack came back to him as he worked.

"And don't take all day," Lonella said.

The potatoes were wet, and his fingertips began to wrinkle from the water and starch.

"Now who is this?" a voice said from the doorway to the dining room. It was a white woman with red hair, wearing a fancy dressing gown with embroidery and ruffles on it. She had a ribbon in her hair.

"He just a boy be helping me," Lonella said.

"We can use some help around here," the woman said.

"Yes, ma'am," Jonah said and bowed his head. It was the first time he'd been caught in the kitchen by the owner of a house. The woman said her name was Miss Linda, and she asked him what kind of work he could do.

"Mos' any kind, ma'am," he answered.

The woman smiled at him, and he had a feeling she knew he was a runaway, or at least someone who was not where he was supposed to be. The woman's gown fell open a little and he could see she had some kind of lace underneath. "Lonella needs a little help, and so does Hettie, the maid," Miss Linda said.

Jonah wanted to say he was on his way to Winchester, Virginia. He wanted to show Miss Linda his note, but with his hands wet he didn't dare, for she seemed to look right into his head. She could call the sheriff and say he was a runaway and he'd be put in chains.

"Yes, ma'am, I be glad to help," Jonah said.

When he finished peeling potatoes, Lonella showed him a room in the basement where he could sleep. There was a cot and nightstand and the place smelled a little damp. But it was far better than the barns and haystacks and thickets he'd been sleeping in. Then Lonella put him to work splitting wood at the woodpile in the backyard. The girls on the second-story porch talked and laughed and called out to him, telling him not to get too hot.

"We don't need much wood this time of year," one said.

When he carried the wood into the kitchen to the wood box, Lonella told him to wash up at the well and then go see Miss Linda in the parlor. Jonah scrubbed his neck and face and hands and felt his heart thumping as he walked through the kitchen into the hallway. The house was finer inside than he'd guessed. A polished wooden staircase glided up to the second story. Pink flowery wallpaper, with white curtains and glass doors, made it look even fancier than the Williams house. Paintings of beautiful women wearing few clothes hung on the walls.

Jonah found Miss Linda not in the parlor but in the sitting room off to the side. The couch had colorful stuffed pillows. Miss Linda sat at a kind of writing desk. A chair nearby had a cushion with a fish embroidered on it. "If it's less than six inches put it back" was written below the fish.

He bowed to Miss Linda and she didn't ask him to sit down.

"People who work for me don't see nothing and they don't say nothing," Miss Linda said. "Do you understand what I mean?"

"Yes, ma'am."

"We're like a family here, and we're a happy family."

"Yes, ma'am."

"This is just a whorehouse," Miss Linda said and laughed. "But we make people happy here, and we make ourselves happy."

"Yes, ma'am."

"Do what I say and you won't have any trouble," Miss Linda said.

She added that she would give him three dollars a week as well as his room and board. He would help out wherever he was needed.

"Sheriff won't bother you long as you work for me," Miss Linda said. She was still pretty, but Jonah could see the wrinkles just under her face powder and rouge.

Jonah had never been in a whorehouse before, but he'd heard of them. There was a place in Greenville that had both white girls and black girls. He'd heard Mr. Williams talk about it with his friend Sampson Hodge. It appeared that Miss Linda had figured out he was a runaway. It was like she'd looked right into his thoughts. That was a power she had over him. If she got mad at him, she could turn him over to the sheriff any time she pleased. He took the note out of the bib pocket of his overalls and showed it to her, and she began laughing and then tossed the note away.

"I like you," Miss Linda said. "What shall I call you?"

Jonah told her his name was Ezra, Ezra Page.

"Well, Ezra, I think we're going to get along just fine." She told him that if he was nice to the girls, they would be nice to him.

"I have a friend named Mr. Wells," Miss Linda said. "If somebody gets out of line he whips them. You understand?"

"Yes, ma'am."

"I will get you some shoes," Miss Linda said. "Nobody goes barefoot at Miss Linda's."

"No, ma'am; I mean yes, ma'am."

There were five girls at Miss Linda's, besides Miss Linda herself, and each had a room upstairs where they lived and took their guests. The youngest of the girls was named Prissy, and she had black hair and honey-colored skin, like she might be Indian, or part Indian. She was a little fatter than the other girls, and from the beginning she was friendly with Jonah.

The maid called Hettie cleaned the rooms, and Jonah had to help her carry things up and down the stairs. When she gathered all the sheets off the beds and heaped them in a basket, Jonah carried the hamper downstairs to the back porch where they would be washed. There was nothing unusual about the bedrooms upstairs. They had fine curtains and furniture, and covers above the beds. Each had a picture of a naked woman, or a nearly naked woman, and that was all. Except for that, you would not have thought it was a whorehouse. The girls slept until noon most days, so most of the cleaning and washing was done in early afternoon.

Jonah's duties, as Miss Linda said, were to do whatever needed to be done. He lit fires in the morning and chopped and carried wood. He peeled potatoes for Lonella and hauled water from the well. He ran to the stores in town when Miss Linda needed cloth or lamp oil. He polished the stove in the parlor and the brass doorknobs on the porches.

Mr. Wells was a tall man with scars on his face and a black mustache. He owned a tavern in town and appeared to be a business partner to Miss Linda. Sometimes he stayed in the kitchen in the evening when the guests were in the parlor or upstairs. He was always friendly, and he sometimes gave Jonah a quarter to shine his boots and brush his coat and hat. "Attaboy!" he liked to say to Jonah. Every time Jonah polished the boots, he saw the knife stuck in a slot inside the left boot.

Miss Linda had said Mr. Wells would whip anybody that got out of line, but Jonah only saw him smile and say teasing things to the girls, at least until the second week he was there. Miss Linda had told Jonah to stay in his room in the evenings unless she called for him. Lonella's room and Hettie's room were in the basement beside his, and they were supposed to stay down there while the guests laughed and talked in the parlor above. The noise didn't bother Jonah; he was usually tired and went to sleep early. It was near the end of the second week of his stay when he heard a scream in the middle of the night. He heard low voices upstairs and then steps outside his door, followed by a knock. "Ezra," Miss Linda called. "Put on your clothes, I need you." Jonah wondered if he should try to run away right then. Had someone found him out and sent for the sheriff? When he put on his shirt and overalls and shoes, he found Miss Linda waiting outside his door, holding a lamp.

"Come with me," Miss Linda said. He followed her up the steps to the kitchen and then up the big stairs to the second story. The door to each of the rooms was open and a girl stood just inside each door. The door to Prissy's room was closed and someone sobbed inside.

Miss Linda opened Prissy's door and Jonah saw Mr. Wells inside holding Prissy down on the bed. Her dress had been pulled off her shoulders and she was naked to the waist. "Are you ready?" Miss Linda said, and Mr. Wells nodded.

"Go out to the icehouse and break off a cake of ice the size of a brick," Miss Linda said to Jonah as she handed him the lamp.

The icehouse was in the backyard near the well. It was mostly underground, where blocks of ice were packed in sawdust. A ladder went down into the cold pit. Jonah set the lamp on a bench and broke a cake of ice off a large block with a hammer. Wrapping the ice in a sack, he climbed out of the pit and took the ice upstairs to Miss Linda. With every step he wondered if he shouldn't just run away while he had a chance. And he wondered if Prissy might be sick and the ice was to be used to bring down her fever.

Miss Linda took the ice from him and thanked him and told him to stand outside the door.

"Don't let anybody in," she said.

A shiver ran through Jonah's guts as Miss Linda slipped back into Prissy's room and closed the door. The other girls looked out their doorways at him.

"No, no, no," Prissy begged inside, sobbing.

“I told you what I’d do if you ever stole from a customer,” Miss Linda said.

“Won’t never do it again,” Prissy said.

“Damn right, you’ll never do it again,” Miss Linda said.

There was more talk inside, but Jonah couldn’t make out what was said. His knees shook so he could hardly stand. The other girls were all staring at him. Jonah looked away, at the darkness at the end of the hall.

“Nobody steals in this house,” Miss Linda said.

“Please,” Prissy said, and tried to repeat the word, but gasped and stammered instead.

Jonah didn’t hear the sound of a slap or a blow. He waited for some indication of a whipping. All he heard was the sound of Prissy begging and sobbing, and water being poured. He shifted from one foot to the other and looked at the girls and then looked away.

And then Prissy began to scream. It was a scream that began as a “No!” and rose to a shriek. It was the sound of a hundred sheets tearing at once and a thousand fingernails on glass. It was a scream of a woman giving birth, and the scream of madness. Prissy’s scream seemed to rise out of the foundation and walls of the house, and soar through the ceiling and roof to the center of the sky and beyond. The scream tore at his ears and cut through his breath.

It was time for the scream to stop, but it went on and on. Whatever they were doing to Prissy didn’t make her faint, but made her hurt in a way she couldn’t escape, even by passing out. The scream made Jonah sick and weak. The other girls had turned away, and some were crying. Jonah thought again of running away. He should escape into the night while he could. He should get far away from Miss Linda’s by morning. He was still thinking about what direction he could take when suddenly the screaming stopped. There were hurried steps inside the room, then the door to Prissy’s room opened and Miss Linda held out to him a pan of water. “Go empty this and wash it,” she said, then closed the door again.

Jonah carried the pan down the hall as the other girls closed their doors one by one. The water in the pan was dark, dark as blood. They must have cut Prissy somehow. But then he smelled the water; it unmistakably smelled of shit. They had hurt Prissy so bad she had fouled herself. They had put the ice inside her in some tender place that hurt and kept on hurting, but wouldn't show on the outside.

They hadn't whipped Prissy, for that would scar her skin, and bruises would make her less valuable. They'd done something inside her with the ice where no one would ever see it. But she and the other girls and he would never forget it. Prissy's scream was a warning to them all. It seemed to Jonah that people were always thinking of ways to be cruel. Miss Linda had treated him well because she could use him. She'd guessed his secret and he had to do what she said. But if he didn't do what she ordered, she'd punish him, hurt him as she had Prissy, and turn him over to the sheriff as a runaway.

Jonah didn't go back upstairs that night. He dumped the pan of water in the toilet in the backyard and washed the pan at the well. Then he set the pan on the shelf on the back porch and returned to his little room. Lonella opened her door when he reached the basement. "Miss Prissy, she alright?" Lonella said.

"She ain't alright," Jonah said and went into his room and closed the door.

Jonah didn't sleep the rest of the night. He sat on his cot and thought about what he was going to do. He thought about how scared he was, scared of Mr. Wells and Miss Linda, of the sheriff with his guns and dogs. He was afraid of white people, and he was afraid of time, for summer was almost over and he was still far from the North. Soon as he got a chance, he had to escape from Miss Linda's. Soon as he saved a little money and maybe found a map. He'd have to wait for the right time, and hope he recognized the chance when it came.

Jonah didn't see Prissy downstairs for several days after that evening. The business at Miss Linda's went on as usual. Men came every evening, men with fine horses and fine buggies, important men with fancy clothes. They came after dark and they left before daylight. Lonella told him that once the governor of Virginia had stopped at Miss Linda's, and a senator always came when he was in the area. That was why Jonah was not supposed to see anything or hear anything or know anything. Most of the time he was supposed to stay downstairs, for too many servants made the guests nervous. They wanted to relax and enjoy themselves without worrying about witnesses. Prissy didn't come downstairs for four days.

Jonah had to carry meals up to her, and empty her chamber pot. The first day Prissy wouldn't speak when he handed the tray to her. Her eyes and cheeks looked swollen, as if she had a bad cold. He took the chamber pot and started out the door.

"Don't you love to carry shit?" Prissy said.

"No, ma'am," Jonah said and closed the door. Lonella had told him that the less he said to the girls, the better it would be. "Don't you say nothing, see nothing, or know nothing," the cook had repeated.

The next day when Jonah brought the tray to Prissy, she sat up in her bed and said she was sorry for what she'd said the day before. "I reckon you got no choice either," she added.

"No, ma'am."

"You don't have to ma'am me," Prissy said. "I'm just a whore, a whipped whore." She laughed, like she didn't think it was funny.

The third day when he came to Prissy's room she asked him to never tell anybody what Mr. Wells and Miss Linda had done to her. "I don't want nobody to ever know what they did that night," she said.

Jonah said he would never tell, but he wasn't sure exactly what they *had* done to Prissy.

"Bless you," Prissy said, and then kept talking. She told him she was born in the mountains of Tennessee. Her mama was a Cherokee and her daddy a soldier. When she ran away from there, Miss Linda had taken her in and given her a home, just like she'd given Jonah a home.

"You'd better keep running while you can," Prissy said, and then went quiet again.

Prissy took laudanum and Miss Linda gave her laudanum every afternoon before the guests arrived. But Prissy gave Jonah a dollar to go to the store in town and buy an extra bottle of laudanum. "Just so I'll have my own supply," she said.

The fourth day Jonah went up to Prissy's room with the tray, Prissy said she liked Jonah and would let him be with her, but Miss Linda wouldn't allow it. Miss Linda knew everything that went on in the house and if she was intimate with Jonah they would both be punished.

"Otherwise you could take your ease," Prissy said, and grinned. It was the first time he'd seen her smile that week. The color was coming back into her cheeks.

"You don't have to stay here," Jonah said in a low voice.

"Where else would I go?" Prissy said and laughed.

The fifth day Jonah didn't take a tray up to Prissy's room. She came down to the dining room for dinner and laughed and talked like she had before. Everybody acted as if nothing had happened, and when Mr. Wells came by he teased Prissy and told her she looked pretty as a princess, a Cherokee princess.

By the time Jonah had been at Miss Linda's for three weeks, he understood that Miss Linda and Mr. Wells had hired him, not in spite of the fact that he was a runaway, but *because* they guessed he was a runaway. That knowledge gave them power over him. Like the girls, he had no choice but to do what they told him to do. And the odd truth was they treated him well, at least as long as he did what he was told. He carried water and wood and lit fires, helped Hettie carry laundry, peeled potatoes for Lonella, and ran to the store in town when anybody wanted something.

Lonella's cooking was good, and Miss Linda had bought Jonah shoes and another pair of overalls, so he now had a change of clothes. Prissy even promised he could be with her, if she ever found a way so Miss Linda and the other girls wouldn't know. Prissy had gotten over her sulk and acted like nothing had ever happened that night when they hurt her.

It was easy being at Miss Linda's, but Jonah knew he was still a slave, and that he was living on borrowed time.

ONE DAY PRISSY WHISPERED to him when he carried out the chamber pot that she'd thought of a way they could be together. Miss Linda insisted that all her girls go to church on Sunday morning. They dressed up in their best and each carried a little Bible as they marched down the street to the Presbyterian church.

"This Sunday I'll say I have a headache and stay here," Prissy said, grinning. Jonah had never been with any woman except Angel that night in the mountains, and sometimes he wondered if he'd only dreamed about that jubilee in the woods. But he knew it was a fact that Angel had traveled with him down the French Broad. He thought about how soft and smooth Prissy's breasts were, and how attentive and kind she'd been to him. All week he thought about the prospect of being with Prissy on Sunday morning. It was lucky Miss Linda didn't make the Negroes go to church. He told himself it was foolish and dangerous to think of being with Prissy. But each day and each night he would study on it. It scared him and thrilled him that Prissy, who'd been with so many different men, wanted to be with him.

On Sunday morning Jonah carried water and wood as usual. And he cleaned ashes out of the stoves and fireplaces. Lonella and Hettie would go to their own church on the other side of the town. While they were gone Jonah was supposed to polish the kitchen stove with black paste and shine the nickel fittings and handles. It was a job he hated, because he had to use the black paste and some of it always got smeared on his clothes.

Miss Linda and the girls dressed up in their best, with bonnets and umbrellas, but Prissy said she had the headache and couldn't go to service.

"I don't want no heathens in my house," Miss Linda said.

"I wish I wasn't poorly," Prissy said.

"You rest up, girl," Miss Linda said, "for tonight is going to be a busy night."

As soon as they were gone, and Lonella and Hettie left, wearing their own bonnets and carrying pink parasols, Jonah hurried to finish polishing the stove. He took another rag and rubbed the fittings until they shone like mirrors. He was so nervous he rubbed extra hard. He saw some of the black polish had fallen on the floor, and he rubbed and washed away the stain.

The house was empty except for him and Prissy. Jonah scrubbed his hands on the back porch and climbed up to Prissy's room. She laughed when he opened the door. She was lying in bed with her nightcap on, but soon as he closed the door she threw back the sheet to show she was wearing nothing else.

"Come here," she said, and reached for him.

When Jonah was naked, he stretched out over her and she fitted him inside and wrapped her legs around his back.

A few moments later he sensed a shift in the room.

"Well, look at that," somebody said from behind him.

Prissy pushed away from him, and when he opened his eyes he saw the fear on her face. He looked behind him and saw Miss Linda and Mr. Wells standing in the doorway.

"Good thing I came back for my tithe money," Miss Linda said.

Jonah rolled away from Prissy and reached for his overalls on the floor.

"I leave you two for a minute and look what you do," Miss Linda said.

"Put on your clothes and come with me," Mr. Wells said. Jonah obeyed. He couldn't look at Prissy or Miss Linda. His hands shook as he slid on his overalls and tied his shoes.

"Didn't mean to do nothing bad," Jonah said.

"Come with me," Mr. Wells said. Mr. Wells didn't seem at all angry or upset. He was calm as if he was asking Jonah to bring him a newspaper or carry in more wood. He told Jonah to walk in front of him down the stairs and around the kitchen to the back porch.

"I don't want to send you back to your master," Mr. Wells said.

"No, sir," Jonah said. "Thank you, sir."

"I don't want to hurt you either," Mr. Wells said.

"Yes, sir," Jonah said.

Mr. Wells was so calm, Jonah began to hope he wasn't going to do anything bad to him. When Mr. Williams whipped him, Mr. Williams had been furious, with his face red and his eyes glaring. Mr. Wells didn't seem at all mad. "Go into the barn," Mr. Wells said.

Just as Jonah stepped into the gloom of the barn beyond the well, he heard a scream from the second story of the house. It was Prissy screaming. Jonah stopped in his tracks, but Mr. Wells ordered him to keep moving.

As soon as Mr. Wells closed the barn door behind them, he told Jonah to turn around. Quick as a flash Mr. Wells grabbed Jonah by the balls and squeezed. Pain roared through him like a hundred fires.

It was the worst pain he'd ever felt. He screamed without knowing he was screaming. Mr. Wells squeezed him tighter and Jonah trembled and peed on himself.

When Mr. Wells let go, Jonah was so weak with pain he fell to his knees on the floor.

"Won't never do it again," Jonah gasped.

"I can send you back to South Carolina, or I can teach you a lesson," Mr. Wells said.

"Please, please, please," Jonah said, not sure what he was asking.

Mr. Well dragged him to a platform where hay had once been piled, and tied Jonah's hands to the slats of a stall. He bound Jonah's feet together and tied the rope to a post on the opposite wall. Then he left Jonah lying there on the boards, bound hand and foot.

Jonah listened as someone drew water from the well, and then he smelled smoke. Through a crack in the barn wall he saw a fire had been started under the washpot. Was Mr. Wells heating water? Was he going to scald him? Was he going to pour boiling water on him? The pain in Jonah's crotch didn't go away. He wondered if Mr. Wells was going to do something to him there. White men were said to castrate Negroes. The barn door opened and Mr. Wells brought in two buckets of water and set them near Jonah. They appeared to be cold, for he saw no steam rising from the buckets. Was Mr. Wells planning to drown him?

Mr. Wells brought in two more buckets of cold water. He appeared to be gathering every bucket on the place. He brought in a dishpan and a small canner, all filled with water. He set the vessels in a row, not six feet from Jonah. Last Mr. Wells brought in two wooden buckets of steaming hot water. And then he came back with a small tub of hot water, and a watering can that breathed a fog. After closing the barn door he unbuttoned Jonah's overalls and pulled them down to his feet, and he unbuttoned Jonah's shirt and pulled it away.

"You must learn your lesson, Ezra," Mr. Wells said, as if he was commenting on the weather.

Mr. Wells poured water from a wooden bucket all over him. The water was not hot enough to burn him, but it made his skin glow. Mr. Wells poured it slowly and gently. Jonah winced and his skin stung a little, as if inflamed. Mr. Wells poured the water over him carefully once, and then again. If he expected to burn Jonah he failed. But the skin on Jonah's chest was hot. I can take this, Jonah said to himself. Mr. Wells poured hot water over him again, and the heat made Jonah almost sleepy. He was sweating and the pain in his groin made him sweat more. Then Mr. Wells picked up another bucket and dashed it on Jonah's chest and belly. The pain was so awful it took Jonah a second to realize the hurt came from cold water. A sick blue lightning shock of pain flashed through his bones, and he released a scream of pain that shrieked from far behind his head. It was worse than the pain from his squeezed balls. It was like some pain from both the beginning of time and the end of the world. The cold water sank through him and he couldn't jerk away. The cold water was a madness and blindness that attacked his spine and his brain and made his bones want to crack.

"Please!" he screamed. "Please don't do it again."

When Jonah stopped screaming, Mr. Wells began pouring hot water on him again. He poured slowly to make the skin glow again. The warmth felt good. The heat opened all Jonah's pores. Mr. Wells paused and lit a cigar and then puffed it while he poured more hot water on Jonah's chest and belly. The hot water stung but felt comforting compared to the blaze of the cold water. Jonah wondered if Mr. Wells had put ice in the cold water buckets.

When his skin was glowing again, Mr. Wells lifted another bucket of cold water and dashed it on Jonah's chest and belly. This time Jonah screamed in anticipation, and when the water licked him with its white cold flames, the scream continued, reaching up through the top of the barn to the sky and beyond to the North Star. His scream was so loud he could no longer hear it, and his eyes stung with the effort of the scream.

When Jonah stopped screaming, Mr. Wells said, “Are you going to listen to Miss Linda?”

“Yes, sir,” Jonah gasped.

“I don’t want to send you back to South Carolina,” Mr. Wells said.

“No, sir.”

Mr. Wells picked up a bucket of hot water to begin pouring it again on his stomach and chest, but Jonah knew he couldn’t stand any more. He begged Mr. Wells to stop. “I do anything,” Jonah sobbed. He’d die if Mr. Wells dumped cold water on his chest again.

“Have you learnt your lesson?” Mr. Wells said.

“Yes, sir, I have,” Jonah cried.

“Have you learned it real good?”

“Yes, sir, I learned it real good.”

Mr. Wells held the bucket of hot water as if trying to decide what to do. Jonah prayed he wouldn’t splash him anymore.

“You don’t have a bruise or a cut on you,” Mr. Wells said.

“No, sir.”

“Nobody can say that I hurt you or tortured you,” Mr. Wells said. “Your skin is not burned or cut in any way.”

“No, sir.”

Mr. Wells carried all the buckets out of the barn except one. “Clean yourself,” he said as he untied Jonah’s hands and feet, then tossed him a feedsack to use as a washcloth.

TEN

ANGEL

After the Goat Man and I ate the peppery mush and tomatoes and roastnears, I brought him another bucket from the river, and he washed the tin pans and the pots and the lids we had eaten on.

"Let me stay the night," I said. I didn't want to go back in that boat and I was scared to start walking in the dark. He smiled and said something in his strange talk.

"I just want to sleep here tonight," I said and leaned my head against my hands like I was going to sleep. He shook his head and jabbered and ran to the wagon and pointed inside. When I looked under the canvas, I saw a little place between boxes with a blanket on the floor and a rolled-up canvas for a pillow.

"No, no," I said and shook my head and pointed under the wagon.

"There's where I'll sleep," I said. He nodded his head quickly and turned away.

As it got darker I sat by the fire while the Goat Man took pieces of bread to the goats. He petted each goat and talked to it like you would speak to a child at bedtime. You'd think the goats were his little children, or his wives. I couldn't tell which, because I couldn't understand what he was saying.

Then I heard horses galloping in the distance and getting closer. And with a jolt I thought maybe they were looking for me. What if they had caught or killed Jonah and were now coming for me? I thought of running off into the woods, but that wouldn't do any good, because the Goat Man could point in the direction I'd gone.

It was still in the July night because the spring peepers were gone and the crickets and katydids hadn't started yet. Master Thomas used to say it was so still in a July night, you could hear the cornstalks groan as they stretched. The river whispered and slurped far below and the hoofbeats grew louder, but the Goat Man didn't seem to pay them any mind. It came to me that he acted the way he did because he couldn't hear anything. If he looked at your face he could tell what you said. And he talked so funny because he couldn't hear what he said, even if it was regular words. He was completely deaf.

I hadn't seen the road and didn't know exactly where it was, except I knew it probably ran close to the river, down the river valley. As the horses got nearer I scrunched down by the fire little as I could make myself. The Goat Man started to sing to the goats, just as three horsemen came out of the dark and stopped. They had rifles across their saddles.

"We're looking for a runaway nigger," one yelled at the Goat Man. The Goat Man took off his hat and bowed to them.

"He robbed a store up the river," another rider shouted. The Goat Man spread his arms to say he didn't know anything.

"Is that your girl?" the third rider said and pointed at me.

The Goat Man smiled and pointed at me and jabbered in his strange tongue.

"He don't know nothing," the first man said and started to turn his horse.

"Goat Man got him a gal," the second rider said and laughed. As they rode off into the dark, I loved the Goat Man for helping me and protecting me. He acted like I was his slave and the riders weren't even suspicious. He was a strange old man who couldn't hear anything, but I was so grateful he could do whatever he wanted with me. When he threw a blanket on the ground for me to lie on, I expected he would get on it with me. I had no choice but to let him take his reward for helping me and feeding me.

But instead the Goat Man climbed into the wagon, and I lay down on the blanket underneath and watched the fire die. I thought he might be taking off his clothes and would climb out and lie with me, but he didn't. Next thing I heard was the Goat Man snoring in the wagon. I lay there a long time listening for horses, listening to the river murmur and goats munching weeds. Dew fell out of the air and stuck to my cheeks, and I wrapped the blanket around me tighter. I wondered if the Goat Man was too old to have any use for me. Or was he the kind of man that didn't care about women? Or did he belong to some kind of religion that taught him to stay away from women? The only thing he seemed to love was the goats.

Next morning I woke before the old man, and I roused myself to go look for sticks to start a fire. I figured if I made myself handy, the Goat Man might let me stay with him and travel with him. I knew he went back and forth, north and south. Traveling with the Goat Man might be a way to get to the North, even without Jonah.

When I came back with an armful of sticks, the old man got up and stood facing the sun and read from a little black book. It looked like a Testament, but I don't think it was. The markings were different from any print I'd ever seen. I couldn't read back then anyhow, but I could tell those letters were different. He was mumbling his prayers or saying the words in the book.

I started a fire and climbed down the bank for a bucket of water. The Goat Man put away his little book and took a coffee grinder from the wagon and ground up some coffee beans. When the coffee started boiling, it filled the clearing with its smell. He got some grits and poured them into a pot of steaming water. Then he got some cornmeal and spread it on a plank for the goats.

As I sipped the black coffee and ate hot grits I saw what I had to do. "Goat Man," I said, "let me travel with you for a while."

He smiled and didn't say anything.

"I can help you look after things," I said. "I can wash dishes and steal eggs out of henhouses and taters out of cellars."

The Goat Man looked like he was thinking. He seemed to be confused, like he couldn't think what he wanted to say.

"I can carry water from wells and springs," I said. The old man looked around like he didn't want to answer me, and he didn't know what he wanted to say. He looked back at the goats browsing on the weeds and brush.

"I can help with the goats," I said. "I can harness them up and feed them and bring them water."

The Goat Man smiled and nodded.

"I can tend to the goats while you sharpen knives and scissors and fix pots and buckets," I said. The Goat Man smiled because he saw I liked his goats. He nodded, which meant I could go with him. Before the sun got above the trees I washed the pots and cups, and then we started out on the road that ran along the bluff over the river.

It was a different thing to travel with the Goat Man. He gave me a colorful scarf to tie around my head, the kind of cloth that must have come from overseas, with purple and gold and green, all shiny and soft. I wore the scarf tied around my chin and hoped nobody would recognize me. I hoped they'd think I was a gypsy or Melungeon, or maybe an Indian. My skin was light enough so I could look like an Indian. Mama would never tell me who my daddy was, but I knew he must be a white man. Eli had whispered to me one time my daddy was Mr. Thomas's nephew that stayed at the Thomas Place one time, but he wouldn't tell me any more.

The first house we stopped at was off in the hills, away from the river. The woman there must have seen the Goat Man coming, or heard the bells on the goats, for by the time we stopped in her yard she had brought knives and scissors out to the porch, and a dishpan with a hole in it and a bucket with the handle torn off. The Goat Man got out his files and hammer, the stone wheel he used to whet blades, and he lit his solder torch. I helped bring the tools from the wagon, but once he started to work on the porch, I wandered around the place. At the side of the yard was a well with a roof over it, and a washpot where the woman washed clothes. There was a woodpile and a woodshed, and a chicken house by the pine woods.

I stepped into the pine woods to relieve myself, and smelled the musty smell pine needles have in summer. And when I came out of the woods I glanced through the window of the henhouse and saw nests along the wall with big brown eggs in them, the kind of eggs laid by red hens. One nest was so close I reached through the window and took two eggs and put them in my pocket. The eggs were still warm.

The lady of the house, when I got back to the front porch, told me to take a bucket and pick some fresh beans in the garden. But just then she saw one of the goats had got into her sunflowers, and I had to run and drive the goat out of the yard. The Goat Man shouted, and though I couldn't tell what he said, I knew he meant for me to stay by the wagon and keep the goats out of the lady's garden.

While I tended to the goats, the lady herself took a bucket to the garden to pick the beans. And when the Goat Man finished sharpening the knives and scissors and soldering the dishpan and fixing the handle of the bucket, she gave him a quarter and the bucket of beans. The Goat Man smiled and bowed to her and put his tools back in the wagon. The woman was happy with his work, and he was happy with the quarter and green beans. And I thought: this is the way the world works, or is supposed to work, away from the Thomas Place. We help each other and live by helping each other. We live by trading, work for money and fresh beans. It seemed so simple. But it *is* the way things work, when they work, trading one thing for another. I felt the eggs in my pocket, but I wasn't ashamed I'd taken them. I'd kept the goats away from the flowerbeds and sunflowers. Two big brown eggs were my pay.

But as we walked along the road and my feet got sore from stepping on rocks and around puddles, I thought how nice it would be to have a place of my own where I could grow flowers, any kind of flowers, and a garden where I could grow potatoes and beans and peas, and tomatoes and sweet corn and squash. When I was on the Thomas Place, I hated to work outside in the garden and fields and wanted to stay in the big house where it was cool and clean. But walking along the road mile after mile with the goats and the Goat Man, I wanted to get far as I could from the Thomas Place, but I wanted more than anything a piece of land that would be my own. At the end of my travel I wanted to stop and grow things to eat and make pretty things to wear. I craved a place where nobody could tell me what to do.

And then I thought: no colored girl is going to have such a place, not in a long life, even if she got to freedom. And then I thought: even if you get to freedom, you've got to have a man. There's no way to have a place without a man. So I had three problems, to get to the North without being caught, get my freedom, and get me a man to help me. Angel, you are far from all three, I said to myself. But it did me good to think on that, and remember the white woman's flowers and her hens in the chicken house by the pine woods laying those big brown eggs every day.

But the Goat Man was not pleased that I took those eggs. When we stopped for the night and I showed him the eggs, he shook his head and said something angry; I didn't understand him at all, because we didn't have anything for supper but mush and green beans, and milk from the goats.

"We can boil the eggs," I said to him.

But he shook his head and waved his arms. When he went to milk the she-goats, I put on water to boil the eggs and cook mush in one pot and green beans in another. And when we started to eat the mush and beans, he still wouldn't touch an egg. He seemed afraid of the egg, so I ate them both, and it was a mighty good supper with coffee white with goat milk.

The Goat Man didn't look at me while he ate and it came to me why he was so mad about the eggs. I saw he traveled all the time up and down the country, north and south, and he didn't steal anything from people because he wanted to be welcomed everywhere. If he stole, they would be afraid of him and drive him away. As it was, he took their quarters and green beans and sweet potatoes. Traveling with the goats, he depended on their friendship and trust as he traded work for their tomatoes and squash. If they didn't trust the Goat Man, they would drive him away and boys would beat him up and steal his wagon and his goats. So he didn't steal anything. That was how he'd lived so long, traveling up and down all over the place. Watching the Goat Man, I kept learning something about how to live. But even so, I knew I was colored and running away, and I was a woman.

"I won't steal any more eggs," I hollered to Goat Man and shook my head. The eggs were so good I doubted I could keep my word if the chance to get more came my way. But I promised it anyway. I had to travel with the Goat Man, and I didn't have any other way to go, and I had to keep on moving.

"I won't steal anymore," I yelled again, and the Goat Man smiled and nodded and said some more of his strange talk. I was glad to have that settled.

After I got more water from the creek and washed up the pots and pans, the Goat Man took a wooden pipe with holes in it from the wagon. It was a kind of whistle, and when he blew it and lifted his fingers from the holes, it made a kind of tune. Some of the notes were sour, but the beat was strong, and he moved his body to the beat. I wondered how he could play at all if he couldn't hear. How could he make music if he was deaf? And then I thought he must be able to hear the music a little bit. Maybe he could feel it in his hands.

I got up and started dancing to the music of the pipe, two steps this way, two steps that way, swung my hips around and clapped. He nodded and played harder, trying to match the playing to my steps. By watching me, he could see the music he was making.

"You old rascal," I said and lifted my skirt a little as I danced. If I was going to wear a gypsy scarf, I might as well dance like a gypsy. I clapped and danced around the fire as it got dark. He knew lots of tunes and he kept playing them. Watching me seemed to please him.

If the Goat Man had guessed I was a runaway, he didn't seem to care. I reckon he lived in a world of his own, on the road with the goats, and didn't take much interest in what happened on plantations and in the towns. Sometimes I thought he must be an Indian from the way he traveled in all weather and lived in his wagon. Except that little book he read out of every morning didn't seem like an Indian thing. It had funny-looking writing, and he made humming sounds when he read from it.

I could tell which way was the north because when the sun came up I looked to my left. That was the way that low-down Jonah said to go. And when the Goat Man left the river, that's the way we tended. I was glad we were working our way in that direction. Jonah might be dead for all I knew, but I was headed in the right way. I didn't know the names of all those places the way Jonah did, but maybe I could get there just the same. Nothing ever works out the way you plan it anyway.

The strangest thing happened after we'd been traveling about a week and got up into Virginia. We shuffled along the road, me leading the goats on a string and the Goat Man whistling and sun crashing down hot as a cookstove. It was so hot, I felt the heat coming up from the ground and the dust on weeds along the road glaring. The Goat Man was looking for a house where he could sharpen knives or a saw and make a little money, and maybe get some new potatoes. In that wild country we hadn't eaten too well in the last few days.

We came creaking over a hill and saw these cherry trees loaded down with black cherries and a woman on a short ladder picking cherries. Now the Goat Man and I thought the same thing: we had to get us some sweet cherries to eat on the way. We needed a change and cherries were just the thing. So we stopped on the road and I hollered to the woman to ask if she wanted any pots and pans mended, or knives and scissors sharpened. She didn't hear me at first and I yelled again. Only then did I see the baby lying on a blanket on the grass at the edge of the orchard. The baby was waving its legs and arms around and crying.

"I have scissors that need sharpening," the woman on the ladder called. "Can you wait till I get to the house?"

"How long will you be?" I hollered.

Now for some reason when I called I looked up and saw this big bird out the corner of my eye. I thought at first it must be a hawk, but then as it came closer I saw it was a golden eagle. You don't expect to see a bird that spreads its wings so wide. And then it dove just like a hawk dropping on a chicken. And I screamed because it was going like a lightning bolt straight for the baby.

"No, can't be!" I hollered and started running toward the baby. I heard the whoosh of the wings, but I was too slow. That awful bird that looked like it was on fire swooped and grabbed the pretty baby in its claws. Its wings were longer than I was tall and I could feel the wind off its wings as they beat to lift back up.

But that baby must have been heavier than the devil bird expected, for it beat harder and blasted up dust from the weeds, and slowly lifted away. It looked like I wasn't going to reach the baby in time. But the awful bird was slower than he meant to be, flogging and flapping his wings to carry off his prize.

"No!" I yelled and grabbed the baby around its belly. "No, you bastard!" I screamed.

The wings beat in my face and the eagle pulled away. But he couldn't lift the baby out of my grasp. Even the hell bird wasn't that strong. He yanked and beat my face and pecked the top of my head like a cold chisel, and I still didn't let go. I thought he was going to peck out my eyes, and I turned my face away, but didn't let go of the darling child.

Now the eagle had to make up his mind. He couldn't carry the baby off as long as I held her, and he wouldn't let go with his claws. His eyes glared at me like squirts of fire. He was as mad as a demon from hell. I jerked my head sideways and he pecked my ear. His claws were dug into the baby's flesh, and I couldn't grab his foot because I was holding on to the baby's belly.

I looked around to see if anybody could help me, but the Goat Man just stood by the wagon like he was frozen, and the woman had fallen off the ladder and was picking herself up in the weeds. For a second I thought of trying to grab the eagle by the neck, but if I let go of the baby he would fly away. He beat his wings more and dust boiled up so

I could hardly see and the baby screamed. That devil was trying to see how determined I was, and when he saw I didn't aim to let go, he gave it up and took his claws out of the baby. But before he flew away he slashed his claws on the side of my head, and I could feel the wet blood.

That terrible bird flapped away and I held the baby that wasn't hurt except for some claw marks. The woman ran up and grabbed the baby out of my hands and she pressed it to her bosom. She laughed and cried at the same time, and then prayed, and started to cry again.

"Your baby's not hurt," I said, blood running down on my forehead. I rubbed the blood out of my eyes and felt the scratch on my head. My hair was all bloody.

The Goat Man came to me and made me bend over so he could see the cuts on my head. Then he stepped into the weeds and got some cobwebs of a writing spider and put the sticky strands on my head to stop the blood.

Still crying, the woman carried her baby to the house and we followed. I stopped at the well to wash my face and hands. The woman stood on the porch a long time holding the baby and when she calmed down, she went inside and came back out with two pairs of scissors. And she handed me a bucket and told me to go pick some cherries to take with us.

All the time I was picking the cherries I kept thinking how strange it was to see that eagle try to steal the baby. Didn't seem like it could happen, except it did. It didn't seem possible for a bird to take a living child. But if I hadn't been there that devil bird would have flown away with the baby.

Now when I carried the cherries back to the house, I went in the back door, but the lady and her baby and the Goat Man were on the front porch where he worked. I could hear the grinding wheel. As I went through the living room I saw this pretty piece of gold cloth folded on the sofa. It would be just perfect to make a dress for myself. The fabric shone and shimmered like sunlight on water. I put the cloth under my dress and walked out the back way, and then I set the cherries and the cloth in the wagon, before going around to the front porch.

The lady of the house was still standing there holding her baby. She reached into her pocket and held out fifteen cents. "Is this enough?" she said.

"That will be plenty," I said and gave a little bow. The place on my head had quit bleeding, but my head hurt like it had been whacked with a stick. The headache came from being scared by that old eagle. Every time I got scared, I came down with the busting headache. When the Goat Man and I got back on the road, I was still shaking from the scare as I walked along.

After we stopped for the night and the Goat Man looked in the wagon, he saw the piece of cloth beside the bucket of cherries. I thought he would be mad, because he feared he'd be blamed. But he held the cloth up in firelight like he was admiring it, and he said something I didn't understand. And he didn't seem mad. I was afraid he would throw the cloth away, or drop it in the fire so nobody could find it and blame him, but he didn't.

"Got to have something for my cuts and scare," I said. The Goat Man just nodded and put the gold cloth back in the wagon bed.

All the time I was getting water and gathering sticks, while the Goat Man was milking the nannies, I studied how to make a dress out of that fine fabric. My own dress was dirty and all torn up and I needed something to make me look decent. To be treated decently, a woman has to look decent. I knew the Goat Man had needles and thread in a box in the wagon, because I'd seen him sew up his own clothes. He even did embroidery on his shirt. But to sew well, you need a pattern to cut out the pieces of a dress. Out on the road I didn't have a pattern and I didn't have a table to lay the cloth on. I couldn't cut fine cloth on weeds and dirt.

As soon as the coffee was boiling and the grits were cooked, the Goat Man and I ate and had cherries with goat milk. The cherries were so sweet and ripe, they burst on my teeth and juice squirted all over my mouth. My head was still sore, but there was nothing I could do about that. After we finished the coffee, I got some more water and washed up the pots and cups and dishes. I was thinking about how I could cut out a dress from the fine cloth so it would fit me. But even if I had a pattern, where would I cut the cloth? And I thought how nice it would be to have a house and sewing table and light to see by. Just to have a chair to sit in would be a luxury. Out on the road with the Goat Man, I had to sit on a rock or a log, or on the ground. Girl, don't you ever run away again, I said to myself. That boy Jonah got you in a bad fix and then up and left you, like any man will.

And then by the fire, after everything was washed up, and the Goat Man was playing his whistle, I saw what to do. Instead of dancing to the music I took my dress off by the fire, so I was not wearing anything but my drawers. The Goat Man looked at my big titties and he kept playing that pipe. I reckon he thought I was going to dance without any clothes on. Instead I pulled a piece of spare canvas out of the wagon, the piece he sometimes used for a tent, and spread the canvas on the ground by the fire. I took a piece of charcoal and tried to draw the sections of my dirty dress on the canvas. It was hard to get it right, but I tried to fit the drawing to the lines and seams of the old dress. It took me several tries to get all the pieces lined out.

The Goat Man watched me, and when I took up the scissors to cut the canvas, he stopped playing and shook his head and ran to the wagon. And he came back with a piece of cheesecloth, the kind he used to strain the goat milk and squeeze the whey out of cheese. It was a kind of light gauze, and I laid it on the canvas and traced out the pattern on the cheesecloth. The gauze was light as a mist when I held it up to the firelight. Taking up the scissors, I snipped out the pieces as carefully as I could.

The Goat Man didn't play any more; he just watched me cut out the pattern. I reckon he was watching my breasts, too. No man can keep himself from looking at breasts, and mine were mighty handsome, if I do say so. I didn't mind being naked in the firelight, which made my skin the color of honey, but I put my old dress back on when the pattern was traced out as close as I could make it.

On the canvas spread out on the dirt, I pinned the pieces of cheesecloth onto my fancy gold fabric, not paying any attention to my sore head. It seemed the fight with the eagle over the baby was all a dream anyway. Nobody would believe that could happen if you told them. I was not sure I believed it myself, except I had the scabs on my head to prove it. And I had the cloth I took from the big farmhouse, too. I sliced out the pieces as neatly as I could in the firelight. And then it was time to go to bed, so I rolled the pieces up and put them in the wagon, and when I lay down in the blanket underneath I expected to go to sleep.

But instead of sleeping, I lay there with my head hurting, thinking about the woman picking cherries and the eagle swooping down, and me holding on to the baby. And when I drifted off to sleep finally, I dreamed about the eagle, and saw the gold cloth was the color of the eagle feathers. My dress would be made from the eagle's feathers. My revenge on the eagle was to cut him in pieces and wear him to show my victory. And in my dream I knew I'm dreaming. But I saw that because I had beaten the eagle I would also beat the road, and I could reach freedom. It would be an awful fight and a long struggle, but I would get there in the end.

Now the strangest thing in my dream was that when I was fighting the eagle and holding on to the baby's belly, I saw the baby's face, and it was not a white face; it was the face of Jonah. I knew that was crazy, and even in my dream I knew it was crazy. But that's what I saw. I saw Jonah crying even as the eagle tried to tear him away. And I thought the story of Jonah was not over yet, and the story of Jonah was my story, too. Silly as it seemed, that's what I saw.

Next day as we walked along way up in the mountains of Virginia, the wagon creaking on rocks and goats cropping grass, I studied on my dream. And I saw it was all a portent. The Bible said a dream told the future, like a prophet, if you knew how to cipher it. I didn't know all the dream meant, and I thought on the eagle and the baby, and I studied on the bright dress I was going to make. That dress flashed in the sun like they said the streets of heaven do. I was going to wear it with the scarf the Goat Man had given me.

That night after all the things were washed up, I start sewing. By the firelight I could just see to thread a needle. Mistress Thomas had tried to make me learn to sew well, but I didn't want to then. But now I wanted to sew more than anything. I had to make my pretty dress. I started joining the pieces of cloth by making tiny stitches. I poked the needle through by feel and pulled the thread tight. I made the most careful stitches I'd ever made. The shiny gold fabric was going to fit my body, the color of the cloth lighter than the deep gold of my skin. But the cloth was no softer or smoother than my skin. With every stitch I was sewing my future. If clothes make the girl, I reckoned I was making myself, what I would be. Pretty cloth to cover my beautiful skin.

The Goat Man played his whistle, and instead of dancing in the firelight, I made my fingers dance with the needle, dancing a stitch at a time, every stitch a step on the long journey.

One morning I woke up under the wagon and it was raining *drip drip drip* off the canvas top on both sides. My blanket was a little wet and the ground was wet. I roused myself because I had to find some sticks to start a fire. But the woods were all wet and the trees streaming water. It was late summer and there was a river nearby.

Where do you find dry wood on a rainy morning out where there's no roof or cover? The Goat Man had rags and paper in the wagon, but you have to have kindling to start a fire, to get enough heat to catch on bigger sticks. You have to have some cobs or pine cones or fat pine wood. I went looking for a pine tree and broke some dead limbs all wet on the outside. With the hatchet from the wagon, I laid one stick on another and split them open so the heartwood was bare. Then I shaved splinters off that sappy wood and put on more and more pumpkin pine till I got a blaze going.

When I reached into the wagon to get the coffee and some pots, I saw the Goat Man hadn't moved. Usually as soon as I rose, he got up. But he just lay there, and when I pulled the canvas back, I saw he wasn't asleep. His eyes were open and he looked scared. He looked at me like he didn't know what to do.

"What's wrong with you, Goat Man?" I said. He made a noise, but it wasn't even the kind of talk he usually made. He moved one arm a little and I saw he could barely shift himself around. And then I smelled him; he smelled like pee and a little like shit, too. He had dookied in his clothes and couldn't do anything about it.

"Goat Man, are you in trouble?" I said. He nodded like he was trying to say yes.

I stepped back out in the rain. My fire was blazing and it was time to put on the coffee and start some grits or mush. I needed to go to the river for water. The goats had to be milked and hitched up to the wagon. And the Goat Man was lying there in the wagon in his own filth. We were out in the woods in Virginia and I didn't know anybody to ask for help.

I looked back in the wagon and the Goat Man opened and closed his good hand like he was milking, and I saw he meant for me to go milk the nannies. He was thinking more about the goats than himself. I didn't know what else to do, so I took the milk bucket and went to one of the nannies. I'd never milked a goat before, but I'd milked cows. But a goat has only two teats and is easier than a cow to milk, once you get down on the ground. There was no stool, so I dropped on my knees and milked the first nanny and then the second.

When I finished the second nanny and stripped her, I took the bucket and set it beside the wagon. And I saw what I was going to have to do, what I had been dreading. I was going have to clean the Goat Man up, because he couldn't lie in his own mess. He was an old man that couldn't even talk, and I had to clean him up. Girl, you are crazy, I said to myself. But I didn't see any other way. I couldn't let the old man lie in his filth. And I couldn't just walk away and leave him like that. Besides, the Goat Man was my protection. The Goat Man was so strange nobody bothered me as long as they thought I was his slave or his girl.

I took a bucket to the river and filled it, and then I warmed half the water over the fire. And then I took a rag and pulled off the Goat Man's clothes and washed him in the wagon. I put a piece of canvas under him and scrubbed him with warm water and then dried him with one of his rags. It wasn't as bad as I thought it would be. Nothing is as bad as you expect, once you get in the middle of it. I'd seen a man's parts before and the Goat Man was no different. He was so helpless, he looked away most of the time, and he groaned like he was in bad pain.

After I washed him up and put on dry clothes, I went to make some coffee, and I made some mush. And then I had to hold the mug of coffee while he drank, and I fed him mush like he was a little baby. I kept thinking, Girl, what are you going to do? Way out here in strange woods with a helpless man and five goats. You don't know anybody and a sheriff could catch you and send you back to the Thomas Place to be whipped and branded on your cheek, and have your ear cut off.

We like to think we can make big choices, that we choose what we do. We like to tell ourselves that. The truth is, we usually do what we have to, what there is to do. We don't really know what we're going to do ahead of time. It just happens, like me running away because I saw Jonah at the jubilee. It was the biggest thing I'd ever done, and it wasn't even a plan, but just a happen.

I didn't know what I was going to do, but we couldn't just sit there in the rainy woods and rot. The Goat Man didn't have any money except what he made sharpening knives and saws and such. I thought I still had the money I took from Jonah on the night of the jubilee, but when I looked in my pocket, it was gone. It must have fallen out somewhere. There was nothing to do but hitch up the goats with the Goat Man lying in the wagon, wash up the pots and pans and put out the fire, and get on up the road the same way we had done before.

The road was muddy with little streams running in the ruts. The wagon splashed and creaked along. The river by the road ran red and angry with flood. We crossed a branch that was ugly and dirty. I tramped alongside the wagon holding my skirt up, but the hem got muddy all the same.

The first house we passed, a woman came out on the porch and hollered at me. I stepped into the yard and she said, "Ain't that the wagon of the Goat Man?" and I told her it was.

"Then where is the Goat Man?"

"He's not feeling too good," I said.

"I need my scissors and knives sharpened," she said.

"I'm doing the work now," I said. I don't know why I said that, because I'd never used the Goat Man's wheel or his files. But I'd watched him use them. I figured that with a little care I could do knives and scissors, maybe file the teeth on a saw. I wasn't ready to use the solder torch though. I took the file and whet rock and wheel from the wagon and brought them to the porch. The woman carried out a half dozen knives, two pairs of scissors, and a handsaw and a bow saw. "I've never seen a woman tinker," she said.

"I am a gypsy," I said.

Sharpening a blade with the wheel was pretty simple. I just held the lip of the metal to the stone and turned it so sparks and dust flew. I kept sharpening the blade till it sparkled and was razor thin at the edge, thin as a whisper. But sharpening a saw was different because the teeth had different angles and directions and the file had to be true to the pitch, this way and that way, changing back and forth along the edge. I tried so hard to file the teeth right I was sweating and my hand trembled.

The goats wandered into the woman's flowerbed and she hollered and drove them out. I stopped working and tied the goats to the wagon and came back and filed on the saws some more. When I was done the woman gave me a quart of sourwood honey and two dimes.

"You are just learning," she said.

"Yes, ma'am," I said and took the honey and the money.

People all along the road were surprised to see me come into their yards with the Goat Man's wagon. Sometimes they went out and talked to the Goat Man lying in the wagon while I sharpened their knives and saws and scissors. And sometimes a woman looked at me and told me she didn't have anything for me to do, and I had to get on up the road. And sometimes, when I could, I stole eggs from a henhouse because eggs made the Goat Man strong, and besides I liked eggs in the morning. It was a habit I'd gotten used to in the big house. While the field hands in the quarters ate mush of a morning, Sally always gave me an egg or two.

And the Goat Man started to move again. First he could push himself around while I washed him, and in a few more days he could take the bucket and rag from me and wash himself. I don't know what kind of sickness he had, but he was getting his strength back little by little, as the leaves along the road turned yellow and orange and it was cool in the morning. We went on up the road past a place with a brick courthouse.

Now I had to stop by a creek to wash out his clothes and my dirty dress. I didn't have a washpot, so I heated water in a kettle and washed in the dishpan and rinsed in the creek. I wore my new gold dress while the old one was being washed and dried by the fire. I was hanging wet clothes on sticks to dry when I looked around and saw the Goat Man slide out of the back of the wagon and fall to the ground. I ran to him, but he waved me away. He pulled himself up off the ground on the side of the wagon, and I handed him a spade to use as a crutch. The Goat Man grabbed the handle and took a step. He arms trembled as he leaned on the spade. He took another little step. I could see his left leg was good and his right leg was bad. He took another step holding on to the shovel. Making tiny hops he moved to the fire. It seemed like he was holding the spade up as much as it was holding him up.

The Goat Man pointed to the spade handle and then he pointed to the woods. He pointed to the hatchet on the side of the wagon and then he pointed to the trees again. Then he pointed to the handle again. For a minute I didn't know what he meant, and then I saw he wanted me to take the hatchet and cut a stick in the woods he could use for a walking stick.

While the clothes were drying, I took the hatchet and went looking for a sapling just the right size. The Goat Man needed something strong to hold him up, but light enough to carry easily. He needed a stick smooth to the touch that wouldn't bend too much. I found a maple, but it was too slim. A white oak would be too crooked. A pine or a poplar would break too easily.

And then I saw this hickory straight as a curtain rod and nearly as thick as my wrist. I hacked it off at the ground and then chopped it to about four feet long. Yellow leaves fell all around me, whispering and cool when they touched my arms.

At the fire the Goat Man looked at the stick and tried leaning on it. And he pointed to the rough end where it was cut and the bark was thick. So I took a knife from the wagon and peeled the bark from the sapling. The bark was stiff as oxhide, but I stripped it off and smoothed the bare wood with the knife, scraping away knots. I rounded off the big end so it felt like a knob, scraping the hickory wood smooth as an egg.

With that hickory stick the Goat Man could hobble around the fire and go to the woods to do his business, and I didn't have to clean him up anymore. When the clothes were dry, we moved on, him riding in the wagon. And when we came to a house, he went to the door, holding on to the stick, and I carried the wheel to the porch, and his other tools. The woman brought out her knives and scissors, saws and hoes.

I never saw anybody so happy to be working again. The Goat Man was so thrilled, he smiled all the time while he filed and turned the wheel and made sparks fling off the metal. I reckon he was that happy to be walking again, happy to not be lying in that wagon. That was the first time I ever saw how happy work can make a man. Being lazy is dreary, and lying helpless is more awful still.

Every day the Goat Man could walk a little better. He still had to lean on the stick I made for him. And he took short steps and favored his right leg. And I reckon his right arm didn't work as well as it had before. But he was soon working almost like he worked before, except he rode in the wagon more. He rode while I walked and led the goats.

Now we came to the place I later learned was Big Lick, between high, dark mountains. There were houses along four streets and the Goat Man went door to door asking if they needed any knives or such sharpened. And then while he was working on a porch, I glanced down the street at a store and saw somebody that looked like Jonah walk into the store. My heart jumped into my mouth and I almost fainted. It couldn't be Jonah, that low-down, trifling boy, I said. But I kept looking, and a few minutes later he came out with a poke in his hand, and I saw it truly was Jonah.

I wanted to go up to that rascal and crack him on the head, because I'd thought he was dead, or in jail, or taken back to South Carolina. But there he was in Big Lick, dressed in new clothes, and walking in the street just like a free man. You trifling, no-count rascal, I thought.

I was still holding a file in my hand, but I started following Jonah. I couldn't help myself. I didn't even think about the Goat Man and his work. I had to follow Jonah and see where he lived, and what he had done to have new clothes and walk in the street like he owned it.

He turned a corner and followed a road that ran into the country going north. I stayed back so he wouldn't see me, but I kept after him. I couldn't do anything else. And then he turned a corner into a yard with a white picket fence, and he went around the house to the back.

I couldn't go right up to the front of the house, but I meant to see what that boy was doing. I stepped into the woods and worked my way around to the back of the yard. There was a barn and woodshed and well there. Three young women sat on the second-story back porch talking and laughing. A black woman opened the back door and dumped a dishpan of water. I stepped around to the side of the barn, but didn't see Jonah anywhere.

I must have waited an hour listening to those girls talking on the porch before Jonah came out with a wooden bucket. He went to the well and I hollered to him from the bushes by the barn. When he saw who I was he turned gray, and hurried over to look at me. "What are you doing here?" he snapped.

"Well, I'm glad to see you, too," I said.

And I saw how scared Jonah was, so afraid he'd be found out as a runaway, and he was afraid I was going to tell on him. He was afraid that if I was caught he would be caught and sent back to South Carolina or sold off to the South. And I saw he was so scared because he was so smart. He knew the names of all the states and towns and rivers he had to cross to get to the North. And he knew what happened to black men caught running away. He was little more than a boy. But he was like my brother now, and my only hope to find my way, and to find love. I can't explain it all, but that was what I felt all of a sudden. That was why I had to tease him a little and say I would turn him in if he didn't take me with him.

Now when a white woman came out on the back porch and saw me talking to Jonah, she called me in, and I had to think quick. This Miss Linda ran this place and I saw quick she wasn't anything but a whore. She had on a fancy dress and perfume, but she was nothing but a hussy. I told her my name was Sarepta, a name from the Bible. And when she called me into the front room and told me what I was going to do, I just smiled and nodded my head and said, "Thank you, ma'am," like I was happy as a pig in mud. I'd do whatever she said because she spotted quickly that I was a runaway. She had the power over me, and I had to do whatever she wanted, because I had to stay close to Jonah. But she didn't know that, I reckon. Working for Miss Linda was the only way I could stay close to Jonah Williams.

While we were eating supper in the kitchen, us four colored servants, including Lonella the cook and Hettie the maid, I saw Jonah was so mad at me and scared of me he could hardly say anything. And I thought that was because he was already in love with me halfway and didn't know it yet. That was why he was so scared, because he knew he couldn't leave me again. He wanted to escape far away to the North, but he couldn't go anywhere without me. He knew how to read, and he had a map in his head, but he was just a scared boy that knew the odds against him. I wasn't going to tell him how I got to Big Lick and found him. I thought: let him be puzzled and think I followed him and tracked him like a hound dog after a fox. That would make him even more scared.

Only then did I remember the Goat Man. I was so surprised and thrilled and curious to see Jonah, and so pleased to be taken in by Miss Linda, I had forgotten all about the Goat Man and his wagon. I had come all that way with the old man and then I forgot all about him. A sour flash of regret passed through my bones. But I didn't say anything. I helped clean up and wash the dishes with Lonella, and then slipped out like I was going to the privy.

But soon as I reached the edge of the yard I hurried to the road and made my way back into town. Everything looked strange, because I hadn't paid any attention to the houses and streets when I was following Jonah. I passed a tavern, and several stores, and came to a courthouse. The house where the Goat Man had stopped to work was on a side street, but I couldn't remember which one. And I wasn't even sure what the house looked like, except it had a porch.

I walked slow and stayed in the shadows, because I didn't want to be noticed. I crossed a street and followed it to the edge of town and I looked in every yard for the Goat Man's wagon. A dog ran out and barked at me. A drunk man stumbling along tried to get hold of me, but I pushed him away and ran on.

The street led out into the country past a warehouse and a mill, but I never saw the Goat Man or his wagon. I turned back and followed all the streets one after another, looking into yards and behind hedges. But I knew the Goat Man wasn't in town anymore. When he finished his job and saw I was gone, he must have driven the wagon on out of town, and would be camped somewhere miles up the road. But I didn't know which road he'd have taken. Roads ran off in all directions. Some led right into the mountains.

There was nothing to do but turn back to Miss Linda's house. It pained me to think I'd run away from the Goat Man. He had taken me all the way from the French Broad River. But at least he could walk again, with his stick, and he could work. He might have trouble carrying water from a creek, but I reckoned he could manage, toting a little at a time. He had managed before he ever saw me, cooking his mush, feeding those goats. And I had done more for him than he had for me. I'd cleaned up his filth and taken care of the goats, and even sharpened knives and saws when he couldn't do anything. Yet when I turned back toward Miss Linda's house, I found my eyes were wet. I walked slow to let myself get calm.

There were lights on in the parlor of Miss Linda's house, and girls were laughing and somebody was playing a piano. I could smell wine or liquor. I went on around to the back of the house.

Now Miss Linda had said I was to sleep in a room down in the basement with Hettie. And when I took a lamp and went down there, I saw there was only one bed. But that was where I was going to have to sleep. Hettie was a kind of dried-up old woman with a stooped back and white hair. She didn't ever say much.

When I got to the bottom of the stairs, I saw this door open, and Jonah standing in the door. He looked at me like he couldn't take his eyes off my breasts. He was scared and he wanted to drive me away, but I saw he hadn't had any company in a long time.

I giggled and shook my butt a little. But the last thing I needed was to get caught with Jonah at Miss Linda's just when I had to behave myself and study on how to survive and keep going to the North. "You look mighty curious," I said and winked at him before sliding into Hettie's room and closing the door.

NEXT MORNING MISS LINDA called me into the parlor and asked if I knew how to sew. She said I needed new clothes and some shoes. She said everybody who worked for her had to have good clothes. "We all have to look decent," Miss Linda said.

"Yes, ma'am," I said.

She said to go down to the shoemaker's and get some shoes, and she gave me two kinds of cloth, yellow and pink, to make two dresses.

"Those that work for me don't see anything and don't say anything," Miss Linda said and looked at me hard.

"Yes, ma'am," I said.

"I hope you understand me," she said.

"I understand you," I said.

ELEVEN

JONAH

After Mr. Wells punished him with the hot and cold water, Jonah was ashamed to look at anyone at Miss Linda's. They all knew he'd been humbled and broken. They knew he'd begged Mr. Wells and promised him to be nothing but his dog. Somehow men like Mr. Williams and Mr. Wells knew that the worst pain, the most lasting pain, was not to the body but to one's dignity. That's what their punishments were intended for, to destroy the last sliver of your dignity.

Lonella and Hettie and the girls knew he'd screamed and begged and cried like a baby. They'd all returned from church while Mr. Wells was torturing him. He couldn't look at their faces. And when he passed a mirror, he couldn't look at his own face. When he was around Miss Linda, he looked at the floor. They'd caught him seeking pleasure with an Indian girl. It was a very personal humiliation, something he knew he would never forget.

After that Sunday morning he and Prissy avoided each other. She'd been punished again and had screamed and screamed. Whether they had used ice to hurt her or not Jonah didn't know. Prissy turned away when she passed him in the hall or saw him in the dining room. He understood that she was ashamed, ashamed of what had been done to her, and what had been done to him. After that Sunday morning Prissy never spoke to him again.

As he regained his strength, Jonah began planning his escape. He knew that Miss Linda and Mr. Wells expected him to try to run away after he was punished. As soon as he was missed, they'd tell the sheriff, and men on horses with rifles and dogs would ride after him. They'd run him down in a few hours. He knew he had to wait until they no longer expected him to run. And he had to convince them he was humble as dirt and happy to be at Miss Linda's.

Whenever Miss Linda spoke to him he bowed his head and said, "Yes, Miss Linda." He took off his hat whenever white folks passed near him. As summer changed into fall, the trees all around took on bright colors. Hickories became rusty gold and maples bright yellow and orange. And some maples on the ridge above the town turned pink orange. Jonah had never seen such intense colors. The mornings were cool and the afternoons sunny and hot. Molasses furnaces steamed in the valley outside town.

Jonah studied the mountains to the north and the mountains to the south. Big Lick was in a trough between two long chains of mountains running to the northeast and southwest. He knew he'd have to run to the northeast. He'd have to go soon if he was to make it to the North before winter came. Because it was getting cool at night, Miss Linda bought him a jacket of heavy jean cloth. It was the kind of coat called a Negro Jacket, the color of blue ink. When he ran away he'd need a jacket, and maybe long underwear. He thanked Miss Linda like she'd bought him his freedom.

Before he tried to escape, Jonah had to do some thinking. A little thinking beforehand could save a lot of effort and danger later. The trick to getting away was to go through water as much as possible, to throw the dogs and trackers off. An idea came to Jonah that was so good he wondered why he hadn't thought of it before. What if he left Miss Linda's during a hard rain? His tracks would be washed away and his scent would be melted away long before they knew he was gone. Why had he not thought of that before? In hard rain it would be difficult for a sheriff to gather his men and set out, much less see the trail. The risk was that he'd get lost in the dark in a heavy rain, or get struck by lightning during a bad storm, but it was a risk he was glad to take. He couldn't carry a torch in a heavy rain. Even a lantern might get drowned out.

Jonah knew the best time to leave was in the evening after supper. When guests were arriving in the parlor, Miss Linda would be busy serving drinks and entertaining. He would help Lonella and Hettie with the dishes and carry in wood and water for the next morning, same as always, and then while the girls were busy upstairs, he'd be gone. It was better not to try to hoard things to take with him. That would only arouse suspicions. He had more than eleven dollars Miss Linda had paid him. He would take that and some matches and his knife and fishhooks, and maybe a bite to eat. He'd carry his writing tablet and pencil inside his shirt. Jonah wished he had a map, but it would be too obvious if he bought a map at the store or cut a map out of the atlas in the parlor. Instead he tried to memorize the maps of Virginia, Maryland, and Pennsylvania in the atlas when he got a chance.

One day, while he drew water from the well, Jonah looked up and saw someone standing in the bushes at the corner of the yard. He put down the bucket and stepped closer, and saw black hair and golden skin, and a big, wide shoulder.

"What are you doing here?" Jonah said.

The person hiding parted the limbs of the yew bush, and Jonah saw it was Angel. He was so surprised he took a step back. "How did you get here?"

"Come up the long road, same as you."

"You can't stay here," he said. With a chill he saw that Angel's arrival might interfere with his plans for escape. It seemed impossible she'd followed him all the way to Big Lick.

"You get away from here," Jonah said.

"That's a fine welcome, after all your good help on the French Broad," Angel said.

"Ain't nothing for you here," Jonah said. But he must have spoken louder than he meant to, for Lonella called from the back porch and asked who he was talking to.

"Ain't nobody," he called.

"Yeah, I see it ain't nobody," Lonella said. "You talking loud enough to raise the dead."

Before he could stop her, Angel stepped out of the bushes and said to Lonella, "I be looking for a piece of cornbread; I be looking for some work." She walked right up to Lonella on the porch. Though she'd lost some weight in the weeks since he'd last seen her, Angel was still big. Instead of the feedsack dress, she wore a gold frock that she must have stolen from a clothesline. Her skin was the color of dark buckwheat honey, and her feet were bare.

"What can you do, girl?" Lonella said.

"I can do most anything," Angel said. "I've done most anything."

Lonella looked the big girl up and down like she was inspecting a piece of pork, looking for maggots. Miss Linda stepped out on the back porch at that moment and saw Angel. She beckoned for her to approach the house. Angel said her name was Sarepta, like in the Bible. "Come with me," Miss Linda said. Jonah watched helplessly as the women started to walk into the kitchen. Lonella turned back and told him to bring that water.

There were four buckets of water to carry into the kitchen, and each time Jonah came inside he heard Lonella and Miss Linda and Angel talking in the parlor. He edged near to the door in the hallway to hear better. He would pretend he'd never seen Angel before, and if she had any sense she'd act like he was a total stranger, too.

"We are just a family here," Miss Linda was saying. "You will help Lonella and Hettie, or whoever else needs help. Looks like you have come a long way."

"I come over the mountain," Angel said.

"And you will go back over the mountain if you give us any trouble," Miss Linda said. "Come, I'll introduce you."

Jonah dashed back to the kitchen just in time to make it look as if he'd been working there, not eavesdropping in the hallway. He tried to avoid looking at either Angel or Miss Linda.

"Sarepta will be joining us," Miss Linda said. "This is Ezra. You will help him when Lonella and Hettie don't need you."

"Yes, ma'am," Angel said.

"You can sleep in Hettie's room until we can fix up a place for you," Miss Linda said. "Now come upstairs to meet the girls."

Jonah was so surprised by Angel's sudden appearance he couldn't decide if it was a good thing or a bad thing. He was pretty sure it was a bad thing, for two runaways had to create more suspicion than just one. He couldn't have the fat girl following him and getting in the way of his plans. It was possible they might help each other, but it was hard to see how that might be. He needed to find out what her plans were, and how she'd gotten as far as Big Lick.

Because there were so many people in the house, and because she pretended to ignore him, Jonah found it hard to get alone with Angel. She worked in the kitchen with Lonella and cleaned the rooms upstairs with Hettie and rarely came outside. She slept next door to him in Hettie's room, but Hettie was always there. It was four days before Jonah got a chance to speak with her alone. It was late at night on Saturday night, and the guests were noisy in the parlor. Someone was playing the piano. Jonah slipped out into the backyard to relieve himself, and then he stood in the dark by the maple trees pondering his escape plans, wondering when a heavy rain would come. He saw Angel step out on the back porch and called to her in a loud whisper to come out in the yard.

"What do you want?" she said.

"Come out here," he said.

"You ain't my boss," she said and giggled. But she stepped off the porch and came to the maple tree. She was wearing a new dress, lavender, with bows on it.

"What are you doing here?" Jonah said.

"Same as you, I got a job." Jonah could smell perfume on her. Her hair was done up in a ribbon.

"Are you working upstairs?" he asked.

"None of your business," Angel said. "Mr. Wells, he likes me."

"You ain't planning on going up north?" Jonah said.

"What if I am?" Angel said. "Don't have to ask your leave to do nothing."

"You followed me here."

"I followed the Drinking Gourd," Angel said. "You think you're the only one know where the North is?"

"You'd better not get in my way," Jonah said.

"You can't do nothing to me, Jonah Williams. You're just mad 'cause you know I'm lying in bed right next to you but you got to sleep alone." She laughed and started back to the porch. In the weeks that followed, there were light rains some mornings, and more colored leaves fell in the yard. But a shower was of no use to Jonah. He needed wind and rain and heavy darkness that would hide him and cover his trail. Only heavy rain would quickly wash away his tracks.

Angel had moved out of Hettie's room to a little room upstairs. She had two fine dresses and new shoes and a red silk scarf. She still worked in the kitchen from time to time, and waited at the table in the dining room. But she did less and less work with Lonella and Hettie and Jonah.

"That girl be putting on airs," Lonella said one day in the kitchen.

"She got what some men want," Hettie said.

"Some mens like black skin and fleshy gals," Lonella said.

Jonah decided that Angel's presence didn't make any difference to his plans. She seemed happy at Miss Linda's, and as far as he knew she hadn't told anybody that she'd known him before. But late one night when he got up to have a dipper of water, he found her on the back porch.

"Ain't you the fancy woman," he said.

Angel ignored his sarcasm. "When you go north I'll go with you," she said.

"Who says I'm going north?"

"I got money, and I can help," Angel whispered.

"I ain't going nowhere," Jonah said. "And if I was, you'd be the last person I'd go with."

"Bet you could use a little company," Angel said and brushed her hip against his.

"Listen, girl, don't get in my way."

"Ain't scared of you," Angel said. "Besides, you think you the only one want to go on to freedom. You're dumb as shit. You gone need my help." A lamp was lit upstairs and Angel slipped back into the kitchen.

Two days later he passed Angel in the hallway and she muttered, "You don't take me with you, I turn you in."

"What if I was to turn you in before I left?" Jonah whispered back.

"I'd send your sorry ass back to South Carolina," Angel said.

The storm he was waiting for never came at the time he needed it. He hoped to escape in the early evening as things got busy upstairs, but no such coincidence of weather occurred. Instead he woke one night around eleven and heard rain lashing the windows above and wind shoving the shutters and roaring in the maple trees in the backyard. Jonah got out of bed and pulled his clothes on as quickly as he could. He laced and tied the brogans Miss Linda had bought him and got his money from under the cot, a box of matches, and his writing tablet and pencil. His fishhooks were wrapped in a folded sheet of tablet paper, and his knife was in his pocket.

There was laughter and movement upstairs and someone was playing the piano. Jonah climbed the steps to the kitchen. If anybody saw him, he'd pretend he was going to the outhouse. No one was in the kitchen, and he hurried to the back door and opened it carefully to keep it from banging in the wind. As he closed the door, he saw the barn lantern hanging on a peg. He grabbed the lantern, hoping it was filled with oil.

When he reached the steps, wind smacked Jonah in the face with cold drops. Rain stung his cheeks, and he pulled his hat lower. He skirted the edge of the yard, staying as far away from the front porch as possible, where guests might be coming and going. Lightning lit the air like magic blue powder flung from the sky. If anyone was looking out the window they'd see him in that flash. In that instant of illumination and flicker, he saw rain flung in sheets across the yard and across the valley. Other houses were dark. It had rained so hard, water stood in the yard and in the road. Puddles stretched to meet each other and appeared to spit and pucker with splashing drops.

Jonah froze and then it was dark again. Thunder growled so loud, he could hear it over the roar of the wind and rain. Thunder was so deep and loud it punched his chest and echoed in his ears. As soon as the rumble passed he hurried to the road and turned to the right. Jonah felt exposed, naked to the wind and lightning. Rain whipped his face and soaked his chest. He carried the lantern under his coat. When he got far enough away, he would light the lantern so he could see the road ahead. In the dark he stumbled through puddles and tripped on ruts and roots and rocks. Only the occasional flares of lightning showed him the way ahead. Several times he wandered into brush beside the road, and once he stepped into a ditch. There was a barn about half a mile up the road, which he'd seen from Miss Linda's yard. When he reached the barn he'd go inside and light the lantern. With a light he'd be able to walk faster. Speed was what he needed most now.

The road was covered with standing puddles that would hide his tracks. In some places the road ran like a stream. Any creeks along the way would be flooded. This was the kind of rain people called a gully-washer. When he got to the barn, a lightning flash helped him find the door, but he was blind as he stepped inside. A horse whickered. Cows stirred somewhere in the dark.

Jonah took the lantern out from under his coat and tried to dry his hands. Every inch of him was wet and dripping. The matches had to be dry and the wick had to be dry. In the dark he could see neither the lantern nor the matches. He would have to tell by touch whether they were dry or not. Whoa, he said to himself. If he made a mistake the matches could be ruined, or the lantern could be ruined, or he could set the barn on fire.

He placed the lantern on the ground and got to his knees. With the inside of his jacket he dried off the lantern, relieved to hear oil sloshing in the bottom. The matchbox he took from his pocket was a little damp, but the sticks inside seemed dry. Jonah dared not try to strike a match on the damp box. He felt around the floor for a rock but found none. What he did find was what felt like a rusty nail. He'd seen Mr. Williams strike a match on his fingernail. Maybe a metal nail would work just as well. He gripped the match near its head and held the nail point to the match head.

When he struck, the match head burst out in blue fire, and then yellow. The flame burned his finger and he put the match in his other hand. The flame faltered and he tipped the match down to make it burn brighter. Quickly he raised the glass on the lantern and screwed the tongue of the wick out longer. When he touched the match to the wick it didn't light at first, and then he touched it lower where the fabric was soaked in oil. The light burst out and he turned the wick down and closed the glass door. As long as he could keep the wick dry, the lantern would burn. But it would be hard to hold the lantern in the high wind.

Jonah buttoned his jacket, gripped the handle of the lantern, pulled down his hat, and stepped out into the storm. The lantern threw a patch of light on the puddles ahead of him, and he hurried to the road and began walking. Terrible as the rain was, Jonah felt a new strength and elation with every step he took. The rain was washing out his tracks as quickly as he made them, washing away any scent the dogs could follow. If he was lucky, Miss Linda wouldn't even know he was gone until next morning. By then he could be fifteen or even twenty miles down the road. He'd heard a man could walk thirty miles a day on a good road. Fifteen miles would be plenty in the dark, in a storm.

Jonah splashed through puddles and strode ahead into the lantern light. Wind lashed his back and pushed him along. The storm roared in the trees above him. After he'd gone a few miles, he saw lightning strike a tree, and the tree fell with a crack and crash into the road ahead. He had to pick his way through brush around the steaming trunk. His shoes were muddy and soaked, but Jonah didn't worry about them.

An animal ran in front of him, and from the flash of white he thought it might be a deer. Whatever it was, it was gone in an instant. Thunder banged the ridge above like barrels and hammers, and seemed to tear the sky to pieces.

As Jonah hurried over the top of a hill, a ball of fire shot out of a lightning bolt and bounced through the trees. And then another and another fireball ricocheted through the woods. One roared over his head and he ducked and looked behind him. A fireball was following the road, and he dropped to the ground, holding the lantern above the puddle. After the fireball hissed by, the woods were dark again and he had only the weak lantern light to guide him down the muddy track. He hurried a little faster. Jonah had always heard of balls of lightning, but he'd never seen them before. He'd assumed it was just an expression people used, a story people liked to tell. But the fireballs had bounced between the mountains and over trees. They'd whizzed just over his head. It was all like a thrilling dream, the storm, the wind, the lightning, and his escape from Miss Linda's.

Jonah walked through the rain mile after mile. He could hardly see the houses he passed or the little hamlets he went through. He crossed a swollen, leaping river on a wooden bridge, and waded through furious creeks and branches. He stalked the little puff of light from the lantern the way a hunter followed prey. He was hunting the way ahead at every step, the way to the North. He knew that somewhere above the rain and wind and thunder, the North Star was shining, calm and bright and everlasting.

As the sky began to lighten over the trees and above the mountains, the wind and rain didn't let up. He turned down the wick in the lantern and blew out the flame to save oil and stumbled ahead through the gray early morning light. He was getting tired and his feet were sore from walking in wet shoes. Jonah knew it was time to stop when he saw a barn at the edge of a field with no house visible nearby. He hurried along the edge of the woods and entered the barn, which he found was used to store hay. A broken-down wagon leaned against a stall. Harness covered with dust hung on pegs. He climbed the ladder to the mow and found in the shadows a pile of hay on one side and a heap of cane and millet on the other. Setting the lantern on the floor, he flopped onto the hay, pulling straw around him and over him. His coat was soaked but the hay would help keep him warm. Rain drummed on the roof and wind whistled in the cracks and made the barn creak. But Jonah was so tired, the barn seemed cozy. He'd traveled at least fifteen miles and had left no tracks that could be traced. He sank into a deep sleep.

When Jonah woke he thought it must be late afternoon; without the sun he couldn't really tell. But he knew he'd slept a long time. The rain on the barn roof was loud as ever, and wind shoved on the walls and banged a loose board. Jonah was hungry and thirsty, but there was nothing in the dusty barn to nourish him. Not for the first time, he wished he'd thought to put a biscuit in his pocket when he left Miss Linda's. He wished there was a store nearby where he could buy cheese and crackers, or a can of sardines or a jar of sausages. After he climbed down from the loft with the lantern, it took Jonah a moment to recall which way he'd come. Yes, the field and the barn had been on the right of the road. He needed to turn right when he reached the track. Only hunger and willpower made him step out into the cold rain again. He pulled his hat down and stomped into the rutted road.

Luck was with Jonah, for he found a little store at a crossroads only a few miles ahead. It was both a store and post office, and half a dozen men sat around a stove opposite the counter. Jonah took off his wet hat and bowed to them. Rain spilled off the brim.

"Don't you get my floor wet, boy," the man behind the counter said.

"No, sir," Jonah said. "No, sir."

Jonah told the storekeeper his master wanted three cans of sardines, a bag of crackers, a pound of cheese, and a jar of sausages.

"Your master must have sent you a long way," the storekeeper said, looking at Jonah's muddy pants and shoes.

"Them roads be awful bad," Jonah said and bowed.

"That will be a dollar and thirteen cents," the man behind the counter said. Jonah paid him and then spent another nickel on a box of matches, because the ones he had were wet. The storekeeper wrapped his purchases in brown paper and tied the package with a string. All the time he was in the store, Jonah felt the men by the stove watching him. No doubt they suspected he was a runaway. It was in his favor that he had money and a new coat. But the mud on his clothes and shoes showed he'd traveled a long way, and he was thoroughly soaked.

As Jonah stepped back into the rain, he was reminded of what a friend the storm was. The men by the stove, even if they were suspicious, wouldn't bother to follow him in this weather, unless they knew for sure he was a runaway and there was a reward for his capture. The storm was a refuge for him. The storm was his friend. Weather this bad was a blessing for the hunted and condemned.

Jonah stopped at another barn a mile farther on to eat some cheese and crackers, sardines and sausages. A bull was penned in a stall in the barn, and while he ate, the bull snorted and slammed into the sides of the stall. Once he heard boards creak, but the slats of the stall didn't give way. By the time he'd eaten it was almost dark. As Jonah lit the lantern he realized he'd forgotten to buy lantern oil at the store. It would only take a little to fill the well of the lantern, but he had no way to carry extra oil unless he bought a jar or a jug. Half the fuel had been used up the night before. He turned the wick down low to preserve what he had left.

As the road got dark and the rain did not let up, Jonah saw he lacked the strength he'd had the night before. His feet were sore and his knees stiff. The crackers and cheese and sardines made him feel numb and sleepy. The earlier sleep in the hay seemed to have taken strength away from him, not refreshed him. But it was also as if the rain had drained him of energy, bleached and leached out the strength in his blood. He lacked the confidence he'd had when he plunged into the storm way back in Big Lick.

FOR THREE NIGHTS JONAH followed the weak light of the lantern through heavy rain. The awful storm seemed to never slacken. One day he slept in an abandoned cabin, and another day he burrowed into a haystack at the edge of a field. He figured he'd gone about a hundred miles from Big Lick, but there was no way to tell. Jonah had no choice but to stumble along in the rain. Every step took him closer to the North and farther from the sheriff and his dogs. The road was nothing but standing water and mud and fallen limbs. Every stream had overflowed its banks. Finally he was able to buy more oil for the lantern at a little store in a hollow between mountains.

By the light of the weak lantern, Jonah crossed footlogs and shaky wooden bridges. He waded through glutted creeks and climbed across fallen trees. He passed a house where a dog barked at him from a shed but didn't come out into the downpour. Fields looked like lakes, and yards were standing water wrinkled by wind and pecked by rain. Jonah walked until his willpower and strength gave way. He figured he had to go another fifteen or twenty miles before stopping. It was still dark, but he had to rest. Slow down there, boy, he said to himself. He looked for another barn, or another shed or cow stall. He was so tired he could sleep in a wet haystack or pile of corn tops. If he had a blanket he could make a tent in the woods. A cellar, smokehouse, or woodshed would serve. Even a chicken house if the chickens were gone. But all Jonah saw were trees and more trees, brambles and brush, vines and thickets. He was on a stretch of wild road. He couldn't lie down and sleep in the woods, for the ground was too wet, and every limb streamed drops. Finally Jonah saw a little house off to the side of the road. He thought at first it was a chicken house, only about six feet by eight feet and made of boards. There was a door and one window, and inside he found a floor piled with broken chairs, a bench, and dusty planks. Jonah cleared a place on the bench and lay down. The floor was inches above the ground and the bench almost dry. There was no straw for a pillow or leaves to keep him warm, but Jonah didn't care. He just needed to get off his painful feet and rest.

Jonah slept better on the hard bench than he had in the haystack the day before. He was so tired he didn't dream, except for a brief dream where he seemed to be wrestling with wind and rain. A dog leapt at him out of the darkness, and the dog turned out to be owned by both Mr. Williams and Mr. Wells. They'd brought the dog all the way from Big Lick.

As Jonah slept, the little building he lay in loosened from its foundation in the rising water and drifted into the current of a nearby swollen creek. Jonah woke with water washing his cheek. At first it felt like tears dampening his temple and ear as he lay on his side on the rough plank bench. But the wetness was cold and didn't go away. In his sleep he wondered if the rain was washing into the little shack, or if there was a leak in the roof. Maybe wind was pushing rain through the low door. And then he felt water on his elbow and on his side. Water soaked into his armpit and covered his thigh. When he pushed himself up from the bench the floor rocked and water sloshed against the wall and swirled around his feet. The floor was unsteady and sank a little when he moved. Jonah reached for the lantern, but it was not where he remembered setting it down. The floor tilted and boards floated loose around his feet. Jonah held to a wall and understood that he was now waterborne.

The drifting shack bumped into something and scraped against an obstacle. It turned and he grabbed the opposite wall. Bushes scraped the side of the building. Jonah could see neither the wall nor the window. It was dark as a cave, and the total dark made Jonah dizzy, and the rocking and shifting made him sick at his stomach. If he was floating out on a creek or river, there might be a waterfall ahead. There was no lightning, but rain whipped the walls and roof and gusts made the shack rock and turn.

Jonah was almost as scared as he'd been when Mr. Wells caught him in bed with Prissy. It was the sense of blindness that made him feel most helpless. He had nothing to hold on to and he had no way to escape. The building could sink or crash over a waterfall. He was wet and cold and sore and confused. It was hard to tell up from down, level from tilted, pitching forward from pitching backward. The water rose to his shins, swirled and whispered and mocked him.

The last of the crackers and sardines he'd eaten hurriedly hours before had not rested well in his belly. And the crackers and cheese may have been tainted with something on his hands or clothes after four days on the road. The rocking and dizziness and fear added to the unsettled feeling. While he clung to the wall, a thrust of sour and bitterness leapt into his throat. He tried to swallow, but it was too late. The charge of vomit pushed into his mouth and over his tongue and flew out between his teeth. He tasted the sardines and cheese now gone sour.

His supper in the rain was coming back to him, leaving him. He puked into the darkness and vomit ran down his chin and on his chest. The shack smelled of puke and dirty water and rotten wood. As he staggered in the darkness and held on, Jonah heaved again and again. He threw up as if he was expelling everything he'd eaten in his whole life. He strained so long, his eyes burned and wept stinging tears. Jonah heaved so deep, he felt his back was going to break, and his throat was raw. When the heaving stopped, he wished he had some clean water to wash his mouth with. His legs were so weak they trembled at the knees, and he was short of breath, as though he'd run five miles.

When Jonah wiped his chin and opened his eyes he saw gray light in the window of the shack. The rain had slackened and almost stopped. The house bumped against something and turned sideways. But all he could see through the door and window was grayness. The light was too faint to make out anything distinctly. Surely there would be more light soon and he could tell where he was, and look for a way to escape. Something nudged his leg, and he reached down and found the lantern floating with pieces of boards and leaves and trash. He picked up the lantern and water spilled out.

Though Jonah was dry inside and empty, spit sweetened his mouth a little. He spat and his mouth felt cleaner. The gray outside was getting lighter. He couldn't make out anything distinct, but he saw something go by, a black tree or post. Things bumped and knocked on the walls of the shack. As his mouth and throat sweetened, Jonah felt the strength of his emptiness. His empty belly had a glow, a rightness, as if he'd gotten rid of a sick burden. He was empty and filled with light. Or maybe he felt that way because there was light in the little house now. He could see boards floating around his knees. Jonah looked out the window and saw something else go by. He studied the gray and found he was looking at fog. More surprising still, he was looking *through* fog, at trees and muddy trash. The fog that had seemed impenetrable before was full of ragged holes, and thinning. Jonah looked through the door and saw water rocking and swooping, and the riverbank beyond. He was drifting in a stream that spread far beyond its banks into fields. The shanty drifted catty-cornered to the current. He weighed one side down so it tilted deeper into the muddy water.

As the fog lifted slowly off the water, Jonah saw what a predicament he was in. The little house had washed out into a swollen stream and was drifting near the middle of a river. He was trapped, knee deep in muddy water, and he couldn't see a way to get out except to plunge into the raging current. If it was possible to climb onto the roof of the shack, he might see what was ahead. He could look out for a log or branch of a tree he might grab onto. He could call to somebody as he passed a town or farm. Maybe somebody in a boat would come and rescue him. When Jonah stood at the door, he tilted the building so far he thought it might tip over. The little house rocked and sloshed. If he climbed onto the roof, he could get out of the dirty, smelly water.

As he studied the little building, Jonah saw that his only hope to escape was through the window. If he could put his feet on the window sill he might be able to hoist himself up to the roof. With the floor slick and so unsteady, it was hard to see how he could get purchase. If he went through the window headfirst he would only push himself out into the flood. Jonah backed up to the window and placed his hands through and felt for the lath outside above the opening. Gripping the slat with all his strength, he pulled himself up through the window, scraping his back on the sill. Only his coat prevented him from cutting his lower back. It took him several heaves to get his butt onto the window sill.

Jonah's raised weight tilted the shack even more. He felt as if he was going to be dumped into the water as the building tipped on top of him. He sat in the window trying to decide what his next step must be. He had to get his feet on the sill to push himself up on the roof. But what was he going to hold to while he shifted his weight to get a foothold? The roof of the little house was rotting cedar shingles, slick and steep.

As the shack drifted and turned in the stampeding water, Jonah studied his chances. If he drowned in the flood, no one would ever know.

His flesh would rot and he'd be eaten by fish. Mama would never know what had happened to him. Mrs. Williams would forget he'd ever been at the Williams Place. If only he had something to hold to, he could pull himself through and stand on the sill and throw himself onto the wet roof. The only possible thing to grip was the corner of the roof to his right. He grasped the eave in his right hand, and moving his left leg an inch at a time, he lifted his knee and slid it under the top of the window. Straining every tendon and muscle in his body, he held the corner of the roof and raised himself on his left foot, pushing on the corner of the window. He began to shake and totter, threatening to fall backward into the flood, but at the last instant made a final effort and heaved himself onto the leaning roof so his fingers caught on the comb, and then his elbows. Hanging by his elbows on the dipping roof, he lay still and looked around.

Trees lined the creek, but water swirled and sucked through the trees. He felt like a sailor clinging to an overturned wreck. The creek was crowded with trees and all kinds of debris, boards and pieces of buildings. And then he saw an oblong box with the lid broken off. It was a shape that made him shiver, a coffin, a new coffin, apparently.

Clinging to the ridge pole of the little roof, Jonah turned to stare at the long wooden box and thought he saw a nose in the end where the lid was broken. The coffin rocked in the current as if someone inside was shaking it. And then he saw another coffin, older and partly rotted and mostly sunken in the river. This box was closer than the first, and the lid completely gone. Current nudged the shack and the older coffin closer, but Jonah couldn't bear to look inside, and he couldn't prevent himself from looking. Muddy water filled the open box, and at first it seemed filled with mud and weathered sticks. Then he realized the sticks were bones, rib bones and arm bones. The box bumped a limb and a skull grinned at him through gray teeth.

Jonah turned away, but when he looked in the other direction he saw another box and another. The stream was full of caskets and burial boxes. The caskets were made of carved wood. The flood must have scoured a hillside and opened all the graves. Since coffins float like boats, they must have raised themselves once the ground was flooded. The current melted the dirt and drew the boxes out of the hillside. The dead had been raised, but not as they were supposed to be at the Second Coming, in shining glory. They'd been summoned forth by the storm and gathered into a convoy down the raging river. I'm traveling in company with the dead, Jonah thought. I've joined the deathly procession. Perhaps I, too, am already dead.

As the fog disappeared and the sun came over the ridge, Jonah saw living people along the edge of the swollen stream. Where roads ran down into the floodwater, people stood watching him pass by. Some in buggies and some on horseback studied the raging flood that stretched hundreds of yards across fields and forests. They studied the angry water as though watching a race. Landslides had torn away whole hillsides where wet soil had given way under its own weight. Red clay showed through like bloody wounds with tangles of roots and stumps, limbs and rocks. Roads seemed to continue on air where bridges had been swept away.

Jonah saw a body floating and at first thought it was a corpse from one of the coffins. But the clothes looked rough and the back full and strong. It was a man in overalls drifting facedown in the muddy tide. And a snake was riding on the dead man's back.

As the sun got higher Jonah saw other snakes. He saw blacksnakes shimmying themselves through the water, and he saw snakes wrapped on limbs or clinging to trunks of floating trees. The snakes in the water were looking for a perch, a place to rest, a boat or raft to ride on. There were snakes on boards and snakes on coffins. The flood had scoured snakes out of dens and stripped them off perches on branches. The current looked stitched and threaded with serpents. Snakes laced themselves around floating brush and stretched on the roofs of floating chicken coops. Snakes hung from the rails of a bridge like ribbons tied there for decoration.

Since he had no paddle or pole, and no way to guide the small house under him, Jonah saw he had no choice but to drift with his awkward craft. The shack had kidnapped him from the shore and could set him down wherever it sank or came to rest. It bobbed along fast in the middle of the river, but if it drifted into an eddy or stuck in the mud he could get off. If he jumped off in midstream he would risk being bitten by snakes, and surely he would drown.

Ahead the river narrowed into a gorge between hills and he saw two boys on a bluff. They waved to him and he waved quickly and grabbed hold of the roof again. It took both hands to hold on, as the shack rocked and tilted every time he shifted his weight. The boys shouted something to him, but he couldn't tell what they said. At first it sounded as if they were asking him a question, and then it seemed they were shouting an order.

Something whistled near him, and at first he thought it was a bird. And then he heard a shot and knew it was a bullet that had twanged by. He looked at the boys on the bluff, and one was holding a stick, but the stick was pointed across the river. It was a rifle. The boy rested the rifle butt on the ground and began to reload it. Out in the middle of the stream, Jonah had no way to turn the little house away or drop out of sight. He hugged to the roof as flat as he could make himself and another bullet stung the air close by. Lying flat on the roof as it drifted in the gorge, Jonah was an exposed target and there was little he could do. He pressed himself to the roof and tried to make himself flat as paper. But there really was no way to shrink himself. He tried to squeeze tight, as if he could make himself disappear. Another bullet whined and thunked into the side of the floating house below his feet. The boys were either bad shots or were just trying to scare him. As Jonah flattened himself against the roof, it occurred to him what river he was on. In the atlas in Miss Linda's parlor he'd seen two rivers north and east of Big Lick. First was the James going generally to the east, and next was the Shenandoah flowing to the northeast. It must be the Shenandoah, or a branch of the Shenandoah, he was on. The Shenandoah ran all the way to the Potomac.

Pling! A bullet spat by and splashed on the river.

As the little house drifted farther from the bluff, Jonah was less afraid of being hit by a rifle shot than he was of the boys telling what they'd seen. If men heard there was a Negro boy floating on top of a building in the flood, they might row out in a boat to seize him. And soon as they rescued him from the river, they'd put him in chains. In the middle of the river, in broad daylight, he couldn't hide. And it would be many hours before it was dark. Jonah saw dead chickens floating in the river, and a dead collie dog. He saw what appeared at first to be a mule, but noticed, because of the small ears, that it was a pony. Though he'd not eaten since the evening before, and he'd puked up most of what he had eaten, Jonah wasn't hungry. The ugly, muddy floodwater, the corpses and snakes and dead animals, had killed any hunger he might have had. But he was thirsty. His lips were dry and his mouth was dry and he felt parched inside. Looking at the muddy water made him thirstier still. He thought of cold spring water. He thought of water sparkling and twisting from the spigot of a pump. He would like some cold cider or lemonade. A bottle of ginger beer or sarsaparilla would be wonderful. The bubble and bite of soda water would taste good in his sticky mouth. Lying against the rotting roof, Jonah must have drowsed off, for he thought he'd come to an even bigger river that must be the

Potomac. All he had to do was get to the left shore and he'd be on his way to the North again.

All that day and into the night Jonah rode on top of the little house. He grew thirstier. In the darkness he saw lights along the shore, far away, at the edge of the floodwaters. The shack rocked and dipped and bumped into logs and other floating buildings. At some point he sank into sleep again, still grasping his perch on the roof. When he woke it was already light, and he saw the mountains beyond the river, long and low and smooth. He slept again.

He was awakened by voices. Jonah raised his head and looked at the far shore and saw nothing but more rushing floodwater. Only when he looked behind him did he see a boat making its way toward him. Two men rowed the boat and a third man stood in the prow holding a rope. The man standing had a pistol in his belt.

"Hey, boy," the man in the prow yelled to him. The boat edged alongside the floating little house. Jonah pretended he didn't hear the man.

"Climb down and take this rope," the standing man called.

Jonah was afraid of the man's pistol. If he didn't obey, the man might shoot him. But even if he got away from this man he would tell others and they'd catch him farther down the river. It was not only fear but thirst that made Jonah obey the man with the rope.

"Jump down," the man ordered.

Jonah tried to slide down slowly, put a foot on the window sill and lower himself to the water. But once he let go of the ridge pole he slid quickly and had no way to brake himself. He clawed at the rotten shingles for a hold, but only slid faster. He hit the water and flailed his arms, trying to find the rope. The boat came to him, and instead of the rope he grasped the prow. "Hold on there," the man with the rope said. It took the man several tries to pull Jonah into the boat. Meanwhile the little house drifted on, rocking and spinning in the current, as the oarsmen directed the boat toward the bank.

"A sorry sight you are," the man with the pistol said, once Jonah rested dripping on the floor of the boat. The man pulled a canteen from his coat and gave it to Jonah. When Jonah put his dry cracked lips to the mouth and drank, he thought it was the sweetest, coolest liquid he'd ever tasted.

TWELVE

ANGEL

As long as I lived down in the basement with Hettie, I could keep my eye on Jonah. I knew he was going to run away as soon as he could. He was going to try to leave me again. He didn't know yet how much he needed me. When he grew up more, he would see things differently. But in the meantime I couldn't lose him again, because he was my only hope it seemed to get to freedom. I couldn't see any other way.

But then Miss Linda called me into the parlor one day and said she was moving me upstairs and I could start entertaining gentlemen. I was going to have a room next door to Prissy. "Every house needs a big girl," Miss Linda said. "Some men likes fat girls, and colored girls best of all." Miss Linda said I had really soft skin. She reached out and touched my arm.

This room upstairs had fancy sheets and pillows and pretty lamps.

The bed had a canopy over it, and carved posts. There were pictures on the walls of women wearing almost nothing. Miss Linda gave me new dresses and perfume and pink satin shoes. And she said Mr. Wells was going to come talk to me.

Sure enough there was a knock at my door that same evening. He was tall and strong and he talked real nice and called me darling, but his look was real hard.

"Sarepta, you're the prettiest girl we've seen in this house in ages," he said. He said colored girls made the best love there was. He talked sweet and gave me a gold necklace, and told me take off my clothes. I saw he was the boss or pimp or whatever they called it of this place. He owned it, and Miss Linda and all the girls. I saw he was going to try me out. He was going to see how I worked. So I said to myself: I'm not going to disappoint him. I can pleasure any man. I've got to stay here and keep an eye on Jonah, and I've got to make a little money. Miss Linda said I would get fifty cents for every man I took upstairs.

I tried hard as I could, to do everything I ever knew or thought of. And Mr. Wells must have been satisfied because when he got up and put on his clothes, he left a silver dollar on the bureau. And when he left I felt ashamed, and then proud of myself, too, for I knew I could make money and live. And Miss Linda wouldn't turn me out as long as I made her and Mr. Wells some money.

Jonah didn't say anything to me after I moved upstairs. He passed me in the hall and looked the other way. He was mad at me but I couldn't help that. A girl that had run away had to live the best way she could. He thought he was finished with me, but I wasn't through with him. He was my only hope to get to the North.

Next thing I knew it turned cold and the leaves started flying off the trees and Jonah built a fire in every room upstairs and carried wood up each morning. I knew he was going to leave, and wondered what he was waiting for. "You can't leave without me," I whispered to him, but he didn't answer.

One night in came an awful storm, and while I was lying in bed under the man they called Judge Hillman, I heard rain beat on the roof and lash against the windowpane. There was lightning and thunder, and rain beat on the wall like the wings of a thousand birds. And it seemed the storm was the end of something, or the beginning of something. The storm was a portent, and it seemed everything outside would be killed by that storm.

And next morning Jonah wasn't anywhere to be found. Lonella said Jonah had gone in the night. We didn't know what direction he took, but I guessed it was up north. The storm hadn't let up. In fact it got worse, blowing leaves up against the house so yellow leaves stuck to the windowpanes, and the walls shook with every powerful gust.

"No way to track him in the rain," Mr. Wells said to Miss Linda. "The sheriff won't even start out till the storm is over."

"We know he's going north," Miss Linda said. "The sheriff will send a telegram to all the towns down the valley."

"I told the sheriff to notify his owner in South Carolina," Mr. Wells said, "but to not mention our names."

Jonah had done it again, left me, abandoned me, and I didn't know where he'd gone. He went north I was sure, but I didn't know where and I couldn't do anything but wait and save my money. Prissy spent her money on laudanum, and other girls bought brandy, but I put my dollars and quarters in an old sock, and I knew I wouldn't stay much longer at Miss Linda's. Nobody needed to tell me Mr. Wells could be mean if you didn't do what he wanted. The other girls whispered about the terrible things he had done, and I could see the cruelty in his eyes, in his mouth.

About a week later I heard Miss Linda and Mr. Wells talking again and they said the sheriff at a place called Winchester had wired the sheriff in Big Lick that he had caught Jonah. It was no concern of Miss Linda's and Mr. Wells, except they didn't want to be accused of hiring a runaway slave. There was no way they could claim the reward.

"The sheriff in Winchester will claim the reward," Mr. Wells said.

"But we sent out the warning," Miss Linda said.

"We can't let anybody know we kept him here for months," Mr. Wells said.

"We had no way to know he was a runaway," Miss Linda said.

All I knew was that Jonah was in jail in Winchester, wherever that might be. That night I studied on what I could do. I had nearly ten dollars in my sock. I had no choice but to follow Jonah, unless I wanted to be a whore the rest of my life. As soon as I got a little older, or got sick with one of those diseases, they would throw me out anyway. So early in the morning while everybody in the house was asleep, I packed my things in a pillowcase, and took my money and slipped down the stairs and out the back door. Lonella and Hettie weren't up yet. The streets were still dark, but I walked all the way to the train station. Everything was closed, and I waited on a bench till the ticket man came and opened the station. I asked for a ticket to Winchester, and he said that would cost a dollar and twenty cents. I bought a ticket and he said the train would come in about an hour. "You want the six-fifty-two," he said.

I figured if I stood in front of the station somebody might see me, so I hid in the corner where they pushed the baggage carts and wagons. I'd never ridden on a train before, but there was no other way to get to Winchester. If I tried to walk along the road, they would catch me before dinnertime and send me back to the Thomas Place. You must be crazy, running after Jonah this way, I said to myself.

When the big huffing and hissing and smelly train pulled in and people got off, I hurried along and climbed into a car. But I'd no sooner taken a seat than a man in a black uniform walked up and said, "What do you think you doing, girl? Go on back to the next car." So I had to pick up my bag and walk back to the next car, where I tried to sit prim and ladylike on the dirty seat there.

When the train stopped at Winchester, it was almost dark. It was just a village, no bigger than Big Lick, and I could see the courthouse down the street. Now I knew the jail would be behind the courthouse, or near the courthouse, so I walked around the building with a clock on its tower, and saw this big log house. A man came out the door with a tray and locked the door behind him. There were bars on the windows and it was dark inside. I walked on by, but when the man with the tray was gone, I turned back.

I walked around the log house and heard something scratching and scraping inside. It was dark now and I couldn't see anything.

"Jonah, is that you?" I said. The scraping stopped, and I said again, "Jonah, is that you?"

The scratching started again, and then I looked closer and saw this hand reach out of the hole under the wall.

"Here, let me help you," I said.

THIRTEEN

JONAH

As soon as the boat touched the bank, the man with the pistol took Jonah by the arm and helped him out onto the ground. "You're lucky we seen you, boy," he said. The man had dried tobacco spit in the corner of his mouth.

"Yes, sir," Jonah said. "I was on my way to see Massa Cyrus's mother in Winchester."

The man led Jonah by the arm up the steep bank to a road leading into a town. The two who had rowed the boat followed.

"What might be the name of your master's mother?" said the man with the pistol. A chill shot through the bottom of Jonah's feet. He should have thought of a better explanation. If he was near Winchester he was caught.

"I got a note here from my massa," Jonah said. "She be Mrs. Page." The note he'd written with his pencil to replace the one Miss Linda had thrown away was still in his pocket, but the paper was waterlogged and the writing blurred. Jonah unfolded the soggy sheet and handed it to the man.

"This nigger boy, Isaac, is going to help my sick mother in Winchester," the man read aloud. "Please help him get there. Cyrus Page, his owner in Knoxville, Tennessee."

The man with the pistol looked Jonah up and down. He said his name was Sheriff Watkins, and he made Jonah empty his pockets of the wet matches, the knife and fishhooks, and the tablet and pencil. He saw the note was written on a sheet from the tablet.

"How did you expect to find your master's mother if you didn't even know her first name?" Sheriff Watkins asked.

"I figured it was writ on the paper," Jonah said. "Figured somebody would read it to me."

The sheriff led him down the road into the town with his deputies following. "What is your name, boy?" the sheriff said.

"Like it say in the paper, I be called Isaac."

"Well, Isaac, you better come with me."

"Maybe somebody help me when I get to Winchester," Jonah said.

"You're already in Winchester," the sheriff said. The three men escorted Jonah through the little town to the brick courthouse, as people on the street turned to watch. They led him behind the courthouse to a building made of locust logs with bars on the windows.

"We heard they's a slave run away from Big Lick," the sheriff said as he unlocked the door.

"Ain't been to no Big Lick," Jonah said.

"Well, Isaac, we'll just hold you here until we find out," the sheriff said. The jail was only one room with an iron cage on either side of an aisle. Jonah had to empty everything out of his wet pockets again, and the sheriff took his pocketknife, then directed Jonah into the cage on the left and locked the door behind him.

"You make a mistake, sir," Jonah said. "I ain't no runaway."

"We'll see about that," Sheriff Watkins said. He told one of the deputies to bring two clean blankets for the cot in the cage, and he ordered the other to draw a bucket of fresh water.

"That is your piss bucket," he said and pointed to a pail already in the cell.

"Ain't done nothing wrong," Jonah said.

"Take your clothes off and wrap one of these blankets around you," the sheriff said. Jonah took off his dripping shirt and pants and laid them beside the cot. The dry blanket felt good around his shoulders.

Sheriff Watkins laid Jonah's wet clothes by the door of his cage. "I reckon you're hungry, Isaac, or whoever you are," the sheriff said.

"Yes, sir, I be hungry, and I be thirsty."

The sheriff left and Jonah looked around the cage. There was one barred window looking out on a side street. A cot made of boards stood in the corner, with a lumpy, straw-filled tick. The floor was dirt and the piss bucket sat in the opposite corner. Initials and names had been scratched on the log walls. JESUS LOVES ME had been inscribed with a nail or knife point.

Jonah stood at the window and watched men repairing a roof. The storm must have blown away some shingles, for they were nailing new shakes among old weathered ones. Puddles stood in streets and in yards along the streets. Sunlight sparkled on the water in a ditch. Jonah was so tired, he sat down on the cot. The sheriff returned after a while with a plate heaped with beans and turnip greens and a pone of cornbread. And he carried a mug of steaming coffee, too.

"We ain't going to let you starve," Sheriff Watkins said. "Whether you're a runaway or not, we won't make you fast." He handed Jonah the plate through the slot in the door, and then he handed him the coffee.

"Thank you, sir," Jonah said. He took the heavy plate and cup to the cot and sat down. He was so hungry he was weak. He was so empty he felt light-headed.

"You forget something?" the sheriff said. The deputy took something from his pocket and tossed it to Jonah. It was a wooden spoon.

The beans and turnip greens needed more salt, but they were hot and juicy. And they'd been cooked with fatback, which gave them a rich and satisfying flavor. The beans were soup beans, sweet and powerful. He savored each bean like it was a morsel of meat soaked in honey. The greens had a golden flavor, as if they'd absorbed all the minerals and salts in the earth, along with the mineral of sunlight and the sparkle of topsoil.

The cornbread sopped up the juice that swirled around the beans and greens. It was hot golden cornbread, sweet as roasted corn picked freshly on a bright August day. The coffee was too hot to drink at first. He set the mug on the cot to eat, and when the deputy brought the water bucket with a dipper, he drank the water with his meal. Hungry as he was, Jonah made himself eat slowly. He knew it was better to eat slowly because he was so empty, and because he'd been sick. And he wanted to make the meal last as long as possible, for he didn't know when he might have another. He munched the cornbread that still had a hint of buttermilk in its taste, and took smaller bites, then began to sip the coffee.

Jonah had always loved coffee, and he'd never tasted coffee better than what the sheriff had brought him. It was dark and nutty, with the glistening, almost bitter sparkle or edge the best coffee had. The coffee tasted vivid, and it made things appear clearer. The other deputy brought a blanket, and as Jonah finished his cornbread and sipped the coffee he began to drowse. He'd slept little the last two nights, and he'd worn himself out clinging to the roof of the lurching little house. Sleep began to take hold of his legs and his arms. It was a kind of numbness that made his ankles itch. His feet were cold and he wished he had some dry socks and shoes to put on.

He felt as if he might go to sleep before he'd spread the blanket on the cot. He set the empty mug and plate on the floor and unfolded the blanket, a gray blanket, a little threadbare but clean. When he sat back down on the cot, he felt the sleep rising in his veins and behind his ears. His shirt and pants were still wet on the floor, but he was too drowsy to think about them. Sleep was a warm bath rising, and soon he'd be floating beyond the touch of gravity. He would float out on the wide, swollen river of sleep. Sleep stretched absolutely level all the way to the horizon.

Jonah lay down and wrapped half the second blanket over him. He was already asleep by the time he put his head down on the cot, drifting far out on the warm river of sleep, clinging to a plank or log. And then he reached for something bigger, something he might climb onto. What he grasped was cold, but he heaved himself onto the flat surface and hoped to lie there and dream. But the thing he'd crawled onto was a coffin. It was a coffin carved from cherry wood. The lid was cracked and he saw through the large crack a skull with its mouth open and the mouth appeared to be laughing in his face.

Jonah jerked away from the coffin and jolted himself awake. He realized it was just a dream and he was still on the cot in jail, not on a coffin lid. A golden beam of late sunlight sliced into the cage from the one window. Jonah dropped back into the dream of sleep.

When Jonah woke again, it was completely dark, and it took him a few moments to remember where he was. A weak light revealed the window, but not enough to show anything about the cell. He knew the plate and mug were on the ground beside the cot, and the water bucket near the foot of the cot. He needed to piss, and got up and stumbled to the other corner, where he found the chamber bucket. At least I have a pot to piss in, he said to himself and chuckled.

But once he relieved himself and lay down again, Jonah began to think about the situation he was in. If Sheriff Watkins telegraphed Big Lick, they might identify him and send him back to Mr. Wells. Or they might even find the wanted posters and contact Mr. Williams in South Carolina. It was only a matter of time before he was put in chains and sent back south. Sheriff Watkins seemed to be the kind of man who would treat him well. But he was also the kind of man who would find your legal owner and hold you until arrangements could be made. A man like Sheriff Watkins liked to believe he was a fair man, an honest man.

As Jonah lay on the cot looking up into the darkness, he knew he would have to think of a way to free himself. The logs of the jail were too thick to cut through, even if he had a knife. The bars on the window were too strong to bend. A hundred men must have been kept in this cage before, and they would have studied ways to escape. If they'd found a weakness in the jail, that weakness would have been corrected. The floor was dirt, and Jonah wondered if he could dig a tunnel under the log wall. But he couldn't make a tunnel with bare hands. All he had was the wooden spoon, and the sheriff would claim that in the morning. They wouldn't give him a metal spoon or knife. The sheriff had taken his pocketknife. With a metal knife he could probably dig his way out under the log wall in a day or two.

Jonah tried to recall what the roof of the jail looked like. Were there iron bars above him, or could he reach the rafters and cedar shingles? If he upended the cot he might climb on the end of it and reach the shakes. He climbed on the cot and found he could touch the eave. The logs or poles that held up the roof were notched snugly into the top log of the wall. Planks nailed to the poles held the cedar shingles. Without an axe it would be impossible to cut through the roof, unless he could find a board that was loose, that wasn't pegged firmly to the rafters.

As Jonah was feeling along the edge of the logs, hoping to find a loose plank, he suddenly heard voices. A man shouted and someone answered quietly. Jonah dropped back on the cot.

"Can't arrest me . . ." a man yelled, his voice slurred with drink. A key turned in the door of the jail and the door creaked open. Lantern light blinded Jonah for a moment, and then he saw Sheriff Watkins and one of the deputies leading a man whose clothes were rumpled and torn.

"No call to arrest me," the man called out as he stumbled into the jail.

"You can rest here tonight," the sheriff said.

"Ain't fair," the man growled.

"I told you to stay away from Thelma," Sheriff Watkins said. "You're not to go near her house."

"My house, too," the drunk man said.

"Not anymore," the sheriff said.

Jonah stayed on the cot out of the lantern light as they unlocked the other cage and led the drunk man to the cot. "You get some sleep, George," the sheriff said.

The sheriff and deputy ignored Jonah, thinking he was asleep. They took the lantern and closed the door and locked it. The deputy complained about not getting any sleep.

"Just be glad old George didn't have his pistol," the sheriff said.

The jail was dark as before. Jonah lay on the cot and listened to the drunk man in the other cell stumble around and grumble. "Ain't got no right, ain't got no call," he said. The man fell and began sobbing, crying like a heartbroken child. It sounded like the man was crawling around on his hands and knees, confused in the dark.

"They will let you out in the morning," Jonah said. He hadn't intended to say anything; the words just came out. The sobbing stopped and there was a moment of stillness.

"Who's there?" the drunk man said.

"Just me in the other cell," Jonah said.

"Are you the devil come for me?" George said.

"I'm locked up, too," Jonah said.

There was a long silence, and then the man called again. "You're the runaway slave!"

"I ain't a runaway," Jonah said.

There was another long pause. Jonah heard a dog barking in the town.

"Won't stay in jail with no nigger," the man grumbled, talking to himself.

Jonah thought of speaking to the man again and reminding him he would be released the next morning, but he knew there was no use to talk to somebody drunk. Jonah lay back on the cot and wrapped the blankets around himself. His shirt and pants were still damp from the river. He felt more hopeless than before. There was nothing he could do now but wait. They'd let the drunk man go free the next day, but hold Jonah until they'd located Mr. Williams. Somebody was certain to connect him with the handbill. Jonah knew there was a good chance Mr. Wells and Miss Linda had learned who his owner was. Jonah wondered what Mama was doing. He wondered who was reading to Mrs. Williams now. Jonah felt hopeless, but the moaning of the drunk man made him ashamed to cry.

"They didn't find my pistol," the man in the other cell said. "You hear that, boy—they didn't find my gun. Had it next to my other gun." The drunk man giggled and repeated, "Had it right beside my other gun."

Jonah heard something metallic. Was it possible the drunk man had a revolver? It sounded like the hammer of a pistol being cocked. Jonah lay very still.

"I won't sleep in a room with no runaway," the man said. There was a flash of fire and an explosion, and the metal of the cage rang. Jonah rolled off the cot onto the floor; he smelled burned gunpowder. There was nothing in the cell for him to hide behind. His best hope was to lie flat on the ground and stay quiet.

"Didn't know I had a pistol, did they, boy?" the drunk man said, chuckling.

The second shot was bright as a flash of lightning, and the jail shook with the report. The bullet hit the wall somewhere above the cot, for Jonah heard the thunk close to his head. He crawled as quietly as he could a few feet away.

"Are you scared?" the man said. "Do you think the devil's coming after you?"

The third blast came from even closer, and Jonah knew the drunk man was reaching through the bars of his cage and firing. Dirt kicked up by the bullet hit his face and his ears rang as if he was deafened. The drunk man was quiet for a full minute. "Won't let me see my children, won't let me in my house," he muttered and began to sob again. If he was holding a regular six-shooter, he had three more shots. Jonah began crawling to the other side of the cell.

"You trying to hide from old George?" the man called. "I ain't got nothing to lose."

Jonah lay as flat as he could, as far away as he could.

The next shot must have gone over his head, for he felt the wind and heard the sickening buzz at the same instant he saw the flash. If the man was not so drunk, he would already have killed him. Jonah crawled halfway back toward the cot.

"Time to die, black boy," the drunk man said.

Jonah hoped the sound of the shots would bring help. Surely the sheriff would hear and come running. But all was quiet around the jail, and Jonah realized that a small building of logs could muffle almost any sound inside it. The crack of the shots might not even be noticed by those sleeping in nearby houses. The fifth shot hit something metal, and the cage rang like it had been slammed by a sledgehammer. The bullet must have ricocheted because something crashed on the far wall of the jail.

"I'll send you to hell!" the man shouted. He fired again, and this time the bullet passed through the blanket near Jonah's waist. He felt he'd been punched there, but when he touched the spot he found no wetness, only torn flannel. The flesh there ached, as if it had been bruised, but there was no blood. It was the last shot in the pistol, if the man had a six-shooter. Jonah listened for sounds of reloading.

"You black bastard," the man said. "Are you dead?"

Jonah lay completely still. He'd crawled to the door of the cage and waited, hoping the drunk man had no more bullets. He listened and heard a kind of whimper. The room smelled of burned powder and urine. The whimper turned into a moan and a growl, and he thought the drunk man was going to scream out. But instead he vomited. The drunk man puked long and hard, and drops splashed all the way across the aisle into Jonah's cage. The room now smelled of rancid alcohol and sour vomit.

Jonah pushed himself away from the bars. He touched the door of the cage and felt it give a little. He pushed again and it gave a little more. Had the gate never been latched? He'd seen Sheriff Watkins lock the door. It was too good to be true! He pushed the gate again and it opened farther. He pushed it quietly open. One of the wild shots must have hit the lock and broken it. There was no other way to explain the unlocked door. A bullet had hit the lock just right to break the bolt.

Jonah stood up as quietly as he could and pushed the door all the way open. He listened and noted the puking had stopped. He waited and thought what he might do if the entrance to the log jail was locked. Just getting out of the cage might do him no good. A snore came from the other cell, and then another. The drunk man must have passed out in his own vomit. Jonah tried to remember what the aisle in the jail looked like. There was a fireplace at the end opposite the door and nothing but a rough wooden table in between. Jonah tiptoed out into the aisle and tried the entrance door. Sure enough, it was locked and the door was made of heavy planks. It would be impossible for one man to shove the door down. In the dark he couldn't tell exactly what kind of lock was on the door. It was likely a padlock on the outside.

The man in the other cell murmured and rolled over. "Ain't got no right," he muttered again. Whatever he decided to do, Jonah knew he should have his clothes and shoes on. He slipped back into the cell and found his shoes beneath the cot. The shoes were still damp but he laced them on and sat thinking. His pants and shirt were mostly dry and he slipped those on. The jacket was still damp. He hung it on the edge of the cot. He wondered if he could reach the roof if he stood on the table. Without an axe to chop through the planks and shakes, it was impossible to get out that way.

It occurred to Jonah that Sheriff Watkins might have left the key in the lock of the drunk man's cell. It was unlikely he had, but was still a possibility. Jonah eased his way out of the cell and across the aisle. For some reason he thought the key would be there, to let the drunk man out in the morning. But there was nothing in the keyhole and the door was locked firm. And then Jonah remembered that even if the key had been there it almost certainly would not have opened the entrance lock. He'd been foolish to even think of it.

As he stood in the aisle and cursed his silliness, Jonah saw there was gray at the window. Daylight was not far away. If he was going to make an escape in the dark, his time was running out. No doubt Sheriff Watkins would get an answer to his telegram today. He might even get a message from the sheriff of Greenville County, if Mr. Wells or Miss Linda had tipped off the sheriff in Big Lick. In the first light Jonah looked toward the fireplace at the other end of the walkway. It was cold and dark, but Jonah suddenly recalled he'd seen a poker and ash shovel beside the fireplace. With the poker he might be able to pry shingles loose from the roof, or even break the lock on the entrance door.

Jonah walked quietly to the fireplace and found the iron tools. The man in the other cell snorted and called out in his sleep like someone lost. With the poker Jonah might hit the sheriff or deputy when they came back to the jail. He would have to find a place to insert the poker into the door to break it open. When Jonah lifted the ash shovel he saw how heavy and strong it was. With such a shovel he might dig under the wall of the log jail. All he needed was a hole deep enough to slip through. He took the shovel into his cell and began digging at the bottom of the lowest log. The dirt was hard at the top, but soon as he cut through the packed crust the ground got softer. He dug in little strokes, removing about a cupful of clay at a time. As he worked it got light enough to see into the corners of the cell.

If the drunk man woke and saw Jonah digging he would call out. He might even have more ammunition for his revolver. He seemed like a man who would not mind shooting an escaped slave. If he merely wounded Jonah, he might be able to collect the reward money for his return. Jonah couldn't tell exactly what time it was. Sheriff Watkins had said he'd come and release the drunk man in the morning. But that could mean any time between six and noon. Jonah placed each shovelful of dirt under the cot, and he hung the blanket over the edge of the cot so the pile of clay was hidden. The shovel was not made for cutting into earth, but to scoop soft ashes off the floor of a fireplace. He reached the bottom of the sill log. The hole would have to be a foot deeper under the sill and maybe eighteen inches wide. The shovel blade banged on the log.

The man in the other cell grunted and pulled himself up off the floor. Jonah froze and waited. The man wiped his mouth and cleaned the vomit off his cheek with the tail of his shirt. He picked up the pistol and looked at its chambers. "Did I shoot this thing?" he said.

"Yes, sir, you did," Jonah said.

"Did I shoot at you?"

"You never hit me, sir."

The man stood and brushed off his clothes. The jail smelled of puke and piss. "I'm sorry," he said and walked to the window. He looked out as though expecting to see someone coming.

"I make a nuisance of myself when I shake hands with the bottle," he said. He sounded entirely different from the man who'd yelled at Jonah and tried to shoot him.

"You was awful drunk," Jonah said.

"Yes, that I was," the man said. "I say things I don't mean when I'm in that condition. And I do things I don't mean." Jonah wondered if the man could remember what he'd hollered in the dark.

The man walked to the bars and looked at the open door of Jonah's cage. "Did I do that?" he said.

"A bullet blowed away the lock," Jonah said.

"Watkins will make me pay," the man said. He stared into Jonah's cell and saw the shovel in Jonah's hands. Even in the shadows he could see the fresh dirt under the cot.

"You go right ahead, son," the man said. "Don't let me stop you. I'm nobody to stop anyone."

Jonah knew that drunks often feel remorse when they sober up, sorry for the trouble and spectacle they've made. But soon as they begin to feel better they get angry and mean again.

"Go ahead, boy, dig yourself out of here," the man said. He ran his hand through his hair and sat down on his cot. Since the man had already seen him with the shovel, Jonah saw no reason to stop digging. If he could dig his way out before the sheriff came, it was worth trying. If not, he would be found with the shovel anyway. Jonah began shoveling at the clay again, but soon there were footsteps outside. Jonah slid the ash shovel under the cot as a key was fitted in the outside lock. The door swung open and the sheriff stepped inside and a deputy followed with a tray. Two mugs of coffee smoked on the tray and two plates of grits and biscuits.

"What is this?" Sheriff Watkins said when he saw Jonah's door open and Jonah standing by his cot.

"It's my fault," the man in the other cell said and pointed to the pistol in his belt. "I'm afraid I scared this boy pretty bad."

The sheriff looked at the broken lock where the catch had been blown away.

"George, you're a damn fool," the sheriff said to the man in the other cell. "One of these days you're going to get yourself hanged."

"I'm awful sorry, Sheriff."

"Are you hurt, boy?" the sheriff said to Jonah.

"No, sir, but he done shot all over the jail."

"Give me that gun," the sheriff said. The man named George handed the sheriff the six-shooter. The deputy passed Jonah a plate and cup of coffee. The grits had a pool of butter right in the middle. The two biscuits were big as saucers. Jonah sat down on the cot and placed the plate on his lap.

"I'm not hungry," the man in the other cage said. "But I'll take some coffee."

The deputy set the second plate just inside Jonah's cell and took the second mug to George.

"You'll have to pay for this," the sheriff said to George.

"I know, Sheriff—I know."

The sheriff sent the deputy for a chain and padlock for the door of Jonah's cage. He hadn't noticed the shovel missing from the fireplace at the other end of the aisle. Jonah figured it was only a matter of time until George told the sheriff that he'd seen Jonah digging. No white man, even a remorseful drunk, was going to let a runaway slave escape from custody, especially if there was a reward for him. As soon as he was out of earshot, George would tell. Then they'd whip Jonah and put him in chains.

Worried as he was, Jonah ate the grits anyway. The biscuits were warm and the butter sweet and the coffee dark and rich. Whatever happened, he needed to fill his belly.

"You can have this plate, too," the sheriff said and pointed to the second plate on the floor.

"Thank you, sir," Jonah said. The more danger he was in, the more important it was to have good manners. When the deputy returned with the chain and padlock, they closed Jonah's door and wrapped it shut.

"George, you ought to be ashamed," the sheriff said, as he opened the other cell and led the prisoner out.

"I am ashamed," George said. "I'm awful ashamed."

When they were gone Jonah finished the first plate of grits and picked up the second. He began to eat slowly, chewing and cherishing every bite. He thought each bite might be his last for a long time. He got half the second plate eaten, and then three-quarters. He ate the last biscuit. He was getting full. He listened for footsteps. No one came. After he finished the second plate, Jonah sat on the cot feeling full and lazy. He sipped the last of the coffee and wondered how the sheriff would punish him for digging the hole. Sheriff Watkins had fed him better than he expected, but once he was angered he might be just as mean as he'd been kind before. That was the way with white men: the best of them might do the meanest things.

Jonah waited a long time, and then he used the piss bucket. Now the jail smelled like shit as well as vomit and piss. He sat back down on the cot and began to be sleepy. The drunk man had kept him awake much of the night. He was tired from worry and digging. It wouldn't hurt to lie down and rest, waiting for the sheriff to come with manacles and chains. Jonah stretched out on the cot and covered himself with a gray blanket. As he slept he dreamed of digging a tunnel. At the other end of the tunnel was a river. Beyond the river lay another country.

It was a key in the lock that awakened him. Jonah sat up, and a deputy came inside carrying a mug and a piece of cornbread on a plate.

"Sheriff said since you had two plates this morning you don't get nothing but coffee and cornbread for dinner," the deputy said.

"That will be fine," Jonah said.

Jonah looked for a whip or chain in the deputy's hand, but he carried only a tray. The deputy handed the plate and mug through the door to Jonah and then he unlocked the padlock and took the dirty plates and mug. The deputy smelled the shit and looked at the chamber bucket.

"I'll bring a rag and hot water and you can clean this place up," he said. "Sheriff don't want no puke in his jail."

"Yes, sir," Jonah said.

"Your shit smells worse than regular shit," the deputy said. But he took the chamber bucket outside and dumped it, then brought it back into the cell.

After the deputy left, Jonah munched the cornpone and sipped the coffee. He was confused, because nothing bad had happened yet. It was not believable that the drunk man called George hadn't told the sheriff

Jonah was digging under the wall. If he'd not told him at first he would certainly tell him later, when he really sobered up and got angry again.

But you could never tell what a white man might do. White men were a mystery to Jonah. All he knew was that he couldn't trust them. They might be kind one minute and cruel the next. He had no choice now but to wait to see what would happen. Might as well let the blanket hang over the end of the cot and hide the dirt pile and shovel as long as there was a hair of a chance he'd not been found out.

When the deputy returned he brought a bucket of hot water and a rag and told Jonah to clean up the puke in the other cell and to wash out the shit bucket, too. As the deputy watched, Jonah wiped up the vomit on the dirt floor as best he could, but the sour had soaked into the ground and he could only scour away some of it. Dirt got on the rag and in the bucket, and soon the water was filthy. The deputy took the bucket outside and dumped it and returned with clean water.

Jonah scrubbed the shit bucket and rubbed it clean. He wished he had some water to wash himself. He was grimy and he smelled bad. He hadn't washed since he ran away from Miss Linda's five or six days ago. The river water had made him even dirtier. But if he asked for water to wash himself that would only complicate things. Every minute the deputy spent in the jail made it more likely he'd spot the shovel missing from the fireplace, or the hole dug beneath the logs. If he could get by until nightfall, Jonah might be able to start digging again. It was a slim chance, but the only hope he had. He washed out the piss bucket and squeezed the rag into the dirty water. The deputy took the cleaning bucket away and locked Jonah's cell and the outside door.

Jonah lay on the cot again and wondered if the sheriff was going to play a trick on him. Maybe they planned to let him dig his way under the logs. They'd be hiding outside in the dark waiting for him. Soon as he crawled through, they'd seize him and put him in chains. Should he give up trying to dig the escape hole? Yet there was a tiny chance they hadn't noticed the missing shovel and the fresh dirt by the logs. It was nearly impossible that the man called George hadn't told the sheriff about Jonah's digging. Could the man have been so sick with a hangover he'd forgotten about the shovel, forgotten about the digging?

FOURTEEN

JONAH

As soon as it was dark Jonah began digging again. Apparently the drunk had not told the sheriff about the shovel, yet. It seemed impossible a white man had protected him, a drunk man at that. Could it mean they were setting a trap for him? Would they beat him and put him in chains as soon as he slipped out under the logs? The second deputy brought a supper of fatback and soup beans and cornbread. Soon as he finished the beans and bread, Jonah started to dig. Without a light it was hard to see where to aim the shovel. No longer trying to hide the dirt, he worked as quick as possible. In half an hour he had the hole a foot deeper. Next he had to reach under the log to make an opening on the other side. That was the hardest work of all because there was no way to get a purchase on the shovel at that awkward angle. He could only stab and jab in the dark.

As he strained Jonah thought he heard a knock on the logs outside, just above where he was digging. He paused and listened. The knock came again and he froze. Somebody had heard him digging. Was it a trick? Was the sheriff making fun of his efforts to dig out?

"Is that you, Jonah?" a voice whispered. It sounded familiar.

"Who are you?"

There was a chuckle. "You don't recognize Angel?" the voice said.

"No," Jonah said.

"I'll help dig from this side," Angel said. Jonah was so astonished he couldn't think of anything to say. If it was a trick, then he was already caught. He started shoveling again. It took another few minutes to make the tunnel reach far enough outside for him to slip under the log. He scraped his shoulders wiggling through. Angel had enlarged the hole from the other side.

"You run off and left me," Angel said.

"How did you follow me?"

"Miss Linda got a telegram that said where you was, and I took the train," Angel said. "I know where to go by that." It was so strange to see Angel here outside the jail that Jonah could hardly think. He stood up in the fresh air, dazed, brushing the dirt from his clothes, and tried to recall the direction of the river. He reached back under the log and pulled his coat through the opening. Jonah seemed to remember the river was to his left, but wasn't sure. The trees and houses all looked different from what he remembered. There was a hedge along the street at the back of the jail, and Jonah paused to listen. He thought he heard something move in the hedge, and stepped as quietly as he could to get a closer look.

"Let's get away from here," Jonah said. He began running in the other direction, stiff from sitting all day and digging in the hard clay. He ran as hard as he could away from the hedge and dark street and he heard Angel following, almost keeping up with him. Lamplight shone in some of the houses and he heard her steps behind as he ran across yards and jumped a fence and continued down the middle of a street.

Jonah ran so hard, his eyes burned and his chest hurt. His only hope was to forget about Angel and vanish into the dark. He ran behind a hedge and jumped over a ditch. He climbed over a picket fence and dashed through a pigpen. He thought he'd left Angel behind, but suddenly she was beside him, her hips bouncing. He must find a creek where he would leave no tracks. Jonah ran so hard he didn't notice the barrier in front of him until he almost slammed into it. It looked like a row of low buildings or sheds. It was too high to climb over. And then he saw the row was *moving*. The walls creaked and rattled and moved to his left. And he heard a whistle.

At that instant he knew it was a train blocking his way. He'd seen trains in Greenville, but had never been this close to one before. The cars appeared in the dark to be long sheds on wheels. In the moonlight he spotted a ladder up one end of a car and he ran and gripped the ladder and found a foothold on a lower rung. Jonah climbed to the top of the boxcar and lay flat on the roof. He didn't know where Angel had gone. He dropped as flat as he could on the roof and listened to the rattle and bang of the wheels on the steel below. He thought he heard men shouting, but he couldn't be sure. The train began to move faster. It was thrilling that he'd gotten away from Sheriff Watkins and his deputies, and that he was riding on a train. And most thrilling of all was the fact that the train appeared to be heading north.

As the boxcar lurched and rattled under him and banged on rough places in the tracks, Jonah began to shiver. In the jail it hadn't seemed very cold, though he'd wrapped himself in the blanket and his coat. But he'd worked up a sweat digging the hole, and had gotten even hotter running across the town. The open air was chilled and the breeze on the moving car made it even colder. He shivered and his teeth chattered. And the air he breathed was filled with smoke that made him cough and sneeze. The wind was full of soot and ashes and winking sparks and glowing cinders. The engine up ahead blurted out cinders that fell around him. He coughed and shivered and knocked a piece of glowing ash off his arm. The train moved under a trail of sparks.

Jonah looked over the side of the car and saw a rail that ran over the doorway. The sliding door rolled along the rail on wheels. The door was half open. It occurred to him that if he grasped the rail with both hands he might pitch forward in a somersault and land inside the car. It was dangerous, but no more dangerous than freezing to death or choking to death on smoke and hot ashes. He would have pneumonia if he stayed on top of the car.

Turning to face the left side of the car, he reached for the rail and gripped it with both hands. Closing his eyes, he pitched forward. But the flat shape of the rail tore out of his grasp as he reached the end of his somersault. Letting go, he fell and his legs hit the floor of the boxcar as his head and shoulders fell outside the door above the clacking rails. Reaching backward, he was able to pull himself into the dark car. Jonah hauled himself deeper into the car until he touched something rough and firm, something bound in ropes and tow sacks. It felt like a bale of cotton. He wrapped his coat around him tighter and pushed himself against the bale to keep warm. As the car rattled and shivered, his teeth stopped chattering. Jonah sat and thought about where the train might be going. He thought about Angel, and the strangeness of her reappearing, just as he dug his way out of the jail. And he thought about where he was going to get something to eat on a moving train loaded with bales of cotton.

As he sank into sleep, Jonah began to dream about Jonah in the Bible, who got swallowed by the big fish and then was spewed out on the beach. That was in the Old Testament. In the dream Jonah was in the belly of the train and he wondered where the train would vomit him out. With luck the train would carry him somewhere far to the north of the Potomac.

During the night Jonah thought he heard something stir in the box-car near him, and wondered if it was a rat or cat trapped on the train. Or maybe he just dreamed that something was moving in the bales and dirt around him.

"Wake up, boy," a voice said. But it was not a dream. It was a voice in front of him. Jonah woke and saw a Negro man holding a knife to his throat.

"You get offen this train," said the man, who wore a gray wide-brimmed hat.

"Ain't hurting nobody," Jonah said.

"And you ain't going to hurt me," the man said.

"You think you own the train?" Jonah said, anger rising out of his sleepy guts.

"I own this knife," the man said. "Don't give me no dumb backsass."

"I'm just going north," Jonah said.

"Well hurrah for you," the man said. "Ain't you the clever one."

Jonah remembered that Sheriff Watkins had taken his knife. He had nothing in his pocket but a pencil.

"Now go on, git," the man said and pushed his knife against Jonah's throat.

"Who are you?" Jonah said.

"Never you mind who I am," the black man said. "I come a long way, and I killed a white man, and I don't mind killing nobody that get in my way."

"I could help you," Jonah said.

"Three runaways is four times more like to be caught than two," the man said and jerked his head sideways. Jonah saw Angel sitting between two bales of cotton.

"Can't get up unless you stand back," Jonah said.

The man with the knife stepped back a foot or so and Jonah raised himself against the cotton bale. Instead of standing he braced his back against the bale and kicked with both feet, hitting the man in the lower belly and crotch. The Negro fell back toward the door of the boxcar and Jonah stood up and kicked him in the groin and in the face. As the man fell backward through the door, the knife clattered to the floor of the car.

Jonah picked up the knife and slipped it into his pocket. His hand trembled, his knees so weak he could hardly stand. He leaned on a bale of cotton and began to cry as the anger and surprise washed through him. He wasn't sure why he was weeping. Maybe it was because he was scared. It frightened him to think that Sheriff Watkins might have let him dig his way out of jail so he could send word ahead to catch him at the next town. It scared him even more that another escaping slave would threaten to kill him with a knife. He was shaken to see how desperate the other man was. It was everyone for himself, which meant that nobody had much of a chance. He might as well have been shot by the sheriff, or drowned in the flooding river, or had his throat cut by the other runaway. He wept because Angel kept showing up and getting in his way and confusing him. After one night of pleasure with her, was he doomed to have her always follow him? Slow down there, boy, he said to himself. The world was empty as a cold fireplace full of ashes. The world was bleached and dead inside. Whoever had made the world made it cruel and crazy. Nothing made sense or was consistent, except the pain.

"You got no call to cry," Angel said. "You done got on the train going north." She sat down beside him and leaned against the bale of cotton. Straw was stuck to her dress and hair.

"Never going to make it," Jonah said. He'd never killed anyone before. The man who fell from the boxcar might well be dead.

"Never going to make it if you cry like a baby," Angel said. She leaned her soft shoulder against Jonah.

"How come you keep following me?" Jonah said.

" 'Cause I got to get to the North," Angel said. "Ain't nobody else to follow." She laughed like everything was all right and there was no need to worry.

"We're a long way from the North," Jonah said.

"I bet we are halfway there," Angel said. "You the one that knows the map. You tell me."

"I learned the map at Miss Linda's."

"Who learned you to read so good?" Angel said.

Jonah told her about the Williams Place, and learning to read from the tutor's lessons. He told about reading to Mrs. Williams and about the Bible she'd given him. He described the whipping Mr. Williams had given him, and running away.

"I found a boat and paddled down the French Broad," Jonah said.

"I seen that boat," Angel said. Jonah leaned his cheek on her breasts. She was acting different, now that they were alone on the train.

"How come you to run away?" Jonah said.

"Because I seen you, seen you was running. Figured if you could go north, I could, too."

"You look well fed," Jonah said.

"I was the prettiest girl on the Thomas Place," Angel said. "Massa Thomas said if I sleep in his bed I don't have to work in the fields. That sound good to me. He give me everything I want. Fatten me up to be his plaything in the dark. All I had to do was let him have his way. He so old he sometimes don't even try. I be his foot-warmer, what they call me."

"And he never whipped you?"

"No need to whip me. I was good to him. But I can't stand it no more. When I see you and know you are on your way, I have to go."

"So you'll blame me when we get caught," Jonah said.

"You the best thing that happen to me, so far," Angel said. They sat like that a long time, swaying together to the rocking of the train. And then they lay down in the straw and enjoyed each other. It seemed impossible to Jonah that two people with nothing in the world but themselves could create suddenly so much comfort and pleasure between them.

When Jonah looked out again it was now full daylight. The train ran on a higher and higher embankment and the clattering and banging got louder. He saw they were on a trestle, on a long bridge, and a wide muddy river ran below them. It was the widest river he'd ever seen, with little islands and rocks tearing the current. The river puckered, shiny as scar tissue. It must be the Potomac, had to be the Potomac. With two steps he could leap out of the car and over the ties of the trestle. He could dive a hundred feet into the brown galloping water below. He could disappear into the mess of water and never have to fear again guns and dogs and sheriffs and men with whips. The water seemed to be waving to him.

Angel lay sleeping on the floor. He didn't want to wake her. When she woke she would be in the North.

Jonah stepped back from the door and rested on the bale of cotton. It occurred to him he was already almost to the North, for the train was crossing into Maryland. He was more than halfway to the light of the North, the promised land.

As THE TRAIN CLANKED and rattled uphill from the river, Jonah looked around in the car to see if the man he'd kicked through the door had left anything besides the knife. He might have had a coat or blanket, some matches or a lantern. Something useful. Nights were getting cold and it would be even colder up north, if he actually got to the North. The car was stacked with bales of cotton at one end. The bales reached almost to the ceiling. But nearly half the car was empty, except for straw and cotton lint on the floor. There was a tow sack folded up, which the man with the knife must have used as a pillow. It appeared other sacks had been used as blankets. In the Bible it talked about people who were sad and repenting, wearing sackcloth and ashes. Maybe that was what was meant, the rough fabric of the tow sack, the ashes from the locomotive. He had to repent and lament like those in the Bible. Except they didn't have trains in the Bible.

An iron kettle sat on the floor with a rope looped through the handle. In the kettle were matches, potatoes, a piece of cornbread. The man with the knife must have carried the kettle slung over his shoulder. He could use it to boil water, cook potatoes, make coffee. Inside the kettle was a metal spoon wrapped in jean cloth. Jonah ate the cornbread. Beside the kettle and spoon lay a piece of paper folded and worn and dirty. It looked as if it had gotten wet and stained by muddy water or coffee. It looked like a scrap that had been thrown away. Jonah picked up the paper and unfolded it and saw there was drawing on the soiled sheet. Someone had drawn lines on the page and written names in pencil. He stepped closer to the light from the door to see what was written. At the bottom of the page ran a curved line with "Potomack" spelled under it. And crossing that line was another line that came to a dot with "Hagerstown" inscribed beside it. That line continued up the page to a dot called "Harrisburg" and then turned to the right. Someone had drawn mountains like little waves, and another line started through the mountains to a place called "Elmira" and then on to "Auburn." The line swung left at Auburn and reached a dot called "Rochester," and then stretched on to "Buffalo." Beyond Buffalo they'd written "Canada" and then "Canaan."

It was a map he'd found, a map that showed how to reach the North, where there was no slavery. Somebody had drawn the map for the man with the knife. According to the sheet the first stop after the train crossed the river was Hagerstown in Maryland. And after that the railroad went on to Harrisburg. At Harrisburg he'd have to get off the train and cross the mountains and follow the river to a place called Elmira.

"What is that?" Angel said. She'd awakened and was rubbing her eyes.

For all his bad luck, Jonah knew he'd had some good fortune, too. Sheriff Watkins had fed him well, and then he'd escaped from Winchester and gotten on the train. The runaway with the knife had not cut his throat, but instead had been thrown from the car himself. Angel had proved a comfort, as well as a complication. And now he'd found a map to the North, to Buffalo, to Canada, to the North Star and freedom. Slow down there, he said to himself. You still have a long way to go. You're maybe halfway to Canada. Even as he thought these words of caution and hope, the train began to slow down. The engine continued to hoof and the wheels creaked, but the rattle was quieter. They were coming into a town, which he guessed was Hagerstown. The train moved steadily but slower past a water tank, some brick warehouses, the backs of houses. He could look down streets that crossed the tracks. A whistle sounded up ahead and the cars slowed down even more. Wagons and buggies had stopped beside the tracks. The train rolled so slow, it took several minutes to reach the station.

"What happens now?" Angel said.

"Get behind these bales," Jonah said. They hunkered down behind two bales stacked one on the other.

Once the train came to a lurching stop, men walked alongside the cars. Jonah didn't know if they were checking the wheels, or the hitches between cars, or maybe the cargo inside the cars. Doors rolled and slammed. Slipping the map inside his shirt, he picked up the kettle and squeezed himself lower down. He and Angel had hidden just in time, for two men came to the door of the car and looked inside.

"What shit-ass left this door open?" one said.

"Maybe it was you," the second man said.

"And maybe it was your grandma," the first man said. They slid the door shut with a bang, and a latch or lock clicked shut. Jonah and Angel looked at each other with alarm: they were locked in, and for all they knew it was impossible to open the sliding door from inside. They could be locked inside until the train reached its destination in New York or Boston. The car must be going where there were cotton mills. They could starve to death or freeze to death before the door was ever opened. They could die of thirst even sooner. A rumble spread through the train, and the car began to move again with jolts and clinks. According to the map, they were off to Harrisburg. He had no way of knowing how long it might take to reach Harrisburg, far to the north. But at least he was going in the right direction.

As soon as the clanks and rocking of the car grew steady, Jonah and Angel came out from behind the bale of cotton and tried the sliding door. There was a kind of handle on the inside of the door, but he couldn't budge the heavy panel. It was locked on the outside, or at least latched securely, and there was no way he could reach the latch. If the door remained closed until the train reached the cotton mills of New England, they were indeed in danger. They might wrap themselves in the tow sacks to keep warm, but they had no water, and no way to get water.

At least it was daylight, and a warm sun sliced through the cracks of the car. He wondered if there could be another door, and examined the walls and looked behind the bales of cotton. The only opening he saw was in the ceiling near the middle of the car. The stacks of cotton bales came about to the middle of the car, but not close enough for him to stand on them and reach the hatchway in the roof.

"What do we do now?" Angel said. The night before she'd seemed all confidence and cheer. Now she was scared and looking to him for a solution.

"Got to think," Jonah said.

Jonah sat on a bale of cotton and studied the problem. He'd heard Mr. Williams say a bale weighed about five hundred pounds, much too big for him to lift or move around. There seemed to be nothing else in the car, no boards or ladder, no wooden box, no pole. He could tell the door above had a latch and a hinge, and the latch had to be released and the lid raised and turned back. He climbed up on the bale to get a closer look at the latch. It was too far to reach unless he had a stick. Even if he got the door open, he couldn't reach the hatch to pull himself through. As far as Jonah could tell, he was trapped until the brakeman or someone else opened the sliding door. The car was made of heavy oak planks too hard to break. Even if he had a crowbar, he wasn't sure he could break out.

"We are stuck here," Angel said. She picked the straw off her dress, one little piece at a time.

"I will find a way," Jonah said.

Jonah sat back down on the bale and studied the floor. It was hard to see the cracks there because of the lint and dirt and straw. The floorboards felt heavy, at least two inches thick. He raked away straw with his foot, and then brushed away more with his hands. It felt as if there was a crack, some kind of break in the floor. He swept away more straw and lint and saw there was a kind of trapdoor. The panel seemed to be attached to hinges on one end. The problem was how to lift the heavy door that fit so flush with the floor. With a crowbar or screwdriver he could have done it quickly. The knife would break if he used it to pry the door. He tried to fit his fingers in the crack but couldn't get a grip there.

"What you gone do now?" Angel said.

Jonah looked around the floor for a stick, a nail, a piece of wood, anything that would fit into the tight crack and lift the trapdoor. As far as he could tell there was no latch or catch. The heavy lid simply lay in its bed. He felt his pockets. The only other thing he had was the kettle. The kettle had a stiff wire handle in the shape of a half moon. It was a very strong handle. Jonah pushed the knotted ends of the rope to either side of the handle and tried to slip the top of the handle into the crack. It fit! Pushing hard on the wire, he lifted the trap door a little. Pressing even harder on the handle, he raised the boards enough to get a grip on the door. He raised the trapdoor back and dropped it on the floor. The clacking and clanking of the wheels came loud through the opening. Crossties and the gravel bed of the railroad blurred below. The track stank of grease and tar, cinders and ashes.

"You gone leave me here?" Angel said.

"I've got to get outside, so when the train stops I can open the door and let you out," Jonah said.

"Don't you leave Angel," she said and laughed. "I am your guardian Angel."

Jonah lowered himself to look under the car. The sleepers rushing by so close made him dizzy and a little sick at his stomach. But he saw rods stretching under the car, rods that strengthened the floor and held the car firm between its wheels. If he could lower his legs through the trapdoor onto the rods he might be able to slide his butt and back onto the rods and ride there. When the train slowed down enough or stopped he could jump off and run before the brakeman could catch him. Easing himself onto the bars was the most dangerous thing Jonah had ever done. If he slipped he would be ground to pieces under the train. But it seemed he had no choice, if he didn't want to die of thirst in the boxcar.

Holding to the sides of the opening, he lowered his legs through and slipped them onto the rods. Pushing with all his strength he slid his behind and his back onto the bars. The clank was deafening and the gravel and crossties were only a foot below him. When he seemed to be firmly in place, he reached back and found the kettle and pulled it through until it rested on his chest.

The creaking and clanking changed their notes and he looked down and saw he was far above a river. Jonah had noticed on a map the river that went through Harrisburg, but he couldn't remember its name. Lying on the bars and holding the kettle, he couldn't reach into his pocket to get the paper. If he shifted two inches, he might slip off the bars onto the ties of the trestle. The water looked far below the bridge, though he guessed it was really not that far down to the river. Jonah shivered and jerked as the cold wind sliced under him. His teeth rattled and his knees jerked. He saw, far below, two men fishing in a rowboat, and he saw the shadow of the trestle and the train across the water. The smoke from the engine cast a ghostly shadow.

As soon as they were across the river, the train began slowing down. The wheels creaked and shrieked on the rails, and the clanking slowed and quieted. Whoa now, Jonah thought. And as if the train were an animal that heard him, it braked even more. He held on tightly as the car came to a complete stop. The gravel and ties below him looked oily and sooty. He had no choice but to push himself off the bars onto the roadbed. Then he rolled over the rail and out into the open, dragging the kettle behind him. The depot stretched alongside the train a little farther on, and beyond the depot, the dome of a big building rose high in the sky. It was the biggest dome he'd ever seen, ten times as big as the courthouse in Big Lick. The dome had windows and doors all around it, and there was a statue on top. Beyond the town a long ridge ran above the river.

"Hey, you there!" someone called. Jonah wheeled around and saw a man sitting in a wagon holding the reins of a horse, not far away. The man must have seen him get out from under the train. Jonah thought of running, but there was nowhere for him to flee except right into the station platform where people were getting off the train and unloading trunks and barrels. And Angel was still locked inside the boxcar.

"Yes, sir," Jonah said and took off his hat.

"Come here," the man said. Jonah crossed a side track, some gravel and a ditch to where the wagon stood.

"Are you looking for work, boy?" the driver said. He wore clean overalls and a heavy jean jacket and a gray hat.

"Yes, sir, I am," Jonah said. It seemed the safest thing to say.

"Then I have a job for you," the man said. He told Jonah to climb up on the wagon seat beside him. Jonah hesitated, and looked back at the train.

"Don't you need a job?" the man said.

"I got to go back and get something," Jonah said. But just then he saw Angel roll out from under the train. He was going to call out to her, but a man in uniform came running toward her. Then he saw another policeman come dashing along the tracks. They grabbed Angel and held her on either side. Jonah mounted the wagon still holding the kettle and didn't look back at the train. He found he'd been holding his breath. There was nothing he could do for Angel. The wagon driver flicked the reins and the wagon began to move. They followed a road that ran along the edge of town and by the river and north into the hills. The farmer said his name was Driver and he lived about three miles above the town. He needed to clean out his well, but couldn't do it by himself because it was a job that took two men, one to hold the ropes while the other was lowered into the well. He'd come into town to find help.

"I've only got girls," Mr. Driver said. "Girls ain't much help on a place."

The farmer looked at Jonah's shoes and at the kettle he held on his lap. "We don't ask no questions here," he said, as if he knew Jonah was a runaway. "I figure a man's business is his business, if you know what I mean."

"Yes, sir, I know what you mean," Jonah said.

Mr. Driver said he would give Jonah a dollar to help him clean the well, a dollar and his dinner. "And there may be other work besides," he added. "Bet you could use a dollar."

"Yes, sir."

"Bet you could use two," Mr. Driver said and laughed.

They passed barns made of stone and houses built of stone and wood. The barns were large and Jonah saw no haystacks or corn top stacks beside them. All fodder must be kept inside the barns. Each pasture had several cows.

"Something fell in the well," Mr. Driver said. "We reckoned it was just muddy. We didn't know it was there until we tasted something foul in the water."

They came around a bend and Mr. Driver pointed to a stone house with apple trees around it and a great red barn behind it. Some kind of design was painted on the gable of the barn. There might have been a dozen cows in the pasture on the hill behind the barn. A few trees in the woods beyond still had yellow leaves.

"The well ain't so deep," Mr. Driver said. "Still, I can't clean it by myself." He turned into the yard and Jonah saw three young women standing on the porch.

"Don't pay no mind to them girls," Mr. Driver said. "They just never laid eyes on a black boy before."

Smoke leaned from the kitchen chimney and Jonah smelled something good like sausage frying. Jonah had eaten nothing but the cornbread in the kettle since he dug his way out of the jail in Winchester. Mr. Driver unhitched the horse and turned it into the pasture. Then he got three long ropes from the harness room at the barn and two wooden buckets.

"I'll tie the rope around your waist and lower you into the well," Mr. Driver said. "You can fill one bucket, then while I'm raising it up to empty you can fill the other one. Clear out everything you see down there, rocks, sticks, leaves, rats, birds. If you see the devil himself down there, clean him out, too." He laughed and handed Jonah the end of a rope.

"Can I help, Papa?" said one of the girls, who'd put on a coat and run into the backyard.

"You go back inside," Mr. Driver said.

"I can help empty buckets," the girl said. Her blond hair glistened in the sunlight.

"You go back and help Mother fix dinner," Mr. Driver said sharply.

The girl glanced at Jonah and turned back to the house.

Mr. Driver said first they had to empty the well. That meant hauling out bucket after bucket of water until the bottom was exposed enough to see what kind of trash was down there.

"Try not to stir up mud," he said. "If the water muddies up, you can't see what has to be picked up."

The well had a little roof over it, and a windlass and rope, but Jonah and Mr. Driver set the cover aside. The well hole itself had rocks around the rim. As Jonah tied the rope around his waist, Mr. Driver went back to the barn for a lantern.

"You'll need this," he said when he returned and lit the lantern.

The well shaft was about a yard across and Jonah braced himself against the sides with his feet and elbows as Mr. Driver lowered him into the darkness. The lantern gave a weak light as he dropped out of the sunlight. The sides of the well had rocks and moss for a few feet down, and below that the walls were clay. Jonah touched the water after maybe fifteen feet, water so cold it burned. When he glanced up at the opening above he saw Mr. Driver looking down and stars in the sky behind him. It was true what he'd heard before: you *could* see stars from the bottom of a well in the middle of the day.

Mr. Driver lowered two buckets and Jonah filled one and then the other. As a bucket was drawn up, water and bits of dirt dripped on his head. His legs ached in the cold water. Mr. Driver emptied the buckets and lowered them again. As the water at his feet got lower Jonah saw something black and gray. It was the hair of an animal. And then he saw the rings on the tail. It was a rotten raccoon. Jonah wished he had gloves to touch the putrid carcass. He should use tongs or even sticks. But he had nothing but his hands for lifting the foul thing.

"They's a coon," he yelled up the shaft.

"Put it in the bucket," Mr. Driver shouted down.

The furry body was so soft Jonah feared it would tear apart before he could lift it into the pail. And he was afraid that if he picked the thing up by the tail the tail would break off. Holding the lantern in his right hand, he scooped up the awful dripping fur and slid the mess into the bucket. He expected to be assaulted by the stench, but there was little smell. The cold water seemed to have absorbed the stink or killed it. He was glad the light was bad and he could hardly see the horrible muck of fur and bones. The eye sockets were empty.

As Mr. Driver hauled the bucket up, water dripped on him, foul water, stink water. He would have to wash with lye soap to get the filth off him. If Mr. Driver dropped the bucket on his head, it would kill him. He was in the worst place he could be, trapped at the bottom of a well. Mr. Driver could go for the sheriff, or one of his daughters could go. Angel was probably in jail and he couldn't help her. Maybe she wouldn't tell the police about him. He was down below grave level and couldn't get away. All for the promise of a dollar, Jonah had put himself in a dozen kinds of danger. You fool, he whispered, you blockhead idiot.

"What was that?" Mr. Driver shouted down.

"Lower the other bucket," Jonah called up the shaft.

As Jonah bailed out more water he saw other animals on the floor of the well, the skeleton of a bird, what appeared to be a squirrel, a snake about two feet long. He promised himself he would never drink out of a well again. There was a black rubber ball, a hair comb, a broken knife, its blade pocked with rust. The clay at the bottom of the well was many colored, streaked with gray and brown, red and yellow. As the water got lower he could see the inlets where water came out of the ground. Sand and bits of trash danced around the nostrils. And there was a place where bubbles came out of the clay and winked into the air. At the side he saw a bigger hole, like a burrow, and he wondered if a giant snake lived there. When he bent to look into the tunnel he saw the blackness went deeper and deeper . . .

"WAKE UP, BOY."

As Jonah opened his eyes he saw a man bending over him. A girl in a gray coat stood behind the man. His chest was sore and his armpits were sore. He felt like his breath had been cut off.

"He's awake," the girl said.

It was Mr. Driver bending over him. Slowly it came back to him and Jonah felt how cold and wet he was. Clay was stuck to his clothes and to his hands. His head ached. In the sky beyond the girl, black birds whirled and circled and disappeared into the trees.

"You got a lung full of gas," Mr. Driver said. "That's what you did." Mr. Driver said that when he called down the shaft to him and Jonah didn't answer, he knew he'd fainted. So he hauled him right up out of the well and laid him on the ground.

"What gas?" Jonah said.

"Natural gas, my boy."

Jonah remembered the bubbles he'd seen coming out of the water and blinking into the air. The headache crashed behind his forehead and thundered between his ears. The headache pushed behind his eyes like a trapped animal. He tried to sit up.

"Take your time, my lad," Mr. Driver said.

When Jonah raised himself, the headache drained off to the side a little.

"We got the well clean," Mr. Driver said. "By God, we done it."

Jonah shivered. His wet clothes and wet shoes, the cold clay on his arms, made him jerk and shudder. The ache deep in his bones told him how thoroughly he'd been chilled. The chill was a numbness in his blood, in every vein of his arms and legs.

"Come into the barn," Mr. Driver said. "I'm going to start a fire to dry you out." He told the girl, who was named Sylvia, to go to the house and get clean overalls and a shirt, dry socks and long underwear. "You could catch pneumony," he added to Jonah.

The farmer led him into a room at the end of the big barn, a kind of toolshed, with a fireplace and forge, where Mr. Driver did his blacksmith work. The walls were covered with tools hanging from pegs. A lathe and different kinds of saws showed Mr. Driver was also a woodworker. Throwing cobs and kindling in the fireplace, Mr. Driver started a blaze that cast orange light all over the toolroom.

"Your color's coming back," he said. "You'd turned all gray."

When Sylvia returned with the clean clothes, her father told her to bring something from the kitchen for Jonah to eat. "A full stomach will warm you faster than anything else," he said. "Bring hot cider and sausages and some bread."

Mr. Driver left Jonah alone to change by the fireplace. The overalls and shirt were too big for him, but the long underwear fit pretty well. Jonah dropped his wet clothes on the floor of wood shavings and transferred his map to the clean clothes. He rolled up the overall legs and shirt sleeves and slipped on the dry wool socks. The clean clothes smelled of lye soap and mild fragrance, as if they'd been taken out of a cedar chest.

As he warmed up, Jonah's thoughts became clearer. He was in the mountains of Pennsylvania and in the North, closer to Canada. He looked at the wet map and saw it was blurred, but still legible. The next place he had to reach was Elmira. He had to go up the river to Elmira, and then to a place called Auburn. From there he'd find his way to Rochester and then Buffalo. It was already cold in Pennsylvania. Jonah wondered if there would be snow when he got to Elmira.

Mr. Driver returned with a plate heaped with sausages, beans, biscuits, and a tankard of hot cider. "See if this will warm your innards," he said.

Jonah sat on the work bench and sipped hot cider. The drink had spices in it, cinnamon and something else, maybe cloves or nutmeg. As he swallowed, his thoughts began to focus better.

"You cleaned out that old well proper," Mr. Driver said. "Why don't you stay a few days and help with getting firewood?" Mr. Driver pointed to a bench with sacks spread on it. "You can sleep right here," he said.

Mr. Driver told Jonah to eat and rest while he did the milking and feeding. "You catch your breath," he said. As he sipped the cider and shifted closer to the fire, Jonah saw black spots flash in front of his eyes, and a black curtain fluttered in his vision and disappeared. Some of the gas must still be in his brain. He was empty. He needed to fill himself to drive away the gas and the blackness. The sausage was juicy and richer than anything he'd tasted in a long time. He ate it slowly, a morsel at a time, and munched the biscuit bread. As he ate, Jonah recalled that he'd last eaten a meal in the jail in Winchester. He'd fainted in the well from hunger as well as from the natural gas.

The girl named Sylvia appeared at the door of the toolroom. In the firelight she looked younger than she had outside. She hugged the gray coat close with one hand and handed him a dish with the other. On the dish was a little cake covered with nuts and honey.

"Mother said to bring you this," the girl said.

"Thank you, ma'am," Jonah said. He expected the girl to leave, but she stood in the doorway watching him. He stopped eating because she was staring at him.

"Where did you come from?" she said.

"From Harrisburg."

"But you don't live in Harrisburg," she said.

"No, ma'am."

She wore a homespun frock under the gray coat. Her skin was very fair and clear and her cheeks red.

"Where are you going?" Sylvia said.

"I'm looking for work," Jonah said.

Sylvia stepped closer to the fire as though studying him. "Do you curl your hair?" she said.

"No, ma'am," Jonah said.

"Would you like some more cider?" Sylvia said.

"No, thank you, ma'am," Jonah said. He began eating again. He wanted to eat all the beans and sausage and bread while he had a chance.

"If you stay till Sunday you can go to church with us," Sylvia said. "Mother and Papa and my three sisters and me ride to church in the wagon."

"Is the preacher good?" Jonah said.

"Elder Herzog talks to the Lord," Sylvia said and giggled.

"How far is it to the church?"

"It's down the river," Sylvia said. "I could get you some more sausages."

"Thank you, ma'am." She disappeared into the long hallway of the barn.

Jonah looked into the fire and imagined he could see glowing mountains behind the flames and a road leading deep into the mountains, and maybe petering out in the mountains. The road turned this way and that way and appeared to stop.

"These are hot," Sylvia said as she came back through the doorway holding another plate.

"Thank you kindly, ma'am," Jonah said and reached for the plate.

Sylvia stared at his head and extended her hand as if to see if his hair was wet. She touched his head and the front of his ear. It was a touch of curiosity. It seemed something she'd planned to do, when she got close enough. She giggled to show she'd not meant to do anything but act a little silly.

"Sylvia!" Mr. Driver came into the room just in time to see his daughter touch Jonah's hair and cheek. "Go to the house," he ordered. When the girl was gone, Mr. Driver told Jonah that he would have to leave in the morning. He could not afford to have a strange man on the place with four daughters. "You'll have to be on your way," he said.

"Yes, sir," Jonah said. He knew it wouldn't do any good to explain that Sylvia had just been curious, that she'd not meant anything. And he'd done nothing but thank her for the sausage.

"You must be gone by daylight," Mr. Driver said before he left Jonah. He didn't mention the dollar he'd promised for cleaning the well, and Jonah didn't remind him. In South Carolina he would have been beaten and cut and hanged if a white man had seen a white woman touch him that way. If Mr. Driver would let him slip away, even without the dollar, Jonah knew he was lucky indeed.

After he finished the sausage and sweet cake, Jonah set the plates by the fireplace. It was already dark outside, and he put another stick on the fire. The flames lit the room in a pulsing orange glow. Jonah had never seen so many tools as hung on nails and pegs on the walls. There were hammers and augers, drawknives and adzes, axes and hatchets, saws and carpenter's levels. One corner had only farm tools, hoes and rakes, shovels and sickles. A scythe hung from a peg. The blade was honed thin as a whisper, and the metal and handle were oiled.

As Jonah lay on the sacks on the bench, he wondered again if Mr. Driver might inform the sheriff he was a runaway. Even now the farmer might be on his way to find the sheriff. Everything was changed because Mr. Driver had seen Sylvia touch him. As Jonah lay on the sacks and stared at the sharp scythe, he began to think of a new plan.

FIFTEEN

ANGEL

It was in that railroad car that Jonah saw how much he needed me. Before that he just wanted to play with me then go on his way, the first chance he got, like most men do. Men want you and then they want to get away. But when he kicked that other runaway out the door of the boxcar and thought that man might be dead, Jonah was more scared than ever, shaking inside his skin. I reckon he wondered how he was ever going to get up north, and he had killed another colored man.

I sat down beside him and leaned against that cotton bale and put my arm around his shoulder, like he was my boy. And Jonah cried like a baby against my bosom because he was cold and afraid and hungry. And he was lost. He'd never been on a train before and he didn't know where it was going, and he was far from home and his mama and everything he knew, and he had been attacked by another black man. He may have had the big map in his head, and all those words, but he was lost all the same.

Now I knew how smart he was and how bold he was to run away, and he'd shown me the way. But without me he was never going to get to freedom. And without him I sure wasn't ever going to make it either. He was my boy, but he was my man, too, scared in his bones, but wild enough in his blood to run away in the first place.

He cried for a while and then he started feeling the warmth of my bosoms. He rested his head on me and then the man in him began to wake up. I could feel when it happened. One minute he just felt helpless and sorry for himself, and the next minute he felt my nipple under the cloth and he started to work his hands over me, seeing how good it felt, how soft and comforting I was. He touched my skin like he'd never felt soft skin before. He started waking up from his misery and confusion and seeing again how big and pretty I was all over.

The fact is I was waking up, too. I'd been with lots of men and given them a good time, but I had never been with anybody like Jonah. Jonah made me feel a spark of sweetness down in my belly and in my head. I liked the way he touched my shoulders and my hair and rubbed me all over like he was finding a new country. And I reckon I was big as a country.

I rolled over and let him take his way whatever he wanted, and it didn't seem possible he could feel so awful before and then so good he could hardly get his breath. It was a miracle. We had nothing but ourselves on that straw floor. But his mouth was on my ear and neck and in my hair and his hands were all over me, and he didn't say anything he was breathing so fast. And I was thinking: this is my man, and nobody else can cheer him up like me, and nobody can give me jubilee like this boy with his serious face and his head full of words and maps and plans for up north and a free life.

"You are my angel," he said.

And I did feel like an angel. Everything I touched was lit like a cloud at sunset, and everything was sparkling like gold. And I saw apples and plums and ripe pears and blue grapes and sweet potatoes full of butter. And I felt wings inside me, in my back and inside my legs, like I was taking off and flying. I was flying over rivers and meadowlands, and fields of waving rye.

And next thing I knew I was laughing, all covered with sweat and straw stuck to my skin. And we were so out of breath we couldn't say anything. It felt like glory had rushed in and flooded all over me.

Girl, you are in love, I whispered to myself. That is what you are. I had never felt like that before. We didn't have anything and we were lying in a dirty freight car with nothing to eat and hardly knew where we were going. And I felt happy as an angel floating on a cloud.

With love in her breast, a woman can go on. When she has her man, a woman can keep moving. A man gives her purpose, like a family gives her purpose. I saw that was why I followed Jonah, because without him nothing meant much. Without him minutes just stretched out forever and didn't go anywhere. Time has no shape to it unless you are in love. Time doesn't go anywhere but to more time, and then one day you are dead. Love makes the hours firm up into something big. I saw, as I lay there on the floor with Jonah, I had no choice, except to be with this man; I had no other way to go on.

We lay there together on the straw till we got cold again. And when Jonah stood up and looked around, he saw the kettle the other man had. It had potatoes and matches in it, and he found a dirty folded paper. When he unfolded and looked at the paper, he said it was a map, a map to Canada and freedom.

"I thought you had a map in your head," I said. He was so tickled with the dirty paper, it made me laugh. It was like he'd found the secret answer to a puzzle. He acted so sure it made me feel sure, too. He now had both the map in his head and the map on the page. He looked out the door of the car and he walked back and forth between the bales of cotton.

But the train started slowing and he said we must be coming to Hagerstown. And then when the car stopped we heard voices and had to hide behind a bale. And next thing we knew the railroad men closed the boxcar door and latched it and we were locked inside that car. The train started moving again and Jonah looked at the ceiling, but he couldn't reach the door up there. He looked around the wall, but there was no way out. He was scared because we were locked in. And I was scared because he was scared. He tried the big door, but that was no good. We were locked in for sure.

Now I saw him study the problem. Jonah got down on his knees and brushed away the straw and dirt. He rubbed the dirt away and found cracks around a trapdoor down there. And using the stiff handle of the kettle, he opened that big trapdoor. You never heard such a racket as came up from the wheels and tracks underneath, a clacking and humming, rattling and snapping.

"Don't you leave me here," I hollered.

But he took the kettle and the knife and lowered himself through the trapdoor onto the rods below.

After the train stopped I tried to squeeze through the trapdoor in the boxcar. It was so narrow I scraped my hip and shoulder, dropping through onto the filthy rocks and crossties. Soon as I rolled over the rails and pushed myself up, I saw Jonah talking to a man on a wagon. Jonah held the kettle and climbed up on the wagon seat. I was going to holler out to him and I knew he saw me. But just then two policemen in blue coats came running up and grabbed me. One took my left arm and the other the right.

I looked back over my shoulder at Jonah riding away in the wagon with the man in a wide-brim hat. He didn't pay any attention to me. They rode up the road out of town toward the mountains. There was nothing I could do, because the policemen jerked me on down the tracks to the station.

"I ain't done anything," I say to the policemen.

"We saw you get off the train," one said.

"Vagrancy and trespass," the other said.

"And maybe there's reward for catching you," the first one said.

"Nobody is looking for me," I said.

"But we found you," the second policeman said and laughed.

They took me to their little jail made of rocks behind the courthouse, and locked me in a room with a cot and a pee bucket. And they brought me in a bowl of beans like soup beans except it was another kind of beans, and a jug of water.

"We'll be back to see you later," one said, and then they left. I didn't know what they meant to do, but then I reckon I did know. I had a good idea. There was nothing for me to do but eat those beans and sit on the cot and wait, because the windows had bars on them and the door was iron bars locked with a big lock. I sat there studying on where Jonah was. All I knew was I was somewhere in Pennsylvania, as Jonah had said. My head felt like a pig bladder full of mud.

A little later the two policemen did come back. One stood outside the room while the other came into the room and took off his clothes. I saw there was nothing to do but let them have their way. They could beat me up and starve me, maybe kill me if they wanted to. There was nothing I could do to stop them. I pulled my dress up and lay back on the cot.

"Now let me see yours," I said, and he laughed.

After the first policeman had a good time, he put on his clothes and the other came into the cell and stripped. And I had to do it all over again. Except this one wanted me to take my dress all the way off. All the while he was huffing and grunting, I wondered if they were going to keep me there to serve them day after day. Or would they send a message down south to Master Thomas and ask him for a reward?

About the time the second policeman finished up, I heard voices outside. The first policeman dashed outside, and I heard more talking. The second man finished putting on his clothes, and the first ran back inside and hissed, “Get her out of here!”

“Put on your clothes,” the second man said to me. And I slipped on my dress and drawers and put on my shoes. He pushed me out of the cell and they marched me to a little side door.

“Get away from here, you big heifer,” one said, and they shoved me out into the cold where the ground was wet and wind slapped my face. A little side street ran behind the jail, and I followed that into the middle of town. A dog barked behind a store and a train whistle ripped the air. I was wondering which way Jonah and that man in the wagon had gone. I was glad I still had the dollars from Miss Linda’s in my pocket, but when I reached into my dress I found the coins gone. The money must have fallen out when I crawled out from under the train, or when I took the dress off in the jail. There was nothing in my pocket but lint. The policeman must have taken the coins. And the policemen had the pillowcase full of my things.

I walked down the street past stores, and houses with smoke coming out of chimneys. I was lucky to be free, but had no place to lay my head. I walked toward the train station and the river, because I wanted to see the place where Jonah got up on the wagon. That seemed the only place to go. Behind a store somebody had thrown out a loaf of bread. It was dirty and had been pecked by something, but I brushed the ashes and dust off and ate it anyway. A few ashes don't hurt when you're hungry.

Eating the bread, I found the spot where I thought Jonah climbed onto the wagon. I followed the direction the wagon went and came to a road that ran along the bank of the river. The wagon must have gone that way, I guessed, and followed the road to the edge of town where there were no more houses. Now the road split there and one fork went off to the right and one ran on up the river. There was no way to tell which road that man on the wagon had taken. I stopped there shivering and studied which way to go.

The road up the river wound into the dark mountains, and I chose that way. The ridges looked like they'd been painted with blue and purple, and the river thrashed over rocks way down below. I followed the road over hills and past several farms and came to this rock house with a big barn behind it, and orchards all around it. There were several women standing in the yard and the man with the wide-brim hat I'd seen on the wagon before was bending over somebody on the ground. I stepped behind an apple tree and watched and saw it was Jonah.

I started to run into the yard but stopped myself, because I didn't know what had happened or who the people were. Maybe they had killed Jonah, and would kill me, too. I knelt behind a hedge at the side of the yard and watched.

"Wake up," the man said and slapped Jonah's cheek. Jonah was all wet and covered with mud. Buckets and ropes lay around him on the grass, beside the well. "Wake up," the man said. The women stood there like they didn't know what to do. The farmer looked in Jonah's pockets and looked in the kettle that sat on the grass.

"He got some gas," the farmer said. And then Jonah started to rouse himself. He woke up and flung his arm out and kicked his foot. Then he rolled over and tried to get up.

"Take your time, my lad," the farmer said.

Jonah looked like he was still half asleep. There was mud on his face like the clay he had painted himself with when we were on the French Broad River. I breathed out relief, seeing Jonah was trying to get up.

SIXTEEN

JONAH

Jonah knew that if Mr. Driver was planning to inform the sheriff and have him arrested, he might not wait until daylight. As Jonah thought about the danger, he knew it was better to leave before the morning. He added wood to the fire to make the toolroom brighter. Anyone watching might think he was there, as long as there was light in the window. He put on his wet shoes and slipped his wet coat over Mr. Driver's clean clothes. The long underwear was warmer than anything he'd ever worn. Jonah took the scythe down from its pegs. Its snath was curved and tapered, the handles smooth and firm. He saw a whetstone on the bench under the scythe and slipped that into his pocket. He placed the damp map in his shirt pocket, and slung the kettle on its rope over his shoulder.

There were two doors out of the toolroom, and he left through the door into the barn hallway, holding the scythe near the head with the blade down. Horses and cows stirred in the stalls. His eyes were used to the firelight and he felt his way along the corridor to the outside, trying to recall the yard of the farmhouse, where the well was, the chicken house, the road. A window near the front of the house showed a light.

Jonah paused to let his eyes adjust to the dark. There was no starlight, and away from the window he saw only shadows, shades of blackness. He listened for the sounds of someone outside the house. Could men be waiting for him behind the hedge? A horse snorted in the barn. A fox barked way off in the woods. Jonah eased his way past the well and the woodshed along the edge of the yard to the road. It would have been a wonderful joy to sleep all night in a warm place. He'd slept little the night before on the train. Mr. Driver would expect Jonah to sleep soundly after the ordeal in the well, after his large meal.

Once he reached the road Jonah found he could tell where the road ran by looking to the left and then to the right. The brush and trees along the way appeared darker than the road itself. If he glanced out of the corner of his eye, he could tell where the tracks ran ahead. Jonah shivered and pulled his hat down firmly on his forehead.

"Where you going with that thing?" a voice said. Jonah whirled around, sure he'd been caught by Mr. Driver or the sheriff. There was no way to explain why he'd taken a scythe out into the night. He wondered if he could run into the woods before they caught him.

"You gone cut somebody's head off?" the voice said, and a chuckle that followed told him it was Angel.

"How'd you get here?"

"Never you mind how I got here," Angel said. "You run off and left me again."

"Had no choice."

"Let's go," Angel said. "You gone carry that mowing blade?"

The inspiration Jonah had in the barn about the scythe was that if a Negro was seen walking along the road with a mowing blade over his shoulder, almost no one would think he was a runaway. Most would assume he was a farmhand, a hired Negro on the way to another job or coming back from a job. It wouldn't occur to anyone that an escaped slave would sally forth along the road in broad daylight with a scythe and a kettle.

Jonah had laughed to think that the devil was supposed to carry a scythe, or maybe it was Death, the grim reaper. He liked to think that he stalked the road like a figure of death. Boys and bullies might leave him alone because he carried the fine-balanced scythe. One swing of the blade could cut a man's head off, or the head of a mad dog. With the scythe he might fend off a charging bull or a bear. He might not have gotten away with carrying a scythe along a road in the Carolinas or Virginia. But in the North, in Pennsylvania, it just might work.

He explained his plan to Angel. "We walk as far as we can before daylight," he said.

"Wouldn't have thought of that myself," Angel said.

"Don't you ride my ass," Jonah said.

"Bet you want to ride my ass," Angel said. Jonah felt his face get hot.

Before daylight Jonah and Angel climbed into a hay barn and buried themselves in straw. Angel did not come near him, but soon dropped into a fast sleep, like someone worn out, who hadn't slept in days. Jonah lay awake for a while. With the scythe beside him, he felt like a soldier with his sword, or a shepherd with his staff. The scythe gave him a new kind of authority. It was an instrument of power and safety.

Jonah woke around noon and heard voices in the yard in front of the barn. Angel was still asleep, almost covered in hay. He looked out the left window and saw a man and two boys digging into a manure pile with pitchforks and loading the manure onto a wagon. As soon as the wagon was loaded, the man giddyupped the horse and held the reins while the boys followed, carrying the pitchforks. The wagon bumped and creaked out toward a distant field, and soon as they were out of sight, Jonah shook Angel awake. "Time to go, big girl," he said.

Angel rolled over and held out a knife pointed at him. He'd not seen the knife before, a small, thin butcher knife. "What are you doing with that?" he said.

Angel saw it was him standing over her in the gloom of the barn loft. She put the knife away somewhere in her dress. "Surprised you didn't leave me asleep," she said.

"I was afraid you'd follow me."

Jonah hurried down the ladder with his scythe and Angel followed, her weight making the ladder creak. He paused to be sure nobody else was in the barnyard, then walked with the scythe and kettle over his shoulder past the opened manure pile to the road, Angel close beside him.

The road was his safety. It might be wet and muddy, puddled in places and rocky in others, but the road was the most neutral ground. In the road he was not trespassing, but just a Negro carrying a tool to another job somewhere farther on. The road was his refuge, if there was any refuge, until he got to Canada. The road was a kind of story he was reading, or telling, step by step and minute by minute, long as a novel. When he got to the end of the story, he would be in chains, or dead, or free in Canada.

"We'll try to look like people going somewhere to work," Jonah said.

"You look silly carrying that thing," Angel said.

"This thing will throw off suspicion," Jonah said.

"Ain't you got it all figured out," Angel said.

"I figured out some things," Jonah said.

As they walked through the thick welts of mud, Jonah thought how, though Mr. Driver had not given him the dollar, he'd provided the long underwear and clothes, which were worth more than a dollar, and the scythe and whetstone were more valuable still. The value of the mowing blade was proved to him the first time he passed through a village along the river.

It was just a little hamlet dominated by a white steeple. As he crossed a hill he saw another steeple farther on. The street ran near the river, but the churches were set back from the main street, and the graveyard was on still higher ground. That was something Jonah had noticed before. Almost all graveyards were placed on higher ground, often on a hilltop, as if the dead preferred a place with a view. But he remembered the coffins washed out by the flood on the Shenandoah River. As they walked past the store, men noticed them. Jonah took off his hat and wished them a good day. With the scythe on his shoulder, he hoped to look like a Negro laborer going from the south side of the village to somewhere on the north side. He hoped Angel might look like someone on her way to do domestic work. Her fine dress was now dirty and torn in two or three places. No one accosted them. They stepped out of the way of two ladies walking by on a plank sidewalk. They passed a small brick courthouse.

A man wearing a blue uniform stepped out of a gate near the courthouse. He wore a black hat and had a pistol in a holster on his belt. He had a long black mustache and stared at Jonah and Angel approaching. Raw fear washed through Jonah's guts. Whoa now, he whispered to himself. He'd have to act like he knew where he was going.

"Good day, sir," Jonah said to the constable and lifted his hat.

"Humph," the man in the uniform muttered.

Jonah thought of asking him a question, such as where was the Smith farm, or where could a man get a good meal. But he decided the less he said, the better his chances would be. A black man who knew where he was and where he was going wouldn't ask such questions. Two laborers returning from work would not be lost. As Jonah walked on he felt the law man watching him. He expected any second to hear, "Boy, where you going?" A wagon approached and he and Angel stepped aside to let it pass. The constable never called out to him. The scythe was like a shield. No one wanted to bother a Negro carrying a mowing blade. They assumed anyone toting a scythe was going about his own business. And maybe having a woman along was not such a bad idea either.

It took Jonah and Angel four days to reach Williamsport, which was almost halfway to Elmira. The mountains were long and low and dark, and he felt they were traveling through a shadow land. They slept in barns and lived on eggs stolen from henhouses. They stopped at a store and bought matches with a penny he found in the road, and he used the kettle as a cooking pot. Boiled eggs were nourishing, and two or three each would fill them up. Boiled eggs helped keep him warm.

They found the best time to steal eggs was just before daylight, when rooster and hens were already stirring, clucking and crowing. If he moved slowly he could take two or three eggs from the nests and not disturb the hens. He was learning the ways of the road. With the old kettle and a few matches and Angel helping, he could go a long way.

The long running ridges of northern Pennsylvania looked like prison walls. But the road followed the river, and the river found its way through gaps and gorges. The river cut through ridges that ran on like a dull-toothed saw. The river came out of the north and they walked contrary to the river and with the river at the same time.

One day, as Jonah and Angel followed the road through a long stretch of woods beside the river, he saw a dog ahead. They'd encountered many dogs, sometimes in packs, sometimes alone. Out in the woods, away from its owner's house, a dog almost always ran from them.

Sometimes a dog would follow from a distance, looking for a handout or companionship or adventure, before disappearing again. But this gray dog watched them approach and did not run away. It stood in the ruts ahead as though studying them, and its tail didn't wag. Jonah whistled as he got closer, to show he was neither scared nor angry. The dog stepped sideways, but continued to stare, its head lowered and tilted to the side. At first it seemed the dog had something in its mouth, a gray animal or a rag. But as Jonah got closer he saw it was foam hanging from both sides of the mouth. And then he noticed the eyes, a little bloodshot and fevered, glazed over like they couldn't really see anything. When the dog took a step, it staggered as if it was drunk.

"That's a mad dog," Jonah said. Angel screamed and backed away.

Slow there, old boy, Jonah whispered to himself, for he saw the dog was truly mad. Slobber hung like an awful beard from its mouth. But it was too late for him to stop and turn around; he was almost even with the dog. He'd not been suspicious because he thought dogs could only be rabid in hot weather, in dog days, but this dog was clearly mad on this chill autumn day. Jonah thought if he just kept walking with the scythe and kettle and Angel beside him, the dog might not bother him. Its eyes were red as a demon's in a nightmare, but they seemed not to see anything. Maybe they could walk quietly by and the afflicted dog wouldn't even locate them. Its brain might be so fevered it couldn't decide what it heard or saw or smelled. Please, Lord, Jonah prayed for the first time in many days, let me get beyond this dog possessed by evil spirits. He took one step, and then another, and another, and Angel walked beside him, and they were almost on the far side of the dog when the animal lurched their way. Jonah knew it was dangerous to run from any dog. Better to act calm and unafraid and try not to excite the cur.

But as he stepped forward on the ruts, not hastening his pace, the sick dog lunged and almost fell, recovered its balance, and then bit down on his leg. Jonah felt the teeth through the heavy jean cloth of his pants, but the dog was too weak to bite hard. Angel screamed and ran into the woods. Jonah jerked away, tearing the fabric out of the dog's mouth. He hit the dog on the head with the butt end of the scythe, and the animal fell on the ground and began jerking.

Jonah started running, but looked over his shoulder and saw the dog wallowing in a fit in the ruts. He ran even harder, but when he looked back again he found the dog had stumbled to its feet and was following him. The mad dog ran sideways, this way and that way. But it was gaining on him. Jonah ran harder, clutching the scythe and kettle, and just before the dog reached him, he came to a little stream that splashed over rocks across the road.

Jonah dashed through the water to the other side, and then looked back. The dog had stopped at the stream's edge and fallen down, quivering in another fit. He'd heard that mad dogs wouldn't cross water. The dog jerked and groaned beside the stream, foam covering its mouth and nose. Jonah knew he had a duty to kill the mad dog. Otherwise it would attack somebody else. It might bite a child, or an old person. It would bite other dogs and animals and pass on its madness. He set the kettle down at the edge of the road. Stepping back into the water, he approached the writhing animal as it groveled in mud and sand. Raising the scythe as though it was a plunger, he drove the butt end down on the dog's head. He pounded again and again until blood seeped out over the ears and jaws and the dog twitched and lay still.

With the blade Jonah pushed the body into brush at the side of the road, and then he washed the mowing blade in the stream, scouring away any blood or fur or slobber. He'd heard you could catch rabies from the spit of a mad dog. Only after the scythe was clean did Jonah look at his pants. There were tooth marks in the cloth, but the fabric had not been cut through. He pulled his trouser leg up, and the long underwear, and saw the skin on his shin had not been broken. With relief he rubbed his hands with sand and washed them in the cold creek water.

Angel stepped out of the woods and looked at his leg. “You got bit,” she said.

“Didn’t break the skin,” Jonah said.

“You ain’t going to be mad?” Angel said.

“No more than usual,” Jonah said.

As they continued along the muddy, rocky road, Angel took care to step around the puddles. Her dress had mud along the hem, and was torn at the waist. “I’d be clean and wearing silk had I stayed at Miss Linda’s,” she said.

“Then why didn’t you?” Jonah said.

“Boy, you sure are a friendly cuss,” Angel said. But she didn’t say any more. They walked along the wet road up a hill and over. The river was so full, it seemed almost level with the road.

“Didn’t want to be the play toy of white men the rest of my life,” Angel said, after a while. “Of course you wouldn’t understand that.”

“I might,” Jonah said. “And then I might not.”

One afternoon Jonah smelled something sweet as he reached the top of a hill above the river. He was used to the smell of rotten things, mud along the stream bank and fester of sinkholes, manure in barns and hogpens, skunks and dead animals along the road, chicken houses and tan yards. But this was a pleasing smell, familiar, though he couldn’t name the scent. The breeze carried fumes where the road ran high above the river.

The sweet smell made him more awake, for it suggested something good. He looked for a house nearby where somebody might be baking, or boiling something. But all he saw were trees on the hill above him and ahead of him. The thought of boiling reminded him where he'd sniffed that scent before. It was the way Mr. Williams smelled when he'd been drinking brandy. It was the smell of the toddy Mrs. Williams had taken sometimes when she was feeling faint.

"That is the smell of brandy," Angel said.

"Or corn liquor," Jonah said.

"Wouldn't mind a sip of that to keep me warm," Angel said. Her feet were covered with mud. She'd washed her dress in the river, but the hem was dirty again. She shivered because she didn't have a coat. If they kept going north she'd have to find a coat somewhere, before they went much farther.

Jonah wondered if there was a liquor still ahead. There could be moonshiners in the mountains of Pennsylvania same as in the mountains of South Carolina. But he didn't see any smoke or smell any smoke, and he thought the scent was sweeter and more subtle than the smell of corn liquor. There was a mustiness in the aroma of fruit on the breeze. And then he saw the apple trees on the hillside ahead of him, stretching evenly in rows all the way to the top of the hill. They turned off the road and climbed through brush to reach the orchard. An apple would taste mighty good, and maybe he could gather a few to carry with him in the kettle.

But when they reached the apple trees, Jonah saw the orchard had already been picked. It was late October and the harvest was over, and most of the limbs were bare. The weeds around the trees had been mashed down by the pickers. Some trees had one or two apples high on limbs where they would be hard to reach. There were a few red apples and pink apples, streaked apples and yellow apples. There were apples so dark they looked purple. He saw one apple still green. He would have to climb a tree to reach each one.

Jonah stepped into the orchard looking for a tree easy to climb, but his foot stumbled on something in the grass, and when he stepped sideways to catch his balance, his other foot crushed something that crunched. The grass and weeds were full of apples, apples that had fallen or apples rejected by the pickers. Some apples were so rotten they looked boiled and ready to melt to pulp. That was where the wonderful smell came from, fruit touched by frost and rotting or fermenting on the ground. The aroma lifted through the weeds and grass and filled the breeze.

But some of the fallen fruit was not rotten, or not completely rotten. A few apples had one good side and others had one good spot. He picked up an apple and wiped the good side on his sleeve and took a bite. The skin had a kind of wax on it, but his teeth cut into the cold and juicy flesh. He ate the good part and threw the rest away and picked up another. After rubbing away dirt and grit on the good section, polishing the shiny skin, he took a bite. Sweet as only a perfectly ripe apple can be, the taste of the second apple was slightly different from the first.

Angel got down on her knees and wiped an apple on her dress before taking a bite. She threw the rotten part away and grabbed another. "Wish it was brandy," she said, and searched in the grass for another apple with a sound spot.

Jonah picked up an apple and rubbed the dirt off and bit into the foamy meat. This one tasted slightly different also. Apples even from the same tree all tasted a little different. He'd never noticed that before. He looked for apples that were mostly sound, and put them in his pockets and in the kettle. Because of the recent rains, the fruit needed to be brushed off. He found a yellow apple tree, but those apples had rotted faster than the red ones. He located only one sound yellow apple to put in with the others.

As he reached into the grass looking for more apples, something pricked his finger. At first he thought he'd touched a briar, but then a buzzing in the grass told him he'd been stung, and sure enough he saw a yellow jacket blur away from the apple he'd grasped. The yellow jacket flew slow in the cold air, but its stinger had worked. After a few seconds the poison from the sting began to take effect, and his finger started to ache. "You put some tobacco juice on that," Angel said.

"Have you seen me with any tobacco?"

"Then squeeze ragweed juice on the sting," Angel said.

Jonah looked around for ragweed. But frost had already singed the weeds in the orchard, turning them into black rags. Only the grass was still green, but he didn't reckon the juice of grass would soothe the yellow jacket sting.

He wished he had a sack to carry more apples, though a sack would weigh him down on the road. He needed to keep moving if he was to reach Canada before winter made the roads impassable. But something about the smell of the apples made him sleepy. It was the smell of cellars and barn lofts, the smell of winter and Christmas.

"Here, I found one by the fence," Angel called. She held up a half-alive ragweed and brought it to him. The leaves were so stiff there was little juice in them.

"Squeeze hard," Angel said. More dust than juice rubbed off the ragweed, but it seemed to soothe the sting a little. Jonah lay back in the grass to rest. Clouds floated above, and as he watched clouds moving at different speeds at different heights, he thought how things just seemed to happen by chance. How many times had he told himself he had to be tough as the world was tough, just to survive. But no matter how tough you were, things still seemed to just happen as they would happen, with little or no connection to how tough he was or how hard he tried. Take these apples. He'd not been looking for apples; he'd not even thought of apples, yet here he was with a kettle full of apples to carry on the road.

Apples had grown in the garden of Eden. Apples had grown on the

Tree of the Knowledge of Good and Evil. An apple was not only a thing of beauty and pleasure, but a sign of temptation and guilt in a way too complicated for him to figure out. An apple was the sign of the knowledge of good and evil. Maybe that's why apples were so pungent and memorable. They grew on the heat of the sun and sap from the roots full of minerals from the soil. They grew on rain and the salts of time. It was the black soil of rottenness that gave apples their richness.

Jonah shook his hand to ease the throb in his finger. His finger would burn until the pain had been diluted. He put his finger in his mouth and sucked. "Want me to kiss it?" Angel said and laughed. Jonah didn't answer. "That's what my mama used to do; she kissed a hurt to make it feel better."

Jonah lay back in the grass and looked at the sky above the trees. He wondered why apples were always planted on hillsides or even on hilltops. There was some explanation he'd heard but had forgotten. Obviously the fruit trees needed to grow where they had plenty of sun. And they needed to grow where they could stay cold in winter so the sap didn't rise too early and the blooms get killed by frost. That was why apples didn't grow well in cotton country, where the winter was too mild.

But on a slope the cold air drained away into the valley on a frosty night in spring and the blooms didn't get killed in April. It was a complicated system, for trees on a hill got more cold wind and were liable to be blown over in a storm. And high on a hill they also got loaded with more ice when an ice storm hit.

Jonah sat in the grass and felt a little drunk from the poison of the sting, and from the smell of all the frost-fermented apples on the ground. The sunlight had an edge to it, and the breeze was sharper. And then he smelled smoke in the updraft. He raised himself up on his elbows and sniffed, wondering if there was a moonshine still on the hill after all. But mixed with the smoke was another smell, not the scent of ferment but something else, something even sweeter.

"What is that burning?" Angel said.

"Smells like blood," Jonah said.

"Smells like something is scalded," Angel said.

If there was smoke nearby, there were people also. They had to move on. Jonah stood up. The pockets of his overalls were filled with apples of all colors, and he gathered a few more red ones to pack in the pockets of his coat. The scent of smoke seemed to be wafting around the hill. They would get back to the road and keep walking. The road was their only place of safety. Jonah picked up the scythe and laid it across his right shoulder, and grasped the kettle with his left hand. The apples were heavy, but he and Angel could eat them in two or three days as they marched along.

"I'll carry that," Angel said and took the kettle from his hand. She was shivering a little from the cold. Jonah knew they'd have to find a coat for her soon.

"You want to eat them all yourself," Jonah said.

"I'm glad you show your thanks," Angel said.

They climbed down the bank of weeds at the edge of the orchard and dropped into the road.

It was only then that Jonah saw the farmhouse around a bend in the road. He'd missed it before because he'd gone into the orchard too far up the hill. The house was made of stone, and an old woman stood in the yard by a fire, stirring a black iron pot. The smoke drifting up the hill smelled of spices. The woman wore a heavy wool bonnet pulled down on her forehead and on both sides of her face. "Howdy," he called to her.

"Howdy to you," the woman said. Jonah figured they'd best keep walking like they were just going about their business. The pockets of his coat bulged and he was afraid apples would start falling out. Apples were stacked in the kettle.

"Who did you buy them apples from?" the old woman called.

"I got them down the road," Jonah said. The woman must have seen them come out of the orchard. He couldn't pretend they'd gotten the apples at some place far away. It was wise to stay on the road and keep going. But if the woman thought they'd been stealing apples, she might send somebody after them. She might call a sheriff. He'd better act friendly, like he had nothing to hide or be afraid of. He stepped into the yard to pretend he was just a friendly neighbor passing by.

The steam from the pot the woman was stirring was the source of the nice aroma. It smelled of cloves and cinnamon and maybe other spices, too. The stuff she stirred was brown and bubbling; he realized that it was apple butter.

"That smells mighty good, ma'am," Jonah said.

"Apples is dear this year," the woman said. "Frost killed half the crop in May." She looked at Jonah's pockets and the kettle Angel held. "Looks like you got about a peck there."

"I just picked them up on the ground among the rotten ones," Jonah said. His face got hot. He wished he'd kept walking.

"Apple trees take lots of work," the woman said. "Pruning and dusting, fertilizing and mowing."

"Yes, ma'am, farming is hard work."

"What will you be doing with that scythe?" the woman said.

"Going up the road a ways to cut some cornstalks."

Jonah didn't see the man until he stepped around beside him from the back. The man wore a wide-brimmed hat and a leather apron, like he'd been working as a blacksmith. He was younger than the woman, young enough to be her son.

"Good day," Jonah said. He tipped his hat with his left hand because he was holding the scythe handle with the right.

"These people have been picking apples," the woman said. She dipped a wooden spoon in the apple butter and blew on the contents.

"So I see," the man said.

"We picked them off the ground," Jonah said.

The smoke from the fire and steam from the pot made Jonah's face sweat. He wanted to leave, but he dared not just break away and start up the road. He would have offered to pay for the apples, but all he had was a penny he'd found in the road. They might get mad if he offered them only a penny.

"That's a nice blade you've got there," the man said.

"Yes sir, I'm going to cut some cornstalks for a neighbor."

"It could use some sharpening," the man said.

"I've got a whet rock right here in my pocket," Jonah said.

"Oliver makes things in his shop," the woman said. "He can make anything out of metal, hoes and rakes, pokers and hinges."

"I even made some irons once," Oliver said and spat on the grass.

"What kind of irons?" Jonah said.

"Irons to put on a runaway slave," Oliver said. "They caught him up here near Williamsport and held him in jail for a month until his owner arrived from Virginia. They needed irons to hold his hands and feet for the trip back, and I made them. I smoothed the irons and rounded all the edges so they wouldn't hurt his ankles and wrists."

"Oliver can make locks, too," the woman said. "Not just anybody can make a lock."

"Want to see the lock I made for the basement?" Oliver said.

"I best be on my way," Jonah said. "I need to cut the cornstalks afore dark."

"Won't take but a second to see the lock," Oliver said.

"Whose cornstalks are you going to cut?" the woman said.

Jonah pretended he didn't hear her. It was too risky to make up a name. "Reckon I could have a quick look," he said. "Ma'am," he said to the old woman, bowing slightly.

"We best be on our way," Angel said.

"Won't take but a minute," Oliver said.

Jonah followed Oliver around a clothesline hung with sheets to get to the back of the house. The backyard was not as neat as the front yard. Tools were scattered around a wheelbarrow, and farm implements littered the ground between the house and the woodpile. The house was bigger than it appeared from the front, with a wing that reached back toward the barn.

"I heard there was a runaway slave spotted in Harrisburg," Oliver said and looked him in the eye.

"A runaway, sir?"

"Actually two runaway slaves."

"Ain't heard nothing about that," Jonah said.

"They say they're dangerous," Oliver said.

At the end of the house, stone steps descended to the basement. A heavy door with a big lock was visible at the bottom of the steps. "This is where we keep cider and store apples over winter," Oliver said. "Also pertaters and other roots."

"I best be on my way," Jonah said.

"What's the hurry, my friend?" Oliver said and slapped Jonah on the shoulder. "Maybe you'd like some pertaters, or a jug of cider to go with the apples."

"Got about all I can carry," Jonah said.

"I could find you a basket or a sack," Oliver said. "Here, let me show you the lock." He put his hand on Jonah's back and urged him toward the steps.

"You can leave your things here beside the steps." He took the scythe from Jonah and set it on the grass. Jonah felt naked without the scythe.

At the bottom of the steps, Oliver drew a large key from his pocket and inserted it in the lock and turned until there was a click. The padlock was big as an iron purse. The door swung open and Jonah saw the floor of the basement was paved with rocks swept clean as the floor of a parlor. The air smelled of apples and cool earth.

"Go ahead and I'll light the lantern," Oliver said. He pushed Jonah forward so hard he fell on the stone floor. Before he could stagger to his feet, the door closed behind him and the lock snapped in place. The basement had no window and was dark as midnight except for a little sliver of light around the edges of the door.

"Hey," Jonah called, "what are you doing?" He thought he could feel a cobweb on his neck. Several apples had fallen out of his pockets and he stumbled on them beside the door.

"I have caught myself a thief," Oliver called on the other side.

"Ain't no thief," Jonah yelled. "I can pay."

"And maybe I've caught something bigger," Oliver said and laughed.

"I be on my way to work," Jonah said. He didn't want to sound like he was pleading.

"What's your name, boy?" Oliver called.

"I be named Jeter," Jonah answered, "Jeter Jenkins."

"Have yourself an apple, Jeter, and think about property, stolen property."

"Open the door," Jonah called.

"I'd better go forge some manacles," Oliver called and laughed again. "You'll need some irons for the journey back to Virginia. I bet your master will pay well."

With the strong wooden door and the heavy lock between him and the steps, Jonah knew it was hopeless. He'd been stupid, and he'd been caught in the most obvious kind of trap. A few ripe apples, his own hunger and greed, had landed him in this dungeon. It wouldn't do him any good to call out to Oliver, to beg or plead or threaten. If Oliver suspected there was a reward for him, he could hold him in the basement until a telegram or letter brought Mr. Williams. Jonah decided he'd say nothing else. He sat down on the swept floor of the basement. The stones were cold, and he got up on his knees to think. The basement was damp and chilly. He looked at the wires of light around the sides of the door.

Jonah knew that at the first sign of danger Angel would have run into the woods. She might have dropped the kettle to run faster. She would run as far away as she could, and there would be nobody to help him escape from the cellar.

"Are you cold, Jeter?" Oliver called. "It'll be warm when you get back down south."

Jonah found tears in his eyes. He'd come all the way from South Carolina and survived a flood and Mr. Wells's cruelty, the jail in Winchester, only to be trapped in the dumbest way possible. He would not answer the smirking Oliver.

"If you get hungry have an apple," Oliver called. "Or a pertater if you want one."

Jonah wiped his eyes and listened. He thought he heard a mouse, or maybe a bat, rustling in the basement. It stirred among leaves or shucks or papers. He shivered, and then he heard another voice outside. It was the old woman talking to Oliver. It was hard to tell what they were saying. Jonah placed his ear against the wood.

"That's enough of that," the old woman said. "Now open the door."

"But Ma," Oliver said.

"But nothing," the old woman said. "The girl has run away. Where is that key?"

"I just wanted to show him the lock," Oliver said. "And he stole the apples. What's the hurry?"

"The hurry is because I say so."

Jonah didn't hear anything else. He thought they'd gone away. Maybe they'd decided to leave him locked in the cellar. Maybe Oliver had persuaded the old woman he was worth reward money. Jonah wiped his eyes again.

There were footsteps outside and he heard the key scratch in the lock. He stepped back from the door as it swung inward. He wondered if he should lunge out and make a run for it. He had nothing to hit Oliver over the head with.

"Come on, old boy," Oliver said. "Time to get out of there."

"I ain't done nothing," Jonah said.

"Everybody has done something," Oliver said and laughed.

Jonah blinked as he climbed the steps. The scythe was still lying on the ground where he'd laid it.

"Didn't mean no harm; just funning you," Oliver said. The old woman stood by the clothesline watching Jonah. "Be on your way," she said. "The girl run off into the woods."

"Yes, ma'am," Jonah said and picked up the scythe. "I be going now."

"You watch out, boy," Oliver said.

Jonah turned away and started around the corner of the house toward the road. Two Plymouth Rock hens pecked in the grass by the woodpile and he walked around them. When he reached the muddy road, he turned north. He knew Angel was watching him and would join him when he got out of sight of the house. Sure enough, as soon as he rounded the first bend, she stepped out of the trees, still holding the kettle full of apples.

"Next time you won't be so sociable," she said.

Jonah saw no point in answering her. His knees were weak from the scare, and he concentrated on avoiding puddles and the worst ruts.

ONE NIGHT A FEW days later Jonah and Angel couldn't find a barn, but they did come upon a haystack at the edge of a pasture. The farmer had stacked his hay close to where his cattle grazed. It was almost dark, but Jonah thought he could see a feeding trough and white block of salt just inside the fence. "We'll have to sleep in that," he said.

"You sure this ain't a snake nest?" Angel said.

"I'm not sure of anything," Jonah said. Angel dropped into the hay and he covered her up with handfuls of straw. Tired and full of boiled eggs cooked beside the river, he left the scythe and whetstone on the ground, parted an opening into the hay, and with his coat wrapped tightly around him slipped inside. The hay was spicy and pleasant as the smell of a warm autumn day.

Jonah must have slept soundly, for when he opened his eyes, gray light came through the hay. It was a special gray light, as if something was glowing close by. He stirred the hay and wet crumbs fell on his face and neck. He wondered if it had rained during the night. When he pushed the straw aside, more crumbs shook in his eyes. As he lifted himself from the hay, he saw everything was white. The haystack was covered with snow, and the field and pasture. Snow stood two or three inches high on the fence rails. The trees on the mountainside were covered with white.

Jonah could smell the snow. It was not a smell he could describe, almost the absence of smell, as if the snow had swept all the dirt and dust and smells from the air. It was the scent of cleanness and freshness. The air had been brushed pure.

"Get up!" he shouted to Angel.

When she pushed the hay aside and looked out, snow fell on her face. "Oh," she yelled, like somebody had dashed cold water on her. "What happened?" she said.

"It has snowed."

"I can see that. I ain't blind."

Jonah swept the hay off his coat and shook the snow off the scythe and located the whetstone under three inches of snow. His hands got wet and cold. He needed gloves, if he was going to be traveling in snow country. With the scythe on his shoulder and the stone in his pocket, he handed the kettle to Angel.

"Maybe the apples are froze," Angel said, her teeth chattering.

"Not likely," Jonah said. They headed back to the road. Every step left a track in the snow that anyone could follow wherever they went. The trackers wouldn't need dogs. If you slipped into a henhouse and took two or three eggs, the farmer could see you'd been there.

Slow down, old boy, Jonah said under his breath. Whoa there now, for sure. The road ran along the edge of the pasture and then over a hill. A wagon had already passed on the road, leaving horse tracks and wheel slices in the snow. Mud puddles stained the whiteness. Jonah's shoes slipped on the steep places and he had to find footholds on the uneven road. Angel walked in her broken shoes in the snow, staining the white cover.

"I've got to find some new shoes and a coat," Angel said.

"How do you propose to do that?" Jonah said.

"Have to think about it," Angel said. "You think about it; you're so smart."

As they crossed the hill Jonah could smell smoke drifting through the trees. It was not just smoke, but something else as well, steam or damp fumes. They descended the hill into the smell. Before they reached the floor of the valley, he knew where the steam was coming from. Two men on hands and knees were scraping hogs beside a pot of boiling water. Smoke from the fire under the pot and steam from the water fogged the barnyard and drifted up the valley. A third man splashed smoking water on the two dead hogs as the other men scraped hair off the carcasses with butcher knives. Smell of scorched hair and blistered skin reached Jonah on the road. Along with the smell of blood and manure, that was the stink of hog killing.

Though he'd never had to do it himself, Jonah hated the smell and sight of hog killing. He knew the ritual well. After the bodies were scraped they'd be hung up and gutted. It took an axe or a saw to break through the breastbone. The entrails and lungs and heart would have to be carried away and buried. Men always got bloody and dirty, tearing out entrails, cutting off the big, fat head, and cleaning out the brains for frying with eggs and onions. Just the smell of hog blood and fat rendering always made him feel a little sick at his stomach. Much as he liked fresh tenderloin and ribs, he dreaded the bloody work, the stink of scalded hair and skin.

Jonah hoped the men butchering hogs wouldn't call out to him or Angel. Much as he would like some fresh meat, he wanted to avoid the bloody mess. There was something almost human about hogs, or something almost hoglike about humans. Their pale skin reminded him of white folks. He had watched hogs squeal when hit over the head, seen them die in mud and manure.

As Jonah and Angel got closer to the barn, the man who dipped the scalding water and splashed it on the carcasses looked toward them. Jonah took off his hat and bowed slightly, and kept on walking. The bucket carrier nodded in his direction and dipped more water from the steaming barrel. Jonah knew it looked odd for a Negro to be walking along the road in these snowy hills, and it looked even stranger for him to be carrying a scythe while the ground was covered with snow. There were not many jobs done with a mowing blade in the snow. Perhaps he could claim to be carrying the blade back to the owner from whom he'd borrowed it.

As Jonah and Angel got even with the barn, the two men scraping hides looked up at them. They stopped work and watched him walk past. "Howdy do?" Jonah said and lifted his hat again. If he'd been in South Carolina one of the men would have yelled, "Where you going, boy?" They would have ragged him and inspected the scythe and asked if he'd stolen it. They would have asked who his owner was.

Jonah expected one of the hog killers to call out to them and ask if he wanted to work. He expected them to ask where they were going, and what he was doing with the mowing blade. He was certain they'd ask who he and Angel belonged to. He'd walked past the barn and was almost even with the farmhouse when he realized they were not going to yell at him or accost him. The men scraping and scalding hogs were going to let him go about his business as they went about their own business. They seemed to have no interest in stopping him. It was too good to be true. He expected every second to be called back and told to do something hard and dirty. He walked farther, almost past the house, and no shout came. The silence of the men was almost as scary as a shout would have been. Jonah wondered if they were quiet because they were afraid of him, afraid of a runaway black man with a mowing blade over his shoulder and a whetstone in his pocket. Afraid of a black man and black woman together? Would they wait until they were out of sight and then run to get a sheriff? Would they follow them and seize them while they slept?

Jonah had walked slow as he approached and passed the men, to show he was in no hurry, that he was not afraid. He'd tried to act as if they were casually going about their own concerns. But soon as they were out of sight of the hog killers he picked up his pace. Better to put as much distance as they could between themselves and the men with sharp butcher knives. The road was slick with snow and muddy water stained through from the puddles. He tried to pick his way through the cleanest, driest places.

"I need some shoes," Angel said.

"We'll find you some shoes," Jonah said.

"I'll believe that when I see it," Angel said.

As THEY MADE THEIR way on the uneven roads, Jonah studied the problem of finding shoes and a warm coat for Angel. Every day it seemed a little colder. The first snow had melted, but there would be more snow any day. Clothes could be taken from clotheslines, but nobody would hang a coat on a clothesline. And Angel would need an especially large coat, big enough to fit over her wide shoulders and belly. A country store would be the most likely place to find both shoes and coat, but every store they passed was in a little crossroads village, with barking dogs and people walking about.

"Maybe we can find a blanket you can wrap around your shoulders," Jonah said.

"Blanket won't do my feet any good," Angel said.

The next day they came to a large stone farmhouse just as a family there was getting into a buggy, all dressed up like they were going to church. Jonah realized it must be Sunday morning. As the buggy pulled out into the road and passed them, Jonah got an idea.

"Maybe they left their house unlocked," he whispered to Angel.

"And maybe they left somebody at home," Angel said.

Soon as the buggy was out of sight, Jonah turned back into the yard and walked to the back door. The ceiling of the porch was hung with dried beans and onions and peppers. He knocked on the door and stepped back, waiting for a cook or some other servant to open it. A dog came around the corner of the house and growled at him. Jonah whistled and held out his hand. The dog barked and backed away.

"That dog ain't too friendly," Angel said. Chickens cackled in the henhouse behind the woodshed. No one came to the door and Jonah knocked again. When no one appeared, Jonah tried the door and found it unlocked. He stepped into the kitchen and Angel followed him. The house smelled of fresh baked bread and roast beef. The Sunday dinner had already been cooked and set on the table with cloths over the dishes, waiting for the family to return. Jonah and Angel each grabbed a roll.

Beside the door several raincoats hung on pegs, and beneath the coats sat rubber boots and galoshes. If nothing else, they could take some rubber boots. The dog whined outside the door and barked. Most likely the clothes were in bedrooms upstairs. Before looking for the stairs, Jonah tore a piece of beef off the roast on the table and crammed it in his mouth. The stairway was just down the hall, and Jonah mounted the carpet-covered steps, followed by Angel. The first room they looked in must have been a child's room, for a rocking horse sat in the corner.

The next room must have been the master bedroom, for women's shoes lined the floor on one side of the bed, and men's shoes stood in a row on the other. Jonah looked in the closet for a coat while Angel dropped to the floor and started trying on the shoes.

"That woman took her good boots," Angel said. But there was another pair of boots, a little worn, made of fine leather with lots of hooks and eyelets. It took some effort for Angel to pull the boots over her dirty feet, but she finally got the shoes on.

"The boots are too little," Jonah said.

"No, they're just the right size," Angel said.

"Then your feet are too big," Jonah said.

"No, my feet are just right," Angel said, "for a woman my size."

There was no heavy coat in the woman's closet. "We'll have to take a blanket," Jonah said.

As soon as she had laced the boots, Angel looked in the man's closet, and took out a heavy black wool coat. "Look here," she said.

"That's a man's coat," Jonah said.

"A warm coat is a warm coat," Angel said and slipped the coat on. It was not a bad fit.

It was at that moment they heard a whimper and a whine in a room down the hall. Both Jonah and Angel froze and listened, then tiptoed to the bedroom door and looked down the hall. The whine came again. Jonah looked at the top of the stairs. To get to the steps, they had to walk past the room where the sound came from. Something metallic rattled, like a chain or coins in a box.

Jonah and Angel stood in the hallway, and Jonah heard the blood thundering behind his ears. The rasp of a chain ran over the floor.

"Let's run," Jonah whispered. He and Angel started toward the stairs, but just as they reached the first step, the bedroom door flung open and a woman with wild hair and scabs on her face glared out. She whimpered and moaned and flung her arms, which were held by chains. Jonah was so startled he just stood there staring at the chained woman for a second, then dashed down the stairs.

Jonah and Angel didn't stop running until they were out the back door and across the yard, with the dog barking and nipping at their heels. When they reached the road they grabbed the scythe and kettle and began walking.

"That woman is a ghost," Angel said, all out of breath.

"That was no ghost," Jonah said, short of breath also. "She was a lunatic." It took them both several minutes before they could breathe normally. When they got out of sight of the house, they stopped to rest. The black overcoat fit Angel pretty well, and the laced-up boots protected her feet from the rocks and mud.

"I wanted to get some more of that beef before I left," Jonah said.

"Don't want to eat anything else from that house," Angel said.

Even though it was cold, and even though the road was rough along the river through the mountains of Pennsylvania, Jonah and Angel were able to travel ten or fifteen miles each day. The mowing blade on his shoulder seemed to give him a special immunity that he didn't entirely understand. With the scythe he seemed to have a citizen's rights. They walked all day and camped by fires in the woods at night. He caught trout in the river and Angel took eggs from henhouses in the hours before dawn. He bought cheese and crackers from a country store with some pennies he found in a church collection box. They slept in their coats on beds of pine boughs with bare feet to their fires. He didn't try to touch Angel again, but some nights she would push up against him and let him warm himself between her breasts and legs. At those times in the dark, she seemed like a different person from the snapping, sarcastic woman who walked beside him in the daylight.

Every day they followed the river north, through dark mountains and snowy fields. The mountains were long-running and steep as walls. He was grateful he didn't have to climb over them. The road always ran near the Susquehanna River. They passed through the towns of Wilkes-Barre and Eatonville. They came to Terrytown and Towanda, and reached the village of Sayre, where the river turned right, toward the northeast. Elmira was a few miles to the west, on the Chemung River.

Jonah's map was so wrinkled and blurred, he could hardly read it. But he'd memorized the names and the directions on it. He knew the names of Elmira and Auburn, Rochester and Buffalo. If they could get to Auburn, maybe they could find what they were looking for. Maybe someone there could help them get to Canada. Instead of breaking away from the river to reach Elmira, he decided to follow the Susquehanna northeast.

Jonah and Angel stopped at a little schoolhouse in a village called Tioga Center. They reached the school at recess when children were playing tag and hide-and-seek, and running around the yard. The children got quiet as they approached, and the teacher came to the doorway to see what caused the sudden quietness. The teacher had a red face and wore an overcoat and gloves with no fingers.

"Good day, sir," Jonah said and took off his hat.

The teacher nodded to him and to Angel.

"What be the best way to get to Auburn?" Jonah said.

The teacher looked at Jonah and the mowing blade as if he knew exactly why a black man wanted to go to Auburn. Auburn was a well-known waystation on the Underground Railroad. Many citizens in Auburn helped runaway slaves reach Rochester and Buffalo and then Canada.

"You're a long way from Auburn," the teacher said.

"I was afraid of that," Jonah said and bowed his head. The children gathered round to hear the conversation.

"If I was you, I'd go to Owego and catch the train to Ithaca," the teacher said. "From Ithaca it's not so far to Auburn."

"Thank you, sir," Jonah said. "Where is Owego?"

"Just a few more miles up the river," the teacher said. He told Jonah he was now in New York State. They'd traveled all the way across the mountains of Pennsylvania.

As Jonah and Angel left the schoolyard, children walked beside them and followed them to the road.

"Where are you going with that blade?" a boy said.

"Going to cut down some cornstalks," Jonah said.

"Too cold to cut down cornstalks," the boy said.

"Not where I'm going," Jonah said.

At the end of the schoolyard, the children stopped and Jonah and Angel kept walking.

"Ain't never seen a nigger before," the boy called after them. Jonah didn't look back.

They slept that night in a hay barn on a hillside, boiled four eggs in the kettle the next morning, and then started up the river again.

At the village of Owego Jonah and Angel found that the main street ran along the north bank of the river. It was a prosperous village with many brick buildings and a courthouse for Tioga County. The railroad station was right on the bank of the Susquehanna. A crane swung cargo from railroad cars onto a platform, and from the platform barrels and boxes, crates and bales, were loaded onto barges in the river. Goods were also being unloaded from boats and barges and stacked in train cars in the railyard. Owego was the busiest place Jonah had seen since Harrisburg. The streets were filled with people, and dozens of men worked in the freightyard and on the barges. Bales of wool were unloaded from one of the boats and winched up to the platform to be packed in a railroad car. Cattle were unloaded from one car, and sheep from another.

"I ain't going to ride on any more trains," Angel said, as they watched freight loaded onto the cars.

"Then how will you get to Ithaca?"

"Maybe I don't want to go to Ithaca."

"How will you get to Canada?"

"Find my own way, I reckon," Angel said.

Jonah could never predict when Angel would get stubborn and arbitrary. She liked to provoke him at the most unexpected times. It angered him that she seemed reluctant to continue, now that they were getting close to their goal. Before he'd hoped to escape from her; now he found he depended on her.

"What do you plan to do?"

"I ain't going on a train and freeze to death," Angel snapped. Jonah turned away from her. He walked away from the waterfront without looking back. He thought she might follow him, but she didn't.

Jonah knew he couldn't get on the train while it was stopped and being loaded. He followed a street that ran along the tracks until he came to the edge of the little town. Then he stepped on the tracks themselves and walked on the ties for maybe a mile, as the rails ascended a grade. Since the train would have to labor up the long hill, he figured that was the place to get on. Twice he looked behind to see if Angel was following him: she wasn't. He stepped off the tracks and slipped behind some sumac bushes at the edge of a field, then sat down on a log that was free of snow and laid his scythe and the kettle in the weeds beside him.

Jonah had to wait a while before he heard the *huff huff huff* of the locomotive coming from the town of Owego. The train had to gather speed as it left the freightyard, and it had to struggle up the grade. It was a small engine and it moved slowly. Jonah hunkered in the brush as the engine puffed past. The engineer leaned out the window looking ahead. The train whistle hooted and startled Jonah. He crouched lower until a passenger car went by and then an open car loaded with coal.

A boxcar passed, but its door was closed. Jonah picked up his scythe in one hand and the kettle in the other and ran to the edge of the rails. The train was rolling slowly, but every car appeared to be locked. He looked down the track and saw there were only four more cars, but they were open beds. He turned and ran after the first boxcar. It was easy to catch, but he wondered how he was going to grab onto the ladder without dropping the scythe and the kettle. He didn't want to lose either, but he had to seize a rung of the ladder with both hands. He threw both scythe and kettle aside and heard them clatter on gravel as he grabbed the rung on the boxcar.

Jonah rode between the cars as the train climbed higher into the hills and then entered a long valley. A light snow glittered on the fields and pastures, and big red barns rose noble as churches from the valley floor, mile after mile. Jonah shivered in the breeze but found if he clung close to the boxcar out of the wind he was not quite so cold. The sunlight warmed him, and when he bowed his head, he breathed less smoke and ash. It would do him no good to climb on top of the car, and there seemed no way to get inside it.

The train kept going up until it appeared to be on top of the world. The tracks crossed the wide valley and climbed around a long, low ridge and ran over rolling highlands. The hills were low and smooth and stretched out for miles, unlike any country Jonah had ever seen. He didn't know that the glacier had once rubbed these hills smooth and rounded them off, but he understood this was a different kind of landscape. Little farms were tucked in coves, and bigger farms stood out boldly on the open plateaus. Jonah felt he'd almost reached the true North. The land seemed to touch the sky in every direction.

As the train rattled and banged along, Jonah saw that each little town they passed had a white church and a red schoolhouse, a store and a village meeting hall. A pump and water trough stood in the middle of each village. Most houses were white and looked recently painted and clean. Jonah held on to the ladder and his teeth chattered, but he was thrilled to be in such high country. After about an hour Jonah was numb with cold. The train began to labor up an even higher hill, and it felt as though the rails ahead must go right off the ground into the sky. Did the ground get higher the farther north you went? Everyone described the North as "up" north. Jonah felt they were already approaching the top of the sky. Spruce trees lined the track. And then the locomotive ahead appeared to drop out of sight. Jonah looked around the corner of the boxcar and saw a great open vista. It was a deep valley with a lake in the distance. He held his breath, looking at the depth and grandeur of the scene revealing itself. A town lay at the edge of the lake, with steeples that shone like points of snowflakes and big brown buildings with many eyes stretched along the sides of hills.

It took several minutes for the train to wind and rumble its way down into the valley and approach the town. The cars rattled and clanked slowly through the outskirts, and soon as Jonah saw the yard ahead where barges and steamboats were pulled up to the docks by the tracks, he knew it was time to jump off. The railroad ended where its cargo would be loaded onto boats for the trip across the lake.

When Jonah touched the ground, he was so stiff with cold, he fell and rolled off the gravel into weeds. He was almost numb, but pushed himself up and looked around. The town was on flat land by the lake, with steep hills on either side. To the east two gorges cut through the ridge and waterfalls milked and smoked over the rims of rocks. Mills with waterwheels jutted out of each gorge. To the south Jonah saw the apron of another waterfall combing and foaming from a lip of rock. It was like no place he'd ever seen. The lake stretched out of sight to the north between rounded shoulders of hills.

With no money, no scythe, no kettle, Jonah had to think first of getting something to eat. He walked away from the tracks toward the center of town as a steamboat blew its whistle. No one he passed on the street paid him much attention. Wind shoving off the lake chilled him more, and he had to get warm before he could think what to do. He had to get out of the biting wind.

SEVENTEEN

JONAH

At the corner of Aurora Street, Jonah came to a brick church with stained-glass windows, and found the door unlocked. It was mostly dark inside, but he saw benches in the light from the colored windows. Out of the wind the air was warmer. As Jonah's eyes adjusted a little, he saw a stove at the side of the church near the altar. He walked toward the front and realized as he neared it that a fire was crackling in the stove. If the stove was lit, someone must be in the church.

"Hello and welcome," a voice said.

Jonah spun around and saw a man in a shiny black robe emerge from a room behind the pulpit.

"Hello, sir," Jonah said and took off his hat. "I just wanted to get warm."

"I'm Timothy Belue," the man in the robe said. "You are most welcome."

Jonah was so surprised he couldn't think what to say. He couldn't claim to be a laborer on his way to work. It must be a Sunday if a fire was roaring in the stove.

"Make yourself at home," Rev. Belue said. He was a short man with glasses and side whiskers. He didn't seem at all surprised to see Jonah. "We'll have worship service in about twenty minutes," the reverend said. "You are very welcome to stay."

"Thank you, sir," Jonah said.

The minister looked at Jonah's boots and his coat, soiled with soot and ashes from the train. "I keep coffee and biscuits in the back room to refresh me while I prepare my sermons," he said. "Could I offer you something to nibble?"

Jonah knew it was impolite to accept, but he was too famished to refuse. "Thank you, sir," he said and bowed his head. Rev. Belue led him to the little room piled with books and papers. Another black robe hung from a hook in the corner. A coffeepot sat on the hearth of a small fireplace where lazy flames beckoned and gestured. The preacher cleared a spot at the table and set a plate of biscuits and a cup of coffee before Jonah.

As Jonah sipped the coffee, he felt the hot liquid warm his belly and begin to spread through him. His bones ached with cold, and the warm coffee didn't touch the marrow at first. The biscuits were sweet as the sweetest cake. There was butter to spread on the biscuits, making them even sweeter.

Mrs. Belue, who was the organist, arrived and also invited Jonah to stay for the service. She was taller than her husband, with dark hair, pale skin, and blue eyes. She invited Jonah to come to their house for dinner after the meeting. "I hope you'll find friends in Ithaca," she said.

When Jonah finished the biscuits and coffee and returned to the meeting room, the room was already half filled with worshipers.

Rev. Belue sat in a chair behind the pulpit and Mrs. Belue began to play a quiet hymn on the organ. Jonah walked to the back of the church and sat on the last bench. Some of those entering in their fine Sunday clothes glanced at him and looked quickly away. An older woman smiled at him. Jonah knew he smelled bad after all the days on the road. He tried to gather himself into himself, to keep his stink from spreading.

As he watched the church fill, Jonah wondered how safe he was here, appearing in public, at a service for everybody to see. There was no guarantee that Rev. Belue, kind as he seemed, wouldn't report him to the sheriff if he knew Jonah was a runaway. And someone in the congregation might be suspicious of him and inform the authorities. But as he warmed up, filled with coffee and biscuits and butter, Jonah felt heavier and heavier. He'd walked many miles, and he'd not slept much the night before. As soon as the Reverend Belue stood up and announced the first hymn and the congregation began to sing, Jonah was already asleep. He dreamed about cliffs and waterfalls and sparkling lakes.

It was only after the church was empty that Rev. Belue woke him. "Service is over," the preacher said and shook his shoulder. "I can see how rousing my sermon was." The preacher laughed and Jonah woke to his laughter.

"I'm sorry, sir," Jonah mumbled.

"No need to apologize," the minister said. "Perhaps you needed sleep more than a sermon."

Jonah had slept so deeply in the warm church, he was befuddled. It took him a minute to understand Rev. Belue's questions.

"Yes, sir," Jonah murmured, as if he was about to go back to sleep.

"Well I have just one question really," Rev. Belue said. "Have you killed anybody?"

Jonah woke and looked the preacher in the eye. "No, sir," he said. "I never killed anybody."

"Well, that settles that," the preacher said. "Come with me to the house and we'll have some dinner."

After they'd eaten, Mrs. Belue put on a kettle to heat water and told Jonah he could bathe in the downstairs bedroom. The pastor and Jonah carried a tub into the bedroom and a bucket of cold water and the kettle of boiling water. When the two waters were mixed the tub was half full of warm water. The preacher brought him soap and a towel and Jonah washed himself thoroughly for the first time since he'd left Miss Linda's. Until he cleaned himself he hadn't realized just how dirty and smelly he'd become.

To wash when you're dirty is almost as satisfying as eating when you're starved or warming when you're cold, Jonah thought. The coffee and biscuits, the nap in church, the dinner with the Belues, and now the bath—they all seemed too good to believe. He wondered when this dream would end.

Slow there, boy, he thought. Easy does it. Don't get too happy. Dangerous to be too happy.

After Jonah dressed and emptied the tub in the backyard, Rev. Belue led him down to the basement of the house, where he had a small printing press. It was the first press Jonah had ever seen. He looked at the large screw that pushed the plates together, and the bits of type in trays. A book could be made from the letters packed in the boxes.

"I haven't asked what your old name is," Rev. Belue said.

"Why is that?" Jonah said.

"Because you will need a new name."

Jonah hadn't thought of that. Of course the reverend was right: he would need a new name. It would be foolish to go by his old name. Jonah tried to think what he should call himself. He'd used different names since he'd run away from the Williams Place. He'd been Julius and Ezra and Isaac and Jeter. Thinking of Mama back in South Carolina, in her little shack behind the mansion, brought tears to his eyes. He could never again be Jonah Williams. He would no longer be Jonah who disobeyed God and was swallowed by a fish and coughed up on the shore. He wanted to be somebody that arrived at the promised land. Moses had gone into the wilderness, but he'd not been allowed to reach the land of Canaan. It was Joshua that led the people on to the promised land. Joshua was the prophet who made it into Canaan.

"I am Joshua," Jonah said, "Joshua Driver."

"That's a good, strong name," the minister said. "Joshua from the Bible and Driver for one who goes forth, and goes far."

The preacher took letters from the tray and arranged them on a plate, then screwed the plate tight. He fitted the plate on the press, inked the letters with a pad, and placed a small sheet of paper on the press. With the wooden arm he turned the big screw until the two halves of the press came together. When he raised the top half and took out the sheet of paper, the words were like tracks with soles of bold new ink.

This certifies that ____________has paid
500 dollars in good money for his freedom.
Robert Montgomery
Frederick, Maryland

Reverend Belue took a pen and wrote "Joshua Driver" in the blank space, and added the date "February 15, 1851" after the address.

"Well Joshua, you must carry this with you at all times," the preacher said.

"Yes, sir," Jonah said.

The reverend said he was foreman in the woolen mill at the foot of Ithaca Falls. They spun the wool that came in bales on the railroad from

Owego into thread and yarn. The yarn was shipped by lake and canal to the cities in the east.

"I think you might find work as a janitor," Rev. Belue said.

"Yes, sir," Jonah said.

That night, before he went to sleep in the clean bed in the room downstairs, Jonah asked himself whether he should continue running, to reach Auburn and Rochester, Buffalo and then Canada. The Reverend Belue seemed to think he would be safe enough with his new name and the forged certificate of freedom. It was impossible to know how safe he was. But Jonah was worn out from running, and he didn't want to go on. And he'd never met anyone as helpful as Rev. and Mrs. Belue. He'd stay here for a while, until he got rested up. He'd stop here for a few days or weeks and see what happened. If he was caught, he would be caught. He just didn't feel like running anymore.

EIGHTEEN

ANGEL

When Jonah left me in Owego, I told myself I would never see that boy again. It was too cold to ride the train. Besides, I couldn't run along a moving train and jump up on it again like he could. If I tried that I might fall right under the wheels and be cut to pieces. He ran away from me on the French Broad, and he ran away from me at Big Lick. And he rode off with that farmer in a wagon at Harrisburg. But I always caught up with him. We lived on boiled eggs all through the mountains of Pennsylvania, tramping through snow and mud and sleeping in haystacks and hay barns. But I wasn't going to run after him anymore.

Still, that left me standing there by the river where they were loading and unloading all the boats and snow whipped sideways in the wind. I walked down that street thinking about what I was going to do. Where was I going, now that Jonah had left me again? What was a big colored girl to do, cold and dirty, way up north on a riverbank?

I walked along the muddy street till I saw a bakery, and I walked behind the bakery and sure enough they had thrown out old bread. Some pieces were soggy and dirty and some were frozen, but I stuffed my pockets with stale bread. And I started to eat a piece that wasn't too dirty.

The train had already pulled out of the depot and I followed the tracks. Didn't seem like there was anything else to do. I figured Jonah had jumped on the train and was riding north in a boxcar or on top a boxcar, and he would freeze to death for sure before he got to the next town. With wind shoving into my face, I munched that old bread and followed, stepping over cinders and turds on the crossties.

As soon as I got out of town, climbing a little hill, I spotted something lying beside the tracks, and when I got closer I saw it was Jonah's kettle and his mowing blade. He must have dropped them when he ran to grab hold of that train. Either that or he fell off and was killed. I looked around but didn't see any pieces of his body or blood on the tracks. I didn't want anything to do with that mowing blade.

In the kettle there were matches and two potatoes, and a busted egg had run all over everything else and frozen. I hung the rope handle over my shoulder to carry the kettle, and started walking along the tracks, for I didn't know where else to go.

Under my breath I cussed that Jonah and told him in my mind he had seen the last of me. But the kettle had brought him luck, and maybe it would bring me luck, too. And soon as I could find an egg or two I'd boil them in the kettle the way we had done so many times. I'd fill my belly with eggs and bread and then maybe I could think about what to do next. I'd sleep in hay barns to stay warm.

After walking along the tracks and almost freezing in the wind, I stopped after dark at a big red barn. It was so dark I lighted a match to see inside and saw cows munching hay. It was so cold steam rose from the cows. By the ladder to the loft there was a feed room, and in the room were shelves with jugs, all shiny and stopped with cobs. If those jugs held molasses, I might just take a sip. I pulled out a stopper and tilted the mouth to my lips. But the stuff inside was sweeter and thinner than molasses. It had a special flavor I'd never tasted before, some kind of syrup I guessed. I tasted it again and swallowed some. The syrup was so sweet, it nearly burned the back of my mouth.

Besides the kettle I hauled the jug up into the hayloft, and sat down in the hay above the cows and ate bread and sipped from the jug. That syrup was so strong it made me warm inside. Girl, you could use some sweetening, I said. Then I wrapped the coat around me tight and lay down and pulled some hay over the coat and went to sleep.

All the time I slept, I dreamed of Jonah and followed him and cussed him out. I wanted to tell him he wasn't worth a fart. He was sorry as a no-count polecat. I'd seen a rotten dog carcass more likable than him. Then in my dream I saw what I'd been trying not to see, which was that I knew I was going to follow that Jonah and see him again. Because he was just a boy that might grow up. He was just scared in a strange place and finding his way. I saw a house where we were going to live, with flowers in boxes on the porch, and I saw children on a floor scrubbed so clean it looked like a mirror to walk on.

And I saw that a woman couldn't quit loving a man just because he was scared and forgetful. She might get mad but she couldn't stop loving him. Besides, a man thinks like a child anyway. He follows his little colonel and the groaning in his belly and gets ideas and makes all kind of trouble. A woman has got to think for him when he can't think for himself. It made me sad to see that, but relieved at the same time. For I could see my way ahead, and I saw how hard it was going to be.

It took me three days following the tracks across the hills before I came to this town by a big lake. It was the biggest lake I'd ever seen, between hills and waterfalls glowing on the hills. I had no idea where Jonah was and what the name of the town might be. I couldn't read the sign at the depot, but stopped at a hardware store behind the station and asked what place this was. The man behind the counter looked at me funny, like he'd never seen a big, fat colored girl in a man's overcoat before. But he said I was in Ithaca, New York.

"Can't you read the sign?" he said and pointed to the depot.

"Just wanted to hear you say it," I said.

Now I'd been thinking what I might do in this cold place. Snow covered the ground and ice hung like fingers from eaves. The wind off the lake cut my face like razors. I had to get inside before I froze to death. I didn't care if I worked in a steaming laundry or washing dishes or cleaning a bakery floor, as long as I could be inside.

At every store along the street, I asked if they had work I could do. They shook their heads and stared at me like I had three eyes or horns coming out of my head. Men sitting around a stove in a store chewing tobacco all looked at me in the dirty coat, carrying the kettle on a rope. It looked like I wasn't going to find anything. But I came to a big house with columns all painted white and there was a man at a desk inside.

He asked if I'd ever mopped floors and washed sheets and I told him I had done that all my life. He asked if I could make beds and clean chamber pots, and I said I'd done that since I was a child.

"Can you read?" he said, and I told him I had never been to school.

He looked at me and said I had to wash up, and I had to wear a uniform. He took me up the stairs to the third floor of the hotel—for that's what it was, a hotel—and showed me a little room not much bigger than the bed that was in it, with a little table. He told me to go wash myself, and he brought me a uniform.

I can't tell you how happy I was to have a room with a real bed, a clean room. There was no fireplace, but it sure was warmer than outside. And there was a blanket on the bed. I didn't care if I had to scrub floors and wash shit out of pee pots, for I had a place to lay my head, in a clean room. And nobody had asked if I was running away. I got some hot water from the kitchen of the hotel and I washed myself all over.

Every day it got colder in that town, and wind came off the icy lake between the hills, and snow blew down the streets like white ghosts and bees swarming. So I stayed inside and worked. I didn't need to go outside because I had to save my money, which was two dollars a week. And besides, I figured the less I was on the streets the less I was likely to be called a runaway. Maybe I would go on to Canada, where there weren't any slaves, when spring came and a girl could travel. I guessed Jonah must already be in Canada.

I worked at cleaning rooms. I swept and dusted and mopped the floors and emptied chambers. One day Tertius, the man at the desk, said to me, "Sarepta"—because I'd told him my name was Sarepta King—he said, "do you want to make some extra money?"

"Sure I do," I said. I looked him in the eye and saw exactly what he meant.

"All you have to do is show a guest a good time," he said.

"What do you mean a good time?" I said, to kind of tease him a little.

"You know what I mean," he said and winked.

"How much extra money?" I said.

"Fifty cents a time," he said.

So he came up to my room from time to time and sent me to a guest room where some salesman or farm boy had come into town, and I did my best to make them happy. Because I had no other way to save extra money for going to Canada. And pretty soon Tertius said I was the most popular girl he had.

"I'm the most girl for the money," I said and laughed.

"That you are," he said. "That you are."

It was getting on toward Christmas when I was walking down the street and saw a black face come out of the hardware store. I stopped in the snow and my heart almost jumped into my mouth when I saw it had to be Jonah. Sure as shooting, it was that trifling boy who I thought was in Canada.

When I called his name, he turned around and looked at me hard. "I'm called Joshua now," he said. I told him I was called Sarepta now, like I was at Miss Linda's. And when I told him I worked at the hotel I could see by his look he already knew what I did.

"Come over and see me," I said. I told him I lived on the third floor of the hotel, and if he came to see me he should climb up by the back stairs. He said he worked at the Ithaca Falls Woolen Mill. Then he turned around and headed back toward the mill, where he worked as the cleaning man. I felt silly that I was so glad to see that no-good boy. I'd been wondering if I would ever see him again, and all that time he was right there in Ithaca. I was all heated up because I'd seen him and talked to him. And I saw maybe I'd stayed in Ithaca because I thought he might be there, or near there. I'd told myself I never wanted to see him again. But in my dream I knew better. And there I was, all out of breath because I'd seen his sorry ass. Girl, you are hopeless, I said.

But I studied on it, and knew Jonah cared for me. He just didn't understand it yet. That boy didn't know his own mind. He was dreaming of something big, like he longed to be a boss man, or president. He lived in a dream that would make him mighty disappointed. There was nobody to help him but me.

Tertius said that black boy named Joshua lived at the boardinghouse on Cayuga Street. Everybody in town knew where he lived, and where he worked. So I began to study on how to help him and how to make him see that he loved me. He was my only hope to have a house and family of my own. There was nobody else to love me.

So I took the old kettle that he'd carried all the way through Pennsylvania, that I'd toted over the hills to Ithaca, and I cleaned it up and polished it with wax until it shined. Then I got cookies and candy and nuts to fill it. Nothing pleased me as much as thinking about Jonah and fixing up a present for him. He liked to read, but I didn't know how to pick a book for him.

Now when it was just before Christmas I went over there to the boardinghouse on Cayuga Street and carried that old kettle tied up in a ribbon. I could hardly get my breath because I wanted to see Jonah so bad. His landlady looked at me funny, when I told her I came to see Jonah, and then I remembered he was now called Joshua.

"If you go to his room you can't close the door," she said.

"I don't want to close the door," I said and gave her a smile. I guessed she had heard rumors about me at the hotel.

Jonah was so startled to see me I almost busted out laughing. He was about to panic I reckon, and then he looked confused. When I showed him the present and he looked in the kettle I saw his eyes get wet. That told me what I already knew, that he cared for me, just like I cared for him. He lifted out the nuts and cookies and candy. And I said real quick, "Now what do I get?" He was so confused, I had to laugh again.

The door was open and the landlady stood at the bottom of the stairs, looking up at us. But Jonah leaned against me and brought his mouth to mine, and I kissed him like he was the dearest thing in the whole world. I just wanted to be with him. I'd been with lots of men, but that didn't mean anything compared to what it was like to be with Jonah again. We had loved in haystacks and barn lofts, and in the woods by the river. I didn't ever want to quit kissing him. But when I did stop, I asked him to come to my room.

"You live in the top of the hotel?" he said.

"Come up the back stairs," I said.

And then I saw the book on the table. He had a black Bible. That boy had been reading again and it made me proud to think he was the one I loved, so smart and with a head filled with words and maps and the stuff he was always talking about.

When I walked back to the hotel in the snow and climbed the stairs to my room, I felt better than I had in a long, long time. I didn't have any presents or company in that cold, windy town. But I knew Jonah cared for me, and that made everything different. Jonah was going to come see me. And giving him presents was better than getting presents. He would see he couldn't do anything without me. He was so young he just didn't know what he wanted yet.

As I got in bed and pulled the old coat over me to stay warm, I thought about the Thomas Place. They would be having a Christmas party there before long. Old Sally would make eggnog and Master Thomas would give everybody fifty cents. And Christmas dinner would be collard greens and baked ham or sausage and sweet potatoes. And master would want me to come down to his room and keep his feet warm and be good to him. Except I wouldn't be there this Christmas; I'd be off in the North and I had my own man and a new name. I had a room to myself and money in a sock. Jonah may not have known I had him yet, but I did. That was the best present I could think of.

NINETEEN

JOSHUA

Now that Joshua had a little money and was living alone in his room on Cayuga Street, he bought himself a leather Bible to read in the evenings by lamplight. It was not as fine as the Bible Mrs. Williams had given him, but it was his, bought with his own money, to be read in his room. As he savored the familiar words, it seemed too good to be true that he was free to read any time he had a spare moment. No one would punish him, even if he was caught with the book open. He would get other books later, and he could read the newspaper every day in the parlor of Mrs. Gregg's house. But first he wanted to pick up where he'd left off reading when Mr. Williams whipped him.

Joshua turned first to the book of Joshua in the Old Testament to read about the man who'd led the Children of Israel out of the wilderness into the promised land. As he read, Joshua was surprised to find the Israelites had to fight the Canaanites to possess the land they'd been promised. Only through a mighty struggle were they able to claim their birthright. And after they had won, Joshua made a covenant with his people and set laws and statutes. Joshua wrote the laws in a book and took a large stone and set it under an oak tree as a sign of God's promise. The favorite verse Joshua found was Joshua 24:27.

"And Joshua said unto all the people, Behold this stone shall be a witness unto us; for it hath heard all the words of the Lord which he spake unto us: it shall be therefore a witness unto you, lest you deny your God."

The passage thrilled Joshua in ways he couldn't explain. Something about the large rock under the oak tree as a reminder of the laws and covenant with the people delighted him every time he thought of it. Just imagining the stone placed as a witness made him feel hopeful and strong. He'd left behind Jonah and his gourd vine for Joshua and his stone and oak tree for witness in the promised land. As soon as it was spring, he'd get his own large rock and place it under an oak tree as testimony of his arrival up north.

On Christmas Eve Joshua sat in his room looking through the first volume of the *David Copperfield*. The pages were crisp and the print vivid. With his knife he slit open every other page. There were pictures illustrating the story. But he couldn't keep his attention on the book. Even though he was invited to the Belues for Christmas dinner the next day, and even though he had a room of his own, he was lonely, more lonely than he'd been since he arrived in Ithaca. Maybe it was the thought that it was Christmas that made him feel so alone, so abandoned. He thought about Mama back at the Williams Place, and the cakes she always made at Christmas. He thought of the presents Mrs. Williams always gave him. He thought of the cedar tree Mrs. Williams had him decorate in the parlor, and the holly and turkey's-paw moss he gathered to put on the mantel and over doorways. He would never see the Williams Place again. An ache shot through his chest so hard he could barely breathe. He'd never before felt such homesickness. He would never eat Mama's cornbread again, and he wouldn't catch catfish in the Saluda River to skin and fry for supper. He'd never read scripture to Mrs. Williams again and get presents from her.

Joshua was surprised by the depth of his loneliness and homesickness. In his room on Christmas Eve he should have been happy and grateful that he had a job and a clean place to live, and he was going to Rev. Belue's tomorrow for Christmas dinner. He should have felt more confident than he had in all the months since he ran away from the Williams Place. Instead it seemed the bottom was falling out of everything he knew. He was sliding down into a blackness he'd never known before, not even when he was humbled by Mr. Williams and Mr. Wells. He was falling and could find nothing to catch onto.

Since fleeing the Williams Place that July night, Joshua had been too busy and maybe too scared to face the loneliness and homesickness he carried somewhere deep in his marrow. Along the road there had been too much danger to ever admit there was such a thing as despair. And anger had borne him up and carried him along at the worst moments. Anger had been the horse he'd ridden and the armor he'd worn after Mr. Williams had whipped him, and after Mr. Wells had hurt him with the hot and cold water. Hate and fury had fueled his long journey from South Carolina and enabled him at desperate moments to go on.

But now that he had plenty to eat at Mrs. Gregg's house, was apparently safe in Ithaca, and had the friendship of Rev. and Mrs. Belue, the fear and pain he'd pushed away before for all those months came crashing down on him. He thought of Christmas Eve at the Williams Place, the carols they would be singing in the quarters, and at church, the pitiful presents Mama would give each of her children, a comb, a ribbon, a stick of horehound candy bought at the store in Travelers Rest. When he thought of the pathetic gratitude he'd felt when Mr. Williams had given him a quarter on Christmas morning, tears filled Joshua's eyes. A quarter had seemed a bounty, a tiny fortune to be carried to the store. Now he could earn that much in a few hours. The cruelty of the Williams Place seemed worse now than it had then. At the time it was all he knew. Now he could see the horror of that way of life. He shuddered, recalling the day Mr. Williams had caught him reading in the barn loft. But even as he shivered, he felt a stabbing homesickness that hurt every part of him, a torment he could not brush away.

At that moment Joshua knew he would crawl a mile on his knees to see the shack where Mama was making mush with molasses sweetening for a Christmas pudding. Since he'd stolen her money she didn't have anything to buy presents with, however small, for the younger children. He would never be able to repay her, and he'd never see her again. He could never ask her for forgiveness.

Joshua felt sick in his bones. He tried to think of something firm and strong to grab hold of. He was sliding down into a pit where there was no air to breathe. He had to catch onto something to stop the tumble or he'd suffocate. He opened one of the volumes of Dickens's novel and tried to read a few lines, but closed the book as the words swam like frog spawn on the page. He opened the Bible he'd bought and saw the name Lamentations. He tried to recall all the people he'd met since he left the Williams Place, on the road in North Carolina and Virginia, Pennsylvania and New York. Miss Linda and Mr. Wells, Hettie and Lonella, Prissy and Sheriff Watkins, Mr. Driver and his daughter Sylvia. Rev. Belue and Mrs. Belue. And then he saw the kettle in the corner of his room, the kettle he'd carried through Pennsylvania, and he began to think of Angel, now Sarepta King, who'd been with him much of the way. He picked the kettle up and saw how Angel had polished the iron with stove polish until it shone like leather.

A chill stung through Joshua as he thought of Angel. He'd run away from her three times on the road: on the French Broad, at Miss Linda's at Roanoke, and at Owego. And he'd avoided her in Ithaca, telling himself it wasn't safe to associate with another escaped slave. Besides, she was ignorant and sold herself at Miss Linda's, and, if rumor was correct, at the hotel in Ithaca. She was fat and her tongue was sharp. She had a special knack for belittling him, and she liked to cross and contradict him.

But he recalled the times she'd been good to him, the night of wonder at the jubilee, the night she'd comforted him on the train after he kicked the other runaway out of the boxcar, the way she'd found him at the jail in Winchester, and waited in the woods for him at the Driver farm in Pennsylvania. He thought of her laugh, and the smoothness of her honey-colored skin. There was a liveliness about Angel he didn't have words to describe. It was as though she was completely *in* her life wherever she was. In comparison, other people, including himself, had their heads off in the clouds or some other vague place. Angel filled her life completely every day.

Joshua saw that the only thing that could cheer him up was to see Angel. She was the only remnant of home he had left. Everything else had been lost. The job he had at the mill and the room he rented from Mrs. Gregg were nice. But they were not home. Not home as he understood it, felt it in his bones and in his blood. Angel was all he had left of his real self. She was the only chance of a home he had.

Suddenly Joshua saw that he must go to Angel and apologize for abandoning her. He'd left her three times, as Peter had denied Christ three times before he repented. She'd seen all along how much he had needed her, and he'd been callous and blind to his true need, and hers. Joshua wiped his eyes and saw what a fool he'd been. He'd acted silly out of fear and arrogance, and his own ignorance. Though she couldn't read, Angel had understood him far better than he had himself.

It was already eight o'clock, but he knew he must go to Angel. He would wish her a Merry Christmas and thank her for helping him reach the North, thank her for stealing those eggs that sustained them through Pennsylvania as the weather turned cold. She'd been his partner and his helpmeet. She'd given him solace and love when he had been most desperate.

Putting on his coat and scarf and cap, Joshua descended the stairs as quietly as he could and stepped out into the cold night. Snow crunched like broken glass under his boots. The stars were brilliant overhead, and candles burned in windows all along the street. He met a group of carolers, their breaths smoking and smelling of brandy as they sang "Joy to the World" at the edge of a yard.

Joshua knew he should take a present to Angel-Sarepta. It was the least he could do to show her his change of heart, his appreciation. He had money in his pocket, but wasn't sure what stores would be open at this hour. He turned onto State Street, which was the main street, and was pleased when he saw lights in Rothschild's dry goods store. A red and gold and blue scarf was displayed in the window, so shiny it seemed like rippling water. He bought it and had it wrapped just as the store was closing for the night. With the package under his arm, he turned the corner and headed toward the hotel.

When Angel had invited him to visit her weeks before, she'd said she lived on the top floor and he should come up the back stairs. But Joshua did not feel like going around to the back and sneaking up to Angel's room. He'd come to a resolution about Angel and he was bringing her a Christmas present and he would not be afraid. He would enter through the front door and lobby for all to see. He'd not be ashamed of visiting his former partner on the road.

As Joshua walked into the lobby lit by gas lamps, a man at the front desk stopped him. "Well Merry Christmas, boy," he said. "Where might you be going?"

Joshua was so surprised he stammered, "Going to see Angel Thomas."

"No Angel Thomas here," the man said. He stared at Joshua and the package under his arm.

"I mean Sarepta, Sarepta King," Joshua said.

"Do you have an appointment?"

Joshua shook his head and anger began to flare in his throat. He swallowed and saw his mistake in coming through the lobby. "She's a friend," he said.

"Sarepta has lots of friends," the man behind the desk said. "You can make an appointment to come later."

"Don't need no appointment," Joshua said.

Just then Joshua saw Angel come out of a hallway with a man in a fur-collared coat and top hat. She wore a coat and big bonnet, but he knew it was Angel by her big figure and dark face. She and the man in fancy clothes started up the staircase to the next floor and Joshua watched them mount until they were out of sight.

"Sarepta will be free later, if you care to make an appointment," the man at the desk said.

Joshua spun around and banged the door as he stepped back into the cold, still clutching the wrapped package. He hardly noticed the chill night air, for the blood inside his face seemed even colder. Snow that had partly melted during the day had now frozen again, and his boots crunched on the hardened tracks. He stomped along the street, hardly noticing where he was going, and almost collided with a tipsy caroler before he stepped aside. "Pardon me," he muttered and hurried on.

With the present held to his chest, he thought of walking to the lake and throwing the gift into the still unfrozen inlet. He thought of climbing the hill past the mill and tossing the scarf over the waterfall. A fire was burning in a barrel at the corner of State Street where boys who had been ice skating warmed their hands. He considered dropping the package into the flames, but he didn't.

Instead Joshua walked back to Mrs. Gregg's house and entered and climbed the stairs to his room without wiping his boots. As he took off his coat he ignored the lumps of melting snow that fell on the floor. He threw the package and the coat on the bed and sat down in his one chair before the little table where the lamp still burned. The Bible lay in front of him and the three volumes of *David Copperfield*. He opened and then closed the first volume.

Joshua had known all along that Angel sold herself to customers at Miss Linda's, after she had moved to the upstairs room. And he knew she'd been a bed warmer for her master at the Thomas place, for she'd told him so herself. He even knew the rumors about her in Ithaca, about her working at the hotel. It was no great secret how she made her living.

He was surprised at himself, and angry at himself, and ashamed of himself for being so affected by seeing her with the man in the top hat and fur-collared coat. He didn't feel like himself but somebody else. Before he had resented Angel going with other men, but he'd been more concerned about getting away from her and making it to the North. He'd liked to be with her himself, but that didn't stop him from abandoning her three times—four times if you counted the train at Harrisburg—and never trying to see her in Ithaca over the past few weeks.

What had changed now was his own feelings. Angel had not changed. She had to find a way to live in this town, until she could make her way on to Canada. How did she know he'd decided to go to her on Christmas Eve? It was his mind that had altered as he saw how much he needed her. Joshua was disgusted with himself for being so foolish. Whoa there, boy, you are dumb as sawdust, he said. But he was still angry at Angel, too.

He looked at the wrapped present on the bed. He'd splurged in his rush of affection for Angel. He'd wasted his money. It was a beautiful scarf, with colors bright as gemstones. The fabric was shimmery, gleaming like sunlight on troubled water. Suddenly Joshua knew what to do with the scarf: he'd give it to Mrs. Belue tomorrow. He hadn't thought of taking a present to the Belues, but he would give the scarf to Mrs. Belue, who'd been so kind to him so many times.

IN THE DAYS AFTER Christmas, Joshua worked at the mill as usual, and he began to read the novel that he'd started that fateful day in the barn loft at the Williams place. But after reading a few pages every evening, his thoughts would return to Angel. He tried to think of other things, but always there was Angel at the back of his mind. He'd been a simpleton to leave her behind, and ignore her after she arrived in Ithaca. She'd followed him all the way from North Carolina. She'd comforted him on the train after following him to Winchester, and she was the only person in Ithaca who could make him happy. He thought of the color of her shoulders in the firelight. He thought of the way she had of nudging him with her big hip. He recalled how deft she was at stealing eggs from a henhouse early in the morning so they could eat breakfast.

In the days before New Year's, a period of heavy snow began. Wind roared across the frozen lake and flung drifts into the streets and yards. Each morning Joshua shoveled a path out to the street from the porch of the rooming house. He walked with head down and ears wrapped in a scarf up the hill to the mill, and returned after dark to his room. Joshua had wondered before how people in the North lived through winters amid ice and snow and bone-cracking wind, and now he found out. They did it mostly by staying indoors. The farms had big barns where hay and grain were stored, and cows and horses stayed inside their stalls until spring thawed out the snowy pastures. Children might play in the snow, sliding and building snowmen, but they soon ran back inside to warm their hands and feet by the fire. Men who had to work outside bundled up and took breaks to warm themselves inside or by bonfires.

The fact was, winter was a sociable time. When blizzards roared down the lake, people were more friendly. They helped each other. Some who were usually glum became cheerful when they had to stumble through deep snow to get to work. In the evenings Joshua read *David Copperfield* or the newspaper by the fire in Mrs. Gregg's parlor. On especially cold nights the landlady served hot cider with spices in it. At the end of every day in the harshest weather, people seemed to feel they'd achieved a victory over the elements just by surviving.

It took almost a week for Joshua to admit to himself that he had to see Angel again. He had to eat his pride and his resentment. He had to humble himself and admit he had a lot to learn about Angel, and about himself. She was less than two years older than him, but she'd experienced far more of life than he had.

It was on New Year's Eve that he finally made up his mind that he had to try once again to see her. It hurt Joshua's pride to think he had to go back to the hotel where he might find her with another customer. But by then it seemed he had no choice. There was nobody else in Ithaca for him to be with and love. Nobody else understood where he'd come from, or cared about him. The choice was inevitable, he saw.

Ithaca was almost as festive on New Year's Eve as it had been at Christmas. Most of the decorations were still in place and candles burned in the windows. New snow had whitened the streets and roofs as if they had been repainted. Stars shivered so bright, they seemed hung just above the houses. But when Joshua reached the corner of Buffalo Street something stopped him. The sky to the north was red, a glowing rose red that stretched from horizon to horizon. And then he saw trails in the red and other colors, green and blue, that hung like curtains and waved and trembled.

In church he'd heard about the Second Coming, the end of the world. Was this the Great Tribulation? Was the sky falling and time coming to an end? But even as Joshua caught his breath and felt his heart thump in his chest, he remembered the description of the Northern Lights he'd heard from Rev. Belue. This was the aurora people talked about, coming like fireworks on New Year's Eve, welcoming in the New Year.

The colors and the curtains wove around far up in the sky, getting brighter in one place, fading in another. It was the green that seemed strangest, a green light in the night sky, eerie and mysterious. No wonder people thought the Northern Lights could foretell terrible things and dramatic changes. But maybe they foretold good things, too. Maybe they were a favorable omen for the coming year.

Joshua watched the display for several minutes. He wished Angel was there to view the spectacle with him; it would be even more beautiful. Maybe if he hurried it would not be too late for her to see the show in the northern sky. Beyond all the color, the North Star blazed just where it always was.

As Joshua approached the hotel, he decided to use the back door and the back stairs this time. He'd not repeat his mistake of Christmas Eve. He would quickly find the back stairs and climb to Angel's room. Surely there would be a name on the door or something to guide him to the right room.

A party was underway on the first floor of the hotel. A band played soft music and people were dancing. He could see their gliding shadows through the candlelit windows. When Joshua entered the building from the rear, he almost bumped into a man and woman in fancy dress kissing at the bottom of the stairs. The smell of perfume charged the air. The light was so dim in the stairwell, Joshua had to feel his way up the steps. Normally people carried a lamp or candle when they climbed to the upper floors, but as he had neither, he touched the wall and took careful steps. When he reached the top landing, he saw a thin string of light under the doorway, and he opened the door to see a hall dimly lit by one small lamp.

There must have been ten doors on either side of the corridor, all looking the same. He walked slowly down the hall, searching for telltale light under a door, listening for the sound of laughter or conversation. In one room he passed there was the sound of snoring. Most rooms seemed deserted. He passed a room where there was a light under the door, but he walked on, hoping to find a clue to tell him which was Angel's room. When he reached the end of the hall and still had found no indication of which room might be Angel's, he returned to the door with light under it and knocked quietly, holding his breath.

It was late March before the snow really began to disappear in the woods on the hills above town. Even after the snow was gone on the streets, and ice had fallen away from the waterwheel at the mill, the hills were still white, and gold and copper in early morning and late afternoon. Sunset turned the lake into a wide boulevard paved with gold.

One Sunday afternoon, when he could see the bare ground in patches on the hills, Joshua decided it was time to fulfill a promise he'd made in the fall after arriving in Ithaca. Wearing his gloves and scarf, he climbed the trail above the mill, which was still muddy from thaw and melting drifts. He took care to find footholds on rocks and roots.

Many pine trees and cedar trees grew along the ridge, on the edge of the gorge. But what he was looking for was an oak tree, preferably a large oak tree with wide, spreading limbs. He followed the path beyond the bluff where you could look down on the mill and all of Ithaca and the lake, and came to a little cornfield enclosed by woods. The corn had never been gathered, and the stalks had been knocked down by wind and snow. Deer tracks, turkey tracks, geese tracks, printed the ground where ears spilled kernels into the mud. Joshua wondered who would have planted a field up there only to abandon it.

To avoid the thaw mud, he walked around the edge of the field, through briars and brush. Beyond the sumac bushes along the clearing, pines gave way to hardwoods, maples, gum trees, shagbark hickories. Joshua entered the woods and picked his way among vines and undergrowth, and then he saw the oak tree.

It was a noble tree with silver, sooty bark, a trunk at least five feet thick at the base, with branches spreading over the other trees. It was older than the other trees, and must have stood there before the white men came to the region. It was a miracle the ancient tree had been spared by the axe. It had dignity and strength, and seemed to stand for a kind of truth. It reached high into the spring sky, but was balanced, perfect all around.

Joshua looked about for a rock. What he needed was a special stone, small enough to be moved, but noticeable. Most of the rocks in the area were flat gray shale, rocks that melted a little when wet or chalked off when rubbed in dry weather. What he wanted was a harder stone, a rounded stone. He searched among the undergrowth, the thickets of vines and briars, the cedars with white shadows, but found only flat rocks. He looked along the edges of the field, avoiding the creamy thaw mud.

And then he saw the rock pile at the corner of the clearing. Some farmer, or more likely his children, had carried rocks out of the field for decades and piled them in a cairn at the corner of the patch. They'd probably dragged stones on sleds and hauled them in carts to clear the ground. Joshua picked among the rocks and found many kinds and shapes. He found blocks and cubes, broken fragments, sheets and plates, and stones shaped like potatoes. And then he saw one rounded almost like an egg, tan colored, about the size of a watermelon. He knew as soon as he spotted it that this was his witness rock. It was a stone that had been waiting for him for years, for ages. With his pocketknife he scratched his initials on the stone.

It took all his strength to lift the rock out of the briars and raise it to his chest. He staggered and stumbled through the underbrush and reeled with the weight. Once he had to drop the stone to the ground to rest, but eventually he brought it to the big oak tree. Out of breath and sore, he placed the rock on bare ground at the base of the great oak.

Joshua knew this would be his special place, the spot he would come to from time to time to remember his escape from the Williams Place and his arrival in Ithaca, to reaffirm his strength and hope, his love. Whatever happened, he had come this far. The oak tree and thawing woods and glowing rock bore witness to his progress, his pilgrimage to this particular place.

And then he turned back toward the town, knowing that Sarepta would be there, waiting for him. She'd probably ask where in hell he'd been to get his boots and his pants so muddy.

TWENTY

SAREPTA

I knew Joshua was going to ask me to marry him long before he knew it himself. He read books and had all those names in his head and could narrate stories and tell facts you never heard of. But he didn't know himself as well as I did. And that is still true to this very day. I saw he was going to come to me out of the cold because he didn't have anywhere else to go. I was the only place he had for comfort and love.

So when he showed up out of the dark to say he loved me and always had, I teased him a little and asked when he was going to up and leave me again. When was he going to run off on his own as he had done already four times. But all the same I told him yes, because I knew he was my only hope, too, in this shivering place. I was all he had left of home, and when that Preacher Belue married us in his fine church, I wore a turban just like the one my mama wrapped around her head for jubilee. There was no jubilee in these winter hills by the lake except what I made my own self.

One thing I liked about Joshua was how he could always spin a tale. He could talk big to the white folks in Ithaca, like he had read a lot of books and knew just what to do. He remembered everything he heard, and he could spread more bullshit with his tongue than ten wagonloads and men with pitchforks. And Preacher Belue loved it, and everybody in the mill and at the church seemed to love it, too. And they made a fuss over Joshua like he was somebody special.

He worked as a janitor at the mill and next thing I knew he was put in charge of fixing things, of keeping all the machines running. And whether he knew what to do or not, he always acted like he did. And that was almost as good as knowing, for he learned quick and remembered.

Now Joshua wanted to teach me to read, but I told him it wouldn't do any good, but he kept on till I gave in and he taught me to write my name and make letters and read a little bit so I could tell street signs and count money and tell time by the clock on the mantel. And once I started reading I kept going, for I found it was fun. And finally I learned almost as many big words as Joshua had, in the Bible and in newspapers, and in the dictionary he bought, and all the novels we got from the lending library.

But I hadn't forgot my dream on the road in Virginia when I saw those houses with pretty flower gardens and apple trees and cherry trees and chicken houses with big brown eggs in pine straw nests. I loved flowers much as I loved good potato patties and hog sausage with pepper in it. After we got the house on Albany Street, the first thing I did was put geraniums in boxes alongside of the porch, red geraniums, a color so bright you thought you dreamed it.

And I put bulbs in the dirt along the walk, so I had tulips and dahlias and such in their season. Such colors you wouldn't think to see this side of heaven. At the Thomas Place I'd hated working in the dirt, but here I was happy to get my hands in soil. And I got grape hyacinths, too, coming early. Those colors show God loves us I reckon. It was a blessing to have these beauties. Joshua said it would break us up, all the money I spent on flowers for yard and porch, but he didn't mean it. He had all those big words and talked to Preacher Belue about things in the Bible and in the paper. I read the Bible, too, and I had my flowers and the floor of my parlor, which I kept shined like a mirror.

When Joshua became the man who fixed things at the mill, I told him not to get too big for his britches, because I'd seen him when he don't have any britches. But he didn't pay any attention to my teasing because he knew I liked his strutting and bragging with all those fine words. But I still gave him the lash of my tongue when he stomped into the house with muddy boots and smeared the floor I'd polished like it was fine silver.

Now I wondered in secret if I would ever have kids after I'd been with so many men and never got pregnant. I didn't mention this to Joshua, because we never talked about all those things I had done back then. There was no use to rake up the memories. But in my own heart I wondered if we would ever have children like I dreamed of way back on the road when I thought of my own house and yard and flowers and it seemed impossible for me to ever have such. I didn't say anything, but fear ran through me like a cold blade stabbing my spine. So much good had already happened to me. Girl, I told myself, how can you expect any more?

I don't need to explain to you how scared and excited I was when my bleeding stopped that next summer, after we got married. I'd never been one for praying much, but I prayed every night that it would be true. After one month the bleeding didn't return, and then a second month. That was when I told Joshua I might be expecting; most likely

I was expecting. I don't think he believed me at first. Then he saw that maybe I was telling him the truth and he was the happiest man I'd seen since the jubilee.

"We'll name him Frederick Douglass," he said. Frederick Douglass was the colored man that published a newspaper called *North Star* in Rochester, New York.

"What if I want to name my baby something else?" I said, just teasing him a little.

"We'll find no name better than Frederick Douglass," he said. He was so excited he didn't hear anything I said anyway.

"How do you know it will be a boy?" I said. "It's just possible we'll be blessed with a little girl."

But I was so tickled I didn't argue with him anymore. I'd be happy with a child of my own, whether a boy or a girl, and I knew it would be as clever as Joshua, and wise and pretty as myself.

ACKNOWLEDGMENTS

I am grateful to the historians of the Ithaca area for their help with local history and the story of African-Americans in the Finger Lakes region in the 1850s. In particular I would like to thank Carol Kammen for her advice, and for her *Ithaca: A Brief History,* and *The Peopling of Tompkins County.* I would also like to thank my agent, Liz Darhansoff, for encouraging this project over the years. My editors Shannon Ravenel and Chuck Adams have generously shared their wisdom as this novel was completed. The staff at Algonquin Books of Chapel Hill, especially Elisabeth Scharlatt, Anne Winslow, and Brunson Hoole, have given invaluable assistance at every step.

CHASING THE NORTH STAR

Little Willie and the Blue Jacket:

A Note from the Author

*

Questions for Discussion

LITTLE WILLIE AND THE BLUE JACKET

A NOTE FROM THE AUTHOR

Writing *Chasing the North Star* was a sharp departure—a change of direction—for me as a fiction writer. At least three things inspired me to tell the story of Jonah and Angel. First, I wanted to write an adventure story, a kind of "on the road" narrative, evoking the landscape and culture of the mid-nineteenth century in the aftermath of the Fugitive Slave of Act of 1850 in the years leading up to the Civil War. I also wanted to tell a story that took place, in part, in the Finger Lakes region of New York, in Ithaca, where I have lived for the past forty-four years and where, up to now, I had never set a novel. Third, I felt drawn to the character of a teenage slave on a plantation in upper South Carolina who feels he has no choice but to escape from bondage and make his way north in search of freedom. I knew he would be on his own, in constant danger from bounty hunters, lawmen, outlaws, and ordinary citizens upholding the law, and at the mercy of the elements.

But there was also a fourth inspiration for me when I began *Chasing the North Star:* a story passed down in my family from my great-grandfather, Frank Pace (1838–1918). In the years just before the Civil War, in the late 1850s, runaway slaves from Georgia and South Carolina often came through the mountains of western North Carolina on their way north. To help or hide a fugitive was a felony, punishable by fines and imprisonment. Posses of men with horses and dogs and guns followed and usually caught the runaways. Those who turned in runaways could collect rewards.

One evening as they sat down to supper, my great-grandfather Frank and his parents, Sarah and Daniel Pace, heard something disturbing the hens in the chicken house. Frank took a lantern out on the porch and saw a man in overalls standing at the edge of the yard.

"Are you stealing chickens?" Frank called.

"No, sir. We just need a drink of water," the black man said.

The man stepped forward into the lantern light, followed by another man and a woman and a boy who limped. They were ragged and exhausted.

Frank's mother came out on the porch and offered the runaways dippers of water and baked sweet potatoes and cornbread from their table. The boy, about five years old, had a bleeding sore on his leg. As they ate, the sound of dogs baying could be heard from the river. The woman pushed the boy toward Sarah and said, "Willie can't run no more. You keep him." And then the two men and the woman disappeared into the night.

The shouts of men and barking dogs came closer. Sarah picked up the boy and carried him to the storeroom behind the kitchen. She placed the boy in the barrel of cornmeal, put tow sacks over him, and sprinkled meal on the sacks. Then she told Frank to scatter black pepper on the porch and in the yard where the fugitives had stood and sat.

When the men on horses and the dogs burst into the yard, Frank and his parents came out on the porch.

"Have you seen four runaways?" the lead man said.

"We were just having supper," Frank answered.

"It's illegal to help escapees," the posse foreman warned.

The slave hunters demanded to search the place. They were heavily armed. Frank told them to search all they wanted: he had nothing to hide. With torches the men looked in the barn and smokehouse and chicken house and other out-buildings. They went through the house, opening closets, searching bedrooms, cellar, attic, cedar chest. One lifted the lid off the meal barrel and looked in but apparently saw nothing suspicious. Before they left they warned Frank that he could go to jail for harboring a runaway or for not reporting one. The hounds were so confused by the pepper they prowled in circles, unable to find the trail.

AFTER THE SLAVE HUNTERS were gone, Frank and his parents had to decide what to do with Little Willie. They assumed the runaways would return for him or send for him. They didn't even know his last name. But in the meantime Sarah doctored the boy's leg with herbs and salves and poultices. They could hide him for a while but knew neighbors were certain to find out about him. Sarah came up with a plan.

When Willie's leg was almost healed, they loaded up their wagon with hams, honey, and molasses and hid Willie under a canvas as they drove down the mountain to Greenville, South Carolina, to peddle the produce door to door. When they returned home, Willie sat on the seat beside them, and Frank told neighbors they had bought the boy in Greenville. It was the only way to protect him.

Sarah became very fond of Willie. Wherever they worked, in the fields and woods, he went along. As the months passed, they waited for someone to come and claim him, but no one ever did. His folks might have been caught, or killed, or made it all the way to Canada. Sarah sewed him a blue jacket, which he was especially proud of.

ONE DAY IN LATE winter Frank and his father were cutting trees on the hill above the spring. Little Willie helped, holding one end of the crosscut saw and pulling it toward him. As the day warmed up he took off his blue jacket and laid it in the leaves. Later, as an oak tree began to fall, he saw the tree would crash right onto his coat. He dashed to retrieve the jacket and would have made it, except he slipped and fell, and the tree hit him, killing him instantly.

They buried Willie in the blue jacket in the family cemetery. When I was a child I was shown the rough stone that marked his grave, and the blue jar in which my great-great-grandmother had placed flowers every year on the anniversary of his death.

ONCE I BEGAN WRITING of Jonah and his escape, of his encounters with bootleggers, storms, and floods and his meeting with the character Angel, also a teenage runaway, the story seemed to take me over. Jonah and Angel are so vulnerable, in so much danger, more danger than they even realize, and I found myself holding my breath as I wrote. I could hardly wait to get up in the morning to find out what would happen next. Jonah and Angel have a lot of courage and initiative, but they are on their own, with no one to guide them. They have no help from the organizations of the Underground Railroad and have no way of contacting such an organization. They have to rely on their own resources, energy, and luck. But most of all they learn that to survive they must lean on each other. It is a lesson that all of us, sooner or later, learn, if we are blessed with the good fortune to find someone to lean on.

QUESTIONS FOR DISCUSSION

1. Most stories of escaping slaves involve the Underground Railroad and the abolitionist organizations that aided those attempting to get to the north. Were you surprised that Jonah and Angel made their way to freedom pretty much on their own? Do you feel that their stories are realistic?

2. Were you surprised at the amount of humor the author inserted into what is otherwise a fairly grim story of two teenage slaves escaping from plantations in the South in 1851? Why do you think the author included these lighter moments in the narrative? Do you think they are effective?

3. Jonah and Angel had many close calls during the course of their journey, barely escaping encounters with bounty hunters, sheriff's deputies, and some simply "evil" people. At which points, if any, did you believe that one or both of them might not make it to the end of their journey?

4. The story alternates between Jonah's point of view and Angel's point of view, and those points of view shift between third person with Jonah and first person with Angel. Why do you think the author chose this format? How did it affect your reading of the novel?

5. It took courage and desperation for any slave to attempt escape and freedom. What are the qualities you see in both Jonah and Angel that give them the resolve to make such a daring move?

6. Many generations of readers were given depictions of slavery that were less than fully accurate, and only in recent years have the real horrors, both physical and psychological, been made a part of the discussion on race in America. Do you feel that the plight of Jonah and Angel in *Chasing the North Star* is an accurate depiction? If not, what do you think the author should have done differently?

7. Given how close Jonah is to his mother, were you at all disturbed by his decision to steal her money and abandon her? What else should he or could he have done?

8. Some book reviewers commented on how vividly the author depicted the landscape through which Jonah and Angel travel, to the point that it almost becomes a character. Do you think that the author succeeded in transporting you to that place and time, the decade leading up to the war and the freeing of the slaves? Which passages were particularly powerful in conveying the spirit of the time?

9. Did the fact that Jonah may have killed another runaway slave and then later denied it change your opinion of him? Why or why not? And likewise did the fact that Angel turns to prostitution make you feel less

sympathy for her? Do you think there were other options she could have chosen?

10. Why do you think it takes Jonah so long to realize that he loves Angel and cannot live without her?

11. What do you make of the differences between Angel's memories of events and those same events recounted in the third-person narrative of Jonah's sections?

12. What kinds of lives do you imagine for Jonah and Angel, once in upstate New York going by the names Joshua and Serepta, following the conclusion of the events described in the novel? Do you believe that they will have a lasting marriage?

13. Based on what you have read, do you think Joshua and Serepta will need to flee later to Canada? Will they be safe in Ithaca?

RANDI ANGLIN

Born in North Carolina, Robert Morgan was raised in the mountains in which much of the story of *Chasing the North Star* takes place. A poet and biographer as well as a novelist, he is the recipient of grants from the National Endowment for the Arts, fellowships from the Guggenheim and Rockefeller foundations, and an American Academy of Arts and Letters Award. He lives in Ithaca, New York, where he is Kappa Alpha Professor of English at Cornell University.

Other Algonquin Readers Round Table Novels by Robert Morgan

Gap Creek, a novel by Robert Morgan

An Oprah Book Club Selection in hardcover, this timeless story chronicles the struggles, disappointments, and triumphs of Julie and Hank, newlyweds facing the complexities of marriage and a changing world in the Appalachian wilderness at the end of the nineteenth century.

"[Morgan's] stripped-down and almost primitive sentences burn with the raw, lonesome pathos of Hank Williams's best songs."
—*The New York Times Book Review*

"Gripping storytelling, indelible sense of time and place . . . Morgan turns the stories of prosaic lives into page-turners."
—*The Raleigh News and Observer*

Winner of the Southern Book Critics Circle Award

AN ALGONQUIN READERS ROUND TABLE EDITION WITH READING GROUP GUIDE AND OTHER SPECIAL FEATURES • FICTION • ISBN 978-1-61620-176-0 • E-BOOK ISBN 978-1-61620-178-4

The Road from Gap Creek, a novel by Robert Morgan

Robert Morgan returns to the vivid Appalachian landscape on which he has staked a literary claim. Set during World War II and the Great Depression, this compelling weaving of fact and fiction explores modern American history through the indelible portrait of an ordinary family persevering through extraordinary times.

"This novel shines with a subtle brilliance." —*Minneapolis Star Tribune*

"Masterful storytelling . . . Unforgettable characters face the tolls of World War II and the changing of their pocket of America."
—Ivan Doig, author of *The Bartender's Tale*

AN ALGONQUIN READERS ROUND TABLE EDITION WITH READING GROUP GUIDE AND OTHER SPECIAL FEATURES • FICTION • ISBN 978-1-61620-378-8 • E-BOOK ISBN 978-1-61620-342-9

Brave Enemies: A Novel of the American Revolution, by Robert Morgan

Sixteen-year-old Josie Summers has run away from home disguised as a boy and is lost in the chaotic Carolina wilderness where the War for Independence rages on. A young preacher invites her to assist in his ministry, and eventually her identity is revealed. But when the preacher is kidnapped by British soldiers, Josie disguises herself once again and joins the militia in a desperate attempt to find him in this page-turning love story of two people brought together by chance and torn apart by war.

"Readers of Morgan's *Brave Enemies* . . . are unlikely ever to take their eyes off the page—or even take a breath." —*The Christian Science Monitor*

AN ALGONQUIN READERS ROUND TABLE EDITION WITH READING GROUP GUIDE AND OTHER SPECIAL FEATURES • FICTION • ISBN 978-1-56512-578-0 • E-BOOK ISBN 978-1-56512-712-8